MIRAC
GIRL N

BY

REBECCA WINTERS

First published in Great Britain 2010
Harlequin Mills & Boon Limited,
Eton House, 18-24 Paradise Road, Richmond, Surrey TW9 1SR

Special thanks and acknowledgement are given to Rebecca Winters for her contribution to The Brides of Bella Rosa series.

ISBN: 978 0 263 87672 7

Harlequin Mills & Boon policy is to use papers that are natural, renewable and recyclable products and made from wood grown in sustainable forests. The logging and manufacturing process conform to the legal environmental regulations of the country of origin.

Printed and bound in Spain
by Litografia Rosés, S.A., Barcelona

Rebecca Winters, whose family of four children has now swelled to include five beautiful grandchildren, lives in Salt Lake City, Utah, in the land of the Rocky Mountains. With canyons and high Alpine meadows full of wild flowers, she never runs out of places to explore. They, plus her favourite vacation spots in Europe, often end up as backgrounds for her Mills & Boon® Romance novels, because writing is her passion, along with her family and church.

Rebecca loves to hear from her readers. If you wish to e-mail her, please visit her website at www.cleanromances.com

To my one and only darling daughter Dominique Jessop, who recently signed her first book contract with Harlequin. Her study experience abroad in Siena, Italy, has caused her to become a lover of all things Italian, just like her mother. With her input on Limoncello, my Mills & Boon® Romance novel MIRACLE FOR THE GIRL NEXT DOOR has been enriched.

CHAPTER ONE

CLARA ROSSETTI had started to descend the steep, narrow steps between the ancient buildings of the hillside town when she heard a deep male voice behind her say, "Hey, Bella—how many men have told you you're a remarkably beautiful woman?"

His seductive delivery had been spoken in the local Italian dialect and had a slightly familiar ring. But Clara assumed he had to be talking to some other female making her way down to the Piazza Gaspare below.

Picking up her pace, she moved across the busy square to the bus stop where she would catch her bus. It would be the last one of the day. Timing was everything when she felt this tired. Once back at the farm she would eat a light dinner and go to bed. Tomorrow she'd feel better.

Footsteps were gaining on her. "Clarissima—surely you haven't forgotten!"

A quiet gasp escaped her throat followed by a burst of joy.

Tino.

After nine years' absence her best friend from childhood was back? Valentino Casali was the only person in the world who'd ever called her Clarissima—a combination of Clara and *bellissima*. Clara had often thought it a joke since from adolescence she had been a chubby girl who'd grown into a heavy young woman. That was the curse of all the Rossettis.

She turned around to stare into the flashing dark brown eyes of Europe's most eligible playboy, but to Clara he represented her exclusive partner in all the craziness of their years growing up. When they'd both turned eighteen and he'd left Monta Correnti, his departure had left a void no one else had ever filled.

Since then he'd become Italy's poster boy, a wealthy, world-renowned adventurer and playboy whose photos appeared in the tabloids on a regular basis. He was constantly on the cover of Italy's hottest celebrity gossip magazine.

"No, I haven't forgotten," she said in a husky voice. Clara had seen him through every stage of his youth, from incorrigible rascal to outrageously handsome teen. His intelligence and daring had distinguished him from all the other guys in the region, leaving an indelible mark. To her he'd always been the picture of precious life itself. Her heart groaned in response to that undeniable reality. "How are you, Valentino?"

Her question seemed to bring him up short, as if he were expecting something else from her while he stared into her eyes. "Better now that I've caught up with my oldest friend."

Delight filled her system to hear him acknowledge it. He might belong to the world now, but those early years she could claim for herself.

After he had kissed her on both cheeks, his narrowed gaze traveled over her classic features as if trying to reconcile the changes that had taken place since she'd grown up and become the slender, five-foot-four woman who'd shed the excess weight she had carried when younger.

"Friend, you say?" she teased. "Whatever happened to the postcards and gifts from the four corners of the world you were going to send me? I don't recall your carrying out any of those periodic visits you once promised to make."

He gave an elegant shrug of his broad shoulders clothed in an expensive-looking open-necked cream sport shirt and jeans. His index finger trailed across her lips, a gesture that appeared as automatic to him as breathing, but he'd never touched her like that in their lives. A shock wave traveled through her body.

"I meant to do it all. You know that," he whispered, always the charmer. The man oozed a sensuality that would be lethal for the many women clamoring for his exclusive attention.

She flashed him a wan smile, struggling to recover from her reaction to his touch. "I *do* know. Your good intentions could pave the road to heaven." Their history went back too far for there to be misunderstandings. In truth Clara could never be angry with the Valentino she remembered—the one who'd always been kind and caring despite his devil-may-care attitude.

From an early age on, the local *ragazzi* had made their typical remarks about her and her younger sister Bianca for being fat, but Valentino had never joined the chorus. That was probably because he'd never looked at her in the man/woman way. They might have been joined at the hip, but he'd had far more important things on his mind than Clara Rossetti.

Having been born in this quiet little mountain village between Rome and Naples, he'd put Monta Correnti on the map. His fame had brought the tourists, as well as a few celebrities from various parts of the world who'd chosen to live here, but there was no question that the heartthrob Formula 1 race-car driver who made his home in Monaco was the most famous celebrity of all.

Valentino cocked his attractive head. She noted

he needed a shave, yet it only added to his virility. In the last nine years, he'd become a man in every sense of the word and so gorgeous she could hardly breathe.

"Are you aware you bear a superficial resemblance to Catherine Zeta-Jones? Only younger, of course."

Clara preferred not to look like anyone else, but since film stars made up part of his world she had to assume he'd just bestowed a serious compliment on her. "No. I had no idea. Have you met her?"

He gave a slight nod. "You're much more beautiful." His white smile faded and he stared at her with increasing intensity. "What happened to your long hair?"

The hair she'd foolishly hoped would hide the rest of her?

Surprised he'd noticed, let alone changed the subject so fast, she said, "This April has been warmer than usual. Besides, I was due for a change." Her silky hair, more black than brown, had become too difficult to deal with recently so she'd had it cut in a jaw-length style that fell straight from a center part.

"I liked it long, not that I don't like it the way you're wearing it now, of course."

"Of course," she teased, wishing she felt better, stronger. "I notice you're wearing your hair shorter these days." His midnight-brown hair was now wavy rather than curly. "Remember when you let it grow out to your shoulders? Signor Cavallo thought you'd be perfect for the role of Prince Valiant in the school play."

A rumble of laughter came out of him. "Are you talking about the time you denuded me?"

"That was *your* fault. You're the one who made me cut your hair off so you wouldn't have to be in *King Arthur*. Can I help it if I made a mess of it? Those poultry shears from your father's restaurant kitchen weren't supposed to be used on humans. I thought Signor Cavallo was going to strangle you when you walked in class the next day."

His grin broadened. "With your help, I got out of the part. What would I have done without you always helping me squeeze out of trouble?"

"Aminta almost strangled me when you told her I was the culprit. She had the most terrible crush on you. Even back then you could have your choice of every maiden in the land."

"Tonight I choose you," he said in a voice of deep velvet. "For old times' sake, come to the restaurant with me and we'll celebrate my return."

"To sneak some *bruschetta* when the chef isn't looking?" She kept up the banter. There was no one more exciting in this world than Valentino. "Those were the days, but we can't get them back."

"No, but there's something we *can* do. Tonight's your lucky night. For a change we'll walk through the front door and I'll *buy* you dinner. Everything up front and aboveboard."

His invitation sounded heavenly, but she was growing weaker by the minute. "That would be a change all right, but, much as I'd love to, I can't. Thank you anyway. It's been wonderful to see you, Valentino."

Over his shoulder she saw the bus pull to a stop. She was thankful it had come to her rescue. Seeing Valentino after all these years had brought back the past and drained her of any reserves she had left. Several people started to board the bus and she moved to get in line behind them.

He put a hand on her arm to detain her. "Wait—where are you going?" She discovered a strange tension coming from him she'd never experienced before. Something was troubling him to produce that slight grimace, but she had to admit the years had been kind to him. Despite the lines of experience in a sun-bronzed face—or perhaps because of them—he was more dashing than ever. No other man came close.

"Home. The family's waiting for me."

"But I just got into town. We have years to catch up on. Is this evening an important occasion? I know it's not your birthday."

He might have forgotten *her* for nine years,

but his razor-sharp memory had an amazing capacity for trivia. Valentino would keep it up until she capitulated. He never did know when to quit, but this was one time Clara couldn't stay around while he managed to talk her into it. She was embarrassed to admit he'd always been able to get her to do what he wanted.

"Mamma has planned a special dinner for my grandmother. I promised to be on time to help."

Again he looked mystified. "Then let me drive you. It will only take me five minutes to go for my Ferrari."

That was too far away. Clara needed to sit down on that bus or she was going to faint from exhaustion. "Thanks for the offer, but my ride is here now. If you're going to be in town for a few days, maybe I'll see you whizzing around and we'll grab a bite together. What color is your car?"

"Black," he muttered.

"You once wanted a red one."

"I did buy one, fire-engine red, but discovered I was somewhat a target for the police."

"Well, you *will* insist on driving too fast. As I recall, you had the police chasing us on your scooter on a weekly basis at least! Sorry, but I have to run now. *Ciao*, Valentino."

She eased away from him and climbed on board, grateful he'd finally let her go without saying anything else. Knowing him, he'd be gone from Monta Correnti by morning to make his next car rally here in Italy or England, probably accompanied by his latest girlfriend.

Clara had seen a clip of him and the newest young French starlet Giselle Artois on the ten o'clock news last month. The journalist had asked him if it was true about the rumors they were planning to marry and settle down in a small palace along one of the fashionable *faubourgs* of Paris.

He had made a noncommittal remark with his breathtaking half-smile, but Clara had noticed the French *vedette* wore a mysterious smile on her face. They looked good together. Maybe this was the woman who'd finally snagged Valentino. Up until now he seemed to try new adventures and change girlfriends with the seasons, but whatever had caused him to run from himself all these years, it was nothing to do with Clara.

Taking a fortifying breath, she worked her way to the back of the bus. Every seat was taken and she finally squeezed in the last row between a stout man and a nun in her habit.

Out of the window on the right she watched Valentino watching her beneath his dark, furrowed brows, his expression devoid of all animation. After the bus pulled away, his brooding image remained. His lean, six-foot body had made millions for the companies that produced posters of him doing a solo trip across the Indian Ocean in a one-man catamaran, or flying around the track in Dubai testing out his latest Formula 1 car.

From childhood he'd been a fascinating adventurer who'd had an obsession with speed and breaking records. Though the Casali family had lived on the shores of Lake Clarissa, fifty kilometers from Monta Correnti, he'd actually spent most of his time in town after school working on his motor scooter.

One of his friends, Luigi, had let him tinker with it in the back of his dad's garage. To hear Valentino speak, none of the existing models were fast enough. Clara had spent many hours in that garage listening to him talk about his dreams of building one that would outperform all existing models.

After he'd left for Monaco to break into the racing world, he'd taken his innovative motor-scooter design with him and it had become the prototype for future scooters. By his twenty-first birthday he'd formed Violetta Rapidita, the Italian scooter company that had catapulted him to international financial success.

Long ago Clara had thought of him as a Renaissance man, pitting himself against the clock, against nature, against anything that would give him a thrill. By listening to him she'd experienced vicarious thrills herself, but there were times when she wondered if his fast living served as camouflage for unexplained demons driving him.

Though she didn't know what they were, she suspected their roots originated from within the complicated Casali family and that they still continued to haunt him. It was interesting that his elder brother Cristiano didn't come home to Monta Correnti very often either.

Only their sister Isabella had been the constant, spending most of her time at Rosa's helping her father run the restaurant. How different was Valentino's family from the huge, hard-working Rossetti clan who always rallied around each other!

She had countless aunts, uncles, cousins and second cousins who helped run the farm, so many in fact you couldn't count them all. Though they lived hand to mouth, even her own four married siblings showed no signs of leaving the farm that had been the hub of the Rossettis' existence for generations.

Clara was no different. As hard as life had been lately, she loved Monta Correnti and couldn't imagine living anywhere else. But fate had been cruel to have allowed her to lay eyes on Valentino today.

Until he'd called out to her, she'd been holding her own, dealing with her challenges on a day-to-day basis, determined not to let them defeat her. But he was like this overpowering force field, a super-bright constellation in the heavens whose magnetic pull drew the world to him.

His appearance had managed to shatter the fragile shell of her existence. She rested her head against the back of the seat and closed her eyes, tortured by her own inner demons that seemed to have magnified a hundredfold by running into him without warning.

The second the bus rounded the corner and was out of sight, a troubled Valentino moved swiftly toward the hub of the village where his father's restaurant was located. Right next to it—in fact adjoining it by a back terrace—sat his aunt's restaurant. The courtyard in front of both opened up into the bustling center square.

Sorella, a restaurant started by Valentino's grandmother Rosa, was now owned by his aunt Lisa Firenzi who'd turned it into a chic, contemporary place serving an international cuisine. His father, Luca Casali, had fallen out with his sister and had broken away from the family business, starting his own Italian traditional family restaurant he'd named Rosa. Isabella was the day manager.

Valentino had kept in touch with her and their father through e-mails, but in the last nine years he'd only come home fleetingly. The most recent had been just last month on the occasion of his father's birthday. Much to his sister's chagrin he'd only stayed the evening.

Just remembering that fateful evening and the fireworks that had ensued caused him to shudder. He always experienced an unpleasant sensation in his gut at the thought that two warring factions of the same family would want to be anywhere near each other. Valentino abhorred confrontation and was continually mystified that two intelligent people like his father and his aunt Lisa, who'd had a jealous rivalry going for years, still maintained businesses side by side.

It was a sick kind of symbiosis. They were like organisms surviving in close approximation, not able to live with or without the other.

As he reached the courtyard he was reminded of the ugly confrontation that had gone on out here during the party. Tempers had flared. Uncaring of who might overhear them, his aunt had lost control. In her rage she'd blurted out a sensitive secret about Luca that had rocked the entire family.

Pain had gutted Valentino. Unable to deal with all the ramifications, not the least of which was his bitter disappointment in his father, he'd left

Monta Correnti after having barely arrived not knowing when he'd ever be back. If it weren't for his father's declining health and Isabella's plea for help with him, Valentino wouldn't have canceled his next two races to be here now.

However, his overriding concern tonight had nothing to do with his father. After leaving the furnished villa he'd just rented at the upper end of the village, he'd been making his way down to the restaurant on foot, never dreaming he would run into Clara Rossetti within hours of arriving back in town.

Their chance meeting had saved him the trouble of looking her up at the farm. The knowledge that he could reconnect with her while he was in Monta Correnti had been the only thing he'd been looking forward to on his return.

Clara had been his saving grace, had always accepted him with his flaws and imperfections. After the party he'd needed desperately to talk to her about what he'd learned, but he'd been in such bad shape at the time he hadn't been willing to inflict himself on her.

He wasn't doing much better now, but seeing her again made him realize how much he wanted to talk to her. There was no one as insightful or as easy to be with as Clara. No one understood him the way she did, but at first glance he hadn't recognized her except for her eyes.

Those incredible irises studded with luminous, diamond-like green dust hadn't changed though everything else about her had. Gone was the overweight teenager with the pretty face who'd been his abiding friend since they'd first attended school as children. In her place stood a gorgeous woman, albeit a little too thin, no longer hidden beneath a cascading veil of glossy dark hair. Just looking at her amazing coloring and figure stopped him in his tracks.

But more startling was the fact that, beyond the drastic alteration in her physical appearance, she didn't radiate that joie de vivre he'd thought inherent in her nature.

Instead of crying out 'Tino', the name she used to call him, she'd proffered the more formal greeting of his name, treating him as she might a former acquaintance. In reality they'd been partners in crime, doing everything together, getting in and out of trouble on a regular basis.

The old fun-loving Clara, always ready for a new adventure, wouldn't have gotten on that bus.

Maybe she was telling the truth and did have to get home, but something had been missing. She'd said all the right words, yet the warm, compassionate girl he'd turned to in his youth—the one person who'd always listened to him and had never scoffed at his bold ideas—had put him off.

That had come as a shock.

He'd been arrogant enough to believe in some corner of his mind that, of all the people who'd come and gone in his life, she'd placed their friendship on a higher par—or at least on a unique plane that meant it was something special, even if he hadn't written letters or sent her pictures. It seemed she didn't want to spend time with him now.

With the Rossettis' farm of lemon, orange and olive groves located several miles south of town, the formerly vivacious Clara wouldn't have turned him down for a ride home. He'd never known a woman who didn't want to take a jaunt with him in his Ferrari. Valentino supposed his ego was hurt that she wasn't impressed, let alone that her memories of him had made no lasting mark on her psyche.

Her dark-fringed eyes might have flared with interest when she'd first seen him, but as they had talked it had felt as if she were staring through him, making him feel at a loss. That spark of life he'd always associated with her had been missing, delivering a one-two punch to the gut he hadn't expected. In truth, he had to reach back to being five years old again to remember that same sensation, leaving him feeling devastated.

He quickened his pace and hurried inside the restaurant where the staff was setting up for dinner. They called out greetings he acknowledged, but he was in too big a hurry to get engaged in conversation. Without hesitation he headed toward the kitchen where his recently engaged sister was probably doing ten tasks at once to keep things running smoothly.

After taking possession of the villa where he planned to live for the next few months, he'd come here with every intention of eating his evening meal, but, after the strange experience with Clara in the piazza, he was now put off the thought of food.

Rosa, named after his grandmother, delivered traditional, home-cooked Italian food in surroundings of frescoed walls and terracotta floors. The rustic restaurant represented his father's dream of owning his own place. He'd wanted it to be evocative of his mother's warm, family-oriented spirit.

In that regard, he hadn't failed. Aside from Clara, who'd made up the best part of the background fabric of his life, Valentino's few good memories included the experience of walking in here to encounter the distinctive aroma of the tomato sauce, Rosa's house specialty, wafting past his nostrils.

William Valentine, his English grandfather, had passed his secret sauce recipe to his sweetheart Rosa who had later passed it on to her son Luca,

Valentino's father. Luca had then improved on the recipe, which was the reason for the restaurant's popularity, even if at this point in time he was heavily in debt.

Valentino had the finances to help him out. At Isabella's repeated urgings, he'd come back home for a while to do just that, but the latest revelation about his father made it damn near impossible to want to approach him.

Being back home brought all the painful memories of the past flooding to the surface, one of them still unbearable if he allowed himself to think about it too much. To make matters worse, he had to maneuver carefully because of his father's declining health and fierce pride.

For two cents he'd leave for Monaco tonight and make arrangements to race in the next Grand Prix. But he couldn't do that and disappoint Isabella again. He'd made her a promise to spend time at the restaurant. Tonight he'd talk to her about some ideas he had to promote the business. With a quick fix he could be out of here a lot sooner!

His sister saw him enter the kitchen. A glance from her expressive blue eyes told him she wanted to talk to him. She took her leave of the chef and signaled with her head that Valentino should follow her out the back door to the nearby stream that ran through the town. In recent years it had been cemented into a channel with bridges where they could lean against the railings and talk in private.

"I was hoping you'd get back in time for dinner," she began without preamble. "Are you going to take the villa? It's been empty for ages. Max hoped you might be interested in it."

Valentino nodded. "I told Max I would rent it on a month-to-month basis. It's roomy and the view is great. It's an ideal solution for my temporary situation."

She looked chagrined. "I thought you said the whole summer."

He'd thought so too until his own pride had suffered a debilitating blow from Clara, the one person he would never have imagined could inflict hurt of any kind, not even unconsciously. It surprised him how much he cared. He was a fool to let it bother him, yet it was eating at him like a corrosive acid and he didn't like the feeling.

"You know me. I have an aversion to being pinned down." Isabella didn't like hearing those words, but she had played mother to him and Cristiano for so many years, she couldn't help but try to manage everything, even now.

Once he'd committed to coming home for a while, she'd insisted he stay at the vacant Casali home on Lake Clarissa now used for vacations. It was only a half-hour's drive from town. When she'd first mentioned it, he'd told her it was too far away to be convenient. In truth, he didn't know if he could ever step inside that building again. What had happened there so many years ago would haunt him to the grave.

"I'm sorry you didn't choose to stay in the apartment with Papa. He was hoping you might move in with him."

Isabella was out of her mind to say something like that. He swore his sister lived in denial. Her constant desire to make everything right between everybody and get along drove him around the bend. He was still furious with her for insisting they get to know their two older half-brothers, Alessandro and Angelo. Until little more than a month ago, no one in the family had known of their existence. Unbelievable!

Yet thanks to his trouble-making aunt, Luca's guilty secret had been exposed and now Isabella was determined to make them a part of their dysfunctional lives. No, thank you.

"I'm afraid I've been on my own too many years, Izzy. Besides, let's be honest. You're always looking in on Papa and don't need a second person being underfoot, even if I am your brother. Please don't take that the wrong way."

She kissed his cheek. "I didn't."

"I admire you for taking care of him." That part was the truth. In her own right she was a terrific person. With her long, wavy black hair and olive skin, he considered her the quintessential Italian woman. "Papa couldn't have made it this long without you." She'd been the glue holding the family together.

"Thank you," she said in a quiet voice.

"I should have said something long before now." When he saw the work she did without complaint day after day, it made him feel all the more uncomfortable that already today he'd been entertaining thoughts of bolting before morning.

Her eyes searched his. "You're in a strange mood. You burst into the kitchen like you were being pursued, and now you're being uncharacteristically reflective. What happened to you after you talked to Max about the villa?"

Like a mother with eyes in the back of her head, his sister saw more than he wanted her to see. He'd run into Clara Rossetti on the way here, but their unexpected encounter hadn't turned out as he'd anticipated, leaving him strangely unsettled.

"I've had an idea on how to expand the business. Unfortunately Papa is such a traditionalist, I don't know if he'll hear me out. I'm the last person he wants advice from."

"How can you say that?" she cried. "You're an international success in business. You could double your fortune showing others how to make it big."

"That doesn't impress a bona fide restaurateur like Papa."

"Of course it does!"

He shook his head. "Let's not play games, Izzy. *You* know why." They stared at each other. "I'm not his biological son. I'm a reminder that I was Mamma's love child from another man."

"Papa raised you as his own with me and Cristiano."

"Yes, and every time he sees me on television or hears about me on the news, he has to wonder about the stranger who was half responsible for my existence. I gave up caring a long time ago when I realized my birth father didn't want anything to do with me either."

Her soulful eyes looked up at him helplessly.

"If he had, he would have made arrangements with Mamma for visitation. Papa had to take me when he took Mamma back. After she died, he was stuck with me. Considering he didn't want his first two sons, let's just say the bastard child comes in last on all counts."

"No, Valentino!" She threw her arms around him. "That's not true. You simply can't believe those things."

"Let's not talk about it anymore, Izzy. It's water under the bridge." He didn't want to get into the subject of their father. The shocking revelation that his first marriage had produced two sons living somewhere else on the planet had done too much damage to Valentino. He felt emotionally wiped out. Erased.

Isabella wiped her eyes. "Then tell me about your idea."

"I don't know if it will work, but I think it's worth a try. This establishment has been Papa's dream. None of us wants to see it go under." In Luca's own way he'd been a good father to Valentino. It was payback time.

"We can't let that happen."

"Agreed. What would you think if we did some advertising with various tour-group operators from Rome and Naples to bring in more people? I'll do the groundwork, of course. If it's a go, I'll contact other operators in Florence and Milan."

"That's pure genius!" she cried excitedly.

He shook his head. "Papa will probably hate it. Secondly I'd like to set up an Internet Web site for us. Anyone seeing our name on a restaurant list can contact us to make advance reservations. Once we're set up on the best search engines, we ought to see an increase in traffic."

"Those are both fabulous ideas. Once people discover us, they always come back for repeat business."

"The trick is to get them here. We just need to spread the word. When do you think would be the best time to approach Papa?"

"Mornings, after he's up and dressed for breakfast."

"I'll come tomorrow. Depending on how he's feeling, I'll broach the subject."

"I'm so glad you're here."

Wishing he could say the same, he hugged her instead. Unfortunately being back meant having to face his old ghosts. The fact that Cristiano was in Australia only reminded Valentino how far the Casali family had grown apart emotionally. Which reminded him of something else unpleasant.

"Did I tell you I happened to see Clara Rossetti in the piazza this afternoon?"

"Oh, yes? You two were inseparable growing up. Sometimes I think she was the only person you ever truly cared about after Mamma died. I used to be jealous of her."

He blinked, not only shocked by her admission, but by the fact that his attachment to Clara had been so obvious, his own sister had been affected by it. "I had no idea."

"Of course you wouldn't. I saw her at church recently. She's grown up to be a real beauty."

"I noticed." Maybe it was the weight loss that had affected her behavior and made her seem less than her herself. The way she'd brushed him off had stung.

"Bianca, too. You remember her sister."

"Very well." She was a year younger than Clara and almost as sweet. Too bad he couldn't say the same about Clara's twin brother, Silvio. The Casalis and the Rossettis had attended the same schools, but from the beginning Silvio had taken a distinct dislike to Valentino.

By high school he'd become Clara's self-appointed guardian, doing his best to keep her away from Valentino, always reminding her she was needed back at the farm. Though it had never come to an actual fight, they'd exchanged heated words on occasion when Valentino had stood up for Clara.

"Rumour has it that Clara has been seeing one of the Romaggio brothers from the valley."

So *that* was the reason she'd seemed changed. "Which one?"

"I think it's Leandro, the really good-looking one who has his own vegetable farm now. Apparently Clara is the envy of all the girls around here."

Izzy had to be kidding—Leandro was the one with more brawn than brains. Valentino had known the Romaggios in school. Clara had an intellect that could run circles around any of the guys. He wasn't her type at all!

For some reason the news made Valentino restless. "Thanks for backing me up in my ideas. Now I've got to go. I left Monaco early this morning and fatigue has caught up with me."

"That doesn't surprise me. I need to go back inside, too. The staff will be wondering where I am."

"I'll see you tomorrow." He kissed her cheek before wheeling around to make his own way through the ancient town and up the hillside to the villa.

Valentino hadn't been completely honest with Isabella. After being up since five that morning to drive to Italy, he would normally be tired and wanting his bed. But the old saying that you couldn't go home again seemed to be in operation here. Meeting up with a changed Clara had disturbed him and he found himself wide awake.

Once he reached his destination, he let himself in the villa originally built in the 1800s by a member of Prince Maximilliano Di Rossi's family for a summer getaway. Because of his love for Izzy, Max had made the villa available to Valentino, who had insisted on paying him rent. He didn't like owing anyone for favors. With no strings attached, he could move about freely in his world.

The villa was much smaller but no different in style from Valentino's home in Monaco. Both had been built around the same period of time and contained similar furnishings. The only real difference besides size was the view. It looked out on the picturesque countryside rather than the Mediterranean.

At the sound of his footsteps echoing throughout the interior, Valentino realized that without warm bodies inhabiting this domicile it was nothing more than an empty tomb. Valentino wasn't used to the peace and quiet. He didn't know if he could stand being here for even a month. Already he was climbing the walls.

He had thought about asking his latest companion, Yvette, to come and bring her friends, and knew she would be here in an instant. But he couldn't do that because then she would read more into his invitation than he meant. Like the other women he'd been with over the years, her hints about settling down weren't so subtle and the last thing Valentino could imagine doing was giving up his freedom.

His thoughts jumped to his father, who'd been married twice. Though divorced from his first wife, he would probably still be with Valentino's mother if she were alive. Valentino wasn't like him. He enjoyed taking risks, but not when it came to women.

Though he knew nothing about his birthfather, he suspected that, since he hadn't shown a fathering instinct where Valentino had been concerned, he'd probably never married either.

At a totally loose end, Valentino headed to the kitchen for a beer. He phoned Roger, his longtime friend at the track. They talked shop for half an hour, then he checked in with Claude, the manager of his bike company in Monaco. Following that, he took a hot shower and got ready for bed.

To his irritation, his scattered thoughts returned to Clara. Throughout his years growing up in Monta Correnti, she'd been the only female constant besides his sister. He couldn't help but wonder how close she was to settling down. For the hell of it, maybe he'd take the time to find out tomorrow.

CHAPTER TWO

WHILE Clara was getting dressed in jeans and a pink cotton top with three-quarter sleeves, Bianca, who was barely pregnant again, walked in the bedroom carrying her six-month-old boy. "Mamma wants to know how you're feeling this morning."

"I'm fine," Clara murmured as she slipped into her sandals. "How's my little Paolito today?" The little boy was old enough now that when she gave him kisses on his tummy, he laughed out loud. "Do you have any idea how much I love you?" She kissed his tender neck.

"He loves his *zia* more."

Together they walked down the hall of the small stone farmhouse to the kitchen where the family ate all their meals. It used to bulge at the seams, but these days it was home to Clara, her parents and grandmother on her mother's side who lived on the main floor. Because of a stroke, the ninety-one-year-old woman was in a wheelchair. Bianca and Silvio lived upstairs with their spouses and children.

The other married siblings and extended family lived in homes on the outskirts of Monta Correnti. Now when they gathered for meals three times a day, there were only twelve at their noisy table.

Her father cast her an anxious glance. "Ah, good. You're up."

Clara kissed him on top of his balding head. "I'm up and hungry." She turned to her mother, who waited on everyone. "I'll get my own breakfast. Sit down, Mamma. You work too hard."

"No, no. You must preserve your strength."

"I have plenty of strength this morning."

"That's good to hear. Now you sit and eat!"

"Yes, *Mamacita*." She took her place across from Silvio, smiling secretly at his three children aged seven, five and three who giggled to hear their *nonna* get mad at her.

Silvio's pregnant wife, Maria, darted her a friendly glance. "You look better this morning."

"I feel good enough to run the stand today." She drank the freshly squeezed orange juice waiting for her.

"Absolutely not!" Silvio barked, so overprotective of her these days she felt smothered.

"Do you think you should?" her anxious mother questioned as she put the hot omelet in front of her. Her devoted mother who did the work of a dozen people went out of her way to make certain she was well fed.

"Of course I do. Thank you, Mamma."

"Are you telling us the truth?"

"If I weren't, I would stay in bed." Clara was getting desperate and wanted to scream, but only because everyone was so good to her and worried about her continually. More than anything she hated being a burden, yet within the last three months that was what she'd become to her hard-working family.

"So you really feel up to it?" Her father stared hard at her.

"*Sì*, Papa," she answered in a controlled voice. "Some days I wake up feeling worse than others. Right now I feel good and want to do my part around here on the days when I can."

His eyes grew suspiciously bright before he nodded. "Then it's settled."

Grazie, she murmured inwardly, but Silvio set his mug of coffee down too hard, telling everyone his opinion. He was the sibling who stifled her most with his concern. As a result, he was the most difficult member of the family to be around.

The hot liquid splashed on the table. Maria told seven-year-old Pasquale to run and get a cloth for his father. While the mess was getting cleaned up, Bianca's husband, Tomaso, walked in the back door in his overalls. He'd been out early setting up the fruit stand for Clara before doing his own work.

His gaze shot straight to Clara. "You've got a visitor." By his awestruck countenance, it told her this was no ordinary person.

"Who is it?" She struggled to keep herself calm, already anticipating the answer with far too much excitement.

"Valentino Casali. He's driving the latest Ferrari 599."

Amidst the audible gasps, Silvio jumped to his feet, letting go with a few colorful expletives their household hadn't heard in a long time.

"*Basta*!" their father admonished him.

"Clara hasn't had anything to do with him in years, Papa. He's no good and he's not welcome on our farm. I don't want him here!" Silvio muttered angrily.

Aghast at her brother's venom, Clara felt a sudden feeling of weakness attack her body, but she fought not to show any vulnerability. She'd thought of course Valentino had only come to Monta Correnti for a few days and might even have left Italy as early as this morning.

In all the years growing up, he'd never once come to the farmhouse to see her for any reason. Every time he'd given her a ride home on the scooter on his way to the lake, she'd insisted on getting off once they reached the road leading into the farm.

"I'll go outside and see what he wants." Out of necessity she'd brushed him off too abruptly at the bus stop yesterday. Since then she'd been suffering guilt…and also regret for missing out on spending more time with him. There was no one like him! Because she'd teased him about not visiting her once in the last nine years, he'd probably decided to stop and say goodbye on his way out of town.

While everyone was reeling from the shock of their hometown celebrity showing up here, she rose from the table and walked out the back door. After rounding the corner of the house she spied the black super-car parked further down the drive.

Valentino levered himself from the front seat and strolled toward her, wearing bone-colored chinos and a black, open-necked sport shirt. He looked so fantastic she could hardly swallow. His sensuous mouth curved into a half-smile. "*Buon giorno*, Clarissima! Forgive me for coming by this early?"

Her assumption had been right. He *was* on the verge of leaving.

His eyes lingered on her soft curves before scrutinizing her from her sandaled feet to the roots of her hair. It didn't surprise her. Three years ago she and Bianca had finally taken off the weight that had plagued them most of their lives.

The diet plan she'd chosen had been part of an article by a film star featured in a celebrity magazine with a photograph of her and Valentino on the front cover. A section had been dedicated to the woman who had claimed to stay thin on the prescribed regimen and swore by it. Naturally there were no pictures of fat girls inside the pages of that magazine or any others.

For some reason seeing Valentino smiling at the slender beauty who'd kept her weight off had annoyed Clara. Out of anger she had started dieting and Bianca had joined her. Once they began to see results, they became local wonders for a while, but now everyone was used to the way they looked, except for Valentino, of course.

"There's nothing to forgive. You know we're a farming family, up with the sun."

His expression sobered. "I could have called your house, but thought I might have more luck talking to you if I came in person."

She was so glad he did. No doubt he was remembering how Silvio used to run interference and decided not to take the chance of her brother answering the phone. It was a good thing. Silvio's jealousy of Valentino had been over the top then. If he should see him now…

"Your car gave Tomaso a big thrill."

"But not you?" He sounded intense again, as he had yesterday.

"Of course it does!"

"It's the only transportation I have at the moment," he murmured in a voice deeper than she remembered. The eighteen-year-old Tino had become an incredibly attractive male. "Come for a drive with me. I need to talk to you."

With that silken tone, Valentino had a way of getting under her skin, but the last thing she wanted was for him to know about what was going on in her life. To spend any time with him when he was no doubt leaving town again would be like standing too near a white-hot conflagration. No more pain…

She shook her head. "I'm afraid I don't have the time. When you drove in, you saw Tomaso opening up the stand for business. I'm running it today."

"Give me five minutes."

Clara got this suffocating feeling in her chest. "Can't we talk right here?"

His striking features darkened with lines. "What are you afraid of?"

The blood hammered in her ears. She backed away from him. "Nothing! I just can't imagine what's so important you would come all this way. It's been years."

"Nine, to be exact. That's too many between old friends. I'm here to atone for my sins." His lips smiled, but for a brief moment his dark eyes looked haunted. "Surely you wouldn't refuse me as easily as you did yesterday when I offered to drive you home—"

"The bus was there. I saw no reason to put you out, but I meant no offense," she added to appease him.

"None was taken." He cocked his head. "Since you're busy now, I'll come by later in the day when you're ready to close up the stand."

Later in the day? "Please don't—" she cried, working up to a panic. After a full day's work, she would need to rest and he'd know something was wrong.

His dark brows lifted. "Have you already made plans for this evening? With a boyfriend, perhaps?"

"Yes." She leaped at the excuse he'd just given her.

Since her weight loss she'd been besieged by different guys from the valley wanting to go out with her. She'd had a lot of dates. One of the guys, Leandro, had been fairly relentless trying to get her to go out with him. When she did, she realized she had no interest in him. But Valentino didn't know any of her dating history and she wanted to keep it that way.

"What time will he be picking you up?"

"When he gets off work," she improvised.

"So when will you close the stand?"

"I—I don't know," she stammered.

"You don't know?" he enquired smoothly. "Four o'clock? Five?"

"Why are you asking me all these questions?" she blurted before realizing she'd displayed her anger. Since Valentino had never witnessed this side of her nature, he stared at her as if she'd turned into a complete stranger. In a way she *had*. Right now her heart was thudding so hard she felt ill.

"I was hoping you'd find a few minutes in your busy schedule for me." To his credit he held onto his temper.

She averted her eyes. "I'm afraid I don't have any time today," she said in a subdued tone.

"I can hear Silvio in your voice," his voice grated. "Forgive me for coming here and disturbing you. That's the last thing I wanted to do." He turned away and headed for his car.

After he'd mentioned her brother's name, she couldn't allow him to think what he was thinking. "How long are you going to be in Monta Correnti?"

He opened the car door. "For as long as it takes."

"What do you mean?"

"My father's not well."

She swallowed hard. "I'm sorry. Is it serious?"

"I hope not." He started to get in the car.

"Wait—" she called out before she realized how anxious she sounded.

His dark head reared back. "Yes?"

"I'm going into town in the morning to do some errands. If you want, I'll meet you at the Pasticceria Bonelli in the Piazza Gaspare where I caught the bus. We could have a cup of coffee or something beforehand."

"What time?"

"Shall we say ten o'clock?"

"I'll be there. *Grazie*, *piccola*."

At eight the next morning Valentino dressed in a polo shirt and jeans before leaving the villa to walk to the restaurant. He entered through the back door into the kitchen with the key Isabella had given him. His plan was to eat breakfast with his father so they could talk business.

Valentino didn't hold out much hope of getting anywhere with him. His father knew the restaurant business inside and out. You couldn't tell him how to run it. Valentino could only try to make a suggestion, but even then his parent would probably resent it.

At first he didn't think anyone was about, but as he passed by the storage area that served as a pantry of sorts he glimpsed someone through the door that stood ajar. On closer inspection he realized it was his father up on a small stepladder with a clipboard. Valentino noticed his cane resting against the leg of the ladder.

Not wanting to startle him by calling out, he moved over slowly to where his father stood, but when the older man saw him, he still jumped and almost fell off the ladder. Valentino rushed to steady him. He was thinner than the last time he'd seen him just a month ago, but he still had a full head of brown hair though it was streaked with silver.

"Why did you sneak up on me like that?"

What a great beginning! Valentino had to tamp down his temper. "I was afraid if I announced myself in the doorway, you'd turn suddenly and fall. I can see you're doing the inventory. Don't you think—?"

"Not you, too—" his father barked, interrupting him. "Go on—say it! Everyone else does. Your aunt Lisa yelled at me the other day that I'm too old and crippled to run my own restaurant. That's the only reason you came back to Monta Correnti, isn't it? Isabella probably sent you in here to stop me!"

Valentino winced. His father didn't want him here. What else was new? "I haven't seen Isabella today. Isn't she at market?"

"Who knows?"

That was a lie, of course. His father knew everything. "Actually I came early so I could help you do whatever needed doing. Inventory is the only thing I'm good at when it comes to running the restaurant."

Valentino had thought he could broach his ideas for promoting Rosa while they worked together, but that was what he got for thinking. Clearly it was too soon to offer Luca anything, let alone money. His father had way too much pride for that and would throw it all back in his face.

Coming home had been a big mistake. Valentino was the last person his father wanted anything to do with. "Why don't you take a break and have breakfast with me?"

"I can't stop now."

That was clear enough. "Is there anything I can do for you today?"

"No, no. You run along and have a good time."

With those words Valentino felt about five years old. All that was missing was a pat on the head. "Then I'll see you later."

As he reached the doorway his father said, "How long will you be in town?"

The temptation to tell him he was leaving right now and wouldn't be back got stuck in his throat. "Long enough to help you. *Ciao*, Papa."

Though Valentino had been a grown man for quite some time, Luca had the power to make him feel small and unnecessary. He left the restaurant and headed through town to the piazza to wait for Clara. He wanted to be here ahead of her, in case she came early.

During their conversation he'd purposely

brought up Silvio's name, knowing she'd always defended Valentino to her brother in the past. His gambit had worked enough for her to feel guilty and agree to meet him.

After ordering a cup of coffee in the pastry shop, he took it to one of the tables outside and drank it while he watched for her. At twenty to ten, Clara got off the bus.

He took a second to study her womanly figure encased in hip-hugging denim capris. She wore a three-quarter-sleeve blouse in a yellow and orange print that buttoned down the front and tied at her waist. The knockout picture she made caused male heads to turn in her direction.

Without doing anything, she elicited wolf whistles and remarks from the drivers in the heavy morning traffic circulating around the piazza, but she appeared oblivious to the attention.

He put the mug down on the table and started toward her. "Looking for someone, *signorina*?" he asked in a quiet voice. She heard him and turned her head in his direction. Obviously she hadn't been expecting him yet.

A tiny cry escaped her throat. "Tino—" Her green eyes played over him.

Good. In that unguarded moment she hadn't forgotten after all. His lips twitched. "Do I dare confess you look good enough to eat this morning?" His comment caused color to seep into her pale cheeks. "Come inside with me. There's a *torta setteveli* with our names on it." She could do with gaining a few more pounds.

"Oh, no, not mine," she said with the infectious laugh he remembered. It made him want to provoke that response from her as often as possible. "Those days are over."

Valentino hoped not. She'd always been so happy before, but he decided not to push it. After they walked in, the woman at the counter smiled at them. "What can I get for you?"

"A large slice of that." He pointed to the *torta*. "Put it on a plate with two forks, and we'd like two cappuccinos, *per favore*."

They always used to drink it together. When she didn't demur, he assumed she still liked it.

"*Bene*, *signore*."

After pulling some Euros out his wallet to pay the check, he cupped Clara's elbow and steered her toward a table for two in the corner away from the window. "We'll hide over here."

"From the paparazzi, you mean?"

"From Leandro Romaggio actually. Is he the jealous type?"

She looked stunned. "How did you hear about him?"

"Restaurant gossip. You can't avoid it. Would he mind?"

Once they were seated across from each other

she said, "If he knew I were here with you, he'd ask me to get your autograph. You're so famous you've become a household word in Italy."

For some reason her comment irritated him. "Does my supposed fame impress you?"

"Of course. It makes me a little sad for you, too."

His brows met. "Why do you say that?"

"Because you were always such a private person. It's quite ironic what's happened to you when I know how much you hate to be recognized everywhere you go. I honestly don't know how you've dealt with it for this long."

Her comment pleased him in ways she couldn't imagine. "Perhaps now you understand why I wanted to see you again. While the rest of the world makes the wrong assumptions about me, you alone know the real truth."

She flashed him a wistful, yet beguiling smile. "You used to complain on a regular basis that you always minded your own business, so why didn't everyone else mind theirs instead of yours!"

A chuckle came out of him. "That doesn't sound so good. I must have been pretty impossible to be around."

"Not at all. You were your own person who spoke the truth. I liked that as much as I enjoyed watching the genius at work."

"Genius—" he scoffed as the woman placed their order on the table.

"Don't be modest, Tino," she said after they were alone again. "All those drawings and experiments you did on that scooter made your fortune. A lot of the guys were jealous of you, my brother among them." She paused. "He was the reason you never stepped on our farm, wasn't he? Mamma always wondered why you stayed away."

"I didn't want him to get upset with you because of me."

"Papa told him to watch over Bianca and me. I'm afraid he took his job a little too seriously."

He took a deep breath. "That's all in the past. I'm sure Silvio does very well for himself these days."

"I'll admit he's a great help to Papa. Out of my three brothers *he* will be the one to take over the farm one day."

"Unlike me," he muttered. "I just came from being with my father. When I offered to do the inventory with him, he told me to run along. I'm a no-account in his eyes."

"You've been away a long time. He's probably so thrilled to see you, he's terrified you'll leave again if he says something you don't like."

Her observation surprised him. "You think?"

"I know."

She said it with such authority he almost believed her. "In his eyes I'm not the dependable type, not like Silvio."

"You've already proven you can be whatever you make up your mind to be." She studied him thoughtfully. "If you're here to help your father, just give it a little time and he'll start to believe it."

Maybe she spoke the truth, but right now Valentino didn't want to talk about his father or her brother, who'd given them both grief growing up. He pushed the *torta* toward her. "The cake of the seven veils. Why don't you eat the top layer, I'll start at the bottom and we'll meet somewhere in the middle." He handed her a fork.

With a mysterious smile, she took it from him. "Maybe one bite."

While she toyed with a couple of mouthfuls, he didn't waste any time making inroads. After swallowing some of the hot liquid he said, "So that's the secret behind your weight loss."

A little chocolate remained at the corner of her pliant mouth, tempting him to taste both. The errant thought took him by surprise. Before he could blink she wiped it away with her napkin.

"The Rossettis have always been a hefty bunch. Three years ago I saw a diet plan in a magazine and decided to try it. Bianca had just gotten married and she went on it with me."

"Does she have an hourglass figure, too?"

Again he watched the blush fill her cheeks. "She looks good. Now she's pregnant again."

"Bianca has a baby?"

"Yes. Little Paolito. He's so sweet. I wish he were mine."

The throb in her voice didn't escape him. "How old is he?"

"Six months."

So much had gone on while he'd been pursuing his dreams. "So tell me what you got up to after I left Monta Correnti."

"You mean besides running the fruit stand?"

"Anything you want to divulge."

She studied him for a minute. "Do you remember Lia?"

"Of course. She was your favorite cousin who had a little white fox terrier named Horatio."

"Yes. I'm afraid he finally died of old age. Anyway, she met a man from Naples who has his own construction company. They got married five years ago and live there with their two children. Last year she begged me to come and stay with them.

"I accepted her invitation thinking I'd only be gone from the farm two weeks. Instead I got a job in his office and started business classes at college."

His dark brows lifted in surprise. "Business?

What aspect of business were you thinking of going into? You told me you would never leave the farm." He'd thought he knew all of her dreams.

"The inspiration didn't come into my mind until after you left for Monaco."

"Which meant I stunted your growth."

"Don't be silly." Though she broke into gentle laughter of denial, Valentino realized he really didn't know all there was to know about her at all. That bothered him. In the past he'd taken everything about her for granted. For the first time it hit him what a shallow man he'd been. That bothered him even more.

"You've got me intrigued." Mystified was more like it.

"As you know, I spent my life in our lemon groves. One day I got this idea for doing something with lemons besides selling them."

"But not lemon furniture polish since it had already been invented, right?"

More laughter rumbled out of Clara. "Actually I came up with my own recipe for limoncello."

"Limoncello—?" In his opinion her mother was the best cook on the planet, so he probably shouldn't have been surprised. Again it showed him he'd been so consumed by his own thoughts and interests back then, he hadn't taken the time to explore hers. "Is it good?"

"My business teacher thought it was the best

aperitif he'd ever tasted. He urged me to work up a model for its manufacture and distribution to present in class."

Valentino felt a sudden onset of adrenalin. "I'm jealous he got to sample it first. When am I going to taste it?"

"There's some left at Lia's, I think. I'll phone her and ask her to bring it when she comes for a relative's party tomorrow. You're welcome to try it."

"I'm going to hold you to that offer. So tell me how your project went?"

"I'm afraid I can't," she said, glancing at her watch. "I'm behind schedule now and have to go."

He stifled a protest of exasperation. Just when he was enjoying this conversation more than anything else he'd done in years, Clara was running off again. Her announcement was unacceptable to him. "Where are you going?"

"Shopping." She took one more bite of *torta*, then drank the last of her coffee.

"I'll come with you. I need to pick up a few things myself."

She laughed and shook her head. "I'm afraid this is an expedition for women only. You stay and finish the *torta*." She stood up. "It's been wonderful talking to you again, reminiscing. Thank you for the treat."

Valentino couldn't believe she was ready to leave so fast. "Why don't we meet up later and I'll drive you back to the farm?" He got to his feet.

"That's a very generous offer, but I've made other arrangements. Now I really do have to run."

To Leandro?

He walked her to the entrance, knowing better than to try to detain her. "Thank you for meeting me, Clara. It meant a lot. I'll be in touch."

She darted him a breezy smile. "That would be lovely."

His body tautened. That would be *lovely*? Clara, Clara. What's going on with you? "*Ciao*, *piccola*."

"*Ciao*!"

Frustrated by her hurried departure, he watched her progress. She had an enticing little walk that fascinated him before she disappeared around the corner. Once she was out of sight he took off in the other direction for the villa.

His father had dismissed him, and the too brief interlude with Clara had knocked him off balance. He needed to get out of Monta Correnti in the Ferrari. Opening it up always cleared his head. Why not strike out for Naples?

He could look up some old sailing buddies and visit a few tour operators to drum up business for his father. Some entrepreneur he was when he *knew* better than to approach Luca before he had something concrete to present.

The change in Clara since their first meeting must have affected him more than he'd realized, or else he was losing his edge. *Diavolo*!

CHAPTER THREE

BEFORE breakfast was over Bianca had asked Clara if she wanted help at the stand, but Clara had turned her down. Her sister suffered from bad morning sickness and helped with their grandmother and took care of Paolito while their mother did the cooking and the dishes. Her sister-in-law Maria did the house-cleaning. Everyone had their chores. Clara liked running the stand.

Their farm did big business with outlets all over the region. Trucks came and went from as far as Naples and Rome. As for the fruit stand, it existed for locals and the occasional tourist wanting a small amount of the spillover fruits or olives they could take with them in a bag. The daily intake of money from the sold produce bought the family's groceries.

After dressing in jeans and a filmy light-orange blouse with a ruffled neckline and three-quarter sleeves, Clara went to the kitchen. On the days she worked at the fruit stand, her mother always packed her a lunch.

Once she'd grabbed it and a bottle of water from the fridge, she headed out of the farmhouse. There were only a few wispy clouds above. The air was soft, just the right temperature so she wouldn't overheat while she waited on customers.

Clara felt brighter than usual today. She could attribute her energized condition to Valentino, who'd made yesterday morning magical for her. He would hate it if she told him he'd been like Cinderella's fairy godmother, transforming her life for that hour they'd spent together. It had been liberating to be treated like a normal person.

With her thoughts so full of him, she didn't realize it was Silvio, not Tomaso, who'd done the setting up with the produce from his truck and was waiting for her at the stand.

That was why he'd left the breakfast table early. Now that they were alone, she braced herself for what she sensed was coming. The knowledge cast a shadow on the beauty of the morning.

His dark eyes squinted at her. "I heard you were at the *pasticceria* with Valentino yesterday morning. Signora Bonelli's son was in the back working and saw you."

"So?"

After a sustained pause, "You shouldn't be letting that scum hang around you."

She took a deep breath. "Don't talk that way about Valentino to me. You know nothing about him. Furthermore, you don't have the right."

His scowl grew more pronounced. "You spent your whole life being his shadow. When he went away, he never gave you another thought. Now that he's back and has seen how beautiful you are, he's decided to make you his next conquest before he leaves town again."

Clara rubbed her temples with her fingers, feeling the beginnings of a headache coming on. If she put herself in her brother's place, she could understand where he was coming from except for one reason. "We're friends, Silvio. He doesn't feel that way about me, nor I him." Valentino doesn't try to protect me.

Silvio's face looked like thunder. "A man like him is capable of using a woman whether he has feelings for her or not. It infuriates me that he has suddenly shown up and taken over like he used to do."

"What do you mean take over? We were close friends all the years we were growing up. Is it so terrible that he wants to see me and catch up while he's in town?"

"What about Leandro?"

"What about him? I wasn't interested in him after our first date."

His features grew hard. "No one wants you to

find love more than I do, but we're talking about Valentino Casali, who isn't capable of it, Clara. You realize it's all over the media that he's been living with that French actress."

"I know, but while he's here to see his father, he has decided to take time to renew some old friendships. We met on the staircase near the Piazza Gaspare by accident the other day. You make this sound so sinister when it's nothing like that."

Her brother wasn't listening. "You're risking your happiness to be with him again. Are you out of your mind to let him come around you?"

"If I am, it's *my* business."

"Clara—" he cried, and put his hands on her shoulders, suddenly contrite. "I didn't mean that the way it sounded."

"I know you didn't." Silvio's heart was in the right place, but he'd forgotten she wasn't a child he could order around anymore.

"Don't you know I'd do anything for you? I love you. That's why I don't want to see Valentino take you for a ride and then dump you like he's done all the other women in his life."

She eased away from him. Valentino had never shown her anything but friendship. But the implication that her brother had only ever thought of her as someone to be exploited by him, rather than be considered a lover, carried its own cruel sting.

To her relief a car pulled up the to the covered stand, preventing further conversation. It was a former customer who got into a lively conversation with her. By the time the man drove away again, Silvio had already taken off in his truck for another part of the farm. Much as she loved her brother, she was glad he'd been forced to get back to work.

For the next five hours business was fairly brisk. Clara sat at the small wooden table with the cash box and ate lunch while she waited for more customers. She'd brought a mystery book to read, but the conversation with Silvio had shaken her and she realized her mind was too focused on Valentino to get into it.

Around two-thirty she saw an old blue half-ton pickup truck coming closer. It lumbered up to the stand. The gears ground before it pulled to a stop. She got to her feet.

"*Buon giorno*, *signore*!" she called to the man in the straw hat and sunglasses climbing out of the cab. With his burgundy T-shirt and jeans covering his well-honed physique, she thought he looked familiar.

"It *is* a good afternoon now that I've arrived and see you standing there."

That voice—like running velvet over gravel. "*Tino*—"

"I guess my disguise isn't so bad."

She laughed so hard she almost cried. He threw his head back and laughed with her. Only Valentino would come up with something so completely outrageous. Beneath the brim, his sensual mouth had broken into a heart-stopping smile she couldn't help but reciprocate.

Everyone else wrapped her in cotton wool, but not Valentino. He was such an original and so charismatic, her heart took flight around him. Right now it was racing too fast and made her slightly dizzy. "Until you got out, the old truck and the kind of hat my grandfather used to wear had me completely fooled."

"Then it's possible I've eluded the usual horde of paparazzi."

Before she could countenance it, he went around to open the truck's tailgate. The next thing she knew he'd produced about twenty new bushel-sized baskets that he stacked near the table.

"Is this all that's left of today's produce?" He motioned to the few remaining baskets of fruits and olives.

"Yes."

Without saying anything else he loaded them in the back of his truck and shut the tailgate. Then he pulled out his wallet and put some bills in the cash box. They represented double the amount she would have received if she'd sold everything by the end of the day.

"Don't worry," he said, reading the question in her eyes. "The produce I've purchased won't go to waste."

She shook her head in amusement. "What are you up to?" The sunglasses hid a lot from view.

"What do you think? I intend to spend the rest of the day with you. Now that you've been bought out, you're free to take the time off and enjoy yourself. *Vieni com me*! I'll drive you up to the house so you can take the money inside, then we'll go." He opened the passenger door.

He'd put her in a position where she could hardly refuse. In truth she didn't want to no matter how tired she was already, no matter how loudly Silvio's warnings rang in her ears. "Will the truck make it that far?" she baited him.

His dark brows lifted. Under that hat he looked devastatingly handsome. "Shall we find out?" He helped her inside, then handed her the box after he'd climbed behind the wheel.

"Where did you get this truck?"

"From Giorgio, the sous chef at the restaurant. He has agreed to let me borrow it for a while. I've given him the use of my Ferrari whenever he wants."

"That's a trade he'll never forget, but he'll probably be terrified to drive it."

"You don't know Giorgio. Before the day is out we'll probably see him whizzing around the countryside racking up speeding tickets."

She laughed. "No doubt with the press hounds in hot pursuit."

"Exactly." He drove them up to the farmhouse, then handed her the metal box after she got out.

"I'll take this inside, then I'll be back."

"There's no hurry. I'm planning to feed you after we get to our destination."

"That sounds exciting, but I hope it's not too far. This evening I have plans I can't break." It was the truth. After a day's work she was too tired to do anything but rest. "I'll need to be home by five-thirty at the latest."

"Message received," he muttered.

She jumped down from the cab with the money box and hurried inside the farmhouse to freshen up. Luckily her mother wasn't in the kitchen at that moment. After the run-in with Silvio, she couldn't take defending her actions to anyone else, least of all her parents, who killed themselves trying to remove the stumbling blocks from her path.

While Valentino waited for Clara, his jaw hardened in frustration because she continually kept him on a short leash. Yet the minute she emerged from the farmhouse the sight of those translucent green eyes lighting up as she smiled at him broke through his borderline anger to mesmerize him.

When she climbed in the cab, he turned his head toward her. "You're meeting Leandro later?"

She averted her eyes. "I haven't seen him for a while. For your information I'm going to watch the children while the rest of the family attends my great-uncle's birthday. It's the party Lia's coming to. None of them gets a break very often. My family wants to go early so they can get home early." She flashed him an impish smile. "Both Bianca and Maria get morning sickness at night."

It was on the tip of his tongue to suggest that, since he had nothing else to do with his evening, he'd be more than happy to help her with the children. However, he thought the better of it when he remembered that, besides Paolito, the other three were Silvio's offspring. Clara's brother would probably explode in a fine fury to discover Valentino in the house. That in turn would place Clara in hot water.

"I had something else in mind for us, but under the circumstances I'll drive us to the Trattoria Alberto. They're supposed to give quick service."

"That's the place where a lot of tour buses stop. It's not too far from here. I haven't been there in years." She sounded so relieved he wondered what in blazes was going on with her.

He started up the truck and they left the farm. "How would you like to play spy?"

A chuckle escaped her throat reminding him of the old Clara. "At the trattoria?"

"Yes. One of the reasons I'm in Monta Correnti

for the summer is to see what I can do to help improve business at Rosa."

"You're here for the whole summer?" The shock in her voice wasn't feigned.

"Your comment yesterday decided me."

"What comment?"

"That it will take time to get anywhere with my father." He could also see that he was going to need that much time to get back in Clara's good graces. Nine years away without checking in had done its fair share of damage.

"But what about your bike business and your racing?"

He shrugged his shoulders. "I can run it with my laptop and phone calls. Missing a few races is of little consequence right now. Papa is heavily in debt. Something needs to be done before he plunges any further. Isabella's doing her best. I need to do my part."

A hand went to her throat. "I had no idea."

"Yesterday I met with some tour operators who gave me their itineraries. They all stop at the Trattoria Alberto when they pass through Monta Correnti. I'd like to find out why they think it's a better place than Rosa. While we're eating, let's make a list of what's good and bad about the place and the food. We'll check prices and the number of menu items."

Her face lit up. "This is going to be fun."

Valentino laughed in pure delight to see her act excited. "I thought it might appeal to you."

It didn't take long before they reached the outskirts of town and pulled into the parking area at the side of the trattoria. He showed her inside and they took a seat that gave them visual access to all areas of the dining room. Without a tour-bus crowd, there were quite a few empty tables because it was still early.

Clara chose chicken and he opted for the veal, the two dishes most tourists ordered. They tested two house wines and ordered the most popular desserts. "Your father will be impressed you went to this much trouble in the name of research."

Valentino let out a caustic laugh before swallowing the last spoonful of his gelato. "To tell you the truth, his opinion of me is so low, I doubt he'll give me the time of day to present my findings, but I have to try. He raised me, after all."

She looked at him in seeming consternation. "Why do you say that? What father wouldn't be the proudest man in the world to have a son who has accomplished so much?"

"You'd be surprised." He studied her through shuttered lids. "You're very sweet, Clara."

He had half a mind to unload his secrets on her, but she seemed to have run out of steam. Her eyelids fluttered like someone who was exhausted. When he saw her glance at her watch, he knew the drill. Defeated for the moment, he laid some money on the table and ushered her outside to the truck.

On the way back to the farm she tried to keep up her end of the conversation, but the spark she'd shown earlier had fled. After he turned onto the road leading up to the farmhouse he said, "Will you have coffee with me at Bonelli's in the morning and we'll compare notes before I head to the restaurant to see my father? I'll pick you up."

"No—I mean y-you don't need to do that," she stammered before opening the door. "I'll come on the bus, but it will have to be early, say nine o'clock. I have a dentist appointment at ten."

That was a lie. He felt it in his bones, but he couldn't prove it. "Understood. Thank you for doing this. I'm anxious for your input."

"After the delicious meal you bought me, it's my pleasure. *Domani*, Tino."

He waited until she'd entered the farmhouse. She couldn't seem to get inside fast enough. By the time he took off for Rosa, he was convinced Clara had been playing some kind of game with him from the beginning. He didn't like it. She flitted in and out of his life like a hummingbird, driving him mad.

Evidently she and Leandro weren't an item. If

she were still afraid of Silvio's opinion, why risk more grief by being with Valentino at all? Her behavior raised more questions than it answered because he knew she enjoyed their time together. So did he.

All the subterfuge and time limits had to end. When he asked himself why he cared so much, the answer hit him smack in the gut. *Every time you're with her, it's harder to say goodbye.*

It came as a shock to discover that when we was with Clara, the thought of chucking it all in and whizzing back to Monaco held less and less appeal. This had never happened to him before.

Valentino drove in the alley at the side of the restaurant and pulled up to the back door behind the Ferrari. He got out of the truck and undid the tailgate to carry the baskets of produce into the kitchen. When he unlocked the door, Giorgio smiled at him and came out to help him bring everything inside.

"The Ferrari is sweet," he said in a low voice, kissing his fingers. "The paparazzi chased me everywhere."

"Better your picture than mine showing up in the newspaper. Many thanks for the use of your truck, Giorgio."

"My pleasure."

"I wasn't harassed once and would like to use it again sometime soon."

"No problem at all. We can make a permanent trade any time you want," he teased. "Look at the size of this!" He picked up one of the lemons. "The olives are big, too. Where did all this wonderful-looking fruit come from?"

"The Rossetti farm."

"Ah. I've heard of it. Did you sign a contract with them?"

Valentino had a hunch the type Giorgio was talking about would have to be done over Silvio's dead body. "That's up to my father. Has he been downstairs tonight?"

"No. I haven't seen him."

"What about Isabella?"

"She's out in front setting up for dinner."

"Then I won't disturb her. I'm going back to the villa. When you see her, tell her I'll be over tomorrow."

"*Bene*, Valentino."

They traded keys before he left Rosa and rocked up the mountainside in the Ferrari full of his plans for tomorrow. Clara posed an intriguing challenge, but no one loved meeting one more than Valentino.

When Clara entered the kitchen, her mother had already started cooking breakfast. She looked over at her. "Up so soon? Do you feel sick?"

"No." Just weak. She rubbed her palms against her hips in a nervous gesture.

"That's good. Your papa will be happy to hear it. He worries on these days."

"I know."

"Sit down and I'll serve you now."

"Not today, Mamma."

"But you have to eat!"

"I know. I'm having breakfast in town early."

"Are you getting together with Gina?"

"No." She hadn't talked to her friend in several weeks. "Valentino asked me to meet him at Bonelli's. He's trying to help expand his father's restaurant business."

"Why would he want to do that? It's been doing well, hasn't it?"

"Between us, his father is in debt." Her mother made a tsking sound in her throat. "We had dinner at a competitor's yesterday. This morning we're going to discuss what worked and what didn't. If he can find a way to increase tourist traffic, it will be good for his family…and him."

Clara had seen suffering in his eyes yesterday. She hadn't realized he'd had serious problems with his father. Evidently the breach between them went back years. The pain in his voice had haunted her all night.

A worried look crossed over her mother's expressive features. "Do you think it's a good idea to get this involved with Valentino?"

"We're old friends, Mamma."

"That may be true for him because you're the best friend any person could ever have and he knows it! But the difference is, you've *loved* him since the first time you met him at grade school."

"Yes, I loved him and I always will. You're confusing it with being *in love*."

"That's good you recognize the difference. You're almost twenty-eight, too old to still be nursing a dream that could never become a reality."

Clara lowered her head.

"Forgive me if that hurts you, but you see the news on television," her mother continued talking. "Valentino's been involved with that French actress lately. Last year it was a German model. Before that, an American Olympic skier." With every word that poured forth, her mother drove the nail a little deeper. "How long is he going to be in town?"

"For the summer. His father's not well."

Her mother looked shaken by the news. "Even if he stays that long, which I doubt, his home and his business are in Monaco. Eventually he'll have to go back. In the meantime you can be sure the women in his life have followed him here and won't leave him alone. Don't forget he can be with them whenever and wherever he chooses because he has the means."

"I know." *I know*.

Her mother sniffed. "If he's sandwiching you in between them for a diversion, it's only natural for him, but you're a Rossetti and Rossettis aren't content to be the crumbs off anyone else's table!"

"I agree, Mamma."

"That's good because I don't want my sweet *bambina* getting hurt in the process."

"Silvio gave me the same lecture earlier."

"Your brother feels more fiercely than the others because you grew up together. What affects you, affects him. That's how it is with twins."

Clara knew that, too. Tears streamed down her cheeks. She took a ragged breath. "When I'm with him, he treats me like we were young again, you know?" She didn't dare say she felt like an invalid around the family or it would hurt her mother. "You think I should just tell Valentino it's time for us to let the friendship go?"

"It's not what I think—it's what you *feel* that matters!" She threw her hands in the air. "I'm just afraid you're too vulnerable right now. He wasn't voted the world's most irresistible playboy for nothing!"

She blinked. "How did you know that?"

"I happened to see it in a magazine Bianca was reading. I'm afraid your sister used to have a terrible crush on him. Do you understand what I'm trying to say? If my words sound cruel, I'm sorry because you know I love you to death."

"I love you, too," she whispered in turmoil.

"I would never say such a thing in front of the men in our family, but I say it to you. And now that I have, it is your decision what happens from here on out."

Her mother's words stayed with her while she washed the tears from her face. "I'll see you later today, Mamma." On the way out the door she grabbed an apple from the bowl to eat on the bus.

By the time she joined Valentino a half-hour later, she'd made up her mind to enjoy this morning's get-together. Maybe by the end of this day she would have gained some wisdom and would know how to tell him she couldn't see him anymore.

The problem was, he was sensitive deep down; Clara knew that and she would never want to hurt his feelings. No one would believe an insecure man lived beneath his famous persona. It stemmed from the troubled relationship with his father. He'd let her see inside him just enough for her to feel a little of his torment.

Oh, Tino.

Valentino stood at the bus stop waiting for Clara. Through his sunglasses he watched the activity in the piazza. So far his navy headscarf and striped sailor shirt with the long sleeves had disguised him enough to keep the paparazzi away.

His outfit must have done a better job than he realized because when she got off the bus at ten to nine, she walked past him in her blue print blouse and denim skirt without realizing it. He followed her into Bonelli's.

There were half a dozen people drinking coffee at individual bistro tables while they read the newspaper. He'd already staked out their table in the same corner as before.

"I'm over here, Clarissima."

She wheeled around in surprise. A slow smile broke out on her stunning face. "I would never have guessed it was you! You look like a French seaman on leave from Marseille or some such port."

"That's the way I'd like to keep it."

"I know," she said in a quiet voice. "I won't give you away."

He held her chair, then sat down opposite her. "Help yourself." He'd already taken their cappuccinos and ham-filled croissants to the table.

"Thank you. After all the food we ate last evening, can you believe I'm hungry again?" She bit into her breakfast.

Valentino smiled as he devoured his. "How did the babysitting go?"

"None of them wanted to go to bed. We ended up having our own party."

He'd wanted to be there. The night had been

endless for him. "Is that why you seem a little tired this morning?"

"Yes," she murmured, but she didn't look at him as she said it.

"Did Lia bring the limoncello with her?"

Her lips curved upward. "She did."

"Good. I'm already salivating for it." Color seeped into her cheeks. "Have you given serious thought to the plus side of the trattoria?"

Clara sipped her cappuccino. "Yes. The placement of the tables was conducive to private conversation. The service was good. The chicken was tender, the gelato excellent." He liked watching her mouth as she spoke. Even when she had been a girl it had a passionate flare.

"What about the negatives?"

"The *bruschetta* was mediocre, the wine so-so, the pasta seemed too greasy and the bathroom needed attention."

He chuckled. "My sentiments exactly, *piccola*. Bravo. I was going to add that the prices were too high."

"Yes, but they obviously lower them for the tour-bus crowds. Oh—something else. The decor wasn't that unique. Not anything like your father's restaurant."

"Well, it's possible Papa will be interested in our findings and can point out the differences to the tour directors when I invite them to Rosa for a meal."

"Rosa's sauce is to die for, Tino."

"My father will be delighted to hear that Signora Rossetti's daughter has given her seal of approval. What Papa really needs is your mother in his kitchen. I ate most of your lunches at school, if you remember."

"I haven't forgotten anything," she admitted in an odd tone before suddenly getting to her feet. "Thank you for breakfast. Now I need to get going to my appointment."

For once Valentino was ready for that and stood up. "I appreciate your taking the time to meet me first." He walked her outside. "After I've met with Papa, I'll call you and tell you what he said."

As she gazed at him her eyes clouded over. "I hope he shows you how thrilled he is that his wonderful son is trying to help him." Her earnestness resonated to his insides. He couldn't hold back any longer.

"I'm not his wonderful anything, Clara. He's not my biological father. You might as well know I'm the product of an extramarital affair."

He heard her long gasp. "Your mother was unfaithful?"

"Yes. She and Luca hit a bad patch in their marriage, but they made up."

She looked devastated for him. "Do you know your birthfather?"

"No, and when I learned about it, I didn't want

to know him. Neither did Luca apparently, so I was raised as a Casali."

"Then he must have loved your mother and you very much."

Valentino studied her upturned features. "You come from a very loving, close-knit family. You see only the good. It's a remarkable trait. Don't ever lose it."

She bit her lip. "You've never told anyone?"

"Isabella and Cristiano know. Our parents told all of us before Mamma died so there'd be no secrets, but it's not common knowledge."

"I'll never say anything," she whispered.

"You think I don't know that?"

"Tino—" She sounded distressed. "I—I'd like to stay longer and talk to you, but I have to go or I'll be late. Forgive me."

"Of course. I'll be in touch."

She nodded before hurrying away across the piazza. Once she disappeared he rushed after her, realizing she'd taken the set of stairs where she'd come down that first day.

When he reached it and mounted the narrow staircase to the next level of the town, she was nowhere in sight. There were more residences than shops in this area. He looked all around, noticing the local clinic on his left. He'd never known a dental office to be in there, but maybe things had changed.

Give her a few more minutes before you burst in looking for her, Casali.

If he did find her inside, he'd be risking her anger because it smacked of invading her privacy. She might never speak to him again.

After the conversation they'd had the other day on the subject of maintaining one's privacy, there was a certain irony to this kind of thinking—and danger. But that was what he thrived on. At this late date he couldn't change his character if he tried and determined to take his chances.

He watched the locals go in and come out the doors of the clinic. He waited another minute, then walked inside. Just as he'd thought, the wall plaque didn't indicate any dentists in the building. Beyond the foyer was a waiting room full of patients. He couldn't see Clara among them. She might not be here at all, but he had to check.

Chagrined that he hadn't followed her more closely, Valentino had no choice but to approach the receptionist at the desk. When she got off the phone he said, "Could you tell me if Clara Rossetti has already gone in for her appointment?"

"I'm sorry. Even if she were a patient here, I can't give you that information unless you're the police or her next of kin."

For no good reason the hairs lifted on the back of his neck. The receptionist had given nothing away, yet for the first time since coming back to Monta Correnti a little frisson of alarm darted through him. It was that same feeling he got on the racetrack when he sensed something wasn't right and braced himself for what was coming around the next curve.

"I'm her fiancé," he lied without compunction. "I've been at sea for a long time, but got shore leave specifically to see her. Her sister Bianca told me I'd find her here for her ten o'clock appointment." If lightning struck him, he didn't care.

"In that case, go back to the foyer and down the hall to the dialysis clinic."

Dialysis—

A shudder rocked his body. That meant kidney failure. People *died* from it.

No. Not Clara. He'd just come from being with her. Though she'd looked tired, she'd seemed healthy to him.

He shook his head, trying to make sense of it.

She couldn't be dying. That was preposterous! Valentino didn't believe it. He must have misunderstood the receptionist.

Bile rose in his throat. He couldn't seem to swallow.

"*Signore*? Are you all right?" The woman at the desk stared up at him anxiously.

"Yes," he whispered.

"You didn't know?"

A groan escaped his throat. Her question made it all too real. It meant that the first day he'd seen her on the staircase between the buildings, she'd just come from the clinic.

And the other morning when she'd said she had shopping to do, she'd been on her way here…

He half staggered out to the foyer where he saw the sign for directions to the dialysis clinic.

CHAPTER FOUR

AFTER having to tear herself away from Valentino, Clara had been plunged into a new low of despair. This time it was for him.

Luca Casali wasn't his birthfather?

Though Valentino might have been living with that knowledge since childhood, a boy would still yearn to know his own flesh and blood father, or at least have *some* information about him. While Cristiano and Isabella had lived with the security of enjoying both parents' love, Valentino couldn't claim the same thing.

If Clara's life didn't depend on this treatment, she wouldn't have left him standing there in front of Bonelli's looking tortured.

Like a slot machine that went chink chink chink, little pieces of memory started fitting together in a mosaic that explained to some extent why he'd been drawn to Clara more than his own siblings during those early years. When he'd lost his mother, he'd needed a friend, no doubt because he didn't feel as if he belonged to the Casali household in quite the same way as the other two.

No one at school had had any comprehension of his struggles, including Clara. While she lay there, she wept for the boy inside the incredible man he'd become.

It was impossible to settle down and concentrate on anything else right now. Normally after she was hooked up to the large hemodialysis machine and the clinician had left the room, she could absorb herself in a good mystery novel. She'd put a new one in her purse, but hadn't opened it yet. She couldn't.

As weak as she'd felt after getting off the bus earlier today, the sight of Valentino wearing jeans that molded his powerful thighs had set off a burst of adrenalin, giving her an extra boost of energy.

He was an impossibly handsome man. In that headscarf and sailor shirt revealing his well-defined physique, he looked like a cross between a dashing pirate and a Gypsy. It couldn't be easy being so famous he had to go to such lengths to avoid the constant crush of the media.

It took a remarkable man to rise above his pain. Valentino made every moment of life exciting. That was one of his many gifts. Who else would have ordered a decadent chocolate dessert they could share and make the moment seem like a fabulous party he'd created just for her?

If Silvio knew the true Valentino the way she did, he wouldn't have grilled her so mercilessly the other morning while she'd been running the fruit stand. He'd fired questions at her she couldn't answer and wouldn't anyway.

When Valentino had come by the farm in the latest model Ferrari, it had reminded her brother of the differences between them, but that wasn't the underlying reason for his bitterness. To her dismay, the girl her brother had been infatuated with in high school had wanted nothing to do with him because she'd been so crazy about Valentino and he had gone through girls like water.

Even though Silvio had moved on to other women and had eventually married Maria, her brother's pride had never got over the rejection. As Valentino's fame grew, so did Silvio's envy for the women—the money—everything that seemed to come to him with what looked like no effort at all. In truth he couldn't forgive Valentino and didn't want Clara to have anything to do with him. In this area, he'd become irrational.

If he knew how hard it had been for Valentino growing up, even if Luca had been good to him, her brother would have a different perspective. Silvio basked in the love of both parents. All of the Rossettis did. How lucky they were!

Depleted physically and emotionally by the distressing revelation, she let out a deep sigh and closed her eyes, aching for Valentino's pain and wishing the treatments didn't take so long. But she couldn't complain, not when they were keeping her alive.

While she lay there on top of the cot fully dressed, she heard the door open. The clinician checked on her every little while. With her eyes still closed she said, "I'm doing fine, Serena."

"That's music to my ears," sounded a deep, familiar male voice.

Her eyelids flew open at the same time her heart clapped inside her chest. She discovered Valentino bigger than life, standing at the side of her bed opposite the machine. He removed his sunglasses and scarf, revealing disheveled dark brown hair. It only added to his potent male appeal.

"You *followed* me!" she cried in a combination of anger and exasperation.

"Guilty as charged."

No one had ever looked less penitent. "How did you get in here?"

"They weren't going to let me in, but I found your clinician. When I told her I was your fiancé she took pity on me."

Of course she did. Serena was a female. No woman was immune to Valentino's charm.

Clara should have been furious he'd found out her secret, but it was so like Valentino to go where angels feared to tread when he wanted answers to questions, she started to laugh and couldn't stop. Maybe it was contagious because he laughed, too. Soon the tears actually trickled from the corners of both their eyes.

They were still laughing when a smiling Serena poked her head inside the door. "I've never heard you laugh before. There's nothing like a fiancé showing up to turn your world around, eh, Clara? I didn't know you had such a gorgeous one. You're a dark horse, you know that?"

After giving Valentino another once-over, she grinned and shut the door again. It wouldn't be long before Serena connected his looks with the legend that preceded him and would know it was all a lie. But right now Clara didn't care.

Those intelligent dark eyes of his searched hers for endless seconds. His expression grew solemn. "How long have you been undergoing these treatments, *piccola*?" he whispered in a shaky voice.

"Three weeks."

He pulled up a chair and sat down next to her with his tanned hands clasped between strong legs. She saw him looking at the graft below the place where she'd rolled up her sleeve. The loop had been surgically inserted in her right arm where her blood was drained and bathed in solution to separate the impurities before returning to her bloodstream.

She heard his sharp intake of breath. "Is this the reason you've lost so much weight?"

"No. I was perfectly healthy until two months ago when I cut my leg on one of the thorny twigs of a lemon tree at the farm. It developed into a blood infection that led to hemolytic uremic syndrome. That caused an acute failure of my kidneys."

A pulse throbbed at the corner of his hard, male mouth. "They don't function at all?"

Clara shook her head. "I have what's known as ESRD."

A bleak look entered his eyes. After a long pause, "Does this mean a kidney transplant is the only cure?" She felt his solemn tone in every sick atom of her body.

"Yes, provided it's the right match. My parents and siblings have tried to donate theirs, but because of weight problems or high blood pressure or pregnancy, they've been turned down."

He rubbed a hand over his face. "Tell me you're on a waiting list—"

"Of course."

"What kind of time are you talking here?" He fired comments and questions at her so fast she was dizzy. In fact she'd never known him to be this intense. The businessman in him had come out.

"I don't know. Waiting for a suitable match is a complicated process. You think there's one available, but then, for one reason or another, it can't or doesn't happen."

"You have a big extended family. Surely there's someone."

"Two of my relatives would be matches, but they have diabetes so that rules them out. One of my aunts was prepared to go through tests, but she has had cancer in the past and the risk is too high for her. My best chance is to receive a kidney from an altruistic donor, but they're hard to come by when thousands of people ahead of me are waiting for one."

"Tell me what you mean by altruistic."

"A non-related person who wants to give a kidney to a loved one, but it's not a match, so they still donate a kidney to someone who is. There are chains of groups of people who do this, but it's a case of finding them and linking up so their serum can be tested against my PRA."

He frowned. "PRA?"

"It means my serum has been mixed with a panel of sixty random donors to see the reaction to the antibodies. Mine is fairly low which is a plus. Kidney allocations are based on a mathematical formula. It awards points for factors that affect a successful transplant."

"What are the other factors?"

"Age and good health. I have all those things going for me."

He reached out to grasp her free hand. "How often do you come here?"

"Three times a week."

"That's virtually every other day—" He sounded aghast.

"It's not so bad when you consider there's no other way for my blood to get filtered."

"Why isn't someone in your family driving you here and picking you up?"

"I don't want to be a burden to them."

He seemed to have trouble sitting there. "You've never been a burden to anyone in your whole life."

Unbidden tears filled her eyes. "I am now. Everyone works so hard at the farm. It's bad enough that I can only do my part on the farm three days a week. There's Nonna who needs taking care of now that she's in a wheelchair and learning to talk again. Bianca has a baby and another one on the way, and Maria's expecting for the fourth time."

Valentino squeezed her fingers gently. "I've upset you when I didn't mean to. Every time we've been together, you've always had to leave.

It has been so unlike the Clara I used to know, I've been at a loss. Because you didn't explain your condition to me, I had to find out the truth for myself. Forgive me for bursting in on you like this?"

His pained eyes were so imploring, she didn't want him to feel bad. After the painful experience he'd had with his father the other morning, she didn't want to add to it. "There's nothing to forgive. I didn't say anything because I've loved spending time with someone who didn't know about my condition and treated me like a normal, healthy person. If anything, I'm the one who needs to ask your forgiveness."

"*Clara*..."

She smiled at him. "You wouldn't be Tino if you hadn't made up your mind to do something no one else would think of doing to get inside this room."

"How did all this start?"

"You don't want to hear all this."

"Let me be the judge of that."

She moved her head back and forth. "Are you sure?"

Lines hardened his features. "You know me well enough to realize I never do anything I don't want to do."

Perhaps that was true once. She had no way of knowing what he was like now, but, since he showed no signs of leaving her bedside, she decided to humor him.

"After I got sick, I had to leave Lia's to come home. The doctor sent me to a specialist, who diagnosed my condition. One thing led to another and I was forced to drop out of school."

A shadow crossed over his handsome features before he found her hand again and kissed the fingertips one by one. His touch melted her like a serving of gelato left in the hot sun. "I'm going to let you rest. Before I leave, is there anything I can do for you?"

She knew it. Now that he'd learned about her condition, he was going to start treating her like all the others. In a matter of seconds she'd gone from being his fun-loving friend to invalid. He'd never held her hand and kissed it before. She couldn't bear it now. Not from him.

"Yes," she said brightly, removing it. "Will you open my purse and bring me the book I brought to read? It's on that table."

Within seconds the task was accomplished. He glanced at the title. "I've heard this is good."

"I hope so." She took it from his hand. "Thank you."

Before he left, taking all the excitement with him, he put on his sunglasses and tied the scarf around his head. "Think I'll still fool the paparazzi?" He flashed her a dazzling white smile, reminding her of the French fictional character Marius who went to sea in the story from Pagnol's *Fanny*.

At the time, she could see that Valentino totally related to the young man who dreamed of seeing the world. Clara, on the other hand, could totally relate to Fanny, who loved him, but knew she had to let him go in order for him to be happy. It was one of their favorite books in lit class. "But of course! *Au revoir*, Marius!"

Marius?

Valentino forced a grin, not having thought about that story or their involved discussions of the characters in a long time. Her humor in spite of her condition humbled him, but inside he was dying.

She looked so damned beautiful and helpless lying there, he couldn't take his eyes off her. The urge to do many things for her was so great, he needed to get out of the room in order to hold onto his sanity.

"*A presto*," he whispered, kissing her forehead.

Once he left her room, he saw Serena and headed in her direction. "Can we talk for a moment?"

"By all means."

"I lied to you before."

She smiled. "I know. If I hadn't recognized you as Valentino Casali, you would never have made it in to see Clara. The way you two were laughing in there, I knew I'd done the right thing. It's the best medicine for her."

He nodded. "Thank you for allowing me in. Would you do me one more favor and give me the name and number of her specialist?"

"Come over to the desk and I'll write it down. Dr. Arno's office is in Rome, but he's overseeing Clara's case."

Once Valentino had it in hand, he thanked her again. After leaving the clinic, he quickly found the secret alleyways through the upper region of the town, not stopping until he reached the villa.

When he checked his watch, he realized Dr. Arno would be in his office for hours yet, that was if it were a normal day for him. No matter what, Valentino needed to talk to him.

The receptionist at his office in Rome answered. When Valentino explained the nature of his emergency, she said the doctor was on vacation and wouldn't be returning for a few more days. But she'd make certain he got back to Valentino ASAP.

Wild with pain, he needed a lot of information pronto! After hanging up, he put in a call to Dr. Rimbaud, his own doctor in Monaco, asking him to phone him back. While he waited for the call, he showered and changed into chinos and a sport shirt. He was drinking some coffee when his phone rang. Valentino grabbed for it.

"Dr. Rimbaud—thanks for getting back to me so fast."

"I thought I'd better in case you've been in another crash," he kidded him.

"Not this time."

"You sound serious, not like yourself. What's wrong?"

"Will you tell me what you can about kidney failure?"

"Uh oh. Anyone I know?"

"No. It's a close friend of mine."

"I'm sorry to hear that. Give me a few particulars."

Once Valentino had unloaded about Clara, the doctor told him what he could. "Those treatments take between four and five hours. Afterward she'll be weak and need rest. Sometimes the patient suffers a sudden loss in blood pressure or gets muscle cramps. One or all of those reasons was why she'd been in a hurry to get on the bus the other day."

"Of course." Valentino had read all the signs wrong. She'd run from him because she wasn't well, and because she had her pride. The Rossettis possessed that in abundance. Clara wouldn't even let her family drive her to the clinic and back.

"Depending on her individual health, she probably needs to eat more animal protein. If necessary she might have to cut milk, cheese, salt and soft drinks. She'll do better on the day after each dialysis treatment. That explains her ability to work at her family's fruit stand."

"How long can she go on like this?"

"Most patients live longer on dialysis these days, but her End Stage Renal Disorder might be more severe. Perhaps she's been diagnosed with anemia. There could be other problems, too, like bone disease, nerve damage or high blood pressure. These are complications you'll have to discuss with her specialist. Naturally the most desired thing would be to find a compatible donor for a transplant as soon as possible."

He closed his eyes tightly. Dr. Arno couldn't call him back fast enough. In the meantime, Valentino intended to be there for her in every conceivable way.

"Thank you, Dr. Rimbaud. What you've told me helps a lot."

"Call me anytime."

As soon as he hung up, he phoned for a taxi to take him to the local market. Once there he did some shopping, satisfied that the paparazzi would be looking in vain for his Ferrari. Until further notice it would stay in the garage. He would wait outside the doors to the clinic in the taxi until she emerged, then offer her a ride home.

"*Signore*?" the chauffeur called to him. "We've arrived."

"So we have."

He instructed him to wait in the loading zone. His pulse picked up speed when he finally saw Clara start out the clinic doors. She looked good, not as pale as she'd been last evening. He stepped out of the taxi into her path so she had to stop.

"How come you keep following me?" he baited her gently.

She lifted her beautiful head so he could see the green flecks in her eyes.

"Tino—"she cried in shock, but her eyes lit up. This was a bonus he hadn't expected after barging in on her treatment.

"Come on. I've brought cold fruit juice and a chicken sandwich for you. You can eat it on the way back to the farm."

He could tell she wanted to argue with him, but she didn't have the kind of strength she needed for that. "Where's the Ferrari?" she asked as he helped her into the backseat.

After he gave the driver directions, he handed her a sandwich and a drink before sitting back to answer her question. "It's out of sight for a variety of reasons."

"That will drive the paparazzi crazy." She took several bites of her sandwich. "I have to admit this tastes delicious. You're spoiling me with good food again."

He'd bought himself a fruit drink and drained

most of it. "I wonder how many hundreds of times you shared your lunch with me at school because I was too busy doing some project to stop and eat. Your mother made the best lunches in Monta Correnti."

A trace of a smile hovered on her lips as she continued to eat. "Our family carried around the excess pounds to prove it."

He flashed her a sweeping glance. "Not any longer."

She avoided his gaze and drank more juice.

"Does your mother know she kept me alive with her cooking?"

"I didn't dare tell her."

Valentino chuckled. "You're lucky you've had her in your life all these years. Do you want to know a secret?"

Clara's head turned in his direction. She'd finished the last of her sandwich. He was thankful she'd had an appetite. "What is it?"

"I was jealous you had a mother who fussed over you every day. You and Bianca always seemed so happy. You didn't know it, but having two parents who were alive and loved you gave you a confidence I would have given anything to feel."

Her expression sobered. "I understand that now, but you did have Luca."

"Yes, and he indulged me without limits."

"That was only natural. After your mother died, he would have tried to play both roles. He loved you, Tino. I know he did. Otherwise his marriage to your mother wouldn't have worked out."

"I guess he wanted her badly enough to include her excess baggage."

In a surprise gesture she covered his hand with her own and squeezed it gently. "I'm so sorry you've carried this pain with you all these years. I often sensed something was wrong, but you never opened up about it."

"I couldn't."

Her head was bowed. "None of us is exempt from problems, but somehow we deal with them because we have no choice, right?"

He marveled at her courage. "*Sì.*"

She let go of his hand. "We're almost to the farm."

Valentino told the driver to turn onto the private road where you could see the sign advertising produce at the Rossetti farm. He told him to follow it all the way in to the farmhouse and pull to a stop.

The minute the taxi slowed down, Clara had the door open. He knew better than to ask her to stay with him and talk. She was probably craving her bed.

"Thank you for the food and the ride, Tino. You saved my life today."

Would that were possible.

"I always enjoy being with you."

She couldn't meet his gaze. "Where are you going now?"

"Home to work on the Web site."

"What did your father say about your ideas?"

"I've decided to wait until I have all the facts at hand, then present them in one go and see how he reacts."

"I think you'll be surprised how accepting he is of your ideas."

"We'll see. Your optimism gives me hope."

"That's good," came her fervent reply.

He leaned toward her. "I'm going to come by for you in the truck after you're off work tomorrow."

Clara felt her pulse race. "What did you have in mind?"

"I thought we'd drive to Gaeta—we went there once, remember? We'll enjoy a meal on the coast. It's not too far. We'll take it in stages. If you feel like sleeping on the way, you can."

He still wanted to be with her?

"I'd love it!" she broke in. To go to the sea with him sounded divine.

His mouth broke into a satisfied smile. "I'm happy to hear it. Get a good sleep. I'll be by about three."

"All right. *Ciao*."

Clara entered the kitchen feeling more light-hearted than she'd been in days. Who else but Valentino would have pretended to be her fiancé so he could gain access to the treatment room? She'd noticed that none of the workers at the clinic were immune to his compelling personality and looks. He'd been the talk of the place. Serena had been totally won over.

As for the taxi waiting for her, it might as well have been a golden coach whisking her away from the castle with her dashing prince while he fed her on the way. Because of his kindness, her body didn't get a chance to feel depleted as it did when she had to walk down to the piazza and then wait for the bus.

She'd been utterly shocked to see him outside the doors. And grateful… He could have no idea how wonderful it was to just get in the car and be waited on as if she were a princess.

Though he'd told her earlier that he had no interest in knowing the identity of the man who'd had an affair with his mother, Clara couldn't help but think his birthfather must have been an extraordinary person with exceptional looks and drive. Otherwise Valentino wouldn't have turned out to be such a brilliant entrepreneur and heart-throb.

"What's the great Valentino Casali doing bringing you home in a taxi?" Silvio had just walked in the kitchen. He wasn't usually home this early.

"He was thoughtful enough to give me a lift from town."

Her brother grimaced. "Did he think that by not bringing you in the Ferrari, the family wouldn't notice?"

"Why would he be concerned about that?" she asked, attempting to control her temper without much success. "If he didn't choose to drive it, it was probably because he was tired of the paparazzi following him every second of his life."

"Why do you let him do it?" he demanded. "Don't you get it?"

"You can stop worrying. It hardly smacks of the kind of attention you're talking about. I'm a dying woman."

"Don't ever say that again!" he cried.

"But I *am* dying, Silvio. You have to face it. We're all going to die some time. I just happen to know that without a new kidney, it will happen to me sooner than later."

"How can you talk that way?"

"How can I not? You've got to stop being angry about it. As things get worse, Mamma and Papa are going to need your strength, not your rage."

His eyes grew moist. "You've been so brave. If the almighty Casali had any idea what you're dealing with now—"

"Actually he does. In fact he sat with me in the clinic today while I was getting my treatment."

"I don't believe it," his voice shook. "You *told* him you have ESRD?"

"No. We met in town before my appointment. After I said goodbye to him, he followed me to the clinic and pretended to be…a relative." She caught herself in time. "He did that so he could get in to see me. At the end of the treatment he brought me home so I wouldn't have to take the bus. He even brought food and drinks because he knew I needed it after dialysis."

Silvio looked dumbfounded.

"Please let's not argue over him. He's been nothing but kind to me and now I'm tired." She felt his eyes on her as she left the kitchen to go upstairs. All she wanted to do was go to bed and dream about tomorrow when he came for her.

One more outing, then she'd tell him that, as much as she enjoyed his company, her illness was slowly draining her to the point that any social life had to end. She was hurtling through space toward a black void from which there could be no return. Where she was going, he couldn't go.

She knew Valentino well enough to know his compassion for her condition would prompt him to continue making himself available to her. She also knew herself well enough to know she would cling more and more to him because he *was* life to her.

Clara couldn't think of a worse scenario for a man whose freedom meant everything to him.

On the way back to town, Valentino had to admit it was getting more difficult to drive away after they'd been together. When he thought about it, he'd never liked parting company with Clara. Until he heard from the doctor, he was going to be on tenterhooks.

In the meantime he needed to keep so busy he wouldn't be able to think. But he soon discovered that work was no panacea for his heartache. Nothing could take it away. It went so deep, he couldn't find solace.

Every time he thought about her pain and what she was facing, he was pierced to the quick. His agony drove him to get in his car. He started driving through the countryside with no destination in mind. While he was en route, the wildflowers seemed to flaunt their fragrance in the night air as if to impress upon him the delights Clara might not be able to enjoy much longer.

Crazed by the thought that a life as sweet and innocent as hers could be coming to an end, he found himself headed for the church. Eventually he pulled up in front of the rectory. It was after nine p.m. when he levered himself from the car and was made instantly aware of the sound of crickets chirping. Tonight all his senses had come alive to nature, sending bittersweet pains through his body.

He took the steep steps two at a time to gain the porch, not hesitating to tug on the bell pull. In a few minutes, a much younger priest he didn't recognize opened the door.

"Yes?"

"I'm here on an emergency to see Father Orsini. Is he still awake?"

"I believe so."

"Will you tell him it's Valentino Casali? If he can see me, tell him I'll be out here waiting for him."

The other man studied him for a brief moment. "*Bene*," he said before shutting the door.

Unable to remain still, Valentino walked to the wrought-iron railing and looked out over Monta Correnti. The lights of the town with its red-tiled roofs and centuries-old palazzos spilled over the undulating hills, creating a fairyland illusion. In the distance, the Rossetti farm made up part of the magical landscape.

Would that what he'd learned at the clinic today were just a bad dream from which he'd awaken at any moment.

"Valentino?" came a familiar voice. "Don't tell me you're here to confess ten years' worth of sins?" He'd asked the question in a joking manner, but the ring of hope lingered in the night air.

Consumed by a guilt so deep he'd never been able to talk about it, he turned to face the gray-haired priest who'd grown much more frail over the last decade. "Not tonight, Father. Otherwise you would never get to bed," he teased. Their easy relationship stretched back to Valentino's childhood.

Father Orsini chuckled. The years hadn't deprived him of a sense of humor, for which Valentino was thankful. "It's good to see you."

"Then you'll understand how pleased I was when Father Bruno told me Monta Correnti's most legendary figure was outside waiting for me."

"Let's not play games, Father. A legendary figure should at least connote someone worthy." He shifted his weight. "Forgive me for calling on you so late, but this couldn't wait."

"Evidently not. Let me put it another way. What's troubling Luca Casali's most famous son?"

"Famous for what?" Valentino muttered in self-abnegation. "Certainly nothing that matters." When the priest blinked in astonishment, Valentino added, "Did Luca or my mother ever take the opportunity to tell you I'm not his birth son?"

"*What is this*?" Father Orsini cried out aghast.

"I don't blame you for being bewildered. Forget I asked."

"My son—"

"It's all right, Father. If you *did* know, you couldn't reveal it anyway. He and Mamma told me the truth years ago. It was a good idea at the time considering I don't look or behave anything like Isabella or Cristiano."

"Do your siblings know?"

"You mean that my infamous qualities can be laid at my biological father's feet?" he mocked. "Yes, but that's not why I'm here. What I'm hoping is that you'll be able to help me over another matter. It's of life and death importance."

The priest cleared his throat. "If I can, but that places a great burden on me."

Valentino squinted at him. "I knew you'd say that, but I have nowhere else to turn." He stared at the priest. "What do you know about Clara Rossetti?"

In the quiet that followed, a sadness entered Father Orsini's eyes and he pursed his lips, giving Valentino the answer. Fresh pain arced through him as surely as if he'd crashed on the track and the paramedics couldn't separate his body from the wreckage.

The compassionate priest put a hand on Valentino's shoulder. "She doesn't want to die and is fighting this with everything she has in her."

Valentino's body trembled. "I know. I've been with her every day since I came home. She's so courageous, I'm in awe of her."

"You two were very close growing up."

A sob got trapped in his throat. "Very. I don't want her to die, Father."

"Of course you don't. After being away such a long time, this news must have come as a great shock."

Shock hardly covered it. Shame for his narcissistic lifestyle had seeped into his soul. Up to now Valentino had lived only for his own pleasures. He'd avoided marriage and children in order to pursue new adventures without suffering any more guilt than he already dragged around.

In the process he'd pretty well abandoned his family, not to mention Clara. Valentino wasn't only selfish, he was a coward unwilling to face certain unpalatable truths. After his aunt Lisa had leaked the latest family secret, his first instinct had been to run away and stay in denial. That had been his pattern over the years.

That was the mortifying part. After spending time with him during their growing-up years, Clara had become so well acquainted with his self-focused obsessions, she'd written him off when he'd left in his late teens. And why not?

What had he ever done for her?

His hands curled into fists.

Nothing! Not a damn thing!

It strained his credulity that she'd given him the time of day since he'd been back. While he'd been off in his superficial world, angry at life while he tried to break barriers and set new bars, she had been battling for her life!

Somewhere in his psyche Valentino had known there'd be a price to pay for always running away, for always taking without giving anything back. He just hadn't expected it to come now, in this particular form. Clara, more than any other human being, had shown him unqualified friendship, but he hadn't realized or understood until it was too late.

"I can see you're in pain, my son."

"I want to help her, but I don't know where to begin."

"She could use a good friend."

Something he hadn't been.

"Is there anything else you'd like to discuss with me?"

Valentino shook his head. "No, *grazie*." He had quite enough on his plate and had said more than he should already. Calling on the priest this late at night constituted a special act of selfishness all its own, the kind for which Valentino was famous.

Luca's "famous" son who really wasn't his son. The negative connotation fit.

"I've intruded on your time long enough. Thank you for seeing me, Father. *Buona notte*." He started down the stairs.

"Don't be such a stranger!" the old priest called after him.

Valentino deserved that particular distinction, too. A stranger was one who was neither a friend nor an acquaintance. Those who knew his name would say that pretty well summed up his existence.

He waved to the priest from the lowered window of the car before he headed back to the villa. His black thoughts drove him to the kitchen where he made a pot of strong coffee. On an empty stomach the caffeine was guaranteed to keep him wired for the rest of the night. He did his best thinking when he prowled around in the dark.

The priest's words wouldn't leave him alone. *She could use a good friend.*

That meant making a commitment you didn't break.

For the rest of the night Valentino searched his soul. By the time morning came eight hours later, he'd determined Clara Rossetti would discover how good a friend he could be, even if she didn't believe it right now.

CHAPTER FIVE

"VALENTINO has come for me, Mamma. We're driving to Gaeta. Just so you know, I've come to a decision. After today, I won't be seeing him anymore. He knows I'm dying, and he'll respect my wishes."

Her mother let out a heavy sigh and stopped stirring the sauce she was cooking. "I'm glad to hear it, for his sake as well as yours. And I'll tell you something else. You're not going to die if *I* can help it! The doctor has assured me they're doing everything to find the right donor for you. God hears me beg for your life every minute of the day and night."

Clara lowered her head, humbled by her mother's love. The doctor had told them they needed a miracle, but she knew that even if a kidney became available from a non-relative, there was always the possibility her body would reject it.

"See you later, Mamma." She hugged her mother, then hurried outside to the old truck. Valentino got out of the cab wearing the same straw hat. When she drew closer, he flashed her a broad smile.

"*Buon giorno, piccola.*" He was hiding something behind his back.

"What have you got there?"

"You need a disguise, too," he said before putting a matching hat on her head. "You look very fetching with it perched at that angle. From a distance we'll look like an old farming couple taking a break after a busy morning."

She loved it! They left the farm and headed in the direction of the coast. The truck made for slow going, but she felt very much at home in it. The Rossettis didn't drive anything but trucks.

They ate some plums he brought and made desultory conversation while they drove through the enchanting countryside. Clara felt so carefree and relaxed that in time she found her eyelids drooping and fought to stay awake.

Nestling against the door, she closed her eyes, telling herself it would only be for a moment. The next time she became aware of her surroundings, she was cognizant of two things: the tangy smell of the Mediterranean and the feel of Valentino's hard-muscled arm against her cheek and shoulder. He'd always smelled so good. It had to be from the soap he used in the shower.

"Oh—I'm sorry—" She sat up horribly embarrassed that she'd been asleep for an hour with her arm against him. Her hat was askew. How was it she'd ended up pressed to the side of his fit body instead of the door? Looking straight ahead, she glimpsed the Gulf of Gaeta spread out before her like a sparkling blue jewel in the sunlight.

Valentino had removed his sunglasses and cast her a sideward glance. "Why apologize? You needed your sleep. I'm hungry and presume you are, too."

"I am." Food had never sounded so good to her before.

"After we eat, we'll take a walk on the beach if it's warm enough for you and you're up to it."

Mentally she was up for everything he suggested, but her body had other ideas. Still she wouldn't think negative thoughts right now, not when this would be her last outing with him. Certainly not when they were passing through hills of rich green vegetation where she spied a fabulous pink hotel surrounded by palm trees and a fabulous garden. "I remember that place from before! Didn't you tell me it was once a monastery?"

"You have an excellent memory. It's the Villa Irlanda. I thought we'd eat by the pool where there's a view of the coast. I was in too big a hurry to stop here last time. It's an oversight I intend to correct now. When I look back on my life, I think I was always in a hurry, but no longer."

Valentino waited in the hotel lounge for Clara, who went into the ladies' room. When she came out again a few minutes later, he escorted her to the pool where they settled on loungers to soak up some sun. They had the place to themselves. He signaled one of the waiters, who came right over.

After greeting them, he named half a dozen entrees on the menu. "But may I suggest that the oven-roasted *abbacchio* with rosemary, white wine and peppers would be a superb choice. You couldn't go wrong with a side dish of *carciofi alla romana*."

"What do you think, Clara?" In the late afternoon sun her eyes glowed an impossibly iridescent green. Fringed by her long black lashes, their color mesmerized him.

"I love lamb. As for artichokes, I've never had them stuffed with mint. It all sounds delicious."

"I think so, too." He placed their order, asking that it be served with his favorite pinot noir. When the waiter walked away, Valentino turned to her. She was a totally feminine creature, one of the few who could wear a blouse with a ruffle like that. "Can you drink wine?"

"In moderation. I have to stay away from sodas."

Valentino thought she looked a little pale. No doubt her work at the fruit stand had drained her. "How are you feeling right now?"

"Good."

"Still, I can tell something's wrong. You don't have to hide anything from me."

She let out a small laugh. "Apparently I'm not able to hide anything from you. To be honest, the air's not as warm here as it was at the farm."

"If you're chilly, that's an easy fix." Valentino was relieved the temperature had turned out to be the culprit for the moment. "Come with me." He helped her to her feet and they walked back inside the hotel to the front desk.

When he told the concierge he wanted a room with a view of the sea, he could see Clara shake her head no, but he pretended not to notice. After making arrangements for dinner to be brought to their room, he escorted her upstairs to a suite with a sweeping vista of the grounds and coastline. It was definitely warmer inside.

"Tino—" She laughed as he moved the table and chairs in the corner of the room to the center of the window.

"I want a view while we eat," he declared. "In the meantime, you can lie down until our dinner comes."

"Have you forgotten I slept in the truck?" Ignoring the suggestion, she sat down on one of the chairs. "Why didn't we just eat in the restaurant?"

He could tell something was bothering her. "Because I wanted you to feel totally comfortable."

"That's very considerate, but are you sure you weren't afraid the paparazzi would sneak in and take pictures of us that will make tonight's ten o'clock news?"

He took a fortifying breath while he tried to understand her sudden burst of heated emotion. "For once the thought hadn't even crossed my mind."

"I don't think Giselle Artois would be happy about it."

Ah. Giselle... Valentino frowned. "She's engaged to her long-time British lover."

Her eyes widened. "But on the news it sa—"

"Forget the news," he cut her off. "They say and print whatever they feel like, but it has nothing to do with the truth. In all honesty there's something I have to say to you and I wanted it to be in private. The restaurant wouldn't have afforded us a moment to ourselves."

To his dismay she paled a little more. It wasn't his imagination that she was all tensed up.

"Tino? Can I speak frankly?"

"Always."

"You said you need to talk me, but there's no point in going to these elaborate lengths in order for us to be alone." More of that hidden temper of hers was showing.

"What are you getting at, *piccola*?"

She plucked at her napkin. "Since you came back to Monta Correnti, don't think I haven't appreciated everything you've done for me, but now it has to stop."

He put his hands on his hips. "Where's all this coming from?"

Before he knew it, she'd jumped to her feet. "Over the last few days you've more than made up for the nine years of silence, and I'll never forget your kindness. But we're going in different directions and I'm not unaware you have personal commitments and a business to run. Entertaining me wasn't your plan when you came here."

A knock on the door interrupted them. He'd never seen her this wound up in his life. Normally unflappable Clara had just delivered the longest impassioned speech she'd ever made, revealing another unexpected side to her nature.

"I'll get it."

One of the staff from the kitchen wheeled in a tea cart with their meal. Valentino gave him a tip, then shut the door and pushed it across the room to the table. With her beautiful body still taut, she held onto the back of one of the chairs while she stared out the window.

Intrigued by her behavior, he put everything on the table and invited her to sit down. "We need to eat our food while it's hot. I wanted this to be special for you. Earlier you admitted you were hungry."

The reminder eventually forced her to comply. Gratified to see her food start to disappear, he poured them some wine and picked up his glass. "I'd like to propose a toast."

Her fingers tightened around the stem of her wine glass as if she were barely holding onto her control and would like to crush it. After a minute she lifted the glass. "Let me go first."

"By all means," he murmured.

"To our old friendship."

He'd seen that one coming. After he touched her glass, they both drank.

"Now it's my turn." Trapping her gaze, he said, "To our new one."

The second the words were out, she looked down without drinking. He swallowed the rest of his wine while he waited for her to absorb what he'd just told her.

She pushed her glass away. "We can't have a new one. I'd like to go home now, Tino."

"Not until you've heard me out."

Her head reared back. Green sparks flew from her eyes. "I'm not trying to be intentionally rude, but I don't want to listen to anything else."

"Not even if this is vitally important to both of us?" When she didn't immediately shut him down he said, "Last night I went to see Father Orsini, but there was one thing I couldn't bring myself to confess to him."

He saw the shiver that ran through her body. "If you're thinking of telling me what you couldn't tell him because I'm dying, please don't. I'm not a priest."

His chuckle permeated to her insides. "No, you're not, *grazie a Dio*. But you *are* the woman I want to marry as soon as possible."

After a long silence, he heard hurtful laughter come out of her. "Me—marry you—" she mocked in a brittle tone.

"Yes."

"It sounds like you've come to the rock bottom of your many excellent adventures. I thought you were the one person who wasn't like everyone else, but I was wrong."

Like the lash of a whip, he felt her salvo. "That's the first unkind remark you've ever made to me."

"Maybe it's because even a dying farm girl doesn't relish the idea of being the object of Valentino Casali's pity."

She got up from the table hot-faced and made a dignified exit from the room. He hurried down to the front desk to pay the bill, then raced after her. When he crossed the parking south of the hotel he found her waiting for him in the cab of the truck with her hat on.

They started back to Monta Correnti. He noticed she stayed close to the door so neither their arms or legs would brush by accident. "Pity comes in many forms, *piccola*," he began. "It depends on the point of view. I'm counting on yours to save me from myself."

Clara didn't want to listen. Valentino had a way of twisting words and meanings until he threw her into a state of confusion. Maybe she was having some strange, distorted dream where the impossible was happening and everything was out of her control.

"Before you consign me to my rightful place, which is a great deal lower than the angels, you need to know I called my doctor in Monaco. Among the things we talked about, he said I can be trained to help you do dialysis at home so you don't have to go to the clinic. They have these new machines so you can even travel with them and carry on your activities."

She couldn't imagine anything more wonderful, but not at Valentino's expense.

"Your mother can show me what kind of meals to make for you. I'm a good cook. I've had to be. The villa has a view of the town and valley from every window. Your family can visit all the time. You can visit them and still run the fruit stand if you want.

"While we're waiting for a kidney, we'll do everything together like we did when we were at school. We'll have fun. When was the last time you had fun? I know I haven't had any. I have to reach back to those years with you to remember what it was like to enjoy a carefree day. Marry me and make me respectable. I need you so much more than you need me."

Oh, Tino. The issues with his father had robbed him of so much confidence. She'd never dreamed they were this serious.

"Allow me to take care of you, *piccola*. Now that I've come home, I can't be around my family, my aunt and cousins, without your help. Since you talked to me about my father yesterday, you've made me realize I have to try harder."

She couldn't believe what she was hearing. "What about the woman in your life? I'm not talking about Giselle now."

"What woman?"

"Don't tease about this, Tino. It's too important."

"I agree. I guess it's confession time. There

have been other women, but not as many as you have imagined. Even the few I had a relationship with didn't inspire me to get married. I suppose I didn't feel I could count on them for the long haul. If I'd wanted to make a lifelong commitment with one of them, I wouldn't be here now."

"Even so—"

"Even so nothing! What about the men in your life? Don't tell me there haven't been any because I wouldn't believe you."

"No. I won't tell you that, but my illness has changed everything."

"Then there's no problem."

She sucked in her breath, trying to keep her wits about her. "Of course there is! You can't just give up your racing and let your team down."

"You haven't been listening to me. Though I haven't officially announced it yet, it's over."

"Since when?"

"It's been over in my mind for quite a while. Isabella has been after me to come home, but it wasn't until I knew I wanted to marry you that the issue was finally settled for me. Our marriage needs to take place right away so we don't lose any more time. Something quiet and private that won't wear you out."

What he was saying had shaken her to the foundations.

"When we get back to the farm, I want to tell

your family so we can make plans right away. The one thing they won't be able to say is that we haven't known each other long enough. From the age of seven to eighteen, I probably saw or spent time with you every day of your life, whether at school or church."

Clara stirred restlessly on the seat, trying to get her bearings. "That's true, but they're going to ask about all the years since then."

A smile hovered around his male mouth. "Surely your parents read about mine or watched it on TV. My last nine years have been lived in a fish bowl. The public seems to know more about my life than I do, but the one thing no one knows except you is my pain. It's time for the pain to end for both of us. Don't you agree?"

She knew what he was asking, but she couldn't answer him. Bands constricted her breathing. They made the rest of the trip home in silence. When he drove them straight up to the farmhouse and turned off the ignition, she started to panic.

"I need an answer, Clara." He turned to her, his eyes blazing. "If it's no, I'll still go on doing everything in my power to help you, but I'm telling you right now it won't be enough for me."

While she sat there trembling from the reasons he wanted this marriage, he got out of the truck and came around to help her down. He'd given her a choice. They could go on being friends as they used to be, always parting company at the end of the day. Or, they could be friends around the clock so he had the support he claimed he needed to be around his family and in return she would get the support she needed through her illness.

If it was an elaborate lie he'd concocted to make her feel better, she couldn't bear it. Finally she turned to him. "I'm afraid the answer has to be no, but I'll never forget your generous gesture. *Arrivederci*, Tino."

While Luca was having a bad morning and stayed upstairs, Valentino got to work and finished the inventory. It had taken him until four in the afternoon.

He found Isabella in the kitchen talking to Giorgio. "The deed is done, Izzy." He put the clipboard in her hands.

She stared at him in shock. "You're a speed demon."

"It's what happens when you're focused." He'd kept up a frantic pace so he wouldn't go crazy waiting for Clara's dialysis to be over for the day. "I would tell Papa myself, but I'll be late picking up Clara." His glance swerved to Giorgio. "Thanks for the use of the truck again."

"Anytime. You know that."

He kissed his sister's cheek and hurried out the back entrance where he'd left the Ferrari.

En route to the clinic he checked with Serena to

be certain Clara hadn't left yet. To his relief she wouldn't be out for fifteen more minutes. That gave him time to pick up some food and drinks for them.

After he'd made his purchases, he parked in the loading zone and got out to watch people as they exited the clinic. Eventually he saw her emerge dressed in a yellow top and white skirt. She looked fabulous in anything, but her features were drawn and pale. To know she was so ill squeezed his heart to a pulp.

"Clara?" he called to her.

She glanced at him, then picked up her pace in order to get away from him. In a few swift strides he caught up to her and spun her around gently.

Her eyes looked tormented. "You shouldn't have come."

"I told you I'd be here for you no matter what."

Clara shook her head. "This has to stop, Tino."

"Let's argue about it in the truck. Come on. I brought food. I know you're starving and so am I after putting in a full day of work at the restaurant. You'll be pleased to know I got the inventory done for my father."

"I'm sure that made him happy."

"We'll see." He helped her into the cab, then walked around and got behind the wheel. "I thought we'd eat at the park by our old school before I take you home. It's on the way."

As they drove off she stared out the passenger window not saying anything. "Was it a bad day, *piccola*?"

"I'd rather not talk about it."

"Then we won't."

Before long they wound around to a grassy section of the park. He slowed to a stop beneath some shade trees. "I think you're too tired to get out, so we'll eat right here." He handed her a sandwich and drink from the bag sitting between them.

Her hunger won out and she ate. After they'd both finished their food he turned to her. "I didn't get to say all I needed to say to you last night."

"You said enough and I told you no."

"Five more minutes is all I ask. If your answer is still no, I won't bring it up again."

She lowered her head. "What is it?'

"I want to tell you the secret I couldn't tell Father Orsini."

"Tino—"

"It's about the details of my mother's death."

Here came his tentacle hooks, grabbing hold of Clara so she was a captive audience, but she kept telling herself she was going to wake up at any second and find herself at home in bed, or at the clinic.

"Did I ever tell you Mamma was a diabetic?"

"No." She hadn't heard that.

"She suffered from dizzy spells, a lot, and was battling a severe one the day she slipped on one of my toys and fell down the stairs. We were alone in the house. I was only five at the time and tried to get her to breathe again, but she wouldn't wake up."

Stop talking, Tino.

"I can still remember my terror because I didn't know what to do. I didn't know how to use the phone and there weren't any neighbors close by. A helplessness went through me the likes of which I'd never known. I loved her so much and remember lying down next to her, sobbing. Cristiano was supposed to be home. I prayed for him to come."

You're breaking my heart.

"The second I heard him come in the house, I ran screaming to him and told him what had happened. He took one look at Mamma and called for the ambulance, but when it came, it was too late. The look he gave me made me want to shrivel up and die."

A moan escaped Clara's throat.

"Her death has plagued me all my life. I always felt the family blamed me, especially since I wasn't Papa's real son."

Her head flew back. "But you *were* his son in all the other ways that counted."

He shook his head. She still couldn't reach him on that point.

"From then on I stayed away from the house as much as possible. You were always kind to me. You were so good and pure and you accepted me for the way I was. I found myself clinging to you."

"Oh, Tino—" Clara had had no idea of the depth of pain he'd suffered.

"I figured that one day when I was older, I would go away so no one would have to be reminded of what a terrible person I was."

"But you didn't do anything wrong!" she cried, shaking her head in despair.

"When I grew to adulthood, I gained an intellectual understanding of what had happened, but emotionally…? To make matters worse, my long absences from home did a lot of damage to the rest of the family. My aunt Lisa took great satisfaction in letting me know I'd let everyone down."

She held her head in her hands. "All this was going on inside you and you never said a word."

"I couldn't. I felt too frozen inside. Isabella kept begging me to come back and help with Papa, but I was too torn apart by my fears to do what she asked. I know Cristiano hasn't come back because deep down he still blames me and would rather not be around to be reminded of what happened."

"That couldn't possibly be true!"

"She was our mother, Clara. He adored her, too. I should have done something—I should have been able to find a way to get help—"

She couldn't stand to hear him go on like this. The torment in his voice was too much. His features were etched in the kind of pain and deep-seated sorrow she wished she could take away.

"Let me ask you a question, Tino. If it had been Cristiano instead of you who was home that day, would you still be blaming him?"

He took a fortifying breath. "You already know the answer to that. He was older and could have prevented her death."

"How do you know she didn't die on impact? If that's the case, then no one could have saved her. Did you ever see the coroner's report?"

Valentino stared at her as if he'd never seen her before. "No," he whispered.

"Then I suggest you ask to see it before you go on crucifying yourself."

Before she could countenance it, he grasped the hand closest to him. "You see how much I need you? How good you are?" He squeezed her hand tighter. "There's only one reason I told you about Mamma's accident. When I saw you lying there getting a treatment the other day, that same feeling of helplessness and despair swept over me. Do you know why?"

She shook her head.

"Because *you* are part of that part of my life, Clara."

"I—I don't understand." Her voice faltered.

"In my mind I can't separate you and our memories from those early years. Since we met again in town and I felt you push me away, a sense of panic took hold of me until I could get to the bottom of your behavior. I swear it was like the angels had shoved me away from heaven's door."

"I'm sorry." Clara bowed her head, her emotions in utter chaos.

"Maybe what you've said is true and no one could have helped my mother stay alive. It's all in the past now anyway, but if I'm your husband, I can help *you* stay alive. I can be there night and day for you to do things no one else can do to ease your burden."

What Valentino was saying went through her like a thunderbolt.

She wasn't prepared for him to pull her into his arms. He buried his face in her hair. "Let me do for you what I couldn't do for my mother," he begged with tears in his voice. "I need to do this, Clara."

His entreaty reached down into her soul. Given the option of being with him all the time, there was no other choice for her, not now that he'd opened up all of his soul to her. He was tortured by his mother's death and the guilt that went with it, but then her soul was tortured, too.

She stayed in his arms for a long time. Last night she'd been so tormented, she hadn't been able to sleep. Though she'd been tempted to accept his proposal, she'd kept remembering her mother's comments about being Valentino's crumbs.

But just a little while ago she'd felt the terrible guilt he carried over *his* mother's death. It went so deep she couldn't ignore his plea.

"While your father's alive, you need to make peace with him, Tino. Otherwise you'll always be unhappy."

"I know," came the surprising admission. "Because of you, I've already begun."

Eventually she lifted her head. Pulling out of his arms, she moved herself next to the door. There was something else he had to understand before things went any further. "You do realize that if we were to get married, you could be a widower within the next six months."

The blood left his face. "That's how long Dr. Arno has given you if you don't get a new kidney?"

"Yes."

His features hardened. "I need you in my life, Clara, so that means we're going to have to find you a new one fast!" Valentino's declaration exploded with a ferocity she didn't know he was capable of. He was a fighter; she'd give him that. To have him on her side was like being handed a precious gift. She felt the blood pounding in her ears.

The next thing she knew he started up the truck and they headed for the road leading out of town. He didn't speak again. They eventually turned into the farm and he pulled up to the house.

"Forgive me for keeping you from your bed. I know you're exhausted." He got out of the truck and went around to help her down. "I'll call you tomorrow."

As he started back to the driver's side of the truck she cried, "Don't go yet—"

There was a sharp intake of breath before he wheeled around. She saw a flare of light in the recesses of those dark brown eyes. His reaction astounded her. "I take it that's a yes."

He *knew* it was.

"Shall we go inside together, or do you want to alert your parents first that they're about to have company?"

Her family would be gathered around the table for the evening meal. She couldn't believe this was really happening and moistened her lips nervously. "I'll tell them you're outside waiting to talk to them."

"I swear you won't regret this." Before she

could think, he cupped her face between his hands and pressed a warm kiss to her mouth, the first one he'd ever given her. It brought heat to her cheeks she could feel as she broke away from him and hurried inside.

Everyone greeted her as she walked in the kitchen filled with noisy conversation. Her mother eyed her with an anxious expression, probably noticing her heightened color. "You were gone so long, we got worried you missed the bus."

Silvio cast her a questioning glance. Her father patted the empty chair next to him. "Come and eat."

"I've already had dinner, Papa." Her heart thundered in her chest. "Valentino is outside and wants to speak to you and Mamma. Is it all right if he comes in?"

She watched her parents share a surprised look before they nodded.

On less than sturdy legs, she hurried back out to the hall and opened the door. "Tino?"

He came inside and followed her through to the kitchen. After all these years the moment was unreal to see him enter her parents' home at last. Her father stood up. Silvio and Tomaso followed suit.

"Please sit down," Valentino urged them. "Good evening," he said to all of them. "Excuse us for this interruption, but Clara and I decided our news couldn't wait." He moved closer and put his arm around her waist. "Today she agreed to become my wife."

Immediately she heard gasps from everyone, her mother's the loudest.

"There's nothing I want more than to take care of her. With my help, I'm hoping we can find her a matching kidney donor as soon as possible."

She saw her father cross himself.

"You have a right to know my plans. I've given up racing. From now on I'll be helping my father at the restaurant and doing consulting work for my business. For the time being we'll be living at the villa here in Monta Correnti. That way Clara can remain close to all of you."

Silvio paled while her father looked knocked off balance.

"I've already asked Father Orsini to marry us."

At that news Clara almost fainted from shock. He held her tighter.

"Because of her condition, he'll waive the normal waiting period and perform the private ceremony at four o'clock on Saturday at the church. He'll make it short so it won't be hard on her."

She saw her mother start to weep.

"The only people we want in attendance will be your immediate family and mine, provided my father is well enough. If everyone will agree to keep this a secret, there won't be any paparazzi around to ruin it. Do we have your blessing?"

Clara saw her parents stare at each other in amazement before her father turned to them. "Is this what you want, *figlia mia*?"

She took a deep breath. This was truth time. *It's what you* feel *that matters*! her mother had counseled her earlier.

"*Sì*."

Her father's dark moist eyes swerved to Valentino. "Since my daughter says yes, then I say welcome to the family." He walked around to embrace him and kiss him on both cheeks. Clara's mother joined them.

Valentino kissed her on both cheeks. "Earlier today I told Clara that when I was a boy, I envied her belonging to a happy family like yours. Sometimes she let me eat the delicious food you made for her lunches."

"That's true," Bianca chimed in with a smile on her face. "I watched it disappear, Mamma. Clara made me promise never to tell."

"You're the best cook in Monta Correnti, Signora Rossetti, but I've never told my father that. I let him think the food at Rosa is superior. Secretly I have to tell you I like the idea of belonging to your family."

Clara knew he meant what he was saying. The

loss of his mother and the tragic circumstances surrounding her death had blighted his life. She could also see his natural charm was lethal. Already he'd seduced everyone in the kitchen except Silvio, who eyed both of them with a hostile expression.

Valentino turned to her. His gaze played over her with relentless scrutiny. "You look tired. I'm going to leave so you can get to bed. I'll let myself out."

After kissing her cheek, he left the kitchen. She didn't want him to go, but, with the family clamoring to talk to her, it was the only thing to do.

"So," her mother said with a new sparkle in her eyes, "we will have to buy you a wedding dress. I always hoped you would wear mine, but look at you—you're so thin it would fall off you and lie in a puddle on the floor."

Everyone laughed including Clara, who needed to be satisfied with the reason Valentino was marrying her and allow her family to be happy for her. Until a few minutes ago they couldn't have imagined another wedding taking place in the Rossetti family. Neither could she.

"Doesn't it bother you that he didn't propose until you lost all your weight?" Silvio's question stunned everyone.

"No," she answered in complete honesty. "If all

he'd wanted was a thin wife, then how come he never married one of the film stars or top models he's been seen with over the years? He's had ample opportunity." He could have married the girl *you* wanted, Silvio—but of course Clara would never have said anything that hurtful to her brother.

His face screwed up in pain. "Just tell me one thing—"

She knew what he was going to ask and took him aside out of earshot. They weren't twins for nothing. Forestalling him, she said, "He needs me, Silvio." Until she'd heard him talking to her mother, she hadn't realized just how much.

Her brother didn't say anything after that, but she knew what was on his mind.

Is he in love with you, Clara? Did he say those words to you? Because if he didn't…

CHAPTER SIX

VALENTINO drove to the restaurant and parked the truck behind the Ferrari. When he stepped inside, he walked over to Giorgio. "The truck's outside filled with gas."

"You didn't have to do that."

"I wanted to. I'm grateful for your help. Do you know where Isabella is?"

"Out in front tabulating the receipts."

"Good. I need to talk to her. See you later. Thanks again for everything." They traded keys.

"*Ciao*, Valentino."

With a nod to the others still cleaning up, he walked through the door into the restaurant.

"There you are," his sister said as soon as she saw him. "Papa is anxious to talk to you."

"Did he find mistakes in the inventory?"

"No. He sounded sorry you ran off so fast."

"That would be a first."

"I told him you had to leave to meet up with Clara."

"Clara's the reason I'm here now. There's something I have to tell you."

"I'm all yours." She finished the last of the receipts and closed up the register. "What's going on?"

He eyed her directly. "Maybe you should sit down. This is important."

A look of alarm crossed over her face and she did his bidding. For the next few minutes he told her about Clara's kidney failure. As he explained the gravity of her condition tears rolled down Isabella's cheeks. "Oh, Valentino. That poor, dear girl."

"I have more news." He sucked in his breath. "Father Orsini is going to marry us in a four o'clock ceremony on Saturday afternoon at the church."

Isabella looked thunderstruck. His stunning revelation actually caused her to drop the money bag she'd been holding. He picked it up for her and put it on the counter.

"I'm not going to let her die if I can help it," he vowed. "Until a kidney is available, she needs help around the clock. The only way to give her the kind of attention she requires is to be with her twenty-four hours a day, so I am going to become her husband."

His sister stared at him in shock. "I don't

doubt your sincerity, but what about your racing?"

"Those days are over."

"Just like that?" came her incredulous question.

"I've been considering it for quite a while now."

"Will you live in Monaco?"

"No. At the villa here."

"You're serious—"

"Clara needs her family around. You and Papa need my help at the restaurant."

The blue eyes studying him swam in liquid. "I take back the ugly things I shouted at you the night of Papa's birthday party while you were driving away." So saying, she threw her arms around him and gave him a surprisingly strong hug.

"Don't get ahead of yourself. I'm everything you called me and more, but that girl doesn't have a selfish atom in her entire body. What's happening to her isn't fair."

"It's awful."

"I'm going to find her a kidney if it ends up taking all my money to do it." That was what he intended to tell Dr. Arno when they talked. Clara's doctor still hadn't called him, which meant he hadn't returned from his vacation yet. "Her chances of a long life will be vastly increased if one is found soon."

"Then you *have* to make it happen! You're known for doing the impossible."

"Is that right?"

She smiled. "You know it's true."

"Let's hope this time it is," he ground out. "I'm going to ask the clinician to start training me how to do her dialysis so she can have it at home when we are married. Right now I'm going upstairs to tell Papa I'm getting married."

"He's always wanted you back home. Your news is going to make him happier than you know."

"Happy enough to attend the ceremony with you?" Valentino knew otherwise, but that wasn't important right now. He'd promised Clara he would try to get along with his father. "I'm not sure he's well enough."

"Papa wouldn't miss it. Do you want me to phone Cristiano?"

In the past he'd always let Isabella do everything, but no longer. This was something Valentino had to do himself, though he dreaded it.

"I'll call him," he murmured. "Except for Clara's immediate family, no one else is invited. I don't want Aunt Lisa or our cousins to get wind of it. This has to be kept so quiet the media won't have any idea of it until long after the fact. I'll do anything to prevent the press from intruding on Clara's private agony."

"I understand."

He breathed in deeply. "Once we've said our vows, we'll drive straight to the villa. Fortunately with the church so close, it'll be a quick trip for her."

She put a hand on his arm. "No celebration?"

"Only if Clara is up to it after we're home. I'm leaving that decision to Signora Rossetti."

"You can count on me for any help."

"I know that." His dark brows furrowed. "Too bad you were let down in the younger brother department. From now on I'll try to do better, Izzy."

As he gave her a hug his father entered the empty dining room with his walker.

"What's going on?"

Valentino intercepted Isabella's glance before they moved toward him. "I was just on my way upstairs to talk to you."

"Giorgio told me you were in here. I decided I'd better find you before you ran out again."

"Let's sit down, Papa."

Isabella patted their father's arm. "I'll be right back."

"I don't need to sit. You did an excellent job on the inventory, by the way."

Incredible. "You're the one who taught me."

They eyed each other cautiously. For the first time in his life Valentino got the impression his father seemed nervous of him. He thought back to what Clara had told him about Luca being terrified Valentino would leave town at the first sign of trouble.

His father squinted at him. "You said you had something to tell me?"

"Wouldn't you rather sit? This could take a few minutes."

"All right." He moved the walker to the nearest table and planted himself on a chair. Valentino sat opposite him.

"I've been doing some research to help bring in more business. It's just an idea, but it might be worth investigating."

"I'm listening."

Valentino presented his ideas about the Web site and attracting the tour-bus crowd. When he'd finished his explanation his father pursed his lips. "That's what you and Isabella were hugging about?"

The question wasn't the response Valentino sought. He couldn't tell what his father was thinking, but at least he hadn't rejected the suggestions out of hand. "No. I was saving my other news until last."

"Go on."

"I've been seeing Clara Rossetti since I've been home. She has agreed to be my wife. We're getting married on Saturday at the church and we'll be living here in Monta Correnti. I would like it very much if you could be there." Despite all grievances, he discovered it was true. "However, I know you're not well," he added to give him an out.

His father stared at him for a long time. "She's a fine girl."

"I agree," Valentino said in a husky voice. I'm in love with her. He'd always been in love with her, but he hadn't known until he'd seen her lying there in the clinic and realized she could be taken from him.

"What do you think?" Clara came out of the dressing room wearing a simple white A-line silk gown with a scooped neck and long lace sleeves that covered her graft.

Her mother, bedecked in the pale blue dress she wore to Mass, let out a sound of approval. Thc tears were never far away. "We bought the right one. You look like a princess."

For once in her life Clara felt like one. It didn't seem possible when just last week she hadn't thought she'd live long enough to see this day. And certainly not with Valentino! How many times in her secret fantasies had she imagined him coming home to Monta Correnti because deep inside he'd always loved her and wanted her for his bride?

When she'd lost all her weight, she'd done it

with him in mind. More than anything in the world Clara had wanted to be the beautiful woman on the cover of the magazine standing next to him.

That first day on the stairs when he'd called her Clarissima and told her she was a remarkably beautiful woman, she'd known he'd meant it. She'd seen it in his eyes, in the tone of his voice. It was the look she'd always hoped to see. Today Clara knew a joy so powerful it was already draining her.

Her family had insisted she stay in bed this morning. For once she didn't fight them. They brought her breakfast and lunch. While Bianca did Clara's nails, her mother washed and combed her hair. They wouldn't let her get up until it was time to drive to one of the local bridal shops in Monta Correnti.

Bianca, also in her Sunday best, carried the shoulder-length, matching lace mantilla Clara would put on right before the ceremony. She kissed her cheek. "The gown is perfect on you. I wish all the relatives could come to the church to see you."

"So do I," her mother said with a sigh, "but we'll just have to take pictures for them to see later. Valentino was right about doing everything possible to keep the paparazzi away. So far no one knows anything."

"Except the saleswoman," Clara reminded her.

"Ah—but she has no idea who's going to be your husband."

"And he's going to be upset if we don't get her to the church right now!" Bianca put her arm through Clara's good one. "We need to hurry out to the truck. Papa is waiting."

The three of them made their way to the outside of the shop. Their mother got in the truck first with a bag holding Clara's regular clothes. Bianca helped Clara in next, taking care with her wedding dress, then she got in Tomaso's truck with the children. Silvio had muttered something about meeting them at the church.

Clara's father drove the truck through the town and they followed the winding road up the hillside to the lovely seventeenth-century baroque church of San Giovanni where their family had been attending for generations.

The air was warmer than the day Valentino had driven her to Gaeta. She couldn't have asked for a more beautiful wedding day. While the others were brimming over with excitement—Silvio being the exception—a calm had descended over Clara.

This was a surreal moment for her. Within the hour she would be Signora Casali, a role many women had coveted. She wasn't naïve. Clara understood exactly the unique place she held in

Valentino's psyche. She knew what marriage to him meant, and what it didn't mean.

No one wanted to live a long life more than she did. If it wasn't her destiny, then Valentino would be given his freedom soon, but it would be with the knowledge that he'd done everything in his power to keep her alive. She'd witnessed that desire yesterday when Serena had spent the four hours teaching him how to administer Clara's dialysis.

His intelligence allowed him to absorb directions quickly. Valentino was at his best when faced with a challenge. Over the last few days she'd watched him take on this new job of health-care giver with a seriousness and dedication that touched her heart.

That plus his assurance that he was working on his relationship with his father meant more to her than he would ever know. For Luca and him to find peace would guarantee they had a happier marriage. She wanted that with every fiber of her being!

When the end came for her, she had every confidence there'd be no demons to torture him the way they had after his mother had died. In the meantime she planned to devote the time she had left to supporting him around his family and making him as happy as her sickness would allow.

Already she was tired, but that was because this

was a day like no other. With so many emotions running rampant inside her, she felt more drained than usual and prayed she'd make it through the ceremony before she wilted.

Her father drove them around the back of the church and pulled to a stop in front of a door used only by the clergy. Tomaso followed in his truck. After the women and children got out, Bianca draped the mantilla over Clara's head. The oohs and ah-h-hs coming from everyone made her smile.

By now her other married brothers, Dante and Cesare, and their families had arrived, bringing her grandmother. She was thankful Tomaso was taking pictures so this day would be preserved.

Father Bruno opened the door and ushered them inside. The younger priest had a serious nature so different from Father Orsini's. Clara got the feeling he didn't approve of this clandestine marriage about to be performed behind doors locked to the public for the next half-hour.

"There you are," Valentino murmured, suddenly appearing in the hallway behind the chapel. He mesmerized everyone as he moved swiftly toward her.

A white rose had been tucked into the lapel of his formal dove-gray suit. Beneath the jacket he wore a darker gray vest. The clothes fit his powerful frame like a glove. In the dazzling white shirt and silk jacquard tie of silver and gray, he could easily have been taken for some important Italian prince. He looked so handsome, her legs almost buckled.

"I can't find the words for how lovely you are," he whispered as his dark, searching eyes played over her face and figure. With that compliment she almost sank to the floor in a puddle, bringing to mind her mother's comment about her wedding dress being too big for Clara.

Valentino seemed to have invisible radar because he put his arm around her waist for support and led her the rest of the way into the chapel. His dark-haired sister Isabella stood nearby.

"Clara? You look beautiful," Isabella said softly and handed her a bouquet of white roses.

"Thank you for coming and for these. The flowers are gorgeous." She buried her face in the petals to hide her emotions while she inhaled their sweet scent.

Next to her sat an imposing Luca Casali with his cane. He'd dressed in a midnight-blue suit for the occasion and looked very distinguished. Valentino helped his father to his feet. The older man patted his son's arm before turning to Clara.

"Welcome to the family," he said in a voice of surprising emotion and gave her a kiss on both cheeks.

"I'm so glad you were well enough to make it," she whispered.

"I wouldn't have missed it and couldn't be more pleased with my son's choice. You were always the best influence on him," he confided sotto voce.

"That's very kind of you to say." He'd sounded as if he meant it. Just then her gaze met Valentino's. Her husband-to-be looked happier than she'd seen him in days. Thank you for coming, Luca. You have no idea what it means to your son and to me.

She wished she could say the same for her twin brother, who sat a few feet away with Maria and the children, unable to pretend something he didn't feel.

While both families greeted each other, Silvio stayed put and only stood up when Father Orsini entered the chapel from a side door. The priest nodded to everyone. "If you will all be seated, I'll ask Valentino and Clara to come and stand in front of me."

Valentino clasped her left hand and drew her toward the priest who'd been their spiritual mentor for the whole of their lives, but the broad smile he'd always had for them was missing. In its place he wore a solemn expression, as if he no longer saw them as children. His wise black eyes seemed to say it was time to put childish things aside for the real test of life.

Father Orsini knew this wasn't a normal marriage between two young lovers desperate to belong to each other. He was a realist who, though he hoped and prayed for the very best for them, had to consider there would probably be dark days ahead in the near future.

"Clara and Valentino? Normally we would celebrate Mass first, but, considering the unique circumstances, I'm going to marry you now. This will in no way make your marriage less sacred."

She could have kissed the priest for his understanding, but she realized it was Valentino who'd prevailed on Father Orsini to keep the ceremony brief.

The older man cleared his throat. "I have one piece of advice for both of you. Strive to lose yourselves in making the other one happy, then you cannot fail."

Since Clara had already determined to do her part no matter what, it wouldn't be hard to take his advice.

"I see Valentino has already taken you by the hand, Clara. If you'll repeat after me."

Within a few minutes they'd both pledged to love, honor and sacrifice for each other, in sickness and in health. Maybe Valentino didn't realize it—or maybe because he did—his fingers tightened hard around hers when the priest said, 'As long as you both shall live.'

"You wish to exchange rings?"

"*Sì*, Father."

Clara couldn't repress a slight gasp as he produced a gold ring with a brilliant light green stone. He slid it onto the ring finger of her left hand. It fit perfectly.

She in turn waited for Bianca to hand her their grandfather's ring so she could slip it on Valentino's finger. Yesterday morning her grandmother had insisted she take it to give to her intended. It was one of those precious moments in life Clara would always treasure.

Father Orsini nodded. "I now pronounce you, Clara Rossetti, and you, Valentino Casali, husband and wife. In the name of the Father, the Son and the Holy Spirit, Amen."

"Amen." Valentino's deep male voice resonated throughout the chapel. Before she could think, he slid his hands to her shoulders and his mouth descended on hers, sending a river of heat through her already weakened body. It wasn't like the warm kiss he'd given her in front of the farmhouse the other night. With this one she felt unmistakable desire arc through her.

Until now she'd had the impression she was in a strange and beautiful dream, but no longer. All of a sudden this man who'd just become her husband felt so alive and real, she was shaken by powerful new sensations. She broke off their kiss and eased away from him in confusion.

"Are you all right, *piccola*?" She could hear the concern in his voice.

"I'm fine."

"No, you're not. The ceremony has exhausted you. Go with your parents. We'll meet at the villa in a few minutes as planned." They'd agreed it would be better if they weren't seen together leaving the church. Soon enough the world would learn Valentino Casali, the world's most exciting, desirable bachelor, had married a little nobody from a town few had ever heard of.

Clara gave a slight nod. Without looking at him she started for the door where they'd come in a little while ago. She was the first down the passageway and out the back of the church, clutching her bouquet in her hand. Everyone hurried after her and rushed to the trucks parked a few feet away.

Once they were in the cab, her mother cried in alarm, "You look like you're going to faint."

"I'm all right, Mamma."

"We're almost to the villa," her father muttered. "Then you will lie down and have a good rest."

Wrong. Valentino had brought her senses alive. For once in her life, rest wouldn't cure what was wrong with her.

* * *

His home was a small, ochre-colored palazzo perched on a summit of vegetation in flower. All the Di Rossi family's royal properties had been built in the prime locations of the region. Any local could point them out, but you couldn't get inside the grounds without passing through the gate.

Valentino had already given her father a remote and directions to the private road leading up to it. Clara's family was still in awe that she would be living in this one with him. For her the only important thing was that she would be an intimate part of his life from now on. The setting was immaterial but lovely as they pulled up to the front with its profusion of flowers and ornamental trees.

Somehow her brand-new husband had beaten them here. He came out the tall paneled doors and pulled her from the truck into his arms.

"Tino—what are you doing?"

He flashed her that devilish smile she remembered from so long ago. "Isn't it obvious?" he murmured against her tender neck.

Once he'd swept her over the threshold, she glanced around her in astonishment. "I've never seen anything so beautiful."

From the elegant foyer to the salon, fresh flowers in every shade possible had been arranged around the period furniture. Flowers reflected in the gilt mirrors, creating the illusion of a wonderful garden.

"You love nature so much, I wanted to bring it inside for our special day."

She was overcome. "I don't know what to say."

"You don't have to say anything. Do you need to go to bed, *piccola*?"

"Not until later." Not after everything you've done to make me happy. "Please put me down."

"Where?"

"How about the love seat over by those tall windows? The view has to be glorious from up here."

Once he'd set her on the small couch and had helped arrange her dress for more pictures, Valentino showed her family through the house. Before long food appeared from the kitchen. He brought her a plate of her mother's cooking. While he sat next to her so they could eat together, Tomaso started taking pictures of the family.

Clara could almost believe she was a normal bride with the normal expectation of a long life with her loving husband and the children who would be born to them.

When she'd eaten all she could, Valentino took her plate. Holding her gaze, he said, "We got away with it, *piccola*. No paparazzi."

"No, thank heaven."

Her father raised his wine glass in salute. "To *all* my married children." He winked at Clara. "I've wanted to say that for many years."

"Papa…" She smiled at him. "Sorry it took so long."

It prompted Valentino to make his own toast. He got to his feet with his powerful legs slightly apart. His gaze fell on Clara. "All good things come to him who waits. To my precious bride."

A blush started at her toes and swept up to warm the crown of her head. With a toast like that coming from such a magnetic personality, there was no question he'd won her family over. But she didn't have to look across the room to feel Silvio's icy glitter.

She'd always been able to read her brother's thoughts…

Valentino's not in love with you, Clara. Personally I can't stand to watch the show he's putting on for the family, let alone that Mamma and Papa are buying into it. Let's not pretend about what's going on here. If you weren't seriously ill, he wouldn't be making a martyr of himself in order to gain the world's attention in a brand-new way.

A new terror seized her heart. Was Silvio right?

Valentino had asked the florist to put flowers in their bedroom. Not as many as in the front of the house, but enough to create atmosphere. While Clara was in the en-suite bathroom taking a shower, he lit the white scented tea-light candles he'd placed around, then he turned out the lights and headed for the guest bathroom at the other end of the hall.

Ten minutes later he returned wearing his navy sweats and discovered her lying under the covers in the middle of the king-sized bed. Her green eyes glowed like jewels above the blue and gold quilt.

"Good evening, Signora Casali."

A smile lit the corners of her mouth. "Good evening, Signor Casali."

"Alone at last."

"My family didn't want to leave."

He sat down on the side of the bed. "It was my idea of the perfect wedding. Short and to the point. The groom gets to whisk away the bride. No endless throngs to navigate. No flashbulbs going off. Fabulous food, compliments of my new mother-in-law. Of course that's the selfish part of me talking. I'm sorry you couldn't have your best friends and the whole town turn out after the banns were posted."

"I had the part that mattered." She smoothed her hand against the sheet, letting him know she had a lot more on her mind. "Why didn't Isabella and your father come to the house after?"

"Papa told me he felt light-headed after the ceremony. I believed him. He rarely goes anywhere, so Isabella drove him home, but she wanted to come."

Clara eyed him soulfully. “He was very sweet to me.”

“How could he not be?”

“I think he was so moved to see you get married, it affected him physically.”

“Tonight I’m in the mood to think only the best thoughts, so I’ll go along with your take on it.”

“Good.”

Valentino held up his left hand. “This ring came as a big surprise.” He had to wear it on his littlest finger.

“My grandfather had smaller hands than you. Nonna wanted me to give it to you. It’s her way of letting you know she approves.”

“I’m honored. Now I need to know if *you* do.”

“That question was answered the first day we met at school years ago. You made me laugh so hard, the teacher got mad at me instead of you.”

“Sorry about that.”

“No, you’re not,” she responded with a quick grin. “You don’t need to fish for compliments, but I’ll tell you one thing if it will make you feel better. You have exquisite taste.”

Looking at her right now, he agreed. She was sitting up in bed and rested against the headboard, allowing him a glimpse of the soft pink robe she’d put on. The color added a tint to her creamy complexion, drawing his attention until he couldn’t look anywhere else.

"I love my ring." Her hand moved so the facets caught the light from the candles, but he found himself mesmerized by the glints in her dark, silky hair. She'd been blessed with perfectly shaped eyebrows the same color. His gaze fell to the alluring contour of her mouth. The desire to kiss her grew so intense, he was shaken by his feelings and got to his feet.

"I hoped you would like it. Is there anything you want from the kitchen before I put out the candles?"

"Nothing, thank you."

In the next minute he'd blown them out. "Are you tired, *piccola*?" he asked in the darkness.

"I'm happy."

He should have known better than to ask his valiant bride, whose exhaustion had probably reached its peak before their guests left the palazzo. "I want to get to know all your habits so I can be of the most help. When you go to bed at night, what do you normally do?"

"Just what I've done tonight. Take a shower and climb in bed. Usually I'm asleep as soon as my head touches the pillow. What about you?"

"The same, but I usually toss and turn for a while first. When my restlessness is bad, I turn on television. The noise usually puts me out."

"Isn't it strange we've known each other since

we were children, yet we don't know all those little things about our everyday lives."

"This is a new adventure for both of us, one I'm already enjoying more than you can imagine. If you'll take the right side of the bed, then I won't worry about rolling onto your arm in the night."

He heard the bedding rustle, then he climbed in and stretched out before pulling the covers over them. Her fragrance was so intoxicating, he feared he'd be walking the floors within the hour.

He turned on his side so he was facing her, but he didn't dare touch her tonight. His fear that she'd push him away was very real. He was still raw from her rejection after he'd taken her to Gaeta. How could he bear it if she accused him of making love to her out of pity? What he needed to do was seduce her slowly; a kiss here, a caress there, until the moment when he knew she wanted all of him.

"Now that I'm your husband, everything has changed. We're going to build a new life together."

He leaned over to kiss her lips. "*Buona notte, mia sposa*."

CHAPTER SEVEN

WHEN Sunday morning came, Clara was awake before Valentino, whose well-honed body took up most of the bed. In truth, after he'd given her that brief kiss, she'd spent the rest of the night in agony because he hadn't reached for her.

Valentino afraid to make love to her because she was ill? Tears smarted her eyes. She'd give anything to go back to a few days ago when he didn't know about her condition. In the natural progression of things she felt sure he would have started kissing her until neither of them could hold back.

While he slept she was able to study her husband's striking features without his being aware of it. To know she would be waking up next to such an exciting man from now on filled her with intense pleasure, but if he never possessed her, she didn't know how she'd be able to stand it.

Already she loved their new life together so much, the thought of it coming to a quick end because of her illness too unbearable to contemplate. Before she gave in to her emotions and kissed him awake, she slid out of bed and hurried into the bathroom to freshen up and brush her teeth.

With her robe still on, she padded down the hall to the kitchen to fix them a meal. The key was to stay busy. For days now Valentino had been doing everything for her. It was time for him to be the recipient.

Her mother had stocked the fridge with food. All Clara had to do was warm things up and they'd have a feast for breakfast. After making cappuccino, she was ready to go get him when she heard him call out her name.

"I'm in the kitchen!"

He emerged from the hallway in his sweats looking disheveled from sleep and sounding the slightest bit out of breath. The shadow covering his firm jaw made him even more disreputably gorgeous. "Why didn't you wake me?"

"Because you were in a deep sleep and needed it."

She could tell he wasn't in a playful mood. "This wasn't supposed to happen!"

"What? That your wife got up to make breakfast?"

"You know what I mean." That hint of anxiety was in his eyes.

"Tino—when I'm feeling good, I intend to do what comes naturally. If I need help, you'll know about it. Unfortunately you haven't always seen me in top form and it has made you think I'm a twenty-four-hour invalid. Come and sit down."

He was clearly out of sorts and raked a hand through his dark hair before doing her bidding.

"Mamma left us a veritable banquet," she chatted. "I don't know about you, but I'm starving this morning. At our house we always put a little chocolate in the cappuccino. If you don't like it, I'll make you regular coffee."

To her delight he drank a whole mug before lifting his head. At last she saw a smile. "I'll never drink anything else again." On that note he popped two sausage-filled rolls in his mouth. "After we eat, I'm taking us for a scooter ride."

The situation was improving. "On your latest model?"

"I think so."

"I can't wait!"

When he looked at her, she could tell he wanted to ask her if she was sure she was feeling well enough, but he refrained. She'd never seen his brown eyes so alive. "Neither can I. Even though the temperature's supposed to climb today, we'll dress you warmly."

She finished munching on a roll. "Where are we going to go?"

"Here and there."

Just as they used to do after school. "I'll hurry and get ready."

Valentino devoured two more rolls. "While you do that, I'll shave."

"No, don't—"

His eyebrows lifted.

"I—I mean, you don't have to do it," she stammered.

An unexpected gleam entered his eyes. "You don't mind my scruffy look?"

"It suits you," she mumbled before clearing the table.

"Leave the dishes, Clara. While we're gone the housekeeper will be in to clean up and unpack the bags your parents brought over in the truck. All you need to do is get ready."

By tacit agreement they left the kitchen and walked back to the bedroom. Valentino disappeared in the walk-in closet and brought out some packages he put on the bed. A ghost of a smile hovered around his mouth. "After you're dressed, put all this gear on. We'll see if I bought the right sizes for you."

The second he walked out the door, she pulled underwear, jeans and a cotton sweater from one of her suitcases and was dressed in a flash. In the first bag she found socks and black boots. The next bag contained a woman's stylish leather jacket in white with green side stripes and a mandarin collar. Another bag held matching gloves. In the last large sack she found a woman's helmet.

"Everything fits!" she cried when he came walking in their bedroom a few minutes later carrying his black helmet. He wore black boots and a black leather jacket with blue side stripes. His powerful body looked even bigger in his riding gear. She felt his dark eyes roam over her in male appreciation.

"You have a stunning figure, *piccola*. In an outfit like this, it's dynamite. You'll have to hold me tight around the waist so some dude doesn't pluck you off the back while we're tearing around."

"Tino—" His absurd remark made her laugh.

"You think I'm kidding—" The sudden seriousness of his tone caused her pulse to race. "Have you looked in a mirror lately? Maybe taking you out in public is going to be too dangerous."

"That's what I've thought about you for years." She spoke her mind before she realized what she'd said. In a quick move she dropped the helmet's shield so he couldn't see how red she'd turned. "Shall we go?"

He led her down the hall to the back of the

villa. They stepped outside into a small courtyard where she could see the garage. With the remote on his key chain he opened the door. Next to the Ferrari sat a gleaming cobalt blue and gold motor scooter.

Valentino put on his helmet before walking it out into the courtyard. "They brought over the deluxe Tourister. See this pillioned seat?" She nodded. "It lets you ride higher behind me. When I designed this, I had you in mind because you always used to tell me you wished you could see better when we rode around together."

He shouldn't have told her that. It meant too much to her. "The Violetta Rapidita is a beautiful machine, Tino." Her voice caught.

"Wait until you ride on it. You'll be totally comfortable. Climb on behind me."

His excitement infected her. After she got settled and wrapped her arms around his torso she said, "Your mother would have been thrilled to know you named it after her."

When her words computed, he squeezed her mid-thigh. She felt the sensation like a dart of flame. "Outside of my family, no one knows its origin. Nothing escapes you, does it? Are you ready?"

"Yes."

He lifted his hands to put on his leather gloves, then they were off. She felt his imprint long after they'd passed through the gate and were zigzagging down the hillside past the patchwork of charming villas partially hidden by lush foliage.

With one of the world's greatest drivers at the controls, Clara gave no thought to anything but the joy of being alive to share this incredible day with Valentino. Sitting on the scooter put you right next to the earth where you could feel and smell nature, hear all the sounds, yet the higher seat allowed her the full sight of her surroundings.

This was so different than riding in a car or a truck or bus. It took her back to her early teens when he offered her rides home after school or church. Sometimes he'd drive haphazardly on purpose, sending her into peals of laughter while the locals shook their fingers at him. Of course they were much younger then and didn't wear the safety equipment they wore now.

In those days the two of them felt invincible. Was he remembering those matchless moments, too? Half the time his old scooter had let him down and he'd had to walk it or push it. Though she would offer to take a turn so he wouldn't have to do all the work, Valentino always refused. Even then there'd been a chivalrous streak in his nature.

Sometimes they ended up walking all the way to the road leading into the farm. When he waved goodbye and kept walking, she always felt a wrench. In truth she'd been so crazy about Valentino, if he'd asked her to go on a walk around the world with him, she would have gone.

Clara had dreamed her dreams, but she could never have imagined that over a decade later she would end up being his wife, riding pillion on this streamlined version of comfort and perfection he'd invented. She nestled tighter against him, resting her chin on his shoulder to feel his body and prove to herself he was flesh and blood, not a fantasy conjured in her imagination.

"Are you all right?" he called to her, turning his head to the side.

"I'm wonderful!" she shouted back. "This is heaven!"

At her comment he twisted the throttle, accelerating them around the next curve where the countryside opened to their gaze. Euphoric, they whizzed past manicured fields and vineyards. Without a cough their scooter ate up the kilometers of rolling hills.

Before long they veered onto a farming road rarely used by tourists. It eventually circled around the furthest end of her family's lemon groves. There was no sight like the straight rows of twenty-foot trees thriving in the sun. Delectable yellow fruit peeked out from the dark green foliage.

It was at the top of one of the trees she could see in the distance where she'd cut her leg, but she didn't want to think about that right now. Please no shadows. Not today.

Valentino didn't slow down. He kept heading south past other farms and cypress trees. This whole area burgeoned with nature and represented paradise to her. She couldn't get enough of it. Eventually they came to the shimmering blue water of Lake Clarissa. Valentino had grown up along this shoreline.

She'd driven past his home many times out driving in her family's truck with Bianca, but that had been when Valentino was winning races in other parts of Europe or the States. Clara had yet to see the inside of his home; knowing it held one of the most painful memories for him, she could understand why he didn't want to stay there now.

He drove them around the west end. When they came to a lay-by, he pulled into it and shut off the motor. They both removed their helmets to take in the lake's beauty. There was a path leading through a meadow-like patch to the water. Anxious to follow it down, she swung her leg over and climbed off the scooter.

"I think we'll rest here and enjoy a snack." He fastened their helmets to the bars, then opened the trunk. To her surprise he'd packed a light blanket. Beneath it she discovered bottled water, apples and a carton of chocolate biscotti. He must have made preparations after she'd fallen asleep last night.

"You remembered—" she cried in awe before reaching for it. "I haven't eaten these since the last time you got sick after splurging on three packs at once."

He tossed back his dark head and laughed. It was a man's deep belly kind of laughter. She felt it rumble through her nervous system with a sense of wonder.

"If you noticed, I only bought one this time. I can't risk becoming indisposed when I'm driving such precious cargo around."

"Indisposed hardly describes your former condition," she quipped to cover her emotions, which were jumping all over the place. Gathering the other items, she started toward the path.

A chuckling Valentino followed her. Several feet from the shore of the lake he spread the blanket over the wild grass and they both sank down. She whipped off her gloves so she could open her water and drink. "Um. That tastes good."

"It does," he agreed after swallowing half of his in one go.

Clara fell back against the blanket and stared up at the sky, where she could see clouds building. "There's going to be a storm later today."

He lay down next to her and opened the carton. "Then it's good we came out here early."

Suddenly he rolled on his side, bringing him breathtakingly close. Without saying anything, he put a cookie to her lips. There was a mirthful glimmer in his eyes. She took a bite. He finished it off and fed her another one.

After three bites she couldn't keep up with him. "No more."

"No? Then how about a different treat?"

"I think I'll save the apple for later."

"I wasn't thinking of fruit." The amusement she'd seen had faded. In its place she glimpsed something else that made her mouth go dry and sent pleasure pains to her palms. "In the past you and I did just about everything together, but we never played six minutes in *paradiso* or spin the *bottiglia da vino*."

A smile turned up the corners of her mouth. "That's because you were too busy playing those games with every other girl in our class. It made the boys furious. As I recall Aminta, Bettina and Crocetta were all enamored of you at the same time."

He traced the line of her mouth with his finger. "I've grown up since then and have developed an appetite for a new treat. Be kind to me, *piccola*."

Valentino didn't give her time to think before he covered her mouth with his own. For once she didn't want to think. His playful mood had infected her, making her want to give in to the sensuous side of her nature. She had one, but had never allowed herself permission to enjoy what other girls took for granted.

Now that there was a time bomb ticking away inside her, she didn't want to leave this world never having known this pleasure with Valentino. "If it's kindness to kiss you back, then I can't think of anything I'd like to do more."

His jacket was open. She slid her hands up his chest and wrapped them around his neck to get closer. In a slow, sweet rhythm she began responding to the urgency of his demands. The pressure of his mouth invading hers melted her insides, sending a languorous warmth through her body.

This was what she'd been waiting for last night. It was ecstasy. She knew what the word meant and had an intellectual knowledge of it, but now that she was experiencing it she didn't want to do anything else. The freedom to do whatever she desired had taken hold of her.

He was such a beautiful man she needed to kiss every centimeter of his face. The best way to do that was to slide on top of him in order to find those favorite spots. She wished they weren't wearing their leather jackets, but she was too enraptured to take the time to remove hers.

"When did you get this scar?" she asked some time later, having discovered it while she was kissing his eyelids.

"I don't remember," he answered in a husky voice. "At sea, I think."

He reversed their position so he was half lying on top of her. "There's not a mark on your skin anywhere. It's like a baby's. Absolutely like velvet and flawless. Everything about you is flawless."

Clara raised her head to kiss the end of his nose. Unused to his compliments, she said, "Except on the inside." But the second the words were out, she regretted them.

With that slip, the enchantment of the moment was gone—not for her, but for him. She knew it by the way he checked himself before moving away from her and lying back on the blanket.

She couldn't bear for this to end and leaned over him. "Don't you want to play anymore?"

Valentino *had* been playing with his wife. He'd never enjoyed anything so much in his life. But if this was just a game to her to make *him* happy, then it changed the rules.

He hated games.

Clara wasn't like other girls who'd passed through his life. She'd been the different one. *His rock*. You didn't trifle with her kind.

When he dug deep down, he realized he didn't want her trifling with him. Anyone else, but not his *piccola*.

Not unless she meant it.

With this new weight troubling him, he felt confused and restless. He raised his hand to smooth some of the hair away from her flushed cheek. "I could play with you all day, but the sky's getting darker and the temperature has dropped. We can't afford to get caught in a storm. The last thing you need is to come down with a cold."

Valentino saw the glint of pain in her eyes before she moved away and got to her feet. Her kidney disease was a fact of life. Since leaving the villa he'd been the one to live in denial. Yet not even the game he'd started—the game he knew she'd enjoyed and would still enjoy if they continued—could make either of them forget. That would be asking the impossible.

Ten minutes after they'd arrived back at the villa, the rain started. While Clara disappeared into the shower to get warmed up, Valentino heated the chicken and pasta her mother had brought.

As soon as lunch was over they were expecting an important visitor. His wife would be surprised, but he knew it would be a good one. "Clara? Lunch is ready," he called to her.

"I'm coming." Within seconds she appeared in the kitchen dressed in a thin light blue cotton wrapper like the one she'd worn last night. It had long sleeves and fell to her knees, barely hinting at the lovely mold of her body beneath. Evidently it was a style and weight she found comfortable for her treatments. "This looks delicious, Tino. Thank you."

"We have your mother to thank for a few more days, then the real test will come when you have to survive on my cooking."

One graceful eyebrow lifted. "You mean *our* cooking. We'll be sharing the work around here."

He let her comment pass and poured them coffee before sitting down at the table with her. Their morning jaunt had depleted her strength. She would never admit it unless she had to, but he'd been around her long enough to tell when she was getting tired. Her eyelids fluttered a little and she lost some color.

As they were finishing the last of their food, he heard the sound of a vehicle pulling up in the rear courtyard. Clara heard it, too, and looked at him in surprise since no one could enter the grounds without authorization. "Are you expecting someone?"

He nodded. "I set the master switch to open the gate. Sit still and I'll get the door."

Once outside, he greeted Serena and the two

other clinicians who'd come with her. After telling her she'd find Clara in the kitchen, he helped the men unload the mobile dialysis machine and wheel it into the villa.

They were good people to come on a Sunday. Even though he was paying them a great deal extra for this service, he was grateful Clara would be able to get a treatment today and wanted them to know it.

He could hear the two women talking and took advantage of the time to show the men to the bedroom where they could set up the machine. Valentino's work with Serena had been instructive.

If Clara could do a longer, slower dialysis every night while she slept, not only would it free up her days and give her more energy, it wouldn't be as hard on her body. She wouldn't get as many cramps and she'd suffer less nausea. Except for a new kidney, he couldn't ask for more than that during this interim.

Serena was scheduled to work with Valentino this afternoon, then the men would each come for two nights to continue training him. By then he'd be able to take care of Clara himself. Provided God was in his heaven, she wouldn't need dialysis once a kidney had been found.

"Hi," his wife said softly as she came in the bedroom with Serena, her gaze finding Valentino's.

"This was an amazing surprise considering it's a Sunday. Thank you. All of you," she added the last. Her moist green eyes reflected her gratitude. It brought a boulder to his throat.

"Shall we get started?" Serena asked. "Since you'll be getting a longer treatment tonight, we'll do a shorter session now. Clara? While you get comfortable on the bed and roll up your sleeve, I'll ask Valentino to wash his hands, then put on rubber gloves. We'll leave a box of them in the bathroom."

Three hours later everyone left with the proviso that Carlo would be back at eleven p.m.

Valentino saw them out, then went back to the bedroom with some juice and a roll for Clara. She was sitting up against the pillows. Her color was somewhat improved. He put her food on the bedside table next to her. "How do you feel?"

"I was just going to ask *you* the same question."

"If you want to know the truth, I'm relieved we've gotten this far."

"You've taken on a huge responsibility." Her voice throbbed.

"It's what I wanted."

She eyed him soulfully. "I believe you, but that doesn't make it any easier on you."

"The job itself isn't difficult."

Her brows formed a delicate frown. "Tell me what's troubling you the most."

"It's something Serena said."

"What was that?"

"She said that humans might have invented a dialysis machine to filter out the impurities that our kidneys can't, yet it can only do fifteen percent of the job done by a four-ounce kidney God created. We're going to find you a kidney, Clara," he whispered almost savagely. "I won't rest until then."

She patted the bed. "I'm the luckiest woman in the world to be married to you. Come and lie down by me. You look tired. Don't deny it."

He flashed her a wry grin. "I won't."

While she ate and drank, he stretched out next to her and closed his eyes. A few minutes later he felt her fingers furrow through his hair. Her touch electrified him. "Did I tell you I had the most wonderful day of my life today?"

Valentino grasped her hand. "Would you believe me if I told you I felt the same way?"

"They say you can't go back, but we did."

His lids opened. "Now I'm anxious to move forward with you. While we were riding on the back roads, I saw that the old Brunello place was for sale."

"I noticed it, too. It used to be a beautiful little farmhouse, but now it's run down. The small lemon grove has been sadly neglected." After she eased her hand from his, she looped her arms around her raised knees covered by the quilt. "Can you imagine any family being willing to give up their land?"

"Maybe there was no one to inherit."

She made a funny sound in her throat. "In the Rossetti family, that would be unheard of."

"In the Casali family, too, believe me." They both smiled. "If you're feeling good tomorrow, how would you like to drive back there and walk around to get a feel for it?"

A curious look crept into her eyes. "Are you thinking of buying it for an investment?"

"I'd like to buy it for us so we can live there."

Clara looked shaken. "I don't understand. What about this villa?"

"It belongs to the Di Rossi family. When Isabella begged me to come home, she talked to her fiancé, Max, about letting me rent it. I was saved the trouble of having to find a furnished place."

"I didn't realize you hadn't bought it."

"There are many things we still don't know about each other. Little did I expect that as soon as I got here, I'd become a married man so fast. Now I want a home of my own to put down roots and build a life with you."

She scrambled out of bed. "But you own a fabulous villa in Monaco. I've seen pictures of it in *Hello* magazine."

"When I made enough money from the motor-scooter sales, I bought it for an investment, but I rarely live there. Maybe this weekend we can drive there and stay over one night before I sell it. Though the economy is poor, I'm still pestered by a few interested parties who are anxious to take it off my hands. I'll put the money to good use on our own plot of ground."

"But, Tino," she cried, "you're not a farmer!"

"Maybe not, but I'm married to a farmer's daughter and Monta Correnti is home to me, too. Does the idea have any appeal, *piccola*?"

Clara's eyes slid away from his. When shadows darkened her features, he felt as if a giant hand had just cut off his oxygen supply. "Of course it does," came a small voice, "but I'm afraid you're getting ahead of yourself."

Her comment coincided with the ringing of his cell phone. Her crushing reply, guaranteed to stifle all hope of a long life together, turned his mood dark. He finally got off the bed and pulled it out of his pocket.

"It's your family," he said after glancing at the caller ID. "Your phone must be turned off. While you talk to them, I'll make certain the house is closed up for the night." He tossed the phone on the bed before striding out of the bedroom.

She sank down on the side and reached for it. "Hello?"

"Clara? Are you all right? Valentino told us he'd arranged for you to start your dialysis at home today."

"He did, Mamma. Serena just left. I—I couldn't be better." Physically it was true. Getting another treatment this afternoon instead of having to wait until tomorrow had already made a difference in how she felt.

Because of Valentino she wouldn't have to go to the clinic anymore. From now on she'd sleep through her treatments and start to live life during the day like a normal person. But the situation with him was unraveling fast. Twice today she'd said something to ruin the moment. Father Orsini had counseled her to make her husband happy.

"You're doing a great job, Clara."

"What did you say?" her mother asked.

"Sorry. I was thinking out loud. Thank you for all the wonderful food. Valentino sings your praises."

"He's a wonderful man." *I know*. "Even your father says so."

Her parents would be overjoyed if they knew about his plans to purchase some farming property. She was in awe of his unselfishness, not just because money wasn't his raison d'être, but because he gave of himself.

Tonight he would have to stay up and work with Carlo till four in the morning while he was trained to perform this service for her. Tears sprang to her eyes and wouldn't stop running down her cheeks.

"Clara? Are you crying?"

"Yes."

"Because he makes you so happy, *sì*? He does everything for you."

"Yes." Her husband did his duty better than any husband alive. It was time she did something for him in return.

"Both Gina and Lia phoned. I hope it's all right that I told them you got married."

"Of course. I'll call them tomorrow."

"By now your father has told everyone else in the family."

Clara smiled. "Pretty soon the word will get out and it will be all over the news. Don't be surprised if the paparazzi come by the farm for an interview and pictures."

Her mother laughed. "Come visit us soon."

"We will, Mamma, and we'll have you come to the villa for dinner. Tell Papa and Bianca I love them, and tell Nonna that Valentino loves his ring."

"That will make her happy."

She bit her lip. "How's Silvio?"

"Grumpy. He misses you."

"I lived in Naples for a long time. He didn't miss me then."

"Oh, yes, he did, but this is different, and *you know why*," she whispered.

Just then her brother's nemesis walked in the bedroom. She needed to talk to him. "Kiss little Paolito for me. *Buona notte*, Mamma."

Wiping the moisture off her face, she hung up. "My parents send their love."

A mask had descended over his arresting features. He took the phone from her. "No doubt they're worried about you."

"Actually they think I'm in the best of hands, which I am." Her voice trembled. "Talking with Mamma brought your father to mind. Could we go visit him tomorrow after we've been out to the Brunello farm?"

He placed his phone and wallet on top of the dresser. "I think we'd better put both those ideas on hold for the time being."

"I don't want to," she said with a pounding heart. He darted her a quizzical glance. "You'll have to forgive me for speaking so impulsively earlier. Ever since I was diagnosed, I'm afraid I stopped planning for a future and have been trying to be content by living day-to-day."

His mouth thinned. "In your shoes I would probably do the same thing."

"But we're husband and wife now, and I'm not the only person in this marriage. Naturally you're not going to be content renting a place when you could have your own home in the countryside we both love. It was shortsighted of me. Please let's drive out there tomorrow and look at the house."

To her relief Valentino rubbed the back of his neck, a sign that he was thinking, listening. "I'll phone the realtor in the morning and we'll go from there."

"Good!" She was pleased he'd agreed to that much. "Do you think your father's too sick for company?"

"No."

When he didn't say anything else she said, "You're tired. I'm going to go in the study and watch television while you get some sleep. The bed in this room is bigger than the one in the guest bedroom. Eleven o'clock will be here before you know it."

She started to leave, but he called her back. "Now I'm the one who's sorry. Forgive me for being abrupt with you." His eyes narrowed on her face. "We'll go over to the restaurant tomorrow only if you're up to it."

"You don't have to apologize for anything."

"Of course I do. You made a perfectly normal suggestion to drop in on my father, but there are things you still don't know."

There was more?

"It meant a lot to me that he came to our wedding, but I still struggle. Bear with me."

"You know I will. Tell me the rest."

He nodded. "Papa and Lisa have never gotten along. Being business rivals, you don't know what it's like when they're together. They have this way of going for the jugular."

"That's horrible."

"Before long their squabbling grows into a major conflict that makes everyone so uncomfortable you want to run for your life. I ran to you a lot during those times. Isabella reminded me I preferred your company to anyone else's."

The revelation took Clara by surprise. She didn't know what to say.

"Growing up I had the sense that something ugly had occurred for them to be at each other's throats all the time. Sure enough it all exploded the night of my father's birthday party. Isabella and I heard angry voices coming from the courtyard. You'd think the party would have given them a reason to try to get along for one night."

He sprang from the bed, unable to sit still. "We got up to investigate. I could hear my aunt announcing to anyone listening that not all my father's children had shown up for the party. She was baiting him relentlessly.

"Isabella and I thought she meant Cristiano, but then she said, 'It's time the secret was out, Luca!' Papa tried to shush her up, but she just kept talking. 'Your children don't know you have two older sons! Don't you think it's time they found out?'"

"What?" Now Clara was on her feet and moved closer to him.

His body tensed. "It seems my father had twins with his first wife, Cindy. She was an American and after their divorce went back to live in the States. Father kept the twins with him for a while, but then, for some reason, he sent them to live with their mother in America and he never bothered to tell any of us about the boys. Of course Aunt Lisa knew all about it and took great delight in exposing his secret. She'd seen the one named Angelo in the newspaper back in New York. The other one is called Alessandro."

Twins. "How old are they?"

"Thirty-eight. Papa gave them up at the time of the divorce. When he married my mother and the three of us came along, he never breathed a word about them."

"No one else ever mentioned them?"

He shook his head. "I found out our cousin Lizzie knew, but she was little at the time and Aunt Lisa told her to keep quiet about it. My aunt has a cruel side. So does my father apparently. I'm not saying he wasn't good to me, but I'm having a hard time dealing with the fact that he has two other children he's never acknowledged."

Luca Casali was an enigma to Clara. There had

to be an explanation for a man who could accept Violetta's love child as his own and raise him, yet abandon his oldest flesh and blood sons and pretend they didn't exist.

Clara was desperate to ease her husband's pain. Knowing he wasn't Luca's blood son had made Valentino insecure his whole life. Now to learn about two older brothers had raised all those old issues of jealousy and feeling inadequate.

Maybe one day when emotions weren't running as high, she'd be able to talk to him about it, but right now Valentino was in no state to hear anything. All she could do was listen.

"Would you believe my sister wants to get to know them?"

Yes. As long as Clara had known her, Isabella had been a do-gooder. She'd been raised as Luca's biological daughter, so she didn't have the same emotional struggles as Valentino. But again Clara had to keep those thoughts to herself.

She put a hand on his arm. "Under the circumstances, do you have any idea how much I admire you for coming back home to help your family? For trying to make peace with your father? You had every right to stay away and refuse to deal with the problems. You could have excluded your father from our wedding. But you didn't do any of those things. That's because you're a real man, Tino."

Rising on tiptoe, she kissed his hard jaw and headed for the study.

CHAPTER EIGHT

WHILE Clara was fixing their breakfast the next morning, the long-awaited call from Dr. Arno came through. Valentino took it in the bedroom where he could talk to him in private.

"Thank you for phoning me, Doctor."

"You're very welcome. I'm sorry you had to wait so long. It isn't often I get someone as famous as Valentino Casali asking me to call him back. I'm a keen fan of yours."

"Thank you very much."

"My receptionist told me you're an old friend of one of my patients."

"Yes. In fact Clara and I were just married."

"*Married*?"

"Yes. We did it quickly so I could be with her around the clock to help her."

"Well, congratulations. She's a courageous young woman. A lovely one, too. You're a lucky man."

"I couldn't agree more. If you have time now, I'd like to hear anything you have to tell me about her condition that Serena might not have shared. Most of all I want to know how I can help find Clara a donor sooner."

"I understand your impatience, Signor Casali, but be assured our department is doing everything humanly possible for her. Since her family hasn't been able to produce one, I'm hopeful we'll find her an altruistic donor."

A tight band constricted Valentino's breathing. "I've thought everything over and would like to be one *if* it's possible."

"She has Type O blood. What's yours?"

Valentino's heart did a kick. "The same. I'm in perfect health. No weight problem, no high blood pressure, no history of diseases, no steroid use, no tobacco, no drugs, recreational or otherwise. Dr. Rimbaud in Monaco will send you all my medical records."

"You sound too good to be true."

"Except that I'm not related to her."

"That isn't necessarily a problem. Over the last several years, immunosuppressive medications have improved to the extent that our transplant center often considers poor tissue matches between donors and recipients. Certainly a kidney matched at four, five or six antigens from a family member may do better in the long term than others, but, as I said, the new medications are proving highly effective."

He gripped his phone tighter. "In that case, let's move ahead immediately."

"Can you come to the hospital in Rome for tests tomorrow?"

"I'll be there in the morning." He would tell Clara he had business. Maybe she could spend the time with her family.

"That's wonderful. I'll set everything up for you and we'll get started on your blood work."

"How long before the transplant can actually take place?"

"If all looks good, I'd say seven to ten days."

"How involved is the surgery?"

"Obviously not as much for you as for Clara, but there are always those normal risks. We have a new technique that takes around three hours and is not as invasive. You'll both be in the hospital four to five days to recover.

"During the transplant operation, you'll both be under a general anesthesia and administered antibiotics to prevent possible infection. Once the new kidney is attached, I may or may not remove her diseased ones. It all depends on the circumstances surrounding her kidney failure. Barring complications, you'll both leave the hospital to face a normal life."

A normal life.

Relief swamped him that they might be able to have a normal life and everything that went with it. "I don't want Clara to know anything about this yet. We can tell her when the time comes, not before."

"That's a very wise decision for both your sakes. If it turns out you're not a good candidate for some reason we don't know about yet, then there's no point in getting either of your hopes up. Before she knows anything, I'd like us to be absolutely certain of optimum results. But I can tell you this much—your being a live donor will give her twice the chance of recovery since your kidney will be healthy and fresh."

Just hearing that made him want to get the surgery done as soon as possible. He thanked the doctor, eager to follow through with his plans.

Clara waved to the realtor as she and Valentino left the Brunello farm on the scooter under more overcast skies. "The man is besotted by you, *piccola*. In that cherry-red cotton sweater you're wearing, I can't say I blame him."

"Don't be silly." She wished her body didn't react every time he made a personal remark. Clara thought it was only redheads whose emotions were too close to the surface. "He's old enough to be my grandfather."

"Didn't you know they have the worst fantasies?"

She chuckled, aware she was feeling different this morning. Better. For the first time in weeks she'd awakened without a hint of nausea. Two treatments since yesterday when she normally wouldn't have had one until today proved the effectiveness of nighttime dialysis. Only Valentino could have made this possible.

He had to be exhausted after his five-hour vigil last night, but he hadn't shown it while they'd inspected the farmhouse. What a disappointment it had turned out to be. The whole place reeked of neglect and was in much worse shape than she'd thought. They'd left without giving the realtor any indication of their true feelings. Naturally Valentino wanted to keep looking.

While she was deep in thought, he said, "On our way back to town, I'd like to stop at your parents' long enough to get that sample of limoncello you told me about. We're almost there now."

"How did you even remember?" Clara had thought he was going to suggest they find a newspaper and see what else was for sale in the Monta Correnti area.

"I've been salivating for a taste of it ever since you mentioned it."

A dissenting sound escaped her lips. "You made that up to make me feel good."

"I'm glad if it did, but, to tell you the truth, the

few times I've been served it, I haven't been impressed."

"Now I'm afraid."

"Not you—you're the most courageous person I've ever known. You *are*, you know, so humor me," he said in his deep voice. "It's possible the daughter of Signora Rossetti, who cooks the best food I've ever tasted, has inherited her mamma's special gift."

"You're so full of it, it's no wonder my mother is crazy about you. She'll be thrilled to see us."

A few minutes later they pulled up to the farmhouse. Valentino waited for her to alight. After they took off their helmets, they went inside. Maria was in the kitchen feeding lunch to her youngest and to Paolito, who was in the high chair.

Clara gave them kisses, then hugged her sister-in-law. "Where's Mamma?"

"Giving Nonna a bath because Bianca is too sick."

"Is it her nausea?"

"That and her pain. Tomaso took her to the clinic. It sounds like a bladder infection."

"I know about those." Clara's voice shook.

Valentino slid his arm around her shoulders and pulled her close. "I'm sure she'll be all right, *piccola*."

"Of course she will," Maria assured her.

"If you and Mamma need help, Valentino and I can stay."

"No, no. Everything's fine."

"If you're sure."

Maria smiled. "You two are still on your honeymoon." But it wasn't the kind Clara's sister-in-law was talking about. "I'll tell Mamma and Bianca you came by."

She nodded, still uncertain.

"Where's the limoncello? I'll get it," Valentino whispered.

"Oh—I forgot. It's right over here." She moved out of his hold and found the corked bottle in the cupboard by the door. She found a sack to put it in. After handing it to him she hurried over to give the children another kiss. "I'll call Bianca later to see how she is."

"She'll probably be home in another hour."

"*Ciao*, Maria," Valentino called out from the doorway.

"*Ciao*, Valentino."

Clara followed her husband out to the scooter. He gave her a kiss on the neck while she was putting her helmet back on. "Do you want me to drive to the clinic in case she's still there?"

"No, Tino, but thank you for offering. She'd think I was crazy. It's just that they've all been wonderful to me, especially Bianca."

They headed down the drive for the main road.

"You two were always close. I'm afraid I can't relate where Cristiano is concerned."

"I'm so sorry." She'd give anything to help him.

"Don't be. I shouldn't have brought him up."

"I'm glad you did," Clara said, emotion clear in her voice. "You need to talk about it."

"Now you're spoiling *me*," he bantered.

"It's about time. What you need is a long nap after being up all night."

"Only if we do it together."

Clara couldn't wait until lunch was over. Sleeping or waking, she craved every second being with her husband.

The next afternoon, Valentino returned from his visit with Dr. Arno in Rome and walked in the kitchen to find Clara just getting off the phone with her friend Gina. He wore an expectant look on his handsome face. "How good do you feel?"

It wasn't an idle question. "Happy now that you're back from Rome. Did your business go well?"

"Better than expected. I think Papa is going to be surprised when I tell him several more tour operators are considering his restaurant very seriously."

"That's wonderful!"

He smiled. "Feel like getting out?"

"I've got lots of energy if that's what you're asking."

"Then I'm going to let you do the honors." He put the Ferrari keys in her hand.

She blinked. "I wouldn't dare drive your car."

"*Our* car," he corrected her. With his hands spanning her waist, he held her a few inches above the ground. "Say it."

"Tino—put me down."

"Say it!"

"All right. *Our* car."

"That wasn't so hard, was it?" He pressed a surprisingly hungry kiss to her mouth before walking her outside to the driver's side of the Ferrari. After he opened the door for her, she was so dizzy with reaction she almost fell into the black leather seat.

He joined her in a minute. She stared helplessly at him.

"Get into the harness first."

After she managed to do that, he fastened the lap belt, then kissed her lips again. He was no stranger to intimacy, but this was new to Clara. He needed to stop doing that or she wouldn't be able to concentrate.

"Tino—I don't know what to do—"

"Sure you do. You've driven a truck before. You can drive this. Feel down the side of the seat and press the button forward until you're close enough."

Going on faith, she reached down. To her surprise it worked just the way he'd said.

"Bravo. Now put the key in the ignition and turn on the power." As soon as she did it, the car came alive like a beautifully tuned instrument. "It's automatic. Just put it in drive. No clutch to worry about."

Pressing her lips together, she did his bidding. The car crept forward. She turned right at the end of the alley and joined in the mainstream traffic. At first she was terrified, but after a few minutes of navigating through the center of town she started to feel braver.

"You're doing fine, *piccola*. There's the sign for Lake Adrina. Let's head that way. If you get too tired, I'll take over."

Tired? What was that? This was so thrilling, she felt that any second now they were going to take flight.

Little by little they left the traffic behind until she couldn't see any cars, then she pressed on the accelerator. The car took off like a rocket, causing her to cry out in sheer delight. Valentino's face had broken into a broad smile. For the moment he looked so carefree, it filled her with joy.

"Oh—I can't believe it! This is the most fun I've ever had in my life!" The car hugged the curves. Her confidence grew as she passed slower cars and trucks. Clara could see the needle on the speedometer climbing, but she didn't care. In no time at all the lake appeared in the distance. They'd already come fifty kilometers!

Valentino leaned closer to her. "Do you want to stop for a drink?"

"No!"

More laughter poured out of him.

She could have gone around the lake, but the drive back to town would allow her to go a lot faster, so she turned and headed back toward Monta Correnti. "I never understood your love of speed, but I do now!" Already she was addicted.

Halfway back she heard sirens, but didn't associate them with her driving until two police cars pulled alongside her. "Uh oh. Tino—" The officer in front motioned to her that she should pull off the road. "How can I stop when the road is this narrow?"

"Do it anyway," he answered in a calm voice. "It's their problem, not yours. After you've stopped, put the window down and start looking for your driver's license."

Valentino had obviously been through this experience before. Hot and flustered, she pulled to the right as far as she dared, then slowed to a stop. Immediately four officers got out. Two waved the traffic past them, while the other two approached the car.

"Do you have any idea how fast you were

going, *signorina*?" the older one with the moustache demanded, but the second he saw Valentino a look of shock altered his fierce expression. He turned to the other officers. Soon everyone knew the famous Valentino Casali was in the car.

"*Mi dispiace tanto*, Signor Casali. We didn't realize it was you."

By this time Valentino had put down his window. "That's all right. My *squisita* bride has been dying to drive my car. Today she took it into her head to take off with it when I wasn't looking. I had to run to catch up with her."

That brought a roar from the men.

"It's a good thing you stopped her when you did because I was starting to get nervous. I was never this nervous at the track."

"Tino!" His comment had the officers reeling with laughter.

They each took turns going around to his side to talk to him about his last race. One of them got a camera from his police car and started taking pictures. She could tell they were ecstatic to have met their favorite hero. Finally the same officer tore himself away long enough to talk to her.

"I'll only give you a warning this time, Signora Casali," he said with a smile.

"Did you hear that, *bellissima*?" He'd undone his harness and leaned over to give her a lingering kiss on the lips. "You're very fortunate they are being so kind to you. Thank them nicely, *per favore*."

While she muttered something indistinct, they took pictures of her, of them, of the Ferrari. If the officers didn't have a job to do, they'd have probably hung around Valentino all afternoon and evening. No doubt they'd never pulled over a celebrity as famous as her husband.

When all the *arrivederci*s had been said and they'd driven off, she finally found herself alone with Valentino. "They did us a great favor today. I saw the way that officer was looking at you. It's a good thing I married such a beauty or your punishment could have been a great deal worse."

Too many emotions were fighting for expression. She squinted at him and could tell his shoulders were shaking. "I'm glad you think this is so funny."

"Don't you? I knew you were brave, but I never dreamed I had such a little daredevil on my hands."

"Neither did I," she admitted before she found herself laughing, too. "It's the car's fault."

"That's as good an excuse as I've ever heard." Their shared laughter filled the empty spaces in her heart.

She started the car and they took off again, but she forced herself to stay within the speed limit. When they reached the town she had the feeling they were being followed.

"Tino?"

"I've already seen them. It's the paparazzi. They no doubt listened in on the police band. We've been found out. Keep driving to the villa. They won't be able to follow us past the gate."

He was so used to being followed and harassed, she could tell he took it in his stride, but this was a new experience for her. "I wish I were in a tank, then I'd mow them down until they resembled a sheet of aluminum foil."

"Putting you behind the wheel has brought out the spitfire in you. I would never have believed it." Valentino was still chuckling after they'd parked the car and gone inside the house.

Once inside he fastened his dark brown eyes on her. "I'm starving and imagine you are, too."

"I have to admit our adventure has given me an appetite."

"Good," he said, getting down two small liqueur glasses. "This is the perfect time to try out your homemade aperitif. A good appetizer should improve our meal." He pulled the cork from the bottle sitting on the counter and inhaled the aroma. "I can smell your family's lemon grove."

Her pulse sped up. "It's the taste that's important. I hope it won't put you off your food."

He poured a little of the yellow liquid into each glass, then took a drink and savored it for a moment before swallowing all of it. She watched him nervously before he poured himself another glass.

Like déjà vu he lifted it. "I'd like to propose a toast." His penetrating gaze sought hers. The way he was looking at her made it difficult to breathe. "To the success of my brilliant wife."

"At least you didn't choke on it." She clinked her glass with his and they both drank. "You're a terrific sport."

His expression sobered. "I don't think you understand. This liqueur is going to put your name on the map."

She smiled. "I don't want it to be on the map, but you're very sweet to say so."

Lines marred his features. "I'm not sweet at all. You've got a recipe here someone would kill for. Does your teacher at the college have a copy of it?"

His question surprised her. "No."

"Do any of the students?"

"No."

"Where is it?"

"In my school notebook at the farm."

"We'll pick it up tomorrow." He put the cork back in the bottle. "This needs to be kept in a safe place."

While he put it in one of the cupboards, she started getting a meal ready. Soon they were able to sit down and eat. She kept looking at him while he devoured his food.

"You're acting preoccupied just like you used to when you were working on your scooter designs. What's going on?"

"This and that," he murmured evasively.

He wouldn't tell her about his trip to Rome until he was ready. "You sound tired. Why don't you take a nap, while I phone Bianca? You're going to be up again most of the night."

Valentino shot her a glance. "We'll take a rest together." They'd done the same thing yesterday. It had been heaven. "No matter how well you've felt today, you need some downtime, too."

"I confess that sounds good."

They left the kitchen and headed into the bedroom where both of them took off their shoes and stretched out across the top of the quilt. "Here. Use my phone."

"Thank you." She took it from him and called her family's home number. Her mother answered.

"Clara? I heard you came by yesterday."

"We were sorry to miss you, Mamma. How's Bianca?"

"She's resting right now, but she's going to be fine."

"The poor thing. She needs to get a lot of sleep."

"We'll see to it. Don't you worry about anything."

She glanced at her husband, whose eyes were

closed. "Tino won't let me. He keeps me too busy to think."

"That's good."

"Guess what I did today?" For the next five minutes she related the experience driving his car.

Her mother gasped several times. "You could have gotten both of you killed!"

Ever since the police had pulled her over, Clara had been regretting her impulsive behavior. If anything had happened to Valentino because of her…

"I won't ever speed again, Mamma."

With those words Valentino's arm caught her around the hips. "Promise me," he whispered.

She'd thought he'd fallen asleep. "I promise."

"What did you say, Clara?"

"I'm sorry, Mamma. I was just answering Tino."

"I can tell you've had a good day."

"A wonderful day."

"That makes me happy."

"Me, too."

"I'll talk to you soon."

"*Ciao*, Mamma."

The minute she hung up, Valentino pulled her closer. "Let me hold you like this for a while."

She made a little moan of consent and nestled against him with her head lying on his shoulder.

If they both slept now, she would read her mystery tonight. They used to read to each other when they had literature assignments. Maybe he'd like her to read aloud to him. They could hash over the plot. She'd lived for their lively discussions. He had the most fascinating mind…

No one knew how much she'd missed him over the years. To have him back in her life like this constituted some kind of miracle. As her eyes closed her hand slid to his chest without conscious thought.

She had no idea how long she slept, but when she was once again cognizant of her surroundings it surprised her that she and Valentino had changed positions. While she lay on her side, he was now turned toward her with his head buried in her neck. His hand roved over her back in ever tightening circles, wringing tiny sounds of pleasure from her throat.

When his mouth found hers, it seemed natural to indulge in a giving and taking that grew more sensual with each breath. "I love the taste of you. Your body feels made for mine." He drew in a deep breath. "I want to make love to you, Clara. Is it selfish of me to want you so badly?"

Her breath caught. He wanted her. "How could it be selfish? I don't understand what you mean?"

"Would it make you feel worse?"

Worse— "I've never felt better, but if you're asking me for health reasons, I couldn't honestly tell you how it would affect me," she whispered against his lips, unable to get enough of them. "My body seems to dissolve a little more with every kiss." She didn't want to talk right now.

"Have you ever been intimate with a man before?"

"Not like this," she murmured, thrilling to each caress.

Maybe it was her imagination but she thought she heard him groan. "Has your doctor given you any guidelines?"

"No. The subject never came up. Does it matter?" She tried to get closer to him. "I don't want you to stop kissing me."

His hands stilled on her arms. "That's my fear—that I won't be able to stop." His breathing sounded shallow.

"Would that be so terrible?" she asked, kissing him more passionately.

"Considering your condition, it would be unconscionable if I got you pregnant, *piccola*. Even the best protection isn't completely safe."

While she was digesting the long-term ramifications, he untangled his legs from hers and rolled out of reach. When he stood up, she couldn't bear it. All her joy evaporated. "Please come back to bed. We'll just hold each other for the rest of the night."

He shook his dark head, taking another step

away from her. "I'm afraid not. Carlo will be pulling up in the drive any moment."

Carlo. She'd forgotten all about his coming again. Valentino had taken her to another world. If the clinician were to walk in right now, he'd find her a throbbing mass of needs her husband had aroused. She couldn't imagine getting to sleep. If he refused to touch hcr from now on, it would be like a second death.

CHAPTER NINE

WHEN Clara awakened early Saturday morning and opened her eyes, she saw that Valentino was already up and dressed in a pullover and jeans. Normally he slept in until ten to catch up on his sleep. During those hours she would get out of bed and leave him alone while she followed through with her own routine. Deprivation was one sure form of self-preservation.

However this morning there was an air of expectancy about him. When he was up to something, he couldn't hide it from her. She loved that quality about him. In truth she loved all his qualities, which were too numerous to count.

Valentino took amazing care of her. What little she did for him by being a listening ear when he chose to divulge his inner thoughts could never make up for the hours he watched over her while administering her treatments. During those hours while she slept, he balanced his time between helping her and running his business from the laptop.

After six consecutive nights of dialysis she felt so normal, she had a hard time believing there was anything wrong with her.

His dark eyes swept over her face and hair. "If you feel as good as you look, I've arranged a surprise for you."

She got excited because his surprises weren't like anyone else's. Every day they went out on the scooter to explore neighboring villages and enjoy picnics. They traveled to all their old haunts and sought new ones, finding delight in everything they did.

But with each passing hour, her physical attraction to him was growing more intense. The only time she could legitimately touch him without worrying what he might think was when she clung to him on the back of his scooter.

He represented the epitome of male sensuality and could have no idea that each time he squeezed or kissed her coming and going he added to the fire raging inside her. If he thought they could go on this way indefinitely, then he truly didn't know how deeply her desire burned for him.

Despite the fact that she was ill, the nature of their relationship would have led to intimacy by now *if* they were in a normal marriage. But they weren't! Valentino needed her as a friend. Though he was a flesh and blood male with the normal urges, he'd been careful not to let things go too far.

She, on the other hand, had to fight not to reveal that a little friendly loving was slowly destroying her.

Feeling his gaze on her, she said, "Judging by the way you're dressed, we're doing some kind of activity outside. Shall I wear my leather jacket?"

"I think you'll prefer a parka, but bring your gloves. I'll meet you out in the kitchen in a few minutes."

Within twenty they'd eaten breakfast and had stolen away from the villa in the Ferrari. Dawn still lay over Monta Correnti. Clara had always considered it a magical time of day when there was a crispness in the air and all was quiet. Valentino must have been enchanted, too, because he didn't talk. They wound their way past the church where the road made a descent and disappeared into the picture-book countryside.

She didn't understand when he eventually turned off onto a dirt road bordered by well-tended farms. Maybe he'd found another property for sale he wanted to show her.

Ahead of them she saw a van pulled to the side.

A couple of men were walking around carrying items. “Uh oh. They must have had car trouble.”

“Let’s find out,” Valentino murmured. He pulled to a stop behind them and got out of the car.

Clara craned her neck to find out what was going on and got the shock of her life to see them unraveling a huge balloon over the ground. A thrill of excitement tinged with alarm shot through her. Valentino had arranged to take them for a balloon ride?

Once she’d extricated herself from the seat harness, she joined him. The men, a father and son, greeted her with broad smiles. Evidently they were good friends of Valentino’s. He introduced everyone.

“*Buon giorno*, *signora*. You have chosen the perfect morning to go up.”

Valentino’s gaze flicked to hers. She saw a definite look of concern in those dark brown depths. “What do you think, *piccola*? Do you want to try it?” He didn’t ask how she was feeling, but she knew he was worried.

Clara had never been on a plane, let alone anything that had ever left the ground. But this was Valentino Casali who’d established a record for the longest solo balloon flight over the Caribbean. She didn’t want to let him down and would show him and his friends that daredevil side he'd accused her of having when she'd driven his Ferrari for the first time.

"I'm dying to find out what it's like!"

Her unintentional slip of the tongue washed over the men, who got busy inflating the balloon, but she saw Valentino's lips tighten for a moment before he moved behind her and slid his hands to her shoulders.

He kneaded them with increasing pressure. "As I've told you several times, you're a woman of great courage, but this is one time when you have to be completely honest with me, or we won't step foot inside the basket."

She took a fortifying breath. "Physically I feel fine, but I'll admit to being scared."

He kissed the side of her neck, sending rivulets of yearning through her body. "That's natural. At first it will feel like you're in a lift that doesn't stop. Then you'll float over a world only the eagle sees. You'll be so full of wonder, you'll never want to come down. I'll have hold of you every second."

Whatever happened, if she could remain in his arms like this, nothing else mattered.

The multicolored balloon straightened as the men filled it with hot air. Valentino knew when the moment was right and helped her into the basket. "While his father is in charge, Agostino will follow our progress in the van. When we descend, he'll drive us back here."

She nodded and clung to him.

In a few minutes he whispered, "Clara?" There was a sense of urgency in his tone that caused her to lift her head. Maybe it was a trick of light, but she thought she glimpsed the heat of desire in his eyes before his mouth covered hers. The moment he deepened their kiss, she forgot where she was or what was happening around them.

Not even she could mistake the force he was unleashing as anything less than a husband's kiss. She'd been needing this for so long, her hunger for him took over and her passion flared. It would have been impossible to hold back even if she'd wanted to for propriety's sake. She had so much to tell him, show him. At this point nothing but a total merging of their bodies would satisfy her.

In the throes of rapture she cried his name with longing.

He drew one more molten kiss from her mouth before he said, "We're up now. Take a look."

She could hardly make sense of what he was saying until she opened her eyes. Then a gasp flew out of her. "Tino—"

They were airborne!

Clara had missed the ascent because she'd been devouring her husband in front of his friend with an eagerness that made her blush scarlet just thinking about it.

Valentino kept her clamped at his side while

she marveled at the vista unfolding several thousand feet below. She'd never seen such a sight, let alone experienced a sensation like it.

"I feel like we're fruit blossoms being carried along by the breeze."

He folded her right up against him and kissed her hard. "You feel a little more substantial to me than that. I wish there weren't so many clothes separating us."

The unexpected admission rang of need rather than playfulness, robbing her of breath. This was the passionate side of Valentino he'd revealed before he'd had the presence of mind to end what was rapidly burning out of control.

In a moment of truth she confessed, "I had the same thought." For the next half-hour she kept her hot face buried in his neck. They passed over the fantastic tapestry best seen from this altitude, but Valentino had just unlocked a door to her own private fantasies.

At the height of her euphoria, sharp searing pain, bitter and real, attacked without warning. Please, God. I don't want to die.

He kissed her hair, increasing her agony. "What did you say, *piccola*?"

"Th-that I wish this day could go on forever," she dissembled in a tremulous voice.

"Why can't it? When we get back, how would you like to drive to Monaco? We'll stay for a few days. I'll take you to the track where we practice. I want to show off my gorgeous wife to the team. I love this new life with you, Clara."

I love it, too, her soul cried out in fresh anguish. Maybe it was wishful thinking on her part, but Valentino *did* seem happier lately, more relaxed. It couldn't all be an act, could it? Not after they'd come close to making love—unless he was carrying his husbandly duty to the extreme.

She'd lived with him long enough to know he was capable of doing anything to make life more enjoyable for her. Knowing her days were numbered, would he go that far? To add to her torment, Silvio's silent questions kept flashing through her mind.

Is he in love with you, Clara? Did he say those words to you? Because if he didn't…

They landed without incident in the middle of another country road. The van was waiting there to take them back to their car. She shook the men's hands. "*Grazie, signori*. It was *stupendo*."

On the return trip to the villa Valentino said, "While you pack, I'll go by the restaurant and talk to Papa and Isabella so they know our plans."

Clara nodded. "Would you like me to put some things in a suitcase for you?"

He kissed the end of her nose. "I'd like that very much. So far there's nothing about our marriage that doesn't make me happy. I can't think why I waited so long. Do you have any complaints?"

"Except for the fact that you fish for compliments when you don't need to, you know I don't. Thank you for another wonderful experience I'll never forget." On that note she leaned over to peck his jaw, then got out of the car and hurried inside the villa to get ready for their trip.

Unless something unforeseen happened, she wasn't going to die today, tomorrow, or even next week. That meant she should make the most of living on the borrowed time dialysis was granting her.

When they reached Monaco, she would forget her illness and love Valentino in all the ways he would allow her. If they both used protection, there would be no worry about her getting pregnant.

Clara had loved him her whole life, but today she realized she was a woman *in love*. She couldn't go back to their platonic relationship. Not now. It wasn't possible.

On the way to the restaurant Valentino's thoughts were on Clara and the way she'd clung to him during their balloon ride. She wanted him as much as he wanted her. For purely selfish reasons this countdown needed to come to an end.

He reached for his phone to let his sister know he was coming, but realized he'd left it on the dresser back at the villa. It didn't matter. When he parked out back and joined Isabella upstairs, he found her still in the apartment making breakfast for their father. The timing was perfect. Valentino could eat with him while she went to market.

As he entered the kitchen it struck him how warm and colorful she'd made the apartment. The place looked lived in and comfortable, the antithesis of his villa in Monaco as well as the one he was living in now. He discovered he couldn't wait to move into his own farmhouse with Clara.

On top of the upright piano in the corner his sister had put photographs of their mother and the family. He wandered over to it and studied the likeness of her he remembered best. Because of a certain conversation with Clara, his stomach didn't clench as it usually did. His wife had changed him so much already, he didn't know himself.

"Izzy?" He headed into the dining room where she'd set the table. "I'm taking Clara to Monaco with me for a couple of days. I have to meet with my sponsor. He knows I've quit racing, but I'd like to tell him in person."

"Is she well enough to travel?"

"The nightly dialysis has made a new woman of her."

Her eyes watered. "I'm so glad, but waiting for a kidney must be so hard on both of you."

"We've been doing our best not to think about it." Valentino didn't tell her that he was waiting for a phone call from Dr. Arno with the results of his own tests.

"Trust me to bring it up."

He gave her a hug. "Thank you for caring so much. I didn't want to leave town without telling you and let you think I was deserting you again."

She shook her head. "I wouldn't think that, but I'm glad you're here. Papa's been asking about you. I'll get him."

"Let me do it," he interjected. "You go. I'll take care of him until you get back."

"Thanks. I realize you're anxious to get going so I won't be more than a half-hour."

"Perfect."

Once she was out the door, he walked down the hall and knocked on his father's bedroom door. "Papa?"

"Is that you, Valentino?"

He always said that, even though he knew who it was on the other side. "Who else? I came to eat breakfast with you."

"Ah—I'm coming."

"Don't forget your cane."

"No one will let me forget it!" he grumbled as he emerged in his tan trousers and matching sport shirt. His eyes stared at Valentino. "How is your Clara?"

"Good, all things considered."

His father's progress was slow. They finally reached the dining room and sat down at the table where Isabella had left warm rolls, fruit and cappuccino. Valentino helped adjust the chair for him and rested his cane against the table leg.

"She's a brave woman. Noble, too."

"That's an interesting choice of words, Papa." Valentino had thought the same thing about her, but didn't expect to hear his father express it.

"Well, isn't she? The way she carries on with that sunny disposition makes me ashamed of the way I've been complaining." He cleared his throat. "While we're alone, I want to tell you how proud I am of you for taking such good care of her."

Valentino sensed his father's sincerity. Another surprise. "Aunt Lisa asked me if I had lost my mind."

"When did she dare talk to you?"

"She phoned me the other night while I was giving Clara a treatment."

His father munched on his roll for a minute. "My sister is a born troublemaker. I happen to know you had a special feeling for the Rossetti girl from the time your poor mamma died. Listen to me, my son, because you *are* my son, even if you aren't my blood."

Valentino lifted his head to stare at this man he thought he knew.

"I can see what a terrible mistake I made by not adopting you years ago, but I was afraid."

"Of what?" Valentino whispered in shock. He couldn't believe they were having this conversation.

To his surprise, Luca's eyes watered. "I was such a failure as a father to my first two sons, I didn't feel I had the right to claim you for my own. Violetta didn't dare talk to me about it. With hindsight I can see she felt so guilty for the affair, she was afraid to ask me. But I was to blame for much of the trouble during that period. Earning a living was always a struggle. It caused difficulties in both my marriages."

In the silence that followed, his father wept quietly. "I didn't feel worthy of the honor to be your father officially."

Valentino lowered his head, unable to talk. Emotion had closed up his throat.

"I don't expect you to understand how it was for me as a young man. I fell for the twins' mother, but she wasn't happy here in Italy. She was an exciting, glamorous American woman who had a high-powered and glamorous job to match. But she didn't feel accepted here and when our twins were born, her partying had to come to an end.

"I was struggling to keep my roadside stall running. Things just didn't work out. When the children turned two, she left them with me and went back to Boston where she divorced me."

"What?" Valentino was incredulous. "From the way Aunt Lisa made it sound, you abandoned them."

"That didn't come until later." Sorrow twisted his features. "My business didn't make any money. By the time the children turned three, I was in desperate financial trouble and asked Lisa for a loan just to buy the boys some food until the situation improved. Sorella was doing well and I promised I would pay her back with interest if she would just help me out for a while."

Valentino could already see the writing on the wall. "She didn't lend you any money, did she?"

"No. Not that she had to, but I had no one else to turn to. She told me I ought to send the boys to their mother in Boston since she had a lot more money and could take care of them properly."

It was always the money with Valentino's aunt, yet she'd never told anyone she'd turned down his father's request for a loan.

His father took a shuddering breath. "I was in dire straits, Valentino. I loved my boys more than you can imagine, but I was unable to provide for them at the time. In the end I had no choice but to send them to their mother. It was the hardest thing I ever had to do, especially when I never knew my own father."

The similarity of Luca's and Valentino's beginnings wasn't wasted on him.

"Don't get me wrong. I'm not making excuses. I'm only trying to give you an explanation for the reason I never told you children about the twins. I was too ashamed over my inability to provide for them. It took me years to start earning enough money to be a family man."

More tears trickled down. "I don't expect forgiveness from anyone. I called the boys on their eighteenth birthdays. They didn't want anything to do with me. Who could blame them?" He put up his hand. "But before you leave here today, I want you to know something.

"When you were born, I named you Valentino in honor of my father, William Valentine. Besides my love, it was the most precious thing I could give you. Your mamma wanted that name for you, too."

The revelations just kept coming.

"How she loved her Tino. The diabetes she suffered from was a terrible disease. With every blackout I feared it was the end and you children would lose your mother."

Valentino's breath caught. "*Every* blackout? You mean it happened more than once?"

"Yes, but we didn't tell you so you wouldn't get alarmed. The doctor said she was dead before she fell down the stairs. Cristiano was just old enough to feel guilty that he hadn't gotten home sooner that day."

"I felt guilty, too, and thought I was to blame because I couldn't revive her."

A heavy sigh escaped. "How sad that both my sons took on that extra burden when you were already suffering."

Clara had been right.

While his mind grappled with information that cleared up the distorted picture he'd carried around for years, they heard Isabella enter the apartment. "I'm back, in case anyone wants to know!"

"Come and join us!" their father called out.

"In a moment."

Valentino eyed him through new eyes. "Papa?"

"Yes?"

"I don't want you to worry about finances anymore. If you don't like my ideas for increasing the business, I'd like to make you a loan to help pay off any debts you have owing because I know you'll pay it back when you can."

His father resisted.

"Let me do this for you. If you hadn't given me a good life, I wouldn't be in the position I am now. Think about it and we'll talk again after Clara and I get back from Monaco in a couple of days."

He patted his arm. "I'm overwhelmed, but you need to keep it for your family now."

"There's enough to do both." Valentino got to

his feet, eager to get back to his wife. He had so much to tell her, it would take the whole drive to Monaco. Only a few more days! Surely Dr. Arno would call any day with the results of Valentino's tests and Clara's transplant could go ahead. Then their lives would truly begin…

Clara had just hung up from talking to her mother to tell her their plans when she heard Valentino's cell phone ring. He'd obviously gone off without it. She lifted it from the dresser to glance at the caller ID, assuming it was someone from his company.

To her surprise it was coming from the Immaculata Teaching Hospital in Rome. Her body shook in reaction. She wondered what it could mean. Dr. Arno's office was there.

She clicked on. "*Pronto*?"

"Signor Casali, *per favore*."

"He's not here, but this is his wife Signora Casali. May I take a message for him?"

No sooner had she said it than her husband walked in their bedroom, his dark eyes searching out her gaze.

"This is the lab calling from Immaculata Hospital in Rome. Your husband asked that he be notified the minute his test results were done. Please tell him they've been sent to Dr. Arno's office."

The person on the other end gave out a phone number before the line went dead, but Clara's mind was reeling.

She stared at Valentino. "That was the hospital in Rome letting you know Dr. Arno had the results of your tests. They must have you mixed up with me, but before I could question it, they hung up. You'd better call them back."

As she handed it to him her cell phone rang. It was still lying on the bed. She reached for it and said hello.

"Clara?"

The familiar voice caused her heart to thud. "Hello, Dr. Arno." Was he calling because the blood Carlo had drawn the other night showed her anemia was worse?

"It's good to hear your voice. How are you doing on the nightly dialysis?"

"Fine. I've been feeling better and better," she said while Valentino stood there watching her in a way that raised the hairs on the back of her neck.

"That's wonderful." After a distinct pause he said, "I have even more wonderful news for you."

As she continued to look at Valentino, pure revelation flowed through her. "You mean about my husband volunteering a kidney for me?" A softness had entered his eyes, too piercingly sweet for her to sustain. She turned away from him.

"Then Valentino told you. We both felt it would be better if the identity of your donor remained a secret until you came into the hospital for the transplant, but as long as you already know…"

Clara bowed her head, praying for the inspiration to make it through this phone call. "To say I'm in shock would be putting it mildly." All this time he'd been laying the groundwork… The extent of his self-sacrifice staggered her.

"The *best* kind of shock there is. You both need to check in the hospital as soon as you can get here."

"You're talking today?" The rhetorical question came out more for herself than for him.

"Preferably in the next two hours so the lab can run a few more tests on you. If all looks good, we'll do the transplant in the morning."

By now Valentino had walked around so she was forced to look at him. Clara closed her eyes tightly.

"I'm afraid we won't be coming, Dr. Arno."

"I don't understand."

"You see, we're on our way to Monaco for a few days so Valentino can talk to his sponsor face to face. He's already turned his home into a hospital and has given up his racing career for me. I won't allow him to give up one of his kidneys, too." Scalding tears ran their course down her cheeks. "That's carrying altruism to an extreme not even God would condone."

"*Piccola—*"

The endearment scorched her to the depths of her soul. She turned away from him again. "Please don't give up searching for a viable donor, Dr. Arno. I know *I* won't."

After hanging up, she walked into the bathroom to wash the moisture from her cheeks. When she came out again, an ashen-faced Valentino was still standing where she'd left him.

"I'm ready to leave for Monaco whenever you are. Our bags are packed."

His features looked chiseled. "We're driving to Rome."

An unnatural calm had come over her. "Father Orsini gave us one charge. To make the other person happy. It would make me very happy to see where you used to live. I'd like to meet your racing buddies. You have no idea how much I've looked forward to this trip."

He studied her for a long time. "We just got married. I don't want you to die. My idea of happiness trumps yours."

Valentino had a way with words and arguments that had always twisted her emotions until she was defeated, but not this time. "Not if it means your death, and it could…I'm not simply referring to the risk you take for undergoing an operation. There's the rest of your life to consider. If it were shortened because of this experience, I couldn't handle that along with everything else on my conscience."

"Then let me remind you of something Dr. Arno told me."

Clara saw the compassion in his eyes. It was too much. "I don't want to hear it."

She grabbed her purse and phone, then reached for her suitcase and started out of the bedroom. He followed with the bag she'd packed for him.

"You'll like it," he persisted after they'd reached the kitchen. "To quote him, 'At times like these, I always tell my patients to be thankful to God. In his wisdom, he gave everyone two kidneys, even though he knew we only needed one. That's so we could give the other one away.'"

She spun around. "I'm sorry, but that lovely little story doesn't make me feel better."

"It should," he fired back. "I don't need both of mine. By this time tomorrow you'll have a functioning kidney again. In four to five more days we'll be home from the hospital. With the medication he plans for you to take to minimize your body's rejection, you'll be ready to throw yourself into the limoncello business before you know it."

She lowered her suitcase to the floor. "The day

could come when one of your kidneys won't work. Then you'll be thankful you still have the other one."

"If that moment should come, then I'll find me a donor."

He always had an answer. "What's the real reason for all this?" she demanded.

His eyes glittered. "The real reason? That covers a lot of territory, but I suppose it was something Father Orsini said that played into it."

Clara didn't know if she could tolerate hearing it, but she needed to know the whole truth now. "What was it?"

"He told me you could use a friend."

"I wish he hadn't said anything."

"How could he not? You're a favorite with everyone."

"That's not true," she cried softly.

"It's pointless to argue the fact. Needless to say his remark shot straight to my gut because I realized you'd always been my one abiding friend, the one person who continually built me up and made me believe in myself without asking anything in return."

The surprising explanation knocked the foundation out from under her.

Valentino moved closer. "I thought about it all the way back to the villa. You were the only reason my visit to Monta Correnti had sounded palatable. You know what happened when we saw each other on the stairs."

Yes. She knew. Her body trembled just remembering how he hadn't left her alone since.

"When I followed you to the clinic, I finally had a way to give you back something of myself for a change."

She felt her limbs dissolve when his hands slid to her shoulders. "You know me," he said in a husky tone. "I don't believe in what I can't see, but if my kidney could make you well, it would probably change my mind for me. Will you at least think about it while we're in Monaco?"

Once again he'd confounded her as only he could do. But even if he'd made her heart bleed, she would never let him go through that for her.

"Yes," she muttered. "Now can we please go?" She eased away, forcing him to relinquish his hold of her.

He carried their cases out the door and put them in the car before helping her in the passenger side. "I'll be back with the machine."

In a few minutes they were ready and left the grounds. The gate closed behind them. "I've never been to the Costa Azzurra or Monaco."

"We'll stop several times along the way to eat and stretch so the drive won't be too much for you."

"Thank you." He never stopped thinking about

her comfort for a second. "How close is your villa to the place where you drove in the Grand Prix?"

"Mine overlooks the main street."

"I know your sponsor has tapes, but it's sad you never got to stand on your own balcony and see yourself driving."

He broke into that male laughter she loved so much. "You're priceless, you know that? Wait till I tell the guys."

"At least you never crashed there."

"How do you know that?" His glance lingered on her profile.

"Bianca and I watched your races and saw every crash you were in." Each time she had almost died from fear.

"I didn't realize that," came the solemn admission. He reached out and grasped her hand to kiss it before letting it go again.

"It's a miracle you're still alive."

"Dr. Rimbaud told me the same thing every time he patched me back together."

She took a shaky breath. "Thank you for taking me on this trip."

"I've been looking forward to it, too, *piccola*."

"Even if there are other things you need to be doing?"

"Like what?" he demanded. "I'm your husband. This is where I need to be."

"I'm the most pampered wife I know." She was still so shaken by his plan to give her a kidney, she couldn't keep the tears out of her voice. "I loved this morning's balloon ride. How lucky was I to have the whole world at my feet?"

"I won't forget it either."

Her emotions were all over the place. "Tell me how it went with your father earlier, or didn't you get to see him?"

He let out a deep sigh. "He was there. Thanks to you, this morning we talked like we've never talked in our lives."

It was clear something monumental had happened. Without forethought she clutched his hard-muscled arm for a moment. "That's good."

"You have no idea."

Clara turned so she could watch him while he drove. She would never grow tired of looking at him. In profile or otherwise, his masculine beauty was stunning. "I want to hear all about it. Don't leave anything out."

Late afternoon of the following day, Valentino left his sponsor's office and walked out to the practice track. It surprised him the sun felt this hot. He was glad for it since he knew Clara welcomed the warmth.

He spotted half a dozen racers on his team surrounding his green-eyed wife seated in the middle of the bleachers. For the occasion she'd worn a wispy, periwinkle-colored blouse and white wraparound skirt with matching Italian sandals. Every color suited her.

Clara's knockout looks were only superseded by a feminine charm that came from someone grateful for life and interested in everyone. She projected that rare selflessness, guaranteed to melt the most cynical heart.

"So, Signora Casali?" He loved calling her that. It was a supreme moment for him to introduce her as his wife. When all this was a new experience for her, he was proud of her and the way she handled herself. "Are the guys giving you a hard time?"

"Oh, no." She flashed him one of her mysterious smiles. "They've been entertaining me with unabridged stories about you." Jocular laughter ensued.

Roger, a three-time world Formula 1 champion, grinned at him, giving him the thumbs-up sign. "Your *belle épouse* has so many statistics in her head, she could write her own book on you. I'm jealous, *mon ami*. You have found yourself a *trésor*."

Valentino agreed with him and nodded before looking around. Most of the journalists who'd come to the track for a photo shoot had gone, but there were still a few left who'd been waiting to get last-minute pictures of him and Clara. They never gave up. Today had been his swan song.

Normally he would have hated the invasion of privacy, but having his wife with him made all the difference. He no longer felt defensive or uptight. In fact the cameramen scarcely impinged on his consciousness.

Pleased that she seemed to be taking it in her stride, he climbed the bleachers two at a time to hunker down behind her and put his arms around her neck. He kissed her tender nape where she smelled of flowers from her lotion. "What do you say we leave and enjoy dinner on the water?"

He felt the little tremor that ran through her body before she whispered, "I'd love it."

A few more pictures while he helped her off the bleachers and they headed for his car. Once inside, he drove them down the zigzag streets of Monaco City to the yacht harbor. Hand in hand they strolled toward the Quai des Savants. This was a local paparazzi hangout, but tonight he didn't care. "I thought you'd enjoy eating at a modern Parisian-style bistro."

The reflected lights off the water from the yachts created an illusion that her eyes were dancing. After they were seated, she smiled at him. "I don't speak French. You order for us."

"They serve a delicious veal escalope with mushroom sauce. I like a Madeira wine with it."

"It all sounds delicious, but will you tell them

to leave the sauce off mine in case there's some dairy in it?"

He'd already anticipated doing it. After the waiter left with their order, Valentino got to his feet. "Let's dance."

"I haven't done it for a long time."

Once he'd pulled her from the chair, he drew her into his arms. "That excuse might have worked years ago, but you're my wife now. I don't care if you can't." He smiled down at her. "We'll just stand here and hold each other."

"Tino—"

He loved it when she blushed. While he was enjoying the moment, and her, and the night, she blew him away with some fantastic moves. They got lost in the music. He couldn't remember ever having this much fun dancing or anything else.

"Don't look now, but our dinner's waiting for us," she reminded him.

With reluctance, he guided her back to their table. "Next time, don't be so modest. You're a sensational dancer."

"Bianca and I used to practice."

Unable to resist, he pressed a kiss to her unsuspecting lips before seating her.

It didn't take long before she moaned. "I can't eat another bite."

"No dessert?"

She shook her head. "But don't let me stop you."

He had no intention of allowing that to happen, but the time wasn't yet…

As soon as they returned to the car, he took her past the Grimaldi Palace. At her request, he drove them around the Grand Prix racing circuit. She expressed a desire to visit the casino. He told her they'd do more sightseeing tomorrow. Though her energy seemed limitless, Valentino knew she had to be exhausted and finally pulled into the back of his empire-style villa for the night.

She hurried to their bedroom and got ready for bed fast. "With you having to be up for my treatment tonight, we shouldn't have stayed out so late, Tino."

"I wanted to. We'll both sleep in tomorrow."

True to what she'd told him on their wedding night, she fell asleep within thirty seconds of her head touching the pillow. It worried him she'd overextended herself. He'd be more careful with her from now on. Unfortunately when she'd refused to go to Rome with him he'd been forced to pull out all the stops to get their marriage back on the right track.

For the last eight hours he'd purposely avoided any talk of kidney donors or her illness. His strategy had paid off. Tonight Clara had acted more relaxed and confident with him than he'd ever seen her.

Little by little they were settling into their

marriage. From the moment he'd approached her parents, it had shocked him how right it had felt.

Once Valentino got her treatment started for the night, he pulled out his laptop. A dozen e-mails from Violetta Rapidita had been sent and needed replies. Isabella had written him, too. He opened it, wondering if this was bad news about their father.

Fratello mio, I didn't know how long you'd be in Monaco. In case you decided to stay there longer with Clara, I thought I'd better tell you what's happening. I don't want you to come back to Monta Correnti and be surprised in case you should run into Lizzie or Aunt Lisa and hear something you weren't aware of.

First off you need to know Lizzie and I have made up because we absolutely hate this war between Papa and Aunt Lisa. More than anything Papa wants the family to be reunited and we're in agreement.

Since the two of you talked the other day, he said he's done with secrets. After regretting that he kept quiet about the twins, he's told the cousins you're not his birth son, but he loves you as if you were. He doesn't want anyone hurting you later on.

Valentino rubbed a hand over his face.

Secondly, I know you're upset with me for getting in contact with the twins, but how can our family ever come together if things remain as they are? As you know, Lizzie and Jack are planning a June wedding, so she has sent invitations to Angelo and Alessandro.

The amazing twins were coming?

She's hoping everyone will show up. I do, too. Please don't be angry with me about this. Life's too short, don't you think?

Talk to you when you get back.

Love, Izzy

The penultimate line gave him pause because he found he couldn't disagree with his sister. Life *was* too short where Clara was concerned. Compared to doing everything to keep her alive, all else paled in significance, even his family's problems.

He stared into space. Before he answered his sister and told her his plans, he needed to send an e-mail to Dr. Arno, who deserved an explanation. The situation was bordering on desperate.

CHAPTER TEN

A WEEK later Clara drove to the farm early to spend the day with her family. She'd left her husband sleeping.

Since the morning she'd told Valentino she wouldn't let him give her a kidney, she'd noticed an alarming change in their relationship. It seemed that her refusal had killed his desire for the little amount of intimacy they'd shared.

On the surface he was the model husband and still affectionate with her, but in bed he didn't even try to hold her anymore. His behavior went beyond his fear that he might make her pregnant. They could have worked around that. To her sorrow he didn't leave himself open to discussion of their situation. For that matter he avoided any talk of her medical condition.

Since their return from Monaco, she'd had one conversation with Dr. Arno. He'd been understanding of the reasons she couldn't let Valentino be a donor, and he'd assured her everything was being done to find her one. Clara was trying to stay positive and stopped by the clinic for routine blood checks.

Because of Valentino's devoted service to her, he'd made it possible for her to lead what seemed like a normal life, but she was terrified he wasn't getting anything out of it. Not even a saint could go on like this much longer. Neither could she…

It all came down to one reality. Her husband was the source of her joy and her pain, and this dichotomy of emotions was tearing her apart.

"I think you need to confront him," Bianca advised her some time later while she let Clara bathe Paolito. Her poor sister was still suffering horrible morning sickness. Until the advent of her nightly dialysis, Clara had lived with nausea and wouldn't wish it on her worst enemy.

She splashed water on the baby, who could sit up in the water if she propped him. "Any suggestions on how to do it?"

"Yes. When you drive back to town, buy yourself something sexy from that little lingerie shop on the Via Romana. Something black and filmy. You're gorgeous in black. Tomorrow morning fix your hair different and put on a different perfume. Be lying there next to him when he wakes up. Tell him it's time he had a treatment from you, then do what comes naturally."

Clara swallowed hard. "Then he'll know."

"You mean that you're madly in love with him?"

As she nodded their mother came in the bathroom. "Your cell phone rang while I was in the kitchen, Clara. I'll take over here with Paolito while you find out if it was important. If it's Valentino, tell him to come for dinner. I'm making his favorite cannelloni."

Clara and her sister shared a secret smile. "I'll tell him," she assured her mamma before hurrying downstairs. Just the thought that it might be her husband caused her heart to thud in anticipation.

She reached for her purse lying on the table and pulled out her phone to check the caller ID. It threw her off balance to discover Dr. Arno had phoned. He'd left a voice message.

"*Clara? You need to come to the hospital as fast as you can. A kidney is suddenly available. Don't eat or drink anything. The nursing staff will alert me as soon as you've checked in and we'll go from there.*"

With hands trembling, she phoned Valentino. Pick up, Tino. Please pick up!

"*Piccola?*" he answered on the third ring. "Are you all right?" The concern in his voice was always there. How she loved him!

"Yes! Where are you?" she blurted.

"Getting ready to walk down to the restaurant. Why?"

"I'm coming for you. We have to drive to Rome immediately. I've got a donor!"

After a pregnant pause, "*Grazie a Dio*." His voice throbbed. "I'll pack a bag for you and meet you below the gate. Whatever you do, don't have an accident on the way. My heart couldn't handle it."

Neither could hers. "I won't." Her voice shook. After she hung up, she shouted, "Mamma?"

"I'm right behind you and heard everything. Someone must have died, making it possible for my precious Clara to live." She wept. "Go, *bambina*! Every second counts! Your father and I will come to the hospital as soon as we can."

Whoever it was had to have signed a donor card while they were still living. As far as Clara was concerned, they were part angel.

Six hours later one of the nurses walked in Clara's hospital room. "They're ready for you, Signora Casali. You have two minutes before they come with the gurney to wheel you to the OR."

Clara nodded, overcome by the outpouring of love from her family. All the adults were here, gathered around her bed. Silvio hadn't left her side since his arrival with Maria. For once he didn't show his resentment of Valentino, which was a blessing in itself.

After her father kissed her one last time, her gaze finally fastened on her dashing husband, whose brown eyes were suspiciously bright.

He squeezed her hand. "This is it, my brave Clarissima."

"Oh, Tino—"

"I'll be with you every step of the way."

"I know that," she whispered in a tremulous voice.

"When you wake up, it will be to a new life." He lowered his mouth to hers in a kiss that felt more like a benediction than husbandly.

A new fear tore at her heart as she was wheeled out of the room.

The minute Clara was gone, Valentino turned to her family. "Dr. Arno says none of us can expect to see or talk to her until at least ten or eleven o'clock tonight. Do whatever you want until then. I'll be here the whole time and plan to catch up on some sleep while I wait."

Clara's mother hugged him. "You do that. No one deserves it more. We will see you tonight."

Once they'd all left the floor, he stepped across the hall to another room prepared for him where he quickly removed his clothes and put on a hospital gown. After he got in bed, a team of medical staff came in to prep him. Soon he was being wheeled out the door and down the hall to the OR.

Throughout his racing career he'd faced surgery several times for a bone to be set, but this was different. He loved the idea that one of his kidneys would be planted inside Clara. They'd had a connection since childhood. With this transplant, that connection would be indelible. Personal. Life-giving. Eternal. Belonging only to the two of them.

One day soon he hoped to plant something else inside her enticing body that would result in bringing both of them ineffable joy.

Clara kept waking up. Each time she did, she became more aware of her surroundings. Where was Valentino?

The next time she opened her eyes, she realized she was back in a different room with a new nurse who was taking her vital signs.

"It's good to see you awake, Signora Casali."

"What time is it?"

"Midnight. You're in the transplant unit."

"I can't believe nine hours have passed."

"How are you feeling?"

"Strange."

"Strange is good."

"Where's my husband?"

"In time you'll be able to see everyone. Relax right now. Let the drugs do their job."

Between the anesthetic and other drugs being fed through the IV, she was feeling no pain, but the sight of the big machine next to her bed alarmed her.

"Did something go wrong with the transplant?"

The middle-aged woman smiled. "Don't you remember Dr. Arno telling you it went perfectly?"

"He did? Then why is the dialysis machine here?"

"In case your new kidney doesn't function right away. You probably don't remember him explaining that to you either." She gave Clara some pills to swallow. "Just take a few small sips."

"The water tastes good."

"Tomorrow you'll be able to drink liquids. Depending on how you're feeling, you'll probably be able to eat a little bit, too. Do you have any questions for me?"

"No, but I would like to see my husband."

"Tell you what. I'll go back to the desk and see how soon a visit is allowed."

"Thank you."

Before long she heard a familiar voice say her name. She opened her eyes. "Hi, Dr. Arno. The nurse told me everything went well."

A broad smile lit up his face. "It certainly did. You're a very lucky woman."

She nodded. "There are so many people I need to thank. You most of all."

"Not most of all. Without a donor, this wouldn't have been possible."

"I know."

"Before I let you talk to your husband, would you like to meet your donor?"

"Meet?" she cried softly. "But Mamma and I thought someone must have…died."

"No. In your case this altruistic donor is very much alive and came through the surgery beautifully, too. He wanted to see the person who received his kidney, but we'll only wheel him in for a moment."

Now that the transplant was over, the reality of the situation was overwhelming. She was about to meet the person who'd willingly given up a kidney for her? Clara couldn't comprehend that kind of sacrifice. Not really. What did you say to someone who'd just granted you a longer life?

Tears from too much emotion blurred her vision as she saw a woman pushing a man in a wheelchair. They came closer until she was able to make out his features.

It was the handsome face of her beloved husband.

She cried out his name on a sob. "*Why did you do it*? *Why*?"

"Don't you understand yet?" He was pushed as close to her as his wheelchair would allow. His intelligent brown eyes blazed with light. "I'm in love with you, darling. I think I was in love with you when we were children, but didn't know it."

To finally hear those words from that deep, silken voice…

More tears flowed down her cheeks. "I've been in love with you forever, but what if something happens one day and you'll need the kidney you gave me?"

"Then I'll give him one of mine."

Clara lifted her eyes to the woman who'd just spoken and received a second shock. "Isabella—" She hadn't realized.

"Yes." His sister smiled. "And if I find I need one, then Cristiano has pledged his to me. Because of you, Clara, our brother has found his happiness at last. This is what families are for, right? The Rossettis and the Casalis stick together."

On the fifth morning Valentino finished showering in preparation for leaving the hospital. Since their surgeries, he and Clara had been walking together, doing all kinds of exercises. They were more than ready to go.

Dr. Arno made his rounds after breakfast and released them. Within the hour a hospital van would be driving them back to Monta Correnti. This day seemed to have taken forever to get here.

As he was pulling on his tan chinos and a blue

sport shirt he heard her call to him but it sounded muffled. He couldn't tell if she was excited or upset about something.

He emerged from his bathroom on a burst of adrenalin and found her standing by his bed.

"Look!" She turned around, giving him an eyeful of her womanly figure. All the tubes and catheters were gone. No more IV stand. She looked incredible and was dressed in the same outfit she'd worn to the track in Monaco. Those green eyes glowed as if they were on fire.

"Your kidney's been working inside me from the time it was transplanted. No more dialysis!"

It was the best news he'd ever heard. He took another step and wrapped his arms around her, careful not to apply too much pressure while their incisions were healing. "I'm glad I've been good for something around here," he teased to cover his emotions.

"Oh, Tino, I'm so happy and so terribly, terribly in love with you!" She raised her hungry mouth for his kiss. They were starving for each other. Dr. Arno had told him they had to wait two weeks to make love. Valentino didn't know how he was going to hold out that long, not with a wife as passionate as Clara, but her comfort had to come first.

They had other rules to follow. Exercise every day. Walk. The longer the walks, the better. No driving a car or motor scooter for three weeks. No heavy lifting until after four weeks.

The fear that her body might reject his kidney had plagued both of them, but no longer. Naturally there was the possibility it might be rejected months or years later, but he refused to think about that right now. The different drugs she was taking were working.

"Signor Casali? Signora? When you're ready, the van is waiting for you at the south entrance downstairs."

Clara pulled away from him in embarrassment. Her face had gone a charming pink color. He would never tire of looking at her. Valentino had definitely come down with a serious case of love for his wife.

The nurse had brought two wheelchairs.

"Do we have to use them?" Clara asked her.

"It's hospital policy."

"Oh, all right," she grumbled and sat down in one. Valentino sank into the other one and reached for her hand. When she looked at him, they both saw the humor in their predicament and started to chuckle. Soon she was laughing. The sound filled him with an excitement he'd never known in his life.

After a short elevator ride, they were wheeled out to the van. The interior felt nice, comfortable. They thanked the staff for everything. Soon the attendant closed the sliding door and they were sealed off from the world for a while.

She darted Valentino a mischievous glance. "I feel like I did when we were little children. I would wait and wait for the end of school so I could run outside and hide from you. Somehow you always found me when nobody else could."

"It wasn't that hard." He grinned. "Whenever I got close, your laughter gave you away. I was attracted to it."

"My laugh?" she asked in an incredulous voice.

He nodded. "It has a happy quality. I liked being around you because of it. Don't ever stop. I couldn't take it."

"*Tino—*"

They were seated across from each other. He wanted to pull her onto his lap, but he didn't dare. After the hell she'd lived through, the thought of anything happening to her before they reached home was anathema to him.

Being a race-car pro, he had a problem letting anyone else drive him. The one hair-raising experience with his wife had been the exception because he adored her. At the moment he needed to have faith in the van driver's skill.

Since he couldn't hold her in his arms right now, he decided this would be a good time to tell her what Isabella had written in her e-mail. He already knew what Clara's response would be. She was a peacemaker. How else would she have survived from birth with a twin like Silvio?

Valentino's relationship with her brother still needed work. It would make her happy if he found a way to ease the tension. He'd have to think about that one.

"Tino?" she called out some time later. "Forgive me for interrupting you, but the driver's going the wrong way. He should have turned north."

"That's true, *if* we were headed for the villa."

"But we're not?"

"I thought we'd do something different."

For once she looked baffled. "Are you taking us to your old house on the lake?"

"No," he drawled.

She made a sound in her throat. "To the farm?"

"That depends on which one."

Silence fell between them before her gorgeous eyes rounded. "You bought the Brunello farm—"

His lips twitched. "Since the day we walked around the property, it's been known as the Casali place."

"Oh, darling—"

They were driving up to the farmhouse now. Her head swiveled around. "There must be a dozen trucks parked outside. My whole family's here! Whose car is that?"

"Isabella's. She brought Papa. He won't be able to stay long, but he came because he loves you."

"I feel the same way about him, Tino. He raised you as his own. I love him for that."

Valentino loved her for saying it and believed it. "They've all planned the celebration we couldn't have on our wedding day. Welcome home, *innamorata*."

She buried her face in her hands. In the next breath she'd broken down in quiet sobs from too much emotion. Valentino could relate.

He heard the van door open. Instead of the driver standing there, it was Silvio. His gaze shot to Clara, then passed to Valentino. For those few seconds he sensed her brother felt unsure of himself.

Taking advantage of the unexpected moment Valentino said, "Why don't you help her in the house while I talk to the driver?" He undid his seatbelt and climbed out of the van in order to give them some time alone.

Noise from the house reached his ears. Only the sounds of a big, gregarious family enjoying themselves could fill the air like that. By marrying Clara, he had entrée into their exclusive club. He'd never thought this kind of happiness could be his.

"Clara? This is for you." Bianca handed her a gaily wrapped gift.

"Another present? Thank you."

"Don't let Valentino open it," she whispered, kissing her cheek. "I'll call you in the morning."

Bianca, whose morning sickness seemed to be letting up, was the last of Clara's family to walk out the door. They'd brought the food and had done the dishes. Her mother had to be the one who'd made up their bed.

After her sister had gone, Clara, still seated on the couch, looked around the living room. She felt sated with food no longer forbidden to her. The wedding presents had been piled high on the coffee table. She couldn't wait to open them, but exhaustion had caught up with her. Tomorrow would be soon enough to dig in.

Seven o'clock wasn't late, but, having just gotten out of the hospital, she was ready for bed and knew Valentino was, too. A little while ago she'd seen him step outside with Silvio. She couldn't help but wonder how they were getting along. Maybe it was a good sign that her husband hadn't come back in yet, but it couldn't be good for him. He'd already been on his feet too long.

On her way to the bedroom with Bianca's gift, her gaze wandered around. Valentino had arranged for the interior of the house to be painted an off-white. He'd had it furnished with enough things for them to get by on. In a quiet aside he told her that, as soon as she was well enough, he expected her to decorate it the way she wanted. "Buy whatever else you want to make this *our* home, *piccola*."

Valentino was a rare man. It frightened her how much she loved him.

After she'd prepared for bed, she opened the present. Inside the tissue lay a black nightgown with lace straps. Definitely decadent.

When she'd asked Dr. Arno about that he'd said, "Two weeks and not before!" That was still nine days away. She smiled to herself before hiding it in the bottom of the drawer under some other clothes. Then she got in bed.

In a minute she saw Valentino's silhouette in the doorway. "We've got a slight problem, *piccola*."

Her heart skipped in worried reaction. "Silvio?"

"No. Amazingly enough he thanked me in a choked-up voice and we talked farming. I told him I would need his advice on how to go about getting started outside. He has offered his services. I never thought I'd see the day."

Contentment washed over her. She let out a relieved sigh. "Neither did I. Come to bed."

"That's the problem. In the hospital I would have sold my soul to be able to hold you. Now that I can in the privacy of our own bedroom, I'm telling you it wouldn't be a good idea."

"Yes, it would. We're both too tired."

"That's how much you know," he muttered.

"I'm wearing the same robe I wore at the villa."

"You think that protects you?" He started getting ready for bed. "Don't you realize how enticing you are when you're buttoned up from hem to neck?" he called out from the bathroom where he was brushing his teeth. "You might as well be wearing a sign that says 'warning—to proceed beyond this point could give you a heart attack'."

Clara laughed so hard it made her incision hurt.

When he finally climbed under the covers, they both lay on their backs. It was the most comfortable position for them. She reached out to touch his arm. He caressed hers. When his fingers came in contact with her graft, the movement stopped.

She heard Valentino suck in his breath. "Now I know why the good doctor left it in. He's a very wise man. You're safe from me for a while longer. *Ti amo*, Clarissima."

"*Ti amo*," she whispered back. It was liberating to be able to tell him *I love you*.

"What do you think, Papa? You're a connoisseur." Valentino had just dropped off Clara at the clinic for a checkup. Now was the perfect time to come to the apartment while he waited. He suggested the two of them sit at the dining-room table to enjoy a drink.

His father took another swallow. “It has a sweet bite. Very unusual.”

“Do you feel it’s good enough for your Rosa clientele to add it to the drinks menu?”

Luca eyed his son intently. “I didn’t know you’d developed a taste for limoncello.”

“In the last month I’ve developed a taste for several new things.”

His father smiled at him. “Marriage obviously agrees with you. I knew it would once you found the right woman. That’s the trick.”

That *was* the trick.

“You’re one of the lucky few who married your best friend and fell in love with her, too. That doesn’t happen to everyone. I’ve a feeling it will last forever. It’s a rare occurrence, just like this tangy liqueur.” He lifted the wine glass and smelled the bouquet before emptying it.

“You’ve hit on the right word, Papa,” Valentino mused aloud. Clara was like the drink she’d created. She had her own tang, her own flavor. His giving wife was no imitation of anyone else.

“Who makes it? This doesn’t smell or taste like it came from Sorrento. It’s sweeter.”

“Your ‘nose’ never fails you. This comes from a local source.”

“Ah…I knew it.”

Among the traits he admired about his father was his insistence on sourcing local produce even if it was more expensive. He paid his staff more and gave them longer holidays.

These were the reasons he was in debt, but, on the other hand, these were the reasons the staff had stayed loyal to him. Giorgio had confided that Lisa had tried to bribe him several times to come and work for her restaurant, but she'd underestimated her brother's influence.

Luca stirred in his chair. "Do I know them?"

"Yes. Quite well, in fact."

He looked surprised. "They've never approached me."

Valentino smiled inwardly. "No. They wouldn't."

"What's their brand name?"

"Limoncello Clarissima."

His father blinked. "How unusual, yet beautiful… Reminds me of your wife. I hope she can one day give you a child because you'll have the most beautiful children around. But more importantly, I have to tell you that you'll make the best kind of father."

A lump lodged in Valentino's throat. "If such a miracle happens and it's a son, Clara has already decided we'll name him Valentino Casali in honor of your heritage."

"Well…" His father had to clear his throat several times. "Where did you say these people live?"

This was fun. "Right here in Monta Correnti."

"Why don't you bring them around to the restaurant tomorrow afternoon or the next afternoon and we'll talk about serving it for a trial period. I can't guarantee anything, of course."

"Of course," Valentino echoed.

He couldn't wait to get back to the farm to tell her. The long wait was finally over. Tonight would be their real wedding night. His papa had just made it possible for Valentino to give her a wedding present she'd never forget.

"About your idea for the tour-bus crowd. I think we should try it and see what happens."

Elated, he got up to kiss his father on both cheeks, then disappeared out the door with the bottle. There was only a little liqueur left. Enough to celebrate her return to life.

Once he took off in the Ferrari, it didn't take long to pull up outside the clinic where she was getting her post-op checkup. He hurried down the hall to the dialysis department. To his frustration she hadn't come out yet.

"She's not here," the receptionist called out. "She told me you were to meet her in the restaurant at the San Gallo hotel."

"*Grazie*."

He had to fight his disappointment that they couldn't simply drive back to the farm. The San Gallo was the best five-star hotel in Monta Correnti and sat on a hill with its own lovely view.

But it was always crowded, especially at this time of year when students and tourists were on spring break. Valentino didn't want to face hordes of people right now. All he wanted was Clara.

"*Buon giorno*, Signor Casali," the maître d' greeted him ten minutes later. "Congratulations on your marriage. I will give you a view table as soon as I can make the arrangements."

"Thank you, but that won't be necessary. I'm looking for my wife. She asked me to meet her in here."

He shook his head. "She hasn't come. No reservation was made."

Valentino took a deep breath. "I'll check with the concierge."

When he asked about her at the desk, the man said, "Signora Casali is in room 152. She'll be happy to know you've come. She was most anxious. Here's another key."

Filled with alarm that something had gone wrong at her checkup and she'd decided to tell him over their meal, he took the card key and raced across the foyer to the stairs. By the time he could let himself in the room on the next floor, his anxiety bordered on terror for fear her kidney had suddenly stopped functioning.

"Clara?" he cried out after flinging the door open.

"*Caro*—" she called from the bathroom "—I thought you would be at your father's longer."

"What's wrong?" he demanded.

"Nothing. I'm fine. I'll be out in a minute."

"You left the clinic without me. You're *not* fine! I know you're not." He raced across the room to open the door, but it was locked.

Frantic, he pressed his forehead against it. "*Piccola*? Don't shut me out."

"I would never do that."

He heard a click, then the door opened.

A barefooted woman stood before him. Except for her eyes that dazzled him with their green fire, nothing else was familiar. A new jasmine fragrance assailed him. Her dark hair was curly like a Gypsy's. She was a vision in sheer black lace over alabaster.

Her seductive smile captivated him.

"You have permission to discover for yourself that there's absolutely nothing wrong with me, *signore*." She wound her soft arms around him and gave him a kiss to die for. "But first, why don't you get out of these clothes? You've been my fantasy for years. Now I want the reality."

Valentino couldn't talk. He couldn't breathe.

"Is that going to be a problem for the famous Valentino Casali?" she teased. "Because if it is, you're in *real* trouble with your farmer wife."

* * * * *

MOTHER OF THE BRIDE

BY

CAROLINE ANDERSON

First published in Great Britain 2010
Harlequin Mills & Boon Limited,
Eton House, 18-24 Paradise Road, Richmond, Surrey TW9 1SR

ISBN: 978 0 263 87672 7

Harlequin Mills & Boon policy is to use papers that are natural, renewable and recyclable products and made from wood grown in sustainable forests. The logging and manufacturing process conform to the legal environmental regulations of the country of origin.

Printed and bound in Spain
by Litografia Rosés, S.A., Barcelona

Dear Reader

When my daughter phoned me (in the supermarket!) to tell me that her boyfriend had proposed, it was hardly a surprise, but still in some ways a shock. Not so the very highly organised way she tackled the wedding planning, and the great fun and fraught emotions and stress that paved the journey. But it was all worth it; the wedding, when it came, was a beautiful, memorable day that will live with me for ever. She was utterly radiant, didn't stop smiling for the entire day, and it was wonderful. My husband's speech recalled things we'd remembered together, and it dawned on me how lucky we were still to be together. And when my editor said, 'Caroline, we'd like you to write a book about a mother and her daughter both making this journey together,' it seemed only natural that the hero should be the bride's father, as well, because they would be forced together to plan the wedding, and in the course of it would have to confront their own failed relationship and rebuild a new one—after all, some day they'll be grandparents. And when, on the way, each of them realises they're still in love… Well, you'll have to read it!

I hope you enjoy this momentous journey as much as I did.

Love

Caroline

For my darling daughter Sarah,
for providing me with so much source material
and inspiration, and for Adam, who had the foresight
to anticipate this book and ask her to marry him!
Thank you both for the most wonderful day,
and here's to many, many happy years ahead.

And for all the other mothers-of-the-bride
with whom I've shared the journey: Petrice, Carol,
Elizabeth, Dee, Linda and Thila, with my love.

CHAPTER ONE

'MAISIE.'

Just the one word, but it curled around her, invading every part of her, swamping her with its gruff warmth. Her heart went into overdrive, her breath stalling at the unaccustomed and yet, oh, so familiar sound of his voice. And then fear kicked in.

'Rob, what is it? What's happened?'

'Nothing's happened—yet,' he said quietly. 'I just wanted to warn you, Alec's going to ask Jenni to marry him this evening, and he wanted my blessing. I thought you should know.'

So the time had come. Maisie's heart sank. For the last three years, ever since her baby had started dating the gentle, humorous Alec Cooper with his smouldering eyes and teasing sense of fun, she'd been waiting for this moment, and now it was here. Her legs felt like jelly, her heart was pounding, her mouth was dry, and she wanted to scream, *'No! She's too young! Don't let her, she's not ready…'*

'Maisie?'

'I'm OK,' she said, sitting down abruptly on the edge of the bed. The bed in which she'd given Rob her virginity over twenty-one years ago.

'Are you sure?'

'Sort of. Thank you for warning me, although it would have been nice if Alec had done it,' she said.

'I know,' he said, his voice sympathetic. 'I suggested he should, but he was afraid you'd try and warn Jenni off.'

'Rob, I'm her *mother*!'

'Exactly. And you have…'

'Issues?' she offered into the silence, and he gave a quiet huff of laughter that clawed at her insides.

'You could put it that way. I told him you'd be upset, but he was very reluctant in case you tried to speak to Jenni, to talk her out of it, because he's been planning it for ages, apparently, and he was desperate for it to be a surprise.'

'Rob, he should have spoken to me, too. I'm the one who's brought her up. Or doesn't my blessing count?'

His sigh was soft. 'Maisie, don't be like that. I asked him to talk to you, he said he'd think about it, but obviously he didn't feel he could, or he hasn't been able to get you. He asked me not to tell you until he had time to ask Jenni, and he's doing that now, as we speak, so I couldn't tell you any sooner. I gave him my word. You have to respect that.'

Of course she did. She just felt out of the loop, as usual, at the bottom of the heap when it came to knowing anything, and it hurt. 'It doesn't matter,' she lied, but he cut in gently.

'It does—and I'm really sorry. If it helps, he only asked me about four hours ago. And my mother doesn't know.'

A small crumb of comfort, but surprisingly perceptive of him to know she'd needed it.

She closed her eyes and gave a tiny, shaky little laugh. 'Rob, they're so young.'

'They'll be fine. I'm sure Jenni'll ring you the moment they're back. It might be nice if you act surprised.'

She swallowed. 'Sure—and, Rob… Thank you for warning me.'

'It's a pleasure,' he said, his voice low and gruff, and she felt the familiar shiver down her spine.

How could he still do that to her, after all these years? She should have got over him by now. She said goodbye and replaced the phone in the cradle, and sat staring at the wall blankly. It really was going to happen. Jenni and Alec were getting married, and even though she'd known it was coming, she was still reeling with shock.

'You're being ridiculous,' she told herself, and, getting up, she went back over to her wardrobe and carried on the weeding process she'd been engaged in when Rob had called.

She pulled out a hanger and stared at it blankly. Good grief, how ever long had she had these trousers? Far too long, she hadn't worn them for years. She dumped them on the growing pile, found a few other things and then realised she'd put her favourite dress on the pile by accident.

She wasn't with it at all, she was miles away, in Scotland, with Jenni, praying that common sense would prevail and she'd tell Alec they should wait. Hoping it would work for them. Worried that it wouldn't, that like their marriage, Jenni's would prove too frail to stand the test of time.

They'll be fine.

Would they? She didn't know, but Rob's deep, warm voice echoed in her ears, and if she let herself, she could almost believe it. But not quite, because he'd said the same thing to her over twenty-one years ago, when he'd asked her to marry him.

'We'll be fine, Maisie. You'll see. It'll be all right.'

But it hadn't been. It hadn't been all right at

all, in the end, even though the beginning had been blissful. Stormy, sometimes, but they'd always, always made up after a row, and sometimes she wondered if they'd had fights just for the hell of it, so they could make up afterwards. She laughed at the memory, but her smile faded and she felt her eyes fill.

She'd married him not only because she loved him, but also because she'd been eighteen, scared, pregnant, and her family wanted nothing to do with her. Her options had been severely restricted, and she'd thought he loved her as much as she'd loved him, but she'd been wrong. She must have been. If he'd loved her, he'd have come after her, but he hadn't, so she'd concluded sadly that he'd only married her out of duty, when they'd hardly known each other—certainly not well enough to weather the birth of Jenni while he was away at sea and she was alone in Scotland with his less-than-enthralled parents.

It wasn't really surprising that it hadn't worked, under the circumstances. They'd been children, out of their depth in the welter of emotions they'd encountered, coping with a situation that would have challenged anyone. And when she couldn't bear it any more up there without him, when she'd left Scotland and come back down here to Cambridge, he'd done nothing about it, to her horror and distress. There had just been a terrible, deafening silence.

He hadn't come to her when he'd had his next shore leave, as she'd expected, hadn't tried to find out what was wrong, but had said nothing, done nothing for six whole months except send money to her account. She'd taken it because she'd had no choice, and she'd written to him begging him to come to her, to talk to her—anything, but there'd been no reply, and then at last there had been a letter asking for access to Jenni in their divorce settlement—a divorce that hadn't even been on her agenda until he'd broached the subject. Shocked, devastated, she'd agreed to everything he'd asked, and the only contact they'd had since then had been over Jenni.

She'd hardly seen him in all this time—scarcely at all since Jenni had grown old enough to spend time with him alone without needing her, and certainly not at all in the last five years. They hardly even spoke on the phone any more. There was no need. If there was anything relating to Jenni, it was discussed with her directly, which was why his call today out of the blue had been so shocking.

She couldn't remember the last conversation they'd had that had lasted more than a very few seconds, but she guessed they'd be having to talk to each other now, and the thought brought all her confused and tumbled emotions about him racing to the surface. Emotions she'd never dealt with, just closed off behind a wall of ice in her heart before they destroyed her.

She still loved him, she realised. She'd die loving him, but it was a one-sided, unrequited love that had never stood a chance. And she was far too old to be so foolish.

The phone rang again, and for a moment she stared at it, her heart pounding, knowing who it was, knowing what she was about to hear, but stalling anyway because until she heard it, it might not be true…

'Mummy?'

'Hello, darling. How are you?'

'Amazing! You'll never guess what—are you sitting down?'

She wasn't, but she did. Rapidly. 'OK. Fire away, what's happened?' she said, trying to sound fascinated and intrigued and enthusiastic instead of just filled with a sense of doom. She'd seen the look in Jenni's eyes, and Alec reminded her so much of Rob as he had been—young, eager, in love—

'Alec's asked me to marry him!'

She squeezed her eyes shut briefly and sucked in a breath. Hard. Her lungs were jammed up tight, her heart was in the way and she wanted to cry.

She didn't. She opened her eyes, forced a smile

and said, 'Oh, my goodness—so what did you say?' As if she didn't know what the answer would have been…

Jenni laughed, her happiness radiating unmistakeably down the phone line. *My baby. My precious, precious baby.*

'*Yes*, of course! What on earth did you expect me to say? Mummy, I *love* him! You're supposed to be pleased for me! You *are* pleased for me, aren't you?'

There was a note of uncertainty, of pleading, and Maisie sat up straighter and forced some life into her voice. 'Oh, darling, of *course* I am—if it's what you really want…'

'You know it's what I want. I love him, and I want to be with him forever.'

'Then congratulations,' she said softly. And then, pretending she didn't already know, she added, 'I wonder what your father will say?'

'Oh, he's really happy for us.'

'That's good.' Her voice sounded hollow, echoing in her ears, but Jenni laughed again, unaware of Maisie's inner turmoil.

'Alec asked him first, apparently. They're really close, and he wanted his blessing—it's so like him. He really wanted to do it right, and I had absolutely no idea. It was amazing. He took me up to the ruin and got down on one knee—and I just burst into tears. I think he was a bit shocked.'

'I'm sure he wasn't, he knows you better than

The Mills & Boon® Book Club™ – Here's how it works:

Accepting your free books places you under no obligation to buy anything. You may keep the books and gift and return the despatch note marked "cancel". If we do not hear from you, about a month later we'll send you 3 brand new books including two 2-in-1 titles priced at £4.99* and a single title priced at £3.19*. That is the complete price – there is no extra charge for post and packaging. You may cancel at any time, otherwise we will send you 5 stories a month which you may purchase or return to us – the choice is yours.

*Terms and prices subject to change without notice.

If offer card is missing write to: The Mills & Boon® Book Club™, PO Box 676, Richmond, TW9 1WU

NO STAMP NEEDED!

MILLS & BOON® Book Club

FREE BOOK OFFER
FREEPOST NAT 10298
RICHMOND
TW9 1BR

NO STAMP
NECESSARY
IF POSTED IN
THE U.K. OR N.I.

that. So, when are you talking about? Next year? The year after?'

'As soon as I graduate—we thought maybe the third Saturday in June, if the church is free?'

'But, Jenni, that's only a few weeks!' she said, her mind whirling. Surely not—please, no, that would be too ironic if Jenni, too…

'Ten and a half—but that's fine. We want to get it over before the really busy summer season, and the weather will be best then. If we wait until autumn the weather up here could be cold and wet and awful.'

'Up there?' she said, the timescale forgotten, blanked out by this last bombshell.

'Well—yes, of course up here, Mum! It's where I live now, where everyone is, except you. We're all here.'

Jenni was right, of course, and she should have seen it coming. They all did live up there, light years away in the wild and rugged West Highlands. Everyone except her. Jenni's fiancé Alec, his family, Jenni's uni friends in Glasgow, Alec's friends—and Jenni's father.

Robert Mackenzie, Laird of Ardnashiel, king of his castle—literally. And she'd been nothing, a nobody; in the words of the taunting kinder-garten rhyme, the dirty rascal, the girl who'd got herself knocked up with the heir's baby and then, little more than a year after their wedding, had walked away. Why had he let her go without a murmur, without coming after her, without trying to fix what was surely not that broken? She didn't know. She might never know.

And now her darling daughter—*their* daughter—was getting married, in the very church where she and Rob had made their vows over twenty years ago. Vows that had proved as insubstantial as cobwebs…

She shuddered and sucked in a breath, the silence on the phone hanging in the air like the blade on a guillotine.

'Mum?'

'Yes, darling. Sorry. Of course you're having it there,' she agreed, squashing the regret that she wouldn't be married here, in Cambridge, from the home where she'd grown up. But that was unrealistic, and she was sensible enough to recognise that now. 'Where else, when you've got such a lovely setting? But—only ten and a half weeks?' she said, her voice perilously close to a squeak of dismay as she thought of the reasons that might exist for their haste. 'Don't you need longer to plan it?' she hedged.

The lovely ripple of her daughter's laughter made Maisie want to cry again. 'Oh, it's all planned! We're having the wedding here in the church, of course, and the hotel in the village can do the catering. They've got a brilliant restaurant, so the food will be great. And we'll have a marquee on the lawn and if it rains there's plenty of room inside, and we can have a ceilidh in the ballroom—it'll be wonderful! But you have to come now, because I need a dress and I've only got a week and a bit before I have to go back to uni, and you *have* to help me choose it. And we have to look for something for you, too—you'll need something really lovely, and I want to be there when you choose it. I need you, Mum. Say you'll come.'

Her voice had dropped, sounding suddenly hesitant, and Maisie knew she had no choice. *Wanted* no choice. This was her baby, her only child, and she was getting married, whether Maisie liked it or not.

'Of course I'll come,' she said, squashing down her apprehension and concentrating on being positive. 'I wouldn't miss it for the world.'

'Great. I can't wait, it's going to be such fun! Look, I have to go, we've got to tell Alec's parents before they go to bed, but I'll hand you over to Dad. He wants to talk to you.'

Oh, lord. Not now. Please, not now, not again. She needed to crawl under the covers and have a really good howl, and the last thing she needed to do was make small talk with the man who still held her heart in the palm of his hand.

'She wants me to come up,' she told him, sticking firmly to business.

'Yes. It needs to be soon, so I hope you aren't too busy. When are you free?'

Never. Not to go there, to the chilly, forbidding castle, with his mother still there despising her and him indifferent to her feelings, doing what was right instead of what mattered and riding roughshod over her heart. Except apparently he wasn't indifferent to her feelings any more. Maybe he'd grown up. Twenty years could do that to you.

'It's not too bad for the next couple of weeks. I interviewed someone today for a feature that I have to write up, and I'm doing a wedding tomorrow—'

'Can't you hand it over to someone?'

She shook her head. 'No. Not this one.'

'Why not? Surely some other photographer…'

She sucked in a breath, stunned that he could dismiss her so easily, implying that any photographer could do the job as well, as if it was just a case of pressing the right button at the right time. So much for him not being indifferent to her feelings!

'I don't think you quite understand the process,' she said drily, hanging onto her temper. 'Quite apart from the fact that they want *me*, not *some other* photographer,' she told him, 'you have to understand that brides are very emotional and there's no way I'd let her down at this point. I gave them my word—to quote you. And you have to respect that.'

There was a heartbeat of silence, then a quiet sigh. 'All right. So you have to do the wedding. What time will you be through?'

'Five? Maybe six, at the latest. It's in Cambridge, so it's local.'

'So—if you get the seven-fifteen from Cambridge to King's Cross tomorrow night, you can pick up the Deerstalker from Euston that gets to Fort William at ten the next morning. Will that be OK?'

The overnight sleeper? It would cost an arm and a lcg—but she'd do it, for Jenni. 'Yes, I'll book it.'

'I've done it. I'm doing it on line now. I'll have the tickets waiting for you at the station to collect, and I'll pick you up in Fort William the day after tomorrow. And, Maisie?' he added, his voice dropping.

'Yes?'

'I know this is going to be difficult for you. It'll be difficult for me, too, but we have to do this for Jenni.'

'Of course we do,' she said wearily. 'And it'll be fine. I just wish I felt they were doing the right thing.'

'It is the right thing. It'll be all right, Maisie. You'll see.'

Those words again, echoing back at her over the years, reminding her of just how frail a thing love could be under pressure. She hoped he was right—heavens, how she hoped it, but she wouldn't bank on it. They were so young, so eager, so unaware of all the pain…

'I'll see you at ten on Thursday,' she said, and switched the phone off.

Thursday morning. Only—she glanced at her watch—thirty-six hours away. No time at all to shore up her defences and get her armour plating up and running.

She'd need days—

Ridiculous. She hadn't done it in twenty years, what made her think a few more days could make any difference?

She got off the bed—the very bed where he'd loved her so tenderly, so sweetly, so patiently. So skilfully. She stroked the quilt smooth, her mind back in the long-ago days when love had been sweet and laughter had been the order of the day.

She'd been about to start her degree here at the local college—not as prestigious as one of the Cambridge University colleges, of course, but it offered a good degree in journalism—and she had needed accommodation. Cheap accommodation. And Rob, who had just graduated with flying colours from one of the Cambridge colleges, had been looking for someone to share his house. He was off to serve in the Royal Navy, a six-year commission, and he needed a caretaker, all running expenses paid in return for maintaining the house in good condition in his absence.

Only one proviso—she had to live in it alone and share it with him occasionally when he was on shore leave, but that suited her fine, because it was the only way she could afford it and it meant she could get away from home, from a repressive father who didn't think she needed to go away to college.

So she'd arranged to view it, and they'd gone out for a drink to discuss the fine detail. Well, that had been the excuse. In fact, they'd just wanted to spend time together, and over the next few days they'd fallen headlong in love. Just a week after they'd met, she'd ended up here in this room, in this bed, giving him her heart.

He still had it. He always would.

She sighed and turned her back on the bed. She wanted nothing more than to crawl under the quilt and cry her eyes out, but she had a feature to write up before tomorrow, clothes to pack for her trip, a wedding to prepare for—and besides, she was all done crying over Robert Mackenzie. She'd worn that particular T-shirt out long ago, and she wasn't going there again.

'How do you think she took it?'

Badly. Especially when he'd implied that

another photographer could step into her shoes at a moment's notice. He'd have to do better than that, Rob thought ruefully.

He smiled at his daughter—his beautiful, clever, radiantly happy daughter—and lied. 'She's fine,' he told her. 'I've booked her train ticket, and I'll pick her up—'

'Let me—please? Give me time with her, so I can talk her down a little. She'll be nervous.'

Nervous? Would she? Quite possibly, he conceded. 'She might not be very thrilled about it, but she's got nothing to be nervous about,' he said, trying to reassure their daughter.

But Jenni looked at him, wise beyond her years, and shook her head. 'Of course she has. She hated it here. She hasn't been here for twenty years and she'll be unsure of her welcome.'

'But—that's silly! She's your mother! Of course she's welcome,' he said, but then he thought about it, about the defensive tone of her voice, about how much she'd seemed to hate it here, and he sighed softly.

'I'll still pick her up. Even more reason. I can talk to her.'

Jenni chewed her lip. 'Dad—she won't want to talk to you. She goes out of her way to be out if you're coming to the house, she won't even look at you—what if she refuses to get in the car?'

'She won't refuse,' he said, wishing he was as

certain as he sounded. 'She's not that fond of walking.'

Jenni gave a splutter of laughter and came over and hugged him, slapping him on the chest simultaneously. 'That was mean. You be kind to her or she'll end up in the hotel in the village, I know she will.'

'I'll be kind to her, Jenni,' he promised, serious now. 'I was always kind to her.'

'Were you? She's never really said anything very much about you, just that it didn't work out.'

'That's about the size of it,' he said, carefully keeping his voice neutral. 'But don't worry. We can do this. It'll be fine, Jenni.'

'Are you sure? You'll probably fight like hell. I don't think you know her. She seems like a pussy-cat, but she can be pretty feisty, you know.'

He laughed, but her words echoed in his head. Feisty? Oh, yes, she'd been feisty, but that wasn't how he remembered her. He remembered her *after* their fights—sweet, tender, passionate—until the end. Then she'd just been withdrawn and uncommunicative, as if all the spark had gone out of her, and he hadn't known how to get through to her. Jenni was right. He really didn't know her, the woman who'd been his wife, who'd taken his heart and broken it into little pieces...

'I'm sure we can be adult about it,' he said, not at all convinced but hoping it was true.

Jenni tipped her head on one side. 'Why did neither of you ever get married again? I mean, I know why you didn't stay married to each other, it's not rocket science, but why didn't you marry anyone else? It's not as if you're hideous, either of you, and you're both so nice.'

He shrugged, not intending to drag his wounds out into the open for his daughter to pick the scabs off. 'Never got round to it, I suppose,' he said casually. 'First I was in the navy, and then I was juggling establishing my business in London and being a father to you, and then my own father died and I had to move up here and take over the estate. And it's hard to meet anyone when you're up here in the backwaters, especially if you work in an almost exclusively male environment. Bear in mind that the majority of women who come to the estate are partners of men who come for the sport. They aren't looking for a husband.'

'Are you sure? Maybe they want to switch husbands? And anyway, that's rubbish. It's never hard to meet people when you're rich, it's just hard to meet the right people,' she said drily, and he could tell from her tone that there was a wealth of hurt there. She'd encountered some gold-diggers at uni, men who'd only been interested in her for her inheritance, she'd told him, but Alec, fiercely protective, had been there for her through thick and thin, and he knew the young man loved his daughter from the bottom of his kind and generous heart.

If only they'd been so lucky, him and Maisie. If only they'd found a love like that. It might not be rocket science, but it was a mystery to him why they hadn't got on. It had been so good at first, so special. Nothing had ever felt like it since, and that, of course, was why he'd never married again. Because to be married to anyone other than his Maisie would have been a travesty, a betrayal of everything he stood for.

He swallowed and stepped back, gently disentangling himself from Jenni's embrace, and headed for the door. 'Sorry, sweetheart, I've got a million things to do. I'll see you for dinner.'

He went out, whistling the dogs, and headed down to the water. He needed a walk, a good, long stretch along the beach and then up over the headland, the point that gave Ardnashiel its prefix. There had been a hut there once, evidently, a shiel, which long ago had given way to the original castle, and he climbed the hill towards the ruins, needing the peace, the solitude that he would find there.

It was his retreat, the place he went to soothe his soul, the harsh wind and savage sea the only things wild enough to match the turmoil in his heart, but today they could do nothing to wipe out the memories of his love, here in this place, where he'd brought her so many times. And now, for the first time, she was coming back, not to him, but to the castle.

It was a step he hadn't been sure she'd ever take, but now she was, and in two days she'd be here.

His beloved, beautiful Maisie was coming home…

The train was on the platform as she collected her ticket, and she only just made it before the doors closed.

The wedding had gone on longer than she'd expected, and it had been harder than she'd imagined. She didn't know why—maybe because now she had become the mother of a bride, and could put herself in Annette's shoes, with the agony of her uncertain future. She'd had a health scare, and was facing a gruelling treatment regime over the next months and maybe years, but today had not been a day for dwelling on that. Today was her daughter's day, and Annette had been radiant.

'I'm so proud of her. Doesn't she look beautiful?' she'd said to Maisie in a quiet, private moment, a little oasis in the midst of the revelry, and Maisie's eyes had filled.

'Yes—yes, she does, she looks absolutely gorgeous, and so do you.'

Annette had met her eyes, her own distressed. 'Take plenty of photos,' she begged, and then added softly, 'Just in case.'

Maisie had swallowed. 'I will. I have. I've got some wonderful ones of you together, and I'll get them to you very soon.'

'Thank you,' Annette had said almost silently, and Maisie had held her gently and shared that quiet moment of knowledge that there might not be very much time left to her, and every second mattered.

So now, on the train to London, she was downloading the photos from her camera onto her laptop, then burning them onto several disks and labelling them. Thank God for mobile technology, she thought as she put the disks in the post on her way from King's Cross to Euston.

She was pleased with the photos. She'd go through them, of course, editing out the dross and cropping and tidying up the images so they could look at them on her website, and she'd produce an album with the family once they'd chosen the ones they wanted, but for now, at least, they'd get them in the raw form almost immediately to look through with Annette.

And hopefully, in the years to come, she'd be showing them to her grandchildren, but if not, at least they'd have a wonderful record of that beautiful day.

She blinked away the tears and stared out of the window of the sleeper at the passing lights. The cabin was claustrophobic—first class, the best it could be, but she was too full of emotion, from the wedding and from the task facing her, to sit still.

She locked up her cabin securely and went to the lounge to order food. She hadn't eaten at the wedding, and she'd had her hands full on the platform at Euston, and her blood sugar was through the floor.

Even so, she didn't touch her supper. Her stomach felt as if someone had tied a knot in it and she gave up and went back to her cabin, lying down on the narrow berth and staring at the window, watching the lights flash past as they moved through stations, but mostly it was dark, the velvety blackness of the countryside all-engulfing as the train carried her north towards Rob.

And Jenni. It was about Jenni, she reminded herself—Jenni and Alec. She had to keep focus, remind herself what she was doing this for, or she'd go crazy.

Actually, what she needed was sleep, not the constant rumble of the rails, the clatter of the points, the slowing and shunting and pausing while goods trains went past, until she thought she'd scream. It wasn't the train's fault. It was comfortable, private—as good as it could be. It was just that she didn't want to be on it, didn't want to be doing this, and the memories were crashing over her like a tidal wave.

She'd done it for the first time when she was pregnant, when she'd just finished her first year's exams at Cambridge and was heading up to Scotland to wait for the birth. She'd wanted to stay in Cambridge, in their little house, but Rob had insisted she should move up to the castle. 'You can be looked after there, and my parents will want to spend time with the baby,' he'd said and so, because he wasn't there to drive her this time, as he had every other time they'd been, because he was already away at sea, she'd got on the train, exhausted, aching, and by the time she'd reached Glasgow, she'd realised she was in labour.

She'd been taken straight to the hospital in Fort William, and the next few hours were still a blur in her mind, but as the train rolled on, she kept reliving it, snatches of the pain and fear, knowing Rob was at sea and wanting him, needing him with her. And when he'd come at last, weeks later, he'd been different—distant, almost as if he couldn't bring himself to touch her. She'd known then that there was something wrong, but they hadn't talked about it, just tiptoed carefully around the cracks in their relationship as if they weren't there. And then he'd gone away again, back to sea, and left her behind to face the cold, dark winter there without him.

She hadn't been able to do it. Leaving the castle, going back south to Cambridge—it had seemed such a sensible move, the only thing she could do to stay sane. It had never occurred to her that Rob wouldn't follow.

She turned over, thumped the pillow, squeezed her eyes shut and pulled the quilt over her head, but the images were still there, crowding into her head, keeping her awake.

She gave up in the end, sitting perched on the lid of the washbasin in the corner and staring out of the window as the dawn broke. The countryside was getting wilder, the hills higher, the gentle ripples in the landscape giving way to crumples and then sharp, jagged pleats as they went further north. It was stark, bleak, with a wild majesty that made something in her ache at the beauty of it, but it terrified her, too, because of all the memories it held for her.

She was washed and dressed before the attendant knocked on the door with her breakfast—a hot bacon roll, tea and some fruit salad—and she sat on the bunk staring out over the wild, untamed landscape as the train slowly wended its way around the hills to Fort William, stopping at every station on the way, tiny outposts of civilisation in the midst of barren wilderness.

Not long now, she thought, and her stomach rejected all thought of the bacon roll after the first bite. She was fraught with nerves, too tense to eat, so she sipped her tea as they climbed up onto the flat and desolate plateau of Rannoch Moor, picked at the fruit because it was ridiculous to have nothing, and then gathered her things together as they pulled into the station in Fort William.

And then, when it was too late to do anything about it, she glanced at the mirror and winced. She looked awful. Dark circles under her tired, strained eyes, her hair in wild red corkscrews, needing attention—she hated travelling, hated the rush and pressure and hanging about. And Ardnashiel was waiting.

I'm not ready for it! she wanted to wail, but she didn't, she just picked up her camera bag, slung it over her shoulder, picked up her laptop and her suitcase and got off the train.

It should be like *Brief Encounter*, she thought, all swirling steam and whistles, but it wasn't, it was loud and noisy, unintelligible and horribly familiar. She took a deep breath and looked up, and he was there, walking slowly towards her in jeans and a sweater, with his rangy, muscular limbs and broad, solid shoulders. His hair was touched with grey now, she noticed in surprise, crow's feet at the corners of his wary, slate-blue eyes, and when he smiled, the crow's feet crinkled and turned her legs to mush.

'Maisie,' he said, and his voice curled round her again, seeping into her heart and unravelling all her resolve.

'Hello, Rob. Here, you can make yourself useful,' she said, and handed over her luggage before he could do anything stupid like kiss her cheek and pretend they were friends.

'Is this all?'

'Three bags? Isn't that enough? I can tell what sort of women you've been mixing with, Mackenzie.'

His smile was wry. 'Yeah, your daughter. I've conveyed her and her clutter back and forth to uni for the last three years, remember. I know how you women travel.'

'I'm only here for a week—two weeks, max.'

'We'll see. Come on, then, let's head back.'

To Ardnashiel. Her heart thumped, and she bit her lip as he led her into the car park and plipped the remote control in his hand. Lights flashed on a car—low, sleek and expensive. She might have known. He'd always liked expensive cars. He stashed her belongings in the boot, then opened the door for her. 'Can I put the lid down, or do you want it up?' he asked as he slid in behind the wheel and turned to her.

She shrugged, unsurprised that the car was a

convertible, a folding hard-top. He'd never been able to get enough fresh air. 'Whatever you like. My hair's a mess anyway. I need a shower.'

'You look fine, Maisie,' he said softly. More than fine. She looked—lovely. Wary, hesitant, out of her comfort zone, but lovely. And he wanted her to himself, just for a little bit longer.

He pressed the button to fold the roof and held her eyes. 'Do you fancy a coffee on the way?'

She frowned then gave a slight smile, the first one since she'd got off the train. 'Actually, that would be really nice. I didn't eat much yesterday—too busy. And I didn't really fancy breakfast. I'm starving.'

'OK. We'll do coffee. There's a lovely place opened since you were here last.'

'Rob, there's been time for dozens of places to open and shut since I was here last,' she pointed out, and he gave a quiet laugh.

'I know. It's been a long time.' Too long.

He started the engine then they purred softly out of the car park and headed out on the road to Mallaig. The air was cool, but it was a beautiful day and the sun was shining, and she put her head back against the butter-soft leather of the seat and closed her eyes, but even so, she couldn't cut him out of her thoughts.

She was aware of every movement he made, every breath he took, every flex of his muscles. Not because she could hear, or see, but because she just *knew*. After all this time, she still knew, her body so aware of him that her nerves were screaming.

How on earth had she imagined she could do this?

CHAPTER TWO

SHE looked wonderful. Tired, with deep smudges under her eyes, but wonderful.

She wasn't asleep, just resting her eyes, but it meant he could look at her out of the corner of his eye without being seen. And he wanted to look at her. Ridiculously badly.

She looked just the same, he thought with a twist to his heart. Well, no, not *just* the same, because she was thirty-nine now and she'd been eighteen when they'd first met, but the years had been kind to her and if anything she was more beautiful than she'd been twenty years ago.

Her skin was like rich cream, smooth and silky, dusted with freckles, and he wondered if it would still smell the way it had, warm and fragrant and uncomplicated. Her hair, wild and untamed, was still that wonderful rich red, a dark copper that she'd passed on to Jenni but which in their daughter was mellowed by his dark-haired gene to a glorious auburn.

She had the temper to go with it, too, the feistiness Jenni had reminded him of. It was something that fortunately neither of them had handed on to their daughter, but although at first they'd had stand-up fights that had ended inevitably in bed with tearful and passionate reconciliation, by the end there'd been no sign of it. And he'd missed it. Missed the fights, missed the making up. Missed his Maisie.

He sighed and turned into the car park of the café overlooking the top of Loch Linnhe, and by the time he'd cut the engine she had her seat-belt undone and was reaching for the door handle.

She straightened up and looked around, giving him a perfect back view, her jeans gently hugging that curved, shapely bottom that had fitted so well in his hands…

'This looks nice.'

He swallowed hard and hauled in a breath. 'It is nice. It's owned by the people who run the hotel in the village. They've got a local produce shop here as well, selling salmon and venison and cheese and the like.'

'And insect repellent?'

He chuckled, remembering her constant battle with the midges. 'Probably.' He held the door, and she went in and sniffed the air, making him smile.

'Oh, the coffee smells good.'

'It is good. What are you having?'

'Cappuccino, and—they look tasty.'

'They are. Do me a favour and don't even ask about the calories.'

'Don't worry, I won't,' she vowed, making him laugh. 'I'm starving.'

He ordered the coffees and two of the trademark gooey pastries, and they headed for a table by the window. He set the tray down and eased into the seat opposite her, handing her her cup.

'So, how did the wedding go yesterday?'

A flicker of distress appeared in her moss-green eyes before she looked down at her coffee. She poked the froth for a moment. 'OK. Lovely. Very beautiful. Very moving. The bride's mother's not well—that's why I couldn't hand it over.'

He frowned. 'Why didn't they postpone it?'

'Because she's about to start chemo,' Maisie said softly. 'They had to rush the wedding forward, and the last thing I could do to them was upset them at this stage. They wanted me, they trusted me, and I'd promised.'

'Of course. I'm sorry, I didn't appreciate that at the time. I can quite see that you had to stay, and I'm sorry if I implied that anyone else could take over from you. Of course that isn't true, especially under those circumstances. You had no choice.'

She blinked. He'd really taken her comments on board, if that was anything to go by, but she wasn't surprised. He'd always been one for doing the right thing—even when it was wrong…

'You'll be wanting to send them the images.'

'I've done it. I downloaded them on the train and posted them at Euston. Just in case…' She sighed softly as she broke off, biting her lip and thinking of Annette.

'Poor woman,' he murmured. 'It must have been hard for the family, dealing with all those emotions.'

She nodded, but then she went quiet, sipping her coffee, absently tearing up the pastry and nibbling at it. 'Rob, this wedding—are you sure it's right for them? They're so young.'

'Not that young.'

'They are! Just like we were. We were far too young.'

'You can't compare them to us. They're three years older than we were—'

'No. I was eighteen, she's twenty. That's only two years.'

'She's almost twenty-one. She'll be twenty-one by the wedding, and Alec will be twenty-four. And those years make a lot of difference. You were only just eighteen and pregnant, and I was twenty-one and committed to the navy for six years, and we didn't know each other nearly well enough.'

'We still don't.'

'No. Jenni said that on Tuesday, and I think she was right. But they're different, Maisie. They know each other through and through. They've been friends ever since they were children, and this has been growing for years. They're genuinely deeply in love, and it's great to see them together. We didn't stand a chance, but they do. I think they'll be very happy together.'

'You don't think they should wait?'

'What for?'

Good question. She stared out of the window over the gently rippling waters of the loch and sighed. 'I don't know,' she murmured. 'To be more settled?'

'They are settled. Alec's got a good job—'

'One you've given him. Rob, you are sure about him, aren't you?' she asked, her anxiety surfacing. 'You don't think he's using her?'

Rob frowned. 'Using her? Of course he's not. They've known each other for years!'

'That wouldn't stop some people.'

'Maisie, Alec's not like that.'

'So what is he like? Tell me—I'm worried, Rob.'

'You don't need to be. They've known each other since they were children—he taught her to ride a bike, for heaven's sake. They used to play together when she came up in the holidays, and they've always got on. He was born in the cottage his parents still live in, and his father was my estate manager until he retired five years ago. He worked for my father, and my uncle before him, and his father before him, so he's the third generation to look after Ardnashiel. It's in his blood, even more than it is in mine, and I can't think of a safer pair of hands either for the estate or for Jenni. He's kind and decent, honest as the day is long, and he really loves her. You honestly don't need to worry.'

She nodded slowly, reassured by his measured assessment of his future son-in-law. 'And your mother? How does she feel about him?'

'She likes him. She's very fond of him, actually.'

'Really? Even though he's one of the estate employees? I'm surprised she thinks he's good enough for her.'

His brows scrunched together in a frown. 'What makes you say that?'

'Well, they made it clear I wasn't good enough for you—or was that just my lack of morals?'

He gave a harsh sigh. 'You don't change, do you?' he said. 'You always were a little too quick to judge.'

'I wasn't judging her, she was judging me! That's unfair!'

'Is it?' he said softly, his eyes searching hers.

'You didn't give my father the benefit of the doubt, you rebuffed all my mother's offers of friendship and you walked off and left me. *That* was unfair.'

She opened her mouth to argue, thought better of it, here in this public place, and shut it again. She'd tell him another time—maybe—just what his mother's offers of friendship had consisted of. And as for his father, there was no doubt to give him the benefit of. He'd hated her, despised her, and he'd made sure she and everybody else had known it. And she hadn't left him, she'd left the castle, and he'd let her go, made no attempt to follow her, to find out what was wrong.

'This is neither the time nor place to go over all of this,' she said, equally quietly. 'And anyway, it's time we got on. I'd like to see Jenni now, she'll be wondering where we are.'

And without waiting to see what he did, she got to her feet and walked out of the café, leaving her coffee half-drunk and her pastry in shreds all over the table.

Stifling a sigh, Rob threw down a few coins for the tip and followed her out, wondering how on earth they were going to get through all the inevitable meetings and discussions and tantrums that would eventually culminate in the wedding.

Ten and a half weeks, he told himself as he unlocked the car and held the door for her, and it would all be over and she'd be gone, and everything would get back to normal.

For some reason, that didn't feel comforting…

The road to Ardnashiel was painfully familiar to Maisie, and they travelled it in a tense and brittle silence.

The first time she'd driven it with Rob all those years ago, it had felt very different. They'd been laughing and holding hands as he drove, their fingers linked on his thigh, and he'd been telling her all about it, about the huge, sprawling estate his father had inherited ten years before from an uncle.

He loved it, he'd told her. He'd loved it as a child, coming up with his parents to visit his widowed uncle, not realising at first that one day it would be his, and he was looking forward to showing it to her. 'Since it's going to be mine. Not for years and years, though,' he'd added, laughing. 'I'm not ready to bury myself up here in the wilderness yet, by a long way, but one day, I suppose, the time will come.'

That day had come sooner than he'd imagined, when his father had died in a shooting accident eight years ago and he'd left London and moved up here for good. She'd never been back, though, not since the day she'd left and vowed never to return.

The road hadn't changed at all since then, she thought, taking it in as her heart knotted ever tighter in her chest. A quiet, winding road that ran between lush green fields with fat cattle grazing contentedly. It was calm, bucolic, and it should have been beautiful, but it was coloured by association. The last time she'd travelled it, she'd been in a taxi, leaving it behind, and part of her was still the lonely, desperate young woman that she had been then.

He reached a junction and turned onto a narrow switchback of a road that clung in the gap between the edge of a loch and the wall of rock where the land met the water. It was an appalling road, and yet the fact that it existed at all in such a tight space was a miracle of engineering in itself.

The loch turned into a river, then the road widened as the land levelled out into a flat bowl around the harbour mouth, houses clustered along its walls, fringing the sea and running up towards the hills, and then beyond the small community, set up on its own on a rocky outcrop above the beach, was Ardnashiel Castle.

Built of stone, grey and forbidding, even with the sun shining on it there was a look of menace about it that chilled Maisie to the bone.

Just as it was meant to, really, since it had been built as a fort, but an ancestor had extended it two hundred years ago, creating a more civilised living area and carving gardens out of the woodland that had encroached on it. He'd added little turrets with tops like witches' hats, and made the windows bigger, and the first time she'd seen it she'd thought it was straight out of a fairy-tale, but then things had changed. It had ceased to be a safe haven and begun to feel like a prison, and looking at it now brought the feelings of suffocation crashing back.

And maybe Rob realised it because, as they crossed the stone bridge and drew up in the stable-yard by the coach-house, he glanced across at her for the first time since they'd left the café and sighed.

'I'm sorry,' he said quietly. 'I realise it's not your fault you don't know Alec, but give him a chance. Please. And my mother. I know you didn't always see eye to eye, but she's worried about seeing you again, worried you'll still dislike her.'

'I didn't dislike her, Rob,' she corrected him quietly. 'She disliked me. And I'm sorry if you felt I was being unfair to Alec. I will give him a chance, of course I will. I've always liked what I've seen of him, but—I'm just worried for Jenni, Rob. She's my little girl, and I'd hate to see her make a mistake.'

'It's not a mistake—and she's my little girl too, remember,' he said with a twisted smile that cut her to the heart. 'Just because she lived with you doesn't mean I didn't love her every bit as much as you did. And I know you feel I've stolen her from you, but she feels at home here.'

She opened her mouth to argue, to say of course she didn't feel that, she knew he hadn't stolen her, but then shut it again, because she did feel like that, did feel that he'd stolen not only her daughter but also her wedding, all the planning and girly excitement she'd seen so often in other young brides and their mothers, the tears and the tantrums and the laughter.

Which was ridiculous, because she was here now, for exactly that, and she would be here for as long as her daughter needed her.

'Rob, it's fine. Let's just move on, can we?' she said, and then the car door was snatched from her hand and Jenni was hurling herself into the car and hugging her, sitting on the sill and cupping her face, staring at her searchingly.

'Are you all right? I know you didn't want to come, but—'

'I'm fine,' she said softly, and gathering Jenni into her arms she hugged her hard. 'It's fine. And it's going to be loads of fun. Come on, let's go inside and we can start planning!'

'Brilliant, I can't wait. Here, look, my ring!'

She held her hand out, eyes sparkling, face alight with love and happiness, and Maisie looked at the ring, a simple diamond in a white gold band, nothing flashy but perfectly suited to her uncomplicated and slender daughter, and she smiled.

'It's lovely. Did he choose it?'

She giggled mischievously. 'I might have hinted a little,' she confessed, and Rob snorted.

'Only slightly,' he said. He was out of the car, taking her bags out of the boot by the time she'd disentangled herself from their daughter and climbed out, and she scraped her windswept hair back out of her eyes and reached for her camera.

Rob was there first. 'I've got it. You go on in with Jenni, I'll put this lot in your room.'

And she was led inside, Jenni's arm round her waist, and it was only as they went in that she realised things had changed.

The house was warm, for a start. Warm and bright and welcoming. It had never felt like that, not even in the summer, the year she'd had Jenni. And Jenni had taken her in through the front door, instead of round the side and in through the kitchen, the way Rob had always taken her in.

Through the tradesmen's entrance?

She was being ridiculous. He'd treated her as a member of the family instead of a visitor, but Jenni—Jenni was treating her as if she was special, a treasured and valued guest, ushering her in, smiling and laughing and hugging her, and as she led her into the drawing room, so familiar and yet so different, Helen Mackenzie got to her feet and came towards them. Older, stiffer, but still beautiful, still the elegant, dignified and aloof woman she'd always been.

'Maisie—welcome back,' she said softly, and held out her hand.

Maisie shook it, glad she hadn't kissed her or embraced her. It would have felt wrong after all the bitterness of the past, and the formal, impersonal contact was enough for now. More than enough. She found a smile and wished she wasn't wearing jeans and had had time to drag a brush through her hair.

'Thank you, Mrs Mackenzie,' she said politely, and then foundered, but it didn't matter.

Rob's mother simply smiled, said, 'Please, call me Helen,' and took up where she'd left off and asked if she'd had a good journey, and if she'd like a drink.

'Tea? Coffee? Or something cold, perhaps?'

'Actually, I'd love a glass of water.'

'Of course. I always get very dehydrated when I'm travelling. There just don't seem to be the opportunities to drink anything civilised. Jenni, my dear, would you ask Mrs McCrae if she could find us a bottle of spring water? Still or sparkling?'

'Sparkling would be lovely. Thank you.'

How stilted. How formal and civilised and polite, when all Maisie wanted to do was head off with

Jenni and hug her and hear all about Alec's proposal.

'Maisie, do sit down. You must be exhausted. I don't suppose you slept a wink on that wretched train. I know I never do.'

'It was very comfortable.'

'But not restful. It's not the same as a decent bed.' She looked down at her hands, flexing her fingers slightly, then met Maisie's eyes again, her own, so like Rob's and Jenni's, troubled. 'I'm glad you've come,' she said frankly. 'I did wonder if you would, but for Jenni's sake, if not for anyone else's, I think we should try and put the past behind us and move on—let bygones be bygones.'

She opened her mouth to speak, found no words that she was prepared to say out loud, and then was saved from answering by Jenni coming back into the room with Alec.

She got up to greet him and found herself wrapped in a warm, firm hug. 'Hi. I'm sorry I wasn't here to greet you when you arrived, I was just welcoming a group of guests, but I saw you drive by and gave them some flannel about checking on the nesting golden eagles and left them to settle in.'

His eyes sparkled mischievously, and Helen gave a rusty chuckle. 'You're a terror, Alec Cooper. Will you stay and join us for a drink, or do you have to be somewhere?'

'Checking the nesting eagles, for instance?' Maisie teased, and he laughed.

'No, I don't have to be anywhere. The guests have all been before, so they know their way around. They're all heading off to the pub for lunch, and I'm free for a while.' He took her hand in both of his, his eyes serious. 'So, will you forgive me? I'm sorry I didn't manage to talk to you, too. I did try, but your mobile must have been off, and I didn't leave a message. It didn't seem to be the sort of thing I could say to a machine, but—well, I know you've had reservations about me, and I really wanted your blessing, too…'

'Oh, Alec, of course I forgive you,' she said, guilt washing over her. He *had* tried to ring—the missed call from a number she hadn't recognised. 'And it's not that I have reservations, Alec. I don't rcally know you, and I just want you both to bc sure, but Jenni knows you much better than I do, and you probably know *her* better than I do, come to that, so I have to trust your judgement. I just want my daughter to be happy, and she does seem to be, so of course you have my blessing. But look after her, Alec, treat her right. That's all I ask.'

'Of course I will. I love her, Maisie. I love her more than anything or anyone in the world. I'll do nothing to hurt her.'

Maisie's eyes filled, and she hugged her soon-to-be son-in-law hard, then reached out for Jenni, drawing her into the hug as well. Please let it be all right, she prayed, and then let them go, just as Mrs McCrae came in, set down the tray and engulfed her in yet another hug.

'Good heavens, lass, let me look at you. You don't look a day older! Oh, it's good to see you again.'

She laughed, delighted to see the kindly housekeeper who had been her saviour and only friend in the dark days after Jenni's birth. 'Oh, Mrs McCrae, how lovely to see you again, too! You haven't changed, either. I would have known you anywhere!'

'A few pounds heavier, mind, but my grand-children keep me fit now when I'm not here running up and down stairs after this lot!'

She heard a door open and close, then Rob came in. 'Sorry to be so long. I was held up by a guest—something about nesting golden eagles?'

Alec chuckled. 'Ah—a little poetic licence. I wanted to greet my future mother-in-law, but it's not a problem. I'll tell them they can't be dis-turbed, and, anyway, we have got nesting eagles.'

'Have we?'

'Aye. I saw them this morning when I was out on the hills checking the deer. We've a stag needs culling, by the way. He's been injured—can't put one hind leg to the ground. It's the big old stag with the broken antler and the scar on his rump.'

Rob nodded. 'I wondered about him. He was lame yesterday, I was going to check on him. Can I leave him to you?'

'Sure.'

That dealt with, Rob turned to Maisie, scanning her face for any clue as to her mood, but she was smiling and talking to Mrs McCrae about her grandchildren and giving his mother a wide berth.

Oh, hell, it was all so complicated, he thought, feeling twenty-two again. If only she'd stayed, if only he'd tried to convince her to come back instead of letting her go without a fight. Or gone with her. They hadn't needed to live up here, they could have lived in London or Cambridge—anywhere, really, that she chose, but she'd chosen to leave him, to take his daughter away, and deny his parents the chance to see their beloved little granddaughter grow up. She'd even done it behind his back, while he'd been at sea, and asked his parents to tell him and give him her letter—a letter that had told him what he'd already known, that she didn't want to stay. She hadn't even had the guts to do it to his face. That, more than anything, had hurt.

He checked the thought and turned to his mother, concentrating on the practicalities. 'So—what time are we aiming to have lunch?'

'Whenever we're ready. Mrs McCrae, how long will lunch take to prepare?'

'It's all ready, Mrs Mackenzie, you just tell me when you want to eat. The bread's fresh out of the oven and I just need a few moments to heat the soup.'

'Ten minutes, then?' Helen said, and Rob wasn't sure if he'd imagined it, or if it was desperation that flickered briefly on her face before Maisie masked it.

'I think,' he cut in smoothly before anyone could argue, 'that Maisie could probably do with a few minutes to freshen up. She's been travelling all night. An hour, maybe?'

He hadn't imagined it. Her eyes met his with relief, and she gave him a grateful smile.

'Thank you. That would be wonderful—if you don't mind, Mrs McCrae? I don't want to put you to any trouble.'

'Och, of course I don't mind! I made cock-a-leekie for you, hen,' she said, beaming at Maisie. 'I know it's your favourite soup, and there's home-made oat bread, and some wonderful Mull Cheddar to follow. You always liked the Mull Cheddar.'

Maisie's face softened, and she smiled warmly at the elderly housekeeper. 'Thank you. That sounds lovely. Fancy you remembering I like cock-a-leekie.'

'I've never forgotten you, pet. I'm making roast beef for you tonight, for Alec's parents coming up. Just to welcome you home.'

She bustled off, and for a moment there was silence while the word 'home' seemed to reverberate around the room, but Rob cut it off swiftly.

'I'll show you to your room,' he said, and opening the door he ushered her out and closed it softly behind them.

'Thank you,' she said. That was all, but it spoke volumes, and he dredged up a smile.

'My pleasure,' he told her, wishing that it wasn't a lie, that every interaction between them, no matter how brief or businesslike, didn't seem to be flaying him alive. 'I've put you in the room you had before. You always used to sit there in the window and look out at the sea. I thought you might like it.'

Maisie felt a chill run over her. She'd wept so many tears in that room, and it was on the tip of her tongue to ask for another, any one, it didn't matter which, just not *that* room, but then she stopped herself and nodded. She had to get over this silliness. They had a wedding to plan, and she couldn't allow herself to keep harking back to the past.

'Thank you,' she said, and followed him up the magnificent old stone staircase to the landing above. He fell into step beside her, hanging back as they reached the room, and she wondered if he could hear her heart pounding with dread.

The door was standing open, and she went in and stopped in her tracks.

It was different. Lovely. The colours were soft and tranquil, muted blues and greens, pale cream, a touch of rose here and there to lift it. A great black iron bed was heaped with pillows and cushions and dressed with a pretty tartan throw so soft she wanted to bury her face in it and sigh with delight.

When had it been changed? And why? Not for her, of course. It would be a favourite guest room, with that gorgeous view out over the sea to the islands, and she realised in surprise it now had its own bathroom off it, in the little room that had been Jenni's nursery.

Progress, she thought in astonishment.

'It looks…'

'Different?' he murmured, and she turned and met his eyes.

'Yes.' Very different from the room she'd been installed in after Jenni had been born. That had been cold and forbidding, but this…

She ran her hand over the throw, fingering its softness. 'This is lovely.'

'It's a pastel version of the Mackenzie tartan,' he told her. 'Jenni's idea. There's one in every room—mohair, to keep out the cold.'

'It's warm in here, though.'

'Well, it is April. The heating works better now, but the wind still sneaks in in January.'

His smile was fleeting, and made her heart ache. She'd loved him so much…

'And an en suite bathroom. That's a bit luxurious,' she said, turning away as if to study it, just to get away from those piercing eyes.

'It *was* twenty years ago, Maisie,' he reminded her gently, as if she needed reminding. 'Things have changed. All sorts of things.'

Him? She said nothing, and after a moment she heard a quiet sigh. 'I'll see you downstairs. Come and find me when you're done—I'll be in my study.'

'Where is it?'

'Bottom of the stairs, turn left, follow the corridor round and it's at the back, by the gun court. Just yell, I'll find you.'

He went out, leaving her alone, and she closed her eyes and thought longingly of the bed. It looked so inviting. So soft and warm and welcoming. And she was shattered.

Later, she told herself. Shower first, then lunch, then talk to Jenni—and maybe later, before dinner, she'd snatch five minutes.

Anyway, her luggage was on the bed, waiting, and she'd have to deal with it before she could lie down.

'Shower,' she told herself sternly, and unzipping her case she pulled out her wash bag and headed for the bathroom.

She didn't dawdle. Lunch was calling her, and she was more than ready for it by the time she'd tamed her hair, pulled on some clean clothes and tracked Rob down in his study overlooking the sea.

He was deep in thought, staring out of the window, feet propped up on his desk and his brow furrowed when she went in. He dropped his feet to the floor and swung round, greeting her with a smile that didn't reach his eyes. 'Everything all right?'

'Lovely, thank you. Much better,' she said with real gratitude, and he got to his feet and ushered her through to the drawing room where his mother, Jenni and Alec were waiting.

He'd gone into the study deliberately, she realised then, to wait for her so she didn't have to come in here alone and face them all. She could have laughed at that. If only he'd realised that he, of all of them, was the biggest stumbling block.

'I'll tell Mrs McCrae we're all ready,' he said, and left her with Jenni, striding down the corridor away from the scent of soap and shampoo and something else he recognised from long ago. Something that dragged him right back to the beginning, to the times when she would come to him smelling like that and he'd take her in his arms and hold her close and breath in the scent of her…

He went down to the kitchen, wishing he could escape, go out onto the hills where the fresh air could drive the scent from his nostrils and bring him peace. But he couldn't, because he had things to do, things that only he could do. His daughter was getting married, and he had to hold it together until then. And dragging Maisie into his arms and breathing her in wasn't an option, either.

'We're all here now,' he said to Mrs McCrae. 'Can I give you a hand?'

'Aye, that would be kind, Robert. You can stir this while I put the bread out.' And having trapped him so easily, in a trap he'd walked into with his eyes wide open, she then started on him in her oh, so unsubtle way.

'She's looking tired.'

'She is tired. She's been travelling all night. She looks better now she's had a shower and changed into fresh clothes.'

'She'd look better still if she'd come home and let me feed her up a bit,' she said, wielding the bread knife like a weapon. 'Poor wee thing.'

'I'm sure Maisie's perfectly capable of feeding herself,' he said firmly, drawing the pot off the heat and closing the lid of the range. 'And she has a home in Cambridge,' he added, reminding himself as much as Mrs McCrae as he glanced at the bare table. He frowned. 'Where are we eating?'

'In the dining room,' she said, her eyes flashing with indignation. 'Robbie, she's come back, wherever you say her home might be! She can't be eating in the kitchen—not today.'

He opened his mouth to argue, shut it again and sighed softly in resignation. 'I'll carry this,' he said, and followed her up the stairs.

'Here we are, hen,' she said, setting the bread down on the table as Maisie sat down. 'And mind you eat plenty!'

She did. She was still starving, the half-eaten pastry just a memory now, and she had two bowls of the delicious hearty soup, a good chunk of cheese and two slices of the soft, warm oat bread that was Mrs McCrae's forte. And while she ate, Jenni took the opportunity to fill her in on the wedding plans to date.

'OK. I've had a few ideas,' she said, making Alec splutter into his soup, which earned him a loving swat from his fiancée. 'You're not here for long, Mum, so I thought we should spend today planning and having a brainstorming session, and then tomorrow we're going to Glasgow to look at dresses. I've made some appointments, and I've made sure they know that there's only two months, but the places we're going all have samples which they can sell us, so we won't have to go through the business of ordering them, which takes ages. Now, they'll probably need altering, so…'

Rob watched her in wry amusement. She'd been planning this for ages, he knew, and Alec's proposal had been like a breath on a hair trigger. He just hoped that Maisie was ready for it.

CHAPTER THREE

'SHE'S amazing. Is there anything she hasn't thought of? She's so organised—it's like a military operation!'

Rob leant back against the ancient stone wall of the gun court, propped his elbows on it and chuckled, to her surprise. 'Did you really expect anything else?'

Maisie shrugged, turning to stare out over the sea below. 'I don't know. I hadn't really thought about it, but it never occurred to me she'd have it all down pat. What if it doesn't work out? What if something can't fit into her carefully orchestrated plan?'

'Then she'll have a little fit and learn the meaning of the word compromise,' he said drily.

Maisie shook her head. 'She's got all these ideas so firmly fixed. How long's she been planning it?'

His broad shoulders lifted in a casual shrug.

'Months? Years, probably. Come on, ever since she knew the meaning of the word bride she's been looking forward to this day. She just wants to be a princess. That's why Alec didn't ask her ages ago, he told me. He knew the second he said anything, she'd be off like a rat out of a trap, and so he had to wait until the time was right.'

'But—two months?' She winced just thinking about it, about all the plans that had to be put into action before the big day, but Rob seemed unperturbed.

'She doesn't need more than that, and he realised that if she had longer, she'd drive herself and everyone else round the bend. You know what she's like. Single-minded, determined, knows what she wants and gets it. Now, who does that remind you of?' he added drily, one brow arched in a mocking salute.

What? He thought she was like that? She nearly laughed out loud, because the one thing—the *only* thing—she'd ever really wanted was standing right there with her now, and she'd failed, lost the only thing she'd really, truly needed in her life.

The love of the man she adored, the man who had given her his child and then turned his back on her when she'd needed him the most.

'I think you overestimate my powers,' she murmured wryly.

'Well, let's hope not, because this wedding is all down to you now. I'll do what I can, but I'm up to my eyes with the estate and the summer's a nightmare with all the guests, so I can't tell you how glad I am that you're here to do it all.'

'But—Rob, I have a life, six hundred miles away! I can't just be here and sort it! I have things to do!'

'Can't you work round them? You can go back for the weddings—heaven knows there can't be that many, and your features you can write from here. You could do one on being a wedding planner.'

'What, and get tax relief on the wedding as a research tool, I suppose?'

'Well, it's a thought,' he said, his lips quirking. It drew her attention to them, to the clean, sculpted line of the top lip, the firm fullness of the lower. He'd kissed her with those lips, trailed them over her skin, driven her crazy with need with just the lightest touch—

Don't go there! Keep focused on the wedding.

She stroked her fingers over the barrel of an ancient cannon, testing the rough surface with her fingertips, searching for compromise. 'I have commitments, Rob. I can't just walk away from my life at a moment's notice.'

'So you'll need to commute. Go back for your weddings, if you've got commitments, and be here when you can. It's not for long.'

'It'll cost a fortune!' she said, horrified, but he just shrugged.

'So? She's your daughter. I'll pay your train fares. Talking of which, you'll need money for tomorrow. I'll give you a card and my pin number so you've got plenty of cash.'

'That won't be necessary. I'm buying her dress.'

'Ah. I wasn't thinking of the dress, I was talking about the train fare and incidentals, but…um… there might be a problem with the dress.'

She tilted her head, searching his eyes. 'A problem?' she echoed, a sinking feeling in the pit of her stomach.

'My mother wants to buy it for her.'

She felt herself recoil. 'No! I'm sorry, Rob. You can do everything else your way, but this is for me to do. She's my daughter. I'm buying her wedding dress. Tell your mother to give her something else.'

He sighed. 'She won't like it.'

'Tough. Sorry, Rob. I'm not backing down on this one, it means a lot to me,' she said implacably, meeting his eyes without flinching.

He studied her face for a moment, then nodded. 'All right. I'll tell her.'

And no doubt it would cause another rift—as if it would show, with something on the lines of the Grand Canyon already yawning between her and the woman who had been her mother-in-law.

'So—we're going to Glasgow tomorrow, is that right?'

'I believe that's the plan. You can park at the station at Fort William—'

'Aren't you coming?'

He smiled at her and shook his head slowly, his eyes laughing. 'Now, Maisie, surely you can work that one out. A girly day in town choosing wedding dresses and mother-of-the-bride outfits? Does that really sound like me?'

Oh, lord. She felt a moment of panic. 'I don't—Rob, talk to me about this wedding. I don't know anything about it, who's coming, how formal it will be, how dressy—anything. And I don't want to let Jenni down or look ridiculously over-dressed, but I have no idea what's expected.'

'Just be there for your daughter, wearing whatever makes you feel good, so long as it doesn't clash with the bridesmaids or the kilts.'

'You're wearing a kilt?'

He smiled patiently. 'Of course I am, Maisie. I'm the Laird. All the men will be in kilts, particularly the groom's party. I'll be in the Mackenzie dress tartan, which is mostly green and blue with broad checks of white and a fine red line, and the Cooper tartan's green and blue but with a mauve line, so I think Jenni's working that in for the bridesmaids and Alec's cravat. The jackets will all be black. As for the day—well, that's a bit more complicated. There will be people who have to be invited, people who will expect to come as well as family and friends. And the villagers will expect it to be done right. My daughter's getting married. It's not often there's a wedding in the castle, so there'll be one hell of a party, make no mistake.'

'And you, I take it, will be footing the bill for this party?'

He chuckled wryly. 'Of course. We'll host a ceilidh for everyone in the evening. The marquee will be outside, and we'll just have to hope it doesn't rain, but if it does, these folk are Scottish, they're used to a bit of mist.'

She laughed at that. 'I seem to remember rather more than mist.'

His mouth tipped in a smile, but then the smile faded and he searched her eyes. 'You never did like the rain, did you? Or much else, come to that. Jenni asked me to be kind to you—she said you hated it here, that you'd be nervous about coming back.'

Oh, Jenni was right, she had certainly hated it here, especially at the end, but nervous?

'No. I'm not nervous. Concerned, perhaps. It wasn't a happy time for me.'

His jaw worked briefly. 'No. She said you'd be

unsure of your welcome, but I hope you're not. You are welcome here, you do know that, don't you? Mrs McCrae's talked about nothing else since Jenni told her you were coming.'

'And your mother?'

She waited, holding her breath in the heartbeat of silence that followed, then he sighed and turned his head to stare out over the sea.

'She's not sure of her place. She's been mistress of the house for thirty-odd years, ever since my uncle died, and she's been unhappy here for most of that time. It's only since Jenni's been coming here regularly that she's seemed more settled, but now, with Jenni marrying Alec and moving out of the house, she's back to that strange limbo.'

'Because you're not married?' she asked shrewdly, and he nodded, his mouth twisting into a wry smile.

'Exactly so. She's mistress, and yet she's not. If I were to marry again, she'd be ousted from her place, and I think she's always wondered if that would happen.'

'Will it?' she asked a little rashly before her brain could control her mouth, but he just tipped his head slightly on one side and looked back at her with a curious, searching expression on his face.

'I don't know.'

'So—does that mean there might be someone? Am I going to have to share the top table with another woman at the wedding?'

He gave a startled laugh and shrugged away from the wall. 'No, Maisie. There's no other woman. I've only ever got close enough once and, frankly, that was enough in one lifetime.'

It should have reassured her, but it didn't. It unsettled her, as if by asking one question she'd prompted him to answer another, and the answer cut her to the quick. Suddenly he was standing too close, so close that she could feel his body radiating heat, reminding her of all she'd lost. She backed away.

'I'm tired,' she said. 'I might go and unpack, sort my things out a little before tomorrow, and the dogs look as if they're expecting you to take them for a walk. What time are we eating tonight?'

'Seven.'

'Fine. I'll see you at dinner. I'm looking forward to meeting Alec's parents. Actually, good point—do you still dress for it?'

He laughed and shook his head. 'No, we don't dress for dinner. We don't stand on ceremony much at all now, although Mrs McCrae still insists on serving us in the dining room. Usually we eat lunch in the kitchen, though. You were honoured.'

Honoured? She felt lost, dislocated from her life, from all the things that kept her sane.

'I'll see you at seven,' she said, and turning on her heel she crossed the lawn swiftly and went in through the door into the side passage, then up the back stairs to her room. She closed the door behind her with relief, then crossed to the window and sat on the padded seat where she'd spent so much time with Jenni as a baby, rocking her for comfort—but comfort for who? For the baby, or herself?

He was right, she thought, looking out of the window. The view was beautiful, and she'd always loved it, loved it for the freedom it brought her, the distance, the ever-changing landscape of the sea music to her soul. Rob was down there now, walking along the shore, heading up towards the ruins of the old castle.

They'd gone up there, sometimes, to be alone, that first September before she'd realised she was expecting Jenni, before it had all changed. It had been magical, their special place, almost sacred to them, but after they were married, of course, they hadn't needed to go there to be alone, and she'd missed it. Missed making love with Rob, the sweet scent of grass and the salt tang of the sea and the harsh cries of gulls all around them. They'd been such good times, infinitely precious. Where had they gone?

She rested her shoulders back against the shutters and let herself feel the warmth of the sun on her face. It was setting now, starting to fade as the evening wore on, and the sky was shot through with purple and gold.

She'd watched so many sunsets from this window in the days and weeks after Jenni's birth, counting the days to Rob's return, marking them off as the setting sun marked the end of each lonely and interminable day without him, and sometimes she'd taken Jenni and gone up to the old castle and stared out to sea, wondering where he was, desperate for him to come home. She'd been so lonely without him, but then, when he'd come back, there had been this strange awkwardness between them, a chasm she hadn't known how to cross, and she'd been even more lonely then.

The memory chilled her, and she rubbed her arms briskly and stood up, opening her case and shaking out her clothes. She'd only packed enough for a few days, but Rob seemed to think she'd need to be here for weeks.

We'll see, she thought.

Days were one thing. Weeks, she was beginning to realise, might be quite another…

'Rob tells me you want to pay for the dress.'

Maisie met Helen's eyes unflinchingly, not wanting to upset her but determined not to back down. 'Yes. I'm sorry, I know you offered, but I really feel it's my place.'

'Are you sure? Wedding dresses can be dreadfully expensive, and I know you only work part time. I wouldn't want you to feel you had to scrimp.'

She hung onto her temper with difficulty. 'Helen, I can afford her dress,' she said firmly. 'And mine. Don't worry, she won't disgrace you—or, more importantly, herself. She can tell you all about it when we get back.' And then, because Helen's eyes were filled with hurt, she went on, her voice softening, 'If you really want to give her something to wear on the day, offer to pay for her veil. She'd be really pleased at that, and she can hand it on to her own daughter.'

As Maisie herself would have done, if she'd had the chance, but her wedding to Rob had been hasty, restricted to immediate members of the family, and under the circumstances the very idea of a veil would have been ludicrous.

She heard voices behind them, and Jenni clattered down the stairs, long auburn hair flying, eyes sparkling with excitement. 'Oh, this is going to be such fun. Are we all ready—? Oh, Grannie, why are you still in your dressing gown? Aren't you well?'

'I'm fine, but I've decided not to go with you, darling. This is for you and your mother to do. I'll look forward to hearing all about it when you get back.'

Had Helen been meant to come? Oh, no, she

hadn't realised that, and for all Helen's faults, Jenni loved her grandmother. She felt a wash of guilt and turned to her. 'We can get a later train. Why don't you come—do what I suggested?' she said softly, but Helen shook her head.

'No. We'll get the veil some other time. You go together, you'll have a lovely day, and I get Jenni all the time now, don't forget.'

She hadn't. It was a constant ache that her darling daughter was so far away from her now, her life almost exclusively up here in the wilds of thc West Highlands. And time spent with her was infinitely precious.

She nodded, touched at Helen's understanding, wondering if perhaps she had misunderstood her years ago, or if Helen had simply mellowed with age. 'Thank you. Come on, then, Jenni, let's go. We've got a lot to do.'

Glasgow was bustling, but the rain which had threatened earlier had cleared by the time they arrived and the sky was a glorious blue. Just as well, since Jenni had orchestrated a tight schedule.

They started at the top of her list and worked steadily downwards through the bridal shops and departments, and as she flicked through the rails of dresses, shaking her head, pulling a face, making 'hmm' noises, it began to dawn on Maisie what this task entailed.

Jenni tried on umpteen dresses in several shops, standing on a box so that the dresses hung without crumpling on the floor, while the ladies adjusted them with huge clips at the back to pull them in if they were too big. Just so she could get the idea.

'How long would it take to alter them?' she asked again and again, and rejected several on the grounds that there simply wasn't time to have them taken in or up or both. Others were rejected because they were encrusted with crystals or smothered in embroidery or just didn't feel right, and in the end they couldn't remember what she *had* tried on. Lots, though.

They paused for coffee after the second shop, to catch their breath and sober up because in both shops they'd been offered sparkling wine, and then they tackled the third.

'That was awful. I hated everything in there,' Jenni said as they emerged, and they had a chuckle and found a café for lunch.

'Mummy, what are we going to do if I can't find anything I like?' she asked, picking her way through a toasted panini with a thoughtful look on her face.

'I don't know, darling. Keep looking?'

'I don't have time. And we've still got to get you sorted out.'

'Don't worry about me, I can get my outfit any time.'

'But I want to be *with* you! And I've got my finals coming up, and if it's all going to be like this, it'll be impossible.'

She looked near to tears, and Maisie squeezed her hand. 'Darling, it'll be fine. I'm sure you'll find something. There are thousands of dresses out there.'

And none of them seemed to suit her, for one reason or another. It wasn't that she was being unreasonably picky, she just hadn't yet seen The One.

'Right, two more to go. Let's get on,' Jenni said, stuffing her list back into her bag and getting to her feet.

And then finally, when Maisie was beginning to think it would take at least another day, they went to the last shop on her list. It was down a side street, tucked away where you would scarcely find it even by accident, and they were led upstairs and ushered to a seating area by a kindly but efficient matron called Mrs Munro.

'What are you looking for? Grecian, retro, sixties, traditional, princess, vintage?'

'Something simple but interesting. I don't know. The feel of the fabric's really important, and I don't want a huge dress. Alec says if I look like a pavlova walking down the aisle, he's leaving.'

Maisie gave a splutter of shocked laughter. 'Oh, Jenni! I'm sure he didn't mean it.'

'I don't know about that.'

'He'll adore it, whatever you have,' Mrs Munro said sagely. 'If the dress is right for you, he'll only see you, my dear, believe me. Right. White, ivory, cream? Or a colour?'

'Not a colour. Ivory, probably.'

'And the wedding's quite soon, you say, so it has to be something in stock—so, will you be needing to allow a little extra room?' she asked with a twinkle, voicing the question that Maisie had been afraid to ask, but Jenni coloured and shook her head hastily.

'No, nothing like that. My fiancé works on a sporting estate. We have to fit round the seasons, and we didn't want a winter wedding and we didn't want to wait till next year.'

She nodded, made Jenni stand up and turn round, and then disappeared.

'Gosh, she's a bit scary, I can't believe she thought I was pregnant,' Jenni whispered, and Maisie suppressed a little flutter of panic.

'Let's just hope she knows what she's doing,' she whispered back, reining in her thoughts. 'I wonder what she'll come up with?'

Trumps. That was what she came up with. She emerged from a cluster of rails with a single dress and hung it on the rail by the door.

'Oh, look, Mum, it's gorgeous,' Jenni breathed. 'Look at the fabric!'

'None of them look anything on the hanger. That's why I don't encourage people to look at them like that, but I've never seen this one on, so let's try it and see.'

So Jenni disappeared into the fitting room, and Maisie sat and sipped spring water—not sparkling wine, because, as the scary matron said, one needed a clear head for these things and there'd be plenty of time for that later!

And then Jenni came out in a dress like nothing else she'd tried. It was exquisite, a beautiful off-white crinkled silk, with a strap over one shoulder and soft asymmetric pleats across the body, hugging her figure to mid-thigh and then flaring out in a flamenco-style skirt that swept the floor.

She looked—heavens, she looked like a bride, Maisie thought, filling up, and put her glass down hurriedly and pressed her fingers to her mouth.

'Oh, darling, you look…'

She couldn't finish, her eyes welling up and flooding over, and Jenni burst into tears and went into her arms.

'Oh, Mummy, I love it!'

'So do I. You look so beautiful—stand back, let me see you again. Turn round—oh, Jenni, it's fabulous.' She met the matron's eye and found an unexpected sheen in them.

Mrs Munro cleared her throat. 'That's the dress,' she said firmly. 'I can always tell when I see it on. I wasn't going to show it to you, because I've only just had it in today and it could do with a wee steam, but I thought the moment I saw you it might be the one for you, and it is. Oh, it most definitely is.' And with a little sniff, she dished out tissues all round, gave Jenni a brisk hug and moved on.

'So the wedding's in mid-June, you say? We need to make sure this dress is ready for then. Now, I promise you I've only just had it in, and you're the first person to try it, so it really is a new dress, so you needn't worry about buying a sample that lots of people have tried on. And I must say, I don't think it needs any alteration at all. What height heel are you talking about?'

'Nothing huge. I haven't looked yet, but Alec's only three inches taller than me, so I don't want to tower over him.'

'Very wise. What size are you?'

She found a pair of shoes with the right sort of heel height that went beautifully with the dress, and when Jenni put them on the length was perfect.

'Oh, they're lovely. Are they for sale?'

'Indeed they are. So, all you need to do now is take your dress home, hang it up in a dark room with a cotton cover over it, and you'll be ready to go. It might need a wee steam just before the day, but we can see to that, if you like, and you can pick it up nearer the time. It's up to you. We just need to choose the veil, if you're having one, and then you're finished. So, where's the wedding? Somewhere windy?'

'Ardnashiel.'

The matron stopped and looked at her. 'Ah, you're *that* Jennifer Mackenzie,' she said, nodding in delight. 'I saw the announcement in the paper yesterday. Well, it could certainly be windy up there on the coast, but you couldn't want a more beautiful setting. A long veil can be a bit of a handful and it'll need anchoring firmly, but they can look wonderful in the photographs on a windy day. Have a look and see if there are any that take your eye.'

The veils were all beautiful, and caused more tears. 'I don't know what Grannie'll think if I choose it without her. She should be here – she's buying it for me,' she explained.

'You can always bring it back and change it,' Mrs Munro suggested.

'That's an idea, Jenni. Or you could bring her with you to choose it, and pick the dress up then. Maybe your father could bring you next week, on your way back to uni, and he could pick the dress up and bring it home.'

'That's a brilliant idea! And it would mean Grannie gets to help me and she'll feel involved, and we don't have to struggle with the dress on the train! Fantastic,' she bubbled, but Maisie hardly heard her, because echoing in her head were her own words.

He could bring the dress home. Not *take* it home, but bring it…

'So have you chosen your outfit yet?'

She dragged herself back from the brink and met the woman's eyes.

'Um—no. This has been sprung on me, really. I only knew about it three days ago.'

'So, do you have any thoughts?'

'Something pretty,' Jenni said, twirling again in front of the mirror and laughing in delight as the skirt swirled out. 'Not mumsy. She's not mumsy at all, she's a bit of a gypsy. She's practical and sensible and down to earth, and she needs something really beautiful to do her justice—and don't argue, Mum. I want you to look beautiful for my wedding, and it doesn't matter if you can't wear it again. But not one of those ridiculous mother-of-the-bride outfits. You're much too young for that.'

She smiled and shrugged, and the matron eyed her up and down. 'What colour are the maids wearing?'

'A soft lilac, I think,' Jenni told her. 'Alec's a Cooper, and the Cooper's got a mauve line. I wanted to pick it up.'

She nodded, and then eyed Maisie again and shook her head. 'You can't wear that colour. It would be awful with your colouring. You need something gentle—cream? That would be all right with the Mackenzie dress tartan the Laird'll be in. Jenni, do you mind if your mother wears cream?'

She stopped twirling in front of the mirror and turned round to face them. 'No. Why? Have you got something?'

'A lace dress—it's very pretty, very beautiful, actually, and it fits like a dream. I got it in for a mother of the bride but she changed her mind and decided to go for something more conventional on the knee. It's sleeveless, shorter at the front with a little fishtail skirt at the back just skimming the ankles, but it's got straps so you can wear a proper bra and it has a lovely little bolero with it. I'll get it.'

It was perfect. The moment Maisie put it on, she knew it was right. It hugged her figure, skimmed her hips and snuggled in under her bottom, and the bolero just completed the look.

'Wow, that's fabulous! Good grief! You look really hot,' Jenni said, and Maisie felt a soft tide of colour sweep her cheeks.

'Are you sure it's not too…?'

'Too *what*?' Jenni asked, and then shook her head and laughed. 'It's *gorgeous*, Mum! You look absolutely stunning. You'll blow Dad's socks off!'

She froze, her breath wedged in her throat, and then gave a strangled little laugh. 'I'm not sure that's a good idea,' she said, but Jenni just flapped her hand.

'Don't be silly. You look really beautiful. You have to have it.'

She did. She absolutely had to have it, even if she never dared to wear it, because nothing she'd put on in her life before had ever made her feel so good.

'I'll take it,' she said. 'I don't even want to know the price.'

'It's reduced, actually, because the lady had paid a non-returnable deposit, so I'm taking that off for you. Just take it as a sign.'

Sound advice. She decided to follow it, and just hoped there was enough space in her account for both it and the wedding dress. She paid for both, and the shoes, and then they said a grateful goodbye to the wonderful and really not so scary Mrs Munro and headed back towards the station.

'So, are we all done?'

'I think so,' Jenni said, and turned to her mother and hugged her. 'Thank you so much. I know Grannie wanted to buy me my dress, but I'm really glad you did. I wanted you to, so much.'

'And I wanted to. Never mind, we'll have to tell her all about it and she can see you in it next week when you choose the veil.'

'I've already chosen it, I think.'

Maisie smiled. 'But she doesn't know that, and if you've got any sense, you'll make sure she doesn't, because I'm still feeling a little guilty.'

'Don't. We've had a fabulous day, and I love her to bits but you're my mother. It should be you. And I just adore your outfit.'

Maisie glanced down at the bag in her hand with a mixture of excitement and trepidation. What if Rob hated it? What if he thought it was inappropriate?

What if it blew his socks off?

'I adore it, too,' she admitted. 'What do you think about shoes? And do I need a hat? Or a fascinator?'

'Oh, they're fun.'

'I think they look as if a chicken's landed in your hair,' she said, and they laughed together, talking accessories over a shared pot of tea in a little café, and then, because neither of them had the energy to keep looking, they caught the next train home—there she went again, calling it home when it was no such thing—and arrived in time for supper.

'So, did you have a successful day?' Helen asked as she dished up Mrs McCrae's delicious cottage pie.

'Brilliant. I'll tell you all about it when Alec's not here,' Jenni said, wrinkling her nose at him mischievously.

'So this is it, then, is it? The One?' he asked.

'Mmm. It's gorgeous—absolutely huge, with a great puffy skirt and hoops and sleeves and—'

He tore a corner off his bread roll and threw it at her, and she giggled and ducked.

Dear heaven, she was still a little girl in so many ways, so full of fun and the boundless enthusiasm of youth. Maisie caught Rob's eyes and found an indulgent look in them she'd seen before, when Jenni was little.

They exchanged knowing smiles, and she felt her heart hitch in her chest. Oh, no. She was too vulnerable to him, and being forced into his company like this was leaving her wide open to hurt.

She wanted him so much—still, even after all this time, felt the same way about him as she had when she'd first met him—but she still didn't know him, couldn't trust him not to turn away from her again if things got sticky. She had to get away.

She looked down at her plate, playing with her food, trying not to think about him, because he was too dangerous for her.

'So I was thinking, as we've got the dress and my outfit sorted, I could go back to Cambridge early next week, perhaps Monday or Tuesday,' she said a little abruptly, and then listened to the echo of her words around the room.

There was a heartbeat of stunned silence, then Rob said, 'But I thought we'd agreed you'd stay longer?'

She met his eyes again with forced calm. 'No. You suggested it, but if we can get the majority of the decisions made this weekend, there's no need for me to stay longer. A great deal of it can be done over the phone or the internet. So long as we've settled the guest list and ordered the invitations and the other stationery, I don't see any point in being here when Jenni's back at uni, and, besides, I have a lot to do at home.'

'She has a point, Dad—the important stuff's done, and she's got a life down there, you know. She can't just drop everything and be here to save you having to make a few phone calls.'

'Fine,' he said, a little curtly. 'Don't worry. I'm sure it'll be all right. I just thought—'

'Well, you thought wrong,' she said, quietly but firmly. 'I'm happy to come back if necessary, but I can't sit around here with my life on hold in case a decision needs to be made.'

'Apparently not. Well, you have to do what you have to do. Right, if you'll excuse me I'm needed—some guests want to plan their weekend's activities and I need to have a look at the website. There's a hitch.'

'It was working fine earlier,' Alec said, sounding puzzled, but Rob had pushed back his chair and was heading for the door as if he couldn't bear to be in the room with her another moment.

'Well, it's not now,' he said over his shoulder, and yanked the door open just as Mrs McCrae reached for the handle.

'Oh—are you away, Robert? I made sticky toffee pudding—'

'Save me some, I'll have it later,' he growled, striding away down the corridor and leaving them sitting there in a strained silence that nobody seemed to know how to break. Jenni got there first, reaching over and covering her hand, her eyes distressed.

'I'm sorry, Mum. I might have known it was too good to last,' she said after a moment, but Maisie just shrugged.

'Well, you didn't really expect it to be plain sailing, did you?' she said lightly. 'We were obviously going to disagree on something. We always did.'

Jenni nodded, and then smiled up at Mrs McCrae who was poised with the spoon and shaking her head after Robert. 'You're going to have to stop feeding me up, Mrs McCrae. I can't put any weight on, my dress fits perfectly.'

She smiled indulgently. 'Does it, hen? That's lovely. Just have a wee piece of the sticky toffee, then, to be on the safe side.'

'Give her a nice big chunk. I'll eat what she

can't manage,' Alec said with a grin, and with his gentle charm he steered the conversation back into safer waters and Maisie felt herself relax again.

CHAPTER FOUR

SHE was going back.

Damn.

Not that he could work out why he wanted her here a moment longer. The whole time she was here he was restless and unsettled, and the last thing he needed was her announcing that she'd cleared her diary and could be here until the wedding, but he hadn't expected her to run away *quite* so fast. There was still so much to do, so many decisions to make, so much to sort out.

'Oh, dammit,' he muttered, flicking on the computer and scowling at the screen. There was nothing wrong with the website. Nothing at all. It was just an excuse to get away, like the guests who wanted to talk about their weekend activities. They'd already done that earlier, and Alec knew it full well.

So he wasn't surprised when there was a knock

on the door a short while later, and Alec slipped through it and closed it softly behind him.

'Problem with the website, is there?'

He shoved the chair back from the desk and propped his feet up on the edge. 'Why's she going so damn soon, Alec? There's still tons to sort out. What have I done wrong?'

'Maybe she's just busy.'

'Bull,' he said shortly. 'It's just an excuse to get away. It's what she's always done when it gets too difficult—she runs away.'

'Well, you should know, you're the expert.' He shoved some papers out of the way and put a tray down on the desk. 'Here—I brought us coffee and some pudding.'

'More?'

He grinned. 'Always room for more. I'm going to have to get Mrs McCrae to teach Jenni how to make it.' He prodded the bowl towards him, and Rob picked it up and toyed with the sauce, dipping the spoon in it and trailing it over the top of the sponge.

'She just gets to me.'

'You don't say. Actually, I think it's mutual. I think the reason she's going is she's having trouble dealing with how she feels about you.'

'She doesn't feel anything about me. Well, that's not true. She hates me.'

'Does she?' Alec murmured. 'I wouldn't be so

sure. She doesn't look at you as if she hates you. Far from it.'

He frowned, prodding the pudding, releasing the gloriously warm, sweet scent of it, and then to stall a little longer he dug the spoon in and scooped up a chunk of sponge. 'I think you're wrong,' he said, pointing the loaded spoon at Alec. 'I think she's just antsy here. She's always hated it.'

'Why?'

He shrugged and put the spoon in his mouth, stalling again.

'She must have loved you once,' Alec persisted. 'Jenni says she's never known her to have a boyfriend.'

He stuck the spoon back in the bowl and dumped it on the table. 'Really?' he said, his voice flat as if the subject bored him, when the truth was he was riveted.

'Really. And she looks at you as if…'

'As if…?'

Alec shrugged diffidently. 'As if she's never really got over you. If you want my honest opinion, I think she still loves you.'

'Loves me?' He snorted and picked up the bowl again. 'Now I *know* you're talking rubbish. She'd got over me by the time she had Jenni. I wasn't here for the birth, and the next time I was home on leave, she could hardly bring herself to look at me. It went from bad to worse.'

'You were in the submarines, weren't you?'

'Yes—and away for months at a time with no contact. It wasn't exactly ideal, but I got such a chilly reception when I did come home that frankly I was glad to go back. She didn't get on with my father either, and she upset my mother all the time. Then when Jenni was six months old, I went back to sea again, and when I came home, she was gone.'

Alec scraped the last trace of sauce off his bowl and put it on the tray. 'Why?'

'I have no idea,' he said flatly. 'We never talked about it. She didn't even tell me to my face, just left a note for me, packed up all her things and took Jenni with her.'

'And you didn't go after her?'

He sounded incredulous, and Rob sighed shortly and rammed his hand through his hair. 'No, Alec, I didn't go after her.'

'Maybe that's where you went wrong?'

He snorted. 'I don't think so. Unlike some people, I can take a hint—and that was a hell of a hint. So forgive me if I think you're wrong about her. I think she was over me by the time I went away to the navy, and the only reason she didn't leave earlier was because Jenni was so small. She hated it here—hated the castle, hated the weather, hated my parents—it was a disaster. The only good thing to come out of it was our daughter, and she took her away from me. Frankly, if we can just get through the run-up to the wedding without killing each other, I think we'll be doing well.'

He met his future son-in-law's thoughtful eyes head on. 'So—was there anything else I can do for you, or are you just here to pick over the bones of my failed relationship with your future mother-in-law?'

Alec gave a huff of laughter and got to his feet. 'No, that was all. Finished with your coffee?'

He glanced at it. It was stone-cold, and it was the last thing he needed. He was wound up enough. 'Yeah, take it away, I'll get a fresh one when I've finished this. And, Alec? Look after Jenni. Make sure this didn't upset her.'

He nodded, picked up the tray and walked out, closing the door quietly behind him.

Rob sighed and dropped his head back against the chair, locking his hands behind his neck and staring at the ceiling. There was a water mark on it, and he made a mental note to check the plumbing in the bathroom above. Another thing to add to the endless list.

He checked his email, sorted out a glitch on the website—poetic justice, he thought drily—and then took the dogs out for a walk along the beach in the moonlight before heading back to the house.

There was a light on in Maisie's bedroom, and he could see her sitting there in the window, staring down at him. Watching him.

Was Alec right? Did Maisie still love him?

He felt his chest tighten at the thought, emotions he'd long put behind him crowding him. They'd walked together on this beach so many times at first, climbed up to the ruins to be alone together. They'd hidden a blanket up there in an old stone alcove, and when the weather was fair they'd stretch it out on the soft, sweet grass inside the ruined tower and make love for hours.

His eyes burned, his chest tight as he remembered the sweet moments they'd shared. She'd been a virgin when he'd met her, his the only hands to touch her. Such a precious gift, and he'd treasured it, but she'd taken it away from him when she'd left.

So long ago. Lifetimes.

Of course she didn't still love him. If she'd loved him, she would have stayed, but she'd walked away without a backward glance, and only a madman would have gone after her.

'Maybe that's where you went wrong?'

He glanced up again, frowning, but her light was off now. Was she still watching him in the dark?

Damn her. He didn't need this. His emotions were like acid inside him, eating at him, and he felt more unsettled than he'd felt in years.

Whistling the dogs, he went back inside, poured himself a hefty malt from the distillery in the village, too restless to sleep, and tackled the sliding pile of paperwork on his desk.

'Mum?'

There was a quiet tap on the door, and Jenni put her head round.

'Oh, you're awake. Good. I've brought us tea.'

She pushed the door open and came in with a tray, setting it down on the table by the window seat and sitting next to Maisie. She put her arm out, and Jenni snuggled up, resting her head on her shoulder as she'd done for years.

'It's so nice, having you here,' she said. 'I miss you.'

'I miss you, too. We haven't had early morning tea together for ages.'

'I know—and it's all going to change when I marry Alec. We'd better make the best of it.'

'Mmm.' She rested her head against Jenni's, then asked the question that had been troubling her for days. Even Mrs Munro had raised the subject yesterday, and Jenni had blushed and denied it, but Maisie wasn't sure, and she wanted to be sure, because it simply wasn't a good enough reason for marriage. So cautiously, tentatively, she said, 'Jenni—you would tell me if you were pregnant, wouldn't you?'

Jenni lifted her head and stared at her mother for a second. 'Of course I would. Mum, I can't be pregnant.'

'There's no such word as can't,' Maisie said drily, but Jenni shook her head, a shy blush warming her pale cheeks.

'There is. I know I can't be,' she said softly, resting her head back down on Maisie's shoulder. 'I really can't. I told him ages ago that I wanted to be a virgin on my wedding night, so if he wanted to sleep with me, he'd have to marry me. And having decided to—well, we don't want to wait any longer. That's the only reason for the hurry. Nothing else, I promise.'

Maisie hugged her tenderly. 'Wow,' she murmured thoughtfully. 'That's novel. I wish I'd had half your sense.'

'I don't,' Jenni told her bluntly, 'or I wouldn't be here now, would I?'

'No, you wouldn't, and I wouldn't change that for anything,' she said, her hug tightening as she dropped a kiss on her daughter's hair. 'I'm just surprised.'

'Maybe all your lectures about respecting myself and being sure about a relationship first have paid off. And I am sure. I'm really, really sure.'

'Good.'

Jenni sighed contentedly and shifted to look out of the window. 'He proposed to me up there, in the tower room of the old castle,' she said, her voice dreamy. 'It was so romantic. He took me up there, with a blanket and a picnic basket, and it was freezing, but he'd got hot pies from Mrs McCrae, and a flask of coffee, and when we'd eaten he got up, and I thought we were going, and I was actually relieved because it was so cold, but then he pulled me to my feet and went down on one knee and asked me to marry him. And I just burst into tears—isn't that silly?'

Maisie hugged her. 'Not silly at all.' It was what she would have done, if Rob had taken her up there and proposed to her like that, instead of telling her that they ought to get married when they hardly knew each other.

'I love the view from here, don't you?' Jenni murmured, and Maisie debated her answer and then avoided it.

'It's beautiful,' she said, because that was indisputable. 'I used to sit here with you for hours when you were a baby, staring out to sea and wondering where your father was.'

'It must have been very odd for you here without him when he went off to the navy. You must have been so lonely without him.'

'I was. I didn't know anybody, and I didn't fit in. And I don't think they liked me.'

Jenni looked shocked. 'Why ever not? Did they think you didn't love him?'

'Oh, I loved him,' she said softly, 'but they knew nothing about me. We were so young, and we'd just met, and then what felt like minutes later he was off into the navy and I was pregnant. Classic timing. It was hardly a great start and not exactly what they'd planned for their only son.'

'But you did marry him, and you had me, and you still managed to do your degree. I think that's amazing.'

She gave a hollow laugh. 'Only in stages, and only because the college was very accommodating and let me take a year off in the middle. And I really struggled that first year, while I was pregnant and he was away so much.'

'Why *did* you move up here?'

She eased Jenni out of her arms and reached for her tea with a quiet sigh. 'I've often asked myself that. Maybe because I thought I'd get more support from them than I was getting from my own family, and maybe I hoped that if I came to love the castle he was so fond of, then our marriage would stand a chance. It didn't work like that, though. It was cold and wet, and I was trapped inside the castle with you for days on end. I couldn't drive then, and there was nowhere to go while he was at sea, and anyway most of the time it seemed to be raining. Then when he did come back he wanted to go out walking on the hills on his own, and I got resentful, and he was withdrawn, and we just stopped talking. Stopped everything, really. If we weren't talking about you, we didn't talk. We never spent any time together that wasn't with you or about you, and most of the time he wasn't here anyway, so what was the point of me being here with you when I felt so unwanted?

'So I took you back home with me, and he let me go. He didn't come after me, didn't ask why—nothing, not for months, and then it was just a letter from the solicitors. I think it was a relief to him. The trouble was, we were both just kids, and we behaved like kids, so it's no wonder it didn't work. Anyway, we got divorced as soon as we could, and I vowed never to come back.'

Jenni's eyes filled with tears. 'Oh, Mum, I'm so sorry. I didn't realise you were that unhappy here. I thought it was just the weather and Dad being away. I mean, I knew you didn't have much in common, but—it must have been awful. No wonder you left.'

She tried to smile, but there was a lump in her throat she was having difficulty swallowing, so she just shrugged and drank her tea, and Jenni snuggled into her side again and said nothing for a while.

'We ought to sort out the guest list,' Maisie said in the end. 'Have you done anything about it?'

'Sort of. Dad and Grannie need to get together

and talk about relatives and things, and you need to tell us who you want on it, but we've done ours, and Alec's asked his best man and ushers and I've contacted Libby and Tricia.'

'Is that all you're having as your bridesmaids?'

'Mmm. They need to come and look at dresses—we can do that in Glasgow one day. And we need to sort out the wedding invitation wording, and get them ordered, and I suppose we need to talk about flowers.'

'Have you had any ideas?'

'Mmm. I want white—just white, with lots of greenery. I think it looks beautiful. Really simple. Maybe white peonies. Apparently they smell gorgeous.'

'Yes, they do. They're lovely. And in mid-June that's perfect. What about table centres?'

'I don't know. Do you think I should have tall vases, or fishbowls, or low posies? There are so many styles and I'm just confused. Can you help me? You go to lots of weddings, you must have tons of ideas.'

'Do you want to look through my portfolio?' she suggested. 'I've got loads of weddings on there, and it might give you some ideas. In fact, the wedding I did on Wednesday was lovely. They had simple hand-ties for everything, and they looked fabulous. And that was just green and white.'

She turned on her laptop and brought up the photos of Annette's daughter's wedding, and they discussed the flowers, the bridesmaids, the favours, the table settings—everything except Annette. Maisie didn't want to add any more emotion into the mix, and some things weren't hers to talk about. She'd only told Rob because she'd ripped his head off when he'd pushed her buttons, and she'd wanted to get them off on a more even keel for this difficult visit.

Not that the uneasy truce had lasted long, she thought with a weary sigh, flicking through to another wedding, another set of options to consider.

'Oh! Mum, who's going to take the photos?' Jenni asked, looking suddenly concerned, but Maisie just hugged her.

'I thought we could ask Jeff. You know, from the paper? He's only young, but he's a good photographer and I can brief him thoroughly. Or we can get someone else?'

'No. No, I like Jeff. Oh, that's pretty,' she said, her attention distracted by another photograph, and they carried on looking through the file—until Maisie's stomach rumbled.

Then she realised what the time was. 'Jenni, it's after nine! We ought to get dressed and go downstairs and get your father and grandmother round the table, even if Alec can't be there.'

'He can. He's coming in for coffee at ten-thirty, and he's bringing Dad. And hopefully he'll stay and talk this time. I can't believe he walked out like that last night.'

'Oh, I can. It's his way, Jenni—or at least, his way with me. But I'll do my best to keep the peace, and hopefully he'll do the same, and we'll be able to get through it all in the next couple of days so I can go home for a while. I didn't even water the garden before I left, I was in such a rush, and I've planted up all my pots.'

'I'll miss you, you know,' Jenni said softly. 'I'm really enjoying having you here. It seems right, somehow.'

Did it? Not to Maisie. Not with Rob on a hair trigger and her stomach in knots because she knew she was falling in love with him all over again. But she'd miss her daughter, too. Unbearably.

'You're going back to uni, don't forget, so you wouldn't see me if I was here—and, anyway, I'll be back,' she said comfortingly, wondering how she'd cope with repeated visits but knowing she would have to in the future if she wanted to get to know her grandchildren.

'You'd better be back! I'm going to need you here before the wedding, Mum, making sure everything's in place. I really, really can't take my eye off the ball at this stage. I have to pass my finals or the last three years will have been wasted.'

'I'll be here,' she said firmly. 'Don't you worry about it, Jenni. I'll be here whenever necessary, and I'll do whatever I need to do to make your wedding day perfect.'

'So, that's the guest list finished, then? Mum, are you sure that's all you want to invite?'

'I'm sure,' she said, and Rob leant across the table to study the list upside down, and frowned at Maisie.

'Your father's not on there.'

She shrugged. 'He won't come. He thinks you're the spawn of the devil and we're well suited, in his words. There's no point in asking him, even if he was well enough to come, which he's not. I've tried and tried and tried to build bridges, and he sabotages every attempt I make, so I've given up.'

'Jenni? Would it make any difference if you asked him?'

His daughter shrugged. 'I never see him, Dad. It doesn't matter, really. He's so cold to Mum, and he ignores me whenever we see him at any family functions, and I don't know him. It's fine.'

'I still think he should be given the option.'

'OK, I'll ask him,' Maisie said shortly, 'but he won't come. He probably won't even reply.'

'And the rest of your family? Your brother and his wife and kids? Will they come?'

'They might. I don't know. It's a long way and he's very busy with school exams at this time of year. He might not be able to get away, but they're on the list.'

'So how many are there?'

'Not quite a hundred,' Jenni said, totting up quickly. 'So I expect by the time some people can't come because it's short notice, we'll be down to ninety or so.

'Which is fine. Alec and I have been looking, and we reckon we can seat a maxiumum of a hundred and twenty in the Great Hall, and it opens onto the side lawn where the marquee will go, so depending on the weather we can eat in or out and the catering tent can be situated so it's convenient for either. We can make a decision the day before, and we can have the reception drinks out on the gun court if the weather holds.'

'So how many invitations do we need to order?' Alec asked, making notes.

'Allow plenty in case of errors. And we need to sort out the wording.' Rob met Maisie's eyes, knowing he was stepping straight into a minefield here. 'Any suggestions?'

'Well, Mr and Mrs Robert Mackenzie won't work,' she said with heavy irony. 'How pompous do you want to be?'

He felt himself frown. 'Pompous?'

'Yes—you know, "The Much Honoured Robert Mackenzie, Laird of Ardnashiel, and Ms Margaret Douglas request the pleasure of the company of—leave blank—at the marriage of their daughter Jennifer to Mr Alec Cooper in St Andrew's church, Ardnashiel, on Saturday 19 June at 2 p.m., and afterwards at Ardnashiel Castle. Carriages at Midnight, or whatever. RSVP to…", blah de blah—or do you think that sounds just a touch stuffy?'

One eyebrow was slightly raised, her mouth twitching, and her eyes flashed with challenge. Jenni was struggling not to laugh, and he took a slow breath.

'I think we could dispense with the "Much Honoured", don't you?' he said drily, refusing to allow her to needle him. He'd had a fairly pointed lecture from his daughter on the subject already that morning, and the last thing he needed was another one. 'How about "Robert Mackenzie and Maisie Douglas"—assuming you refuse to use your married name?'

'I do. I'm not married any more. I go by Douglas.'

'So "Robert Mackenzie and Maisie Douglas request the pleasure of your company at the marriage of their daughter Jennifer to Alec Cooper", et cetera, et cetera. I think that's pompous enough. What do you two think?'

'How about "Alec and Jenni would love you to join them for their wedding on" blah blah?' Jenni said, folding her arms and leaning back, her eyes every bit as challenging as her mother's, and he had to press his lips together to stop himself from laughing.

'Mother?'

'I think your version, Robert. It says enough and not too much. I think you could work "of Ardnashiel" into your name, though. You are the Laird, like it or not, and it'll be expected.'

'I agree,' said Maisie. 'We ought to write it down. I don't suppose anyone can remember what we said?'

How much more?

The guest list was finalised—at last—and they'd done the invitation format and discussed the inserts, such as map, directions and gift list, discussed the wording of the evening invitations, and then a thought occurred to her.

'I suppose the church is free on that day, before we rush ahead and get the invitations printed?' she murmured, and there was a little nod from Jenni.

'It's free, I checked this morning. It's all sorted and booked, subject to him talking to us. Alec, we have to go and see him later, and he'll read the banns tomorrow. Mum, Dad, you'll both have to come. I really want you there, and Alec's parents. You'll be there, too won't you, Grannie? You always are.'

'I most certainly will, darling. As you said, I'm always there, every Sunday morning.'

Polishing her halo, Maisie thought, and then squashed the unkind thought. There was no room for her old resentments, and she had to try and let them go, for everyone's sake.

'Good. That's that sorted. Right, what else? Oh—flowers. I was looking at Mum's photos, and we've decided just white with greenery—'

She was interrupted by a soft gasp from Helen, and Maisie looked at her distressed face and her heart sank. Now what?

'Not green and white—please, Jenni. Something colourful, darling. It's a wedding.'

'But I don't want colourful. I want just white.'

'No—!' And without another word, Helen pushed back her chair and hurried from the room, her hand pressed to her mouth.

'What on earth's the matter with Grannie?' Jenni asked, utterly confused. 'Whatever's wrong with green and white? It's not exactly controversial.'

'I don't know. I'll go and find out,' Rob said, and followed his mother out of the room. He came back a short time later, and sat down heavily.

'They were the colour of the flowers at my father's funeral,' he said softly. 'I'd forgotten. Can you bear to have something different?'

Jenni swallowed, shrugged and said, 'I suppose so. I'll have to, won't I? I can't upset Grannie,' and then she, too, left the room in tears, followed by Alec.

Maisie met Rob's eyes across the table.

'Are you going to burst into tears and rush off?' he asked, and she gave a low laugh.

'No, I think you're safe.'

'Thank God for that. Do you fancy a coffee?'

'We've just had one.'

He smiled conspiratorially. 'No, I mean a *real* coffee. With a wicked pastry and lots of froth and no overwrought emotions.'

She regarded him steadily, suppressing the chuckle in her throat. 'I can't promise that, but for the sake of the pastry, I'll give it my best shot.'

He grinned. 'That's my girl,' he said, and, standing up, he ushered her out of the door and round to the stableyard, grabbing a couple of jackets off the hook by the back door on the way out. He unlocked his car and folded down the roof while she pulled the fleecy jacket on, settled herself in the car and fastened her seat belt, then they set off, while she sat there and listened to his voice saying '*That's my girl*' over and over in her head.

CHAPTER FIVE

'SO, what did you want to talk about?' she said, once they were seated with their coffee and pastries, and he arched a brow.

She couldn't quite hold in the smile. 'Let me guess—Jenni had a go at you and told you to apologise?' she asked, and he snorted quietly, his mouth quirking in a reluctant grin.

'Actually, Alec got there first. He had a go at me last night. And Jenni had a go this morning. But for what it's worth, I was going to apologise anyway. I didn't mean to walk out like that, but the thought of you bailing out on me and leaving me to cope with the tantrums was more than I could take, and this morning just underlined it all.'

'I'm not bailing out on you,' she said softly. 'But I do have things to do, as I told you before. I've got to sort the wedding photos for two weddings now, and get the albums ordered, and there's a rush job for the one I did on Wednesday because until Annette's had her chemo there are still question marks, so I absolutely can't let them down, and I've still got to do my regular column in the paper as well as other features. I can't just walk away from my commitments.'

He sighed and scrubbed a hand through his hair, making it stick up so her fingers itched to reach out and smooth it back down, to touch it, to sift it through her fingertips and see if it still felt as soft, as thick and rich as it had…

'No, I know you can't. I'm sorry if I implied you weren't taking the wedding seriously. Of course you've got a life down there, and I don't underestimate the importance of your work. I think you've done amazingly well, forging your twin careers while you've been bringing Jenni up, and of course you have to honour your commitments. I was just panicking.'

'You, panicking?' she teased. 'That doesn't sound like you.'

His smile was wry. 'My daughter's never had a wedding before.'

'Oh, well, at least we've only got the one—unless you've got any others stashed away somewhere that I don't know about?'

'Hardly. One's quite enough to worry about.' He sat back, stirring his coffee thoughtfully. 'So how are you getting on with Alec?'

Maisie smiled, feeling a little wave of affection for the decent young man her daughter had fallen in love with. 'Very well. You're right, he adores her.'

'He does.' He put the spoon down with exaggerated care. 'Do you know why the wedding's so rushed?'

'Jenni did tell me—when I asked her if she was pregnant.'

He chuckled softly, then his eyes locked with hers and his smile faded. 'I envy them. I envy them for being so sure, for having the time to learn how to love each other, for having the common sense to wait and do things properly. Maybe if we'd done that, things might have been different.'

'They would. We wouldn't have had Jenni, for a start, so I can't wish it undone, Rob. But I might wish it done better. Differently.'

'How?'

She sighed softly, fiddling with the crumbs on her plate, her hair falling forward and shielding her eyes from his searching gaze. 'Maybe if you hadn't gone away to the navy? If my father hadn't thrown me out?' She lifted her head and met his eyes. 'If your father hadn't thought I was a tramp?'

He went very still. 'Oh, come on, he never thought that.'

'Oh, he did. He said so. I heard him, talking to your mother. You were away—it was just after I'd had Jenni.'

Emotions chased through his eyes, and she watched them, watched as the truth registered. He let out his breath on a quiet, slightly uneven sigh. 'I took you away from your familiar surroundings and brought you here because I thought you'd be happier here, better looked after, but it was a disaster, wasn't it?'

She nodded. 'They didn't want me. Why would they? My own family didn't, what on earth made either of us think yours would?'

He dropped his elbows back onto the table and steepled his fingers, pressing them thoughtfully against his mouth. 'Maisie, I'm so sorry,' he murmured. 'No wonder you left.'

'And you didn't follow me.'

'You didn't want me to.'

'Oh, I did, Rob,' she said softly. 'But you couldn't cope with it all, any more than I could.'

His eyes clouded. 'No, you're right. I couldn't. I was spending months at a time under the sea, desperate for the feel of the wind in my hair and the sun on my face, and when I was home you were sad and withdrawn, the baby was crying, and I didn't know what to do to help you.'

'Because you didn't know me. And I didn't know you, Rob,' she said softly. 'I didn't even know you were going to be a Laird until we came up here.'

'What's that got to do with anything? It's not as if I'm the clan chief. I'm just a squire, really. It's virtually meaningless—feudal nonsense.'

'No, it's not. It has implications for where you live your life. There's no choice, if you're going to do it properly. The Laird of Ardnashiel lives in the castle on the estate. End of.'

'It's not exactly Siberia,' he said defensively, but she just arched a brow.

'Really? It feels like it in the winter, believe me, when you can't drive and you're stuck there with a little baby and her father's out there somewhere under the sea out of reach for months at a time. And it doesn't help when his parents despise you and only tolerate your presence because you've got their grandchild.'

'I had to go to sea. You knew I was committed to the navy for six years.'

'But not the subs,' she said, feeling the old frustration and disappointment rise up. 'You could have switched—even if you'd been at sea, we would have been in touch then, I could have talked to you from time to time, but no. You *chose* to go into the submarines, you *chose* to isolate yourself from us for months at a time, and left me there alone.'

'You weren't alone!'

'Wasn't I?' she asked softly. 'Who was there for me, Robert? Not your parents, that's for sure. Your father thought I was a slut, and your mother thought I was a gold-digging little whore, deliberately getting pregnant to get my hands on the estate I didn't even know you had coming to you, though who knows why anyone in their right mind would want to live in a forbidding pile of rock somewhere just shy of the Arctic Circle? If it hadn't been for Mrs McCrae taking me under her wing, I seriously think I wouldn't have survived it.'

He stared at her, his face expressionless, and then he stood up. 'Come on, we're leaving,' he said, and walked out.

She heard his footsteps crossing the room, then someone coughed, breaking the silence, and the conversation resumed around her, a low hum, and speculative glances…

She followed him out, and found him standing down by the shore, hands rammed in his pockets.

He turned to her, his eyes searching.

'Was it really that bad, Maisie?'

She gave a choked laugh. 'Oh, yes, Robert, it really was that bad. And now they all know,' she added, gesturing to the café behind her.

He waved a hand dismissively. 'They're tourists. They don't know who we are, it doesn't matter.'

'So why didn't you stay and finish the conversation?'

'Good idea. You can tell me why you left me, and took my daughter with you.'

'You left me, Rob! You left me here, at the mercy of your parents. I felt utterly abandoned. Is it any wonder I walked away? And I didn't leave you, I left Ardnashiel. Maybe I should have stayed away and let sleeping dogs lie.'

He held her eyes for several seconds, then without another word he turned on his heel, strode back to the car and got in, staring straight ahead while he waited for her to join him.

Once again, the drive back to the castle was conducted in a screaming silence.

'Where did you go? We were looking for you everywhere, and then Alec spotted the car was missing.'

Rob put the roof up and got out without a word, leaving Maisie to talk to Jenni. His emotions were at fever pitch. He and Maisie needed time and space to talk, but of course there wasn't any, and there was probably no point in any case. It was all water under the bridge, over years ago, but he was deeply troubled by her description of her time there without him.

If it hadn't been for Mrs McCrae taking me under her wing, I seriously think I wouldn't have survived it. You left me there. I felt utterly abandoned. I didn't leave you, I left Ardnashiel.

'Where's your grandmother?' he said a little shortly, and Jenni's eyes widened with distress.

'Have you two been fighting *again*?' she said, and turning to Alec she threw herself into his arms and sobbed.

'Damn,' he muttered, and strode off into the castle, looking for his mother. He found her in the drawing room, reading a book, of all things, while the world went to pieces. He took it out of her hand. 'Talk to me,' he demanded abruptly. 'I want to know what went on here while I was at sea.'

She went very still. 'Robert, nothing went on.'

'That's not how Maisie sees it.'

'Well, that doesn't surprise me, she never did make any attempt to see it from our point of view.'

'And what point of view was that?'

'Oh, come on. You were young, rich, poised on the threshold of your life—you were a good catch, Robert, and she caught you. Your father said she was a tramp—'

'Don't—ever—call her that again,' he said, his voice deadly quiet. 'Not that it's any of your damn business, but Maisie was a virgin when I met her. And besides, if she'd been after my inheritance, don't you think she would have stuck around? She hasn't even taken maintenance from me all these years!'

She bristled. 'Why would she need maintenance? You gave her a house—the house we'd given you for your eighteenth birthday! What more could she want?'

'A home? A husband? Someone to love her—someone whose parents didn't think she was a gold-digging little whore? She heard you, Mum. She heard you and Dad talking.'

His mother went white, her eyes widening with distress. 'No! She wasn't meant to hear—'

'You're damn right she wasn't. You weren't meant to have said it! I trusted you to look after her, to keep her safe, to make her welcome, and all you did was regard her with disgust and suspicion.'

'But your father said—'

'I know what my father said, and I have no need to ever hear it again. That doesn't excuse you. I think you owe her an apology, and I think you should do it now, before she leaves.'

'She's leaving? So soon?'

He gave a short laugh. 'Give me one good reason—just one—why she should stay another minute!'

She couldn't. Of course not. There wasn't one.

He walked away, looking for the dogs, needing to escape, and found them in the kitchen, sitting hopefully at Mrs McCrae's feet.

'Lunch is all ready when you are,' she said, and

he stared at her blankly. Lunch? What did lunch have to do with anything?

'You'd better hold it,' he growled. 'I don't think there's a snowflake's chance in hell of us all sitting down together at a table right now. Dogs?'

'Oh, dear, no, no' another scrap, Robert,' she tutted, but he ignored her, slapped his leg for the dogs and went out. They dragged themselves away from Mrs McCrae and followed him along the shore and up to the ruins of the castle, and he stood there, in the broken remains of the tower where he and Maisie had spent so much time, waiting for his emotions to subside, for some semblance of peace to come.

It didn't.

But Maisie did, her footsteps almost silent on the soft grass, any noise drowned out by the whisper of the wind. The dogs alerted him, running to greet her, and he waited, turning towards her, arms folded, letting her set the tone.

'Can we talk?'

He gave a short laugh. 'I don't know—can we? We can't usually manage it but it's probably about time.' He looked down, scuffing the grass with his toe, then he looked up and met her eyes again. 'I owe you an apology—again. We all do.'

'I've seen your mother. Apparently she didn't know I'd overheard those things, and she's mortified.'

'Good. She needs to be. I'm so angry with her.'

'You upset her, Robert.'

He snorted. 'Not nearly as much as she upset me, I can tell you.'

'I'm sorry.'

'What for?'

She shrugged. 'Causing a scene in the café?'

He laughed softly and held out his arms, the fight going out of him. 'What a mess. Come here, Maisie. You look as if you could do with a hug, and I know I could.'

She hesitated, looked around at the place where he'd held her so many times, and for the first time in twenty years, she went back into his arms.

They closed around her, folding her firmly against the solid warmth of his chest, and she rested her head against his heart and listened to its even, steady beat while the tension drained out of her. Lord, how she'd missed this—missed the feel of his arms, the strength of his body, the sound of his heart under her ear.

They stood like that for an age, silent, unmoving, just holding on, and then she lifted her head and met his eyes, easing back a little but still standing in the loose circle of his arms.

'We should go back,' she said. 'Jenni's terribly upset. She hates rows at the best of times, and she's got her finals coming up, the wedding to organise—the last thing she needs is us coming to blows. We need to put this on one side and concentrate on her for now.'

'I agree. And the wedding's only the start of it, Maisie. OK, it might be a bit soon to start thinking about it, but—well, one day we're going to be grandparents. It might be an idea if we were at least friends. It's a pity you don't live closer.'

'I know, but my life's in Cambridge, Rob. And as you said yourself, it's not exactly Outer Mongolia up here.'

'Siberia.'

She felt herself smile reluctantly. 'Whatever. I can see Jenni and Alec and the grandchildren whenever I want. I can come and stay with them—presumably they'll be living on the estate?'

'Yes, they're moving into the gatehouse. It's pretty, it's got a safe, enclosed garden, it's the closest to the village for Jenni to socialise with other mums when the time comes, and it's ideal. It's got four bedrooms, so there'll be plenty of room for you, and there are always other cottages we can put you in if you'd rather. And ultimately, of course, they'll have the castle.'

'Not for a long while, I hope.'

His mouth quirked into a gentle smile. 'Hopefully not. And in the meantime, do you think we can try and be friends? Maybe get to know each other, at last?'

'Not before time.' She smiled up at him wryly.

'Did you know Alec brought Jenni up here for a picnic on Tuesday night and proposed to her?'

'Here? No, I didn't.' He gave a soft laugh. 'How ironic they should choose the place she might have been conceived.'

'I know. She said it was freezing, but very romantic.' She swallowed, trying not to think about the past, about lying with him under the stars on the blanket he'd hidden here, huddled together for warmth. They'd been cold, too, but it had been worth it, just to be alone with him away from prying eyes.

Until it had all gone wrong.

'I'm not surprised he planned it like that. He adores her—and he's picking up all the pieces at the moment,' he said with a sigh. 'I suppose we'd better go and pour oil on the troubled waters and let him off the hook.' He let her go, stepping back so she felt the chilly wind cooling her body where it had been in contact with his. It made her shiver, and she turned and headed back down to the castle, Rob behind her and the dogs running around their feet, while she wished—oh, how she wished—that things could have been different.

They walked in through the kitchen door to a welcoming committee of anxious faces and reddened eyes.

'So, Mrs McCrae, what's for lunch? I'm

starving, and we've got a wedding to finish planning,' Rob said, and there was a collective sigh of relief as she bustled to the stove and pulled the stockpot onto the hob.

'A good rich broth to keep the wind out, and I found some more cheese yesterday at that café and shop on the way to Fort William. You know the one. It's new, Maisie. You might not have seen it, lass.'

Rob met Maisie's eyes and one brow hitched—a tiny movement only she would have noticed, she was sure, and she smiled wryly and looked away. 'I do know the one,' she said blandly, and pulled a chair out and smiled at everyone. 'Right, what else needs considering?' she asked, settling herself down at the scrubbed old table where she'd spent hours in that long-ago winter, keeping Jenni warm by the stove while Mrs McCrae had bustled around them.

'Tons,' Jenni said, looking despairing.

'What are you doing about the wedding cake, hen?' Mrs McCrae asked her, spoon poised over the pot. 'Because a good fruit can't be hurried, and you've only got ten weeks today. I'll need to be getting on wi' it.'

Jenni and Alec exchanged glances. 'Um, we don't really like fruit cake,' Jenni said carefully. 'In fact, lots of people don't like fruit cake. We thought we might not bother.'

Mrs McCrae turned to them, her face scandalised.

'Y'have tae have a cake!' she exclaimed in horror.

Oh, no, another fight brewing, Maisie thought, and chipped in.

'At some of the weddings I've been to, they've had a cake made of cheese. That's very popular now.'

'A *cheesecake*?' Mrs McCrae said, sounding hugely unimpressed. Helen opened her mouth, thought better of it and said nothing, to Maisie's surprise and relief.

'No, a stack of whole cheeses, like the tiers of a wedding cake, only made of cheese. They can look wonderful decorated with grapes and things, and people have them as the centrepiece of the buffet, or just as a huge cheeseboard to follow the meal. The bride and groom cut them in the normal way. You could source local cheeses—there are some wonderful ones apart from the Mull and Orkney cheddars, and you could add others. Just a thought.'

'I really like that idea,' Alec said slowly, a smile dawning on his face, and Maisie let out a slow, quiet sigh of relief.

'So do I—and it's easily dealt with,' Rob said. 'Brilliant, Maisie. Thanks for that.'

'I sha' still make a wee fruit for 'e, it'll be

expected,' Mrs McCrae muttered, stirring the pot as if she was beating the demons out of it, and then she smacked the spoon down and Maisie stifled a smile. 'Right, then, who's for Scotch broth? Or do you no' like that today, either?'

They tackled the rest of the things after lunch, until Jenni and Alec had to see the minister, and then Helen went to lie down for a while and Maisie and Rob were left alone together in the drawing room.

'So what else is there?'

She shrugged. 'I don't really know. I imagine table linen will be included in the table hire. Or do the caterers supply it with the crockery and glassware and so on?'

'Probably—to both. I'll get onto the hotel in the village and check they can do the catering, ring the marquee people for a quote and book the piper in the morning, and I need to track down a ceilidh band for the dance. There's one in the village and they're pretty good, but I don't know how Alec feels about them. We'd better ask.' He slumped against the chair back and shook his head slowly. 'There can't surely be much more, can there?'

'The order of service? Choosing a menu, then printing or ordering the menu cards, place names, table plan—that can only be done when you've got the replies—'

'Maisie, do you have to go back? I mean, I know you do, but couldn't you just go for the weddings and do the rest from here? I take it it's all digital?'

'Oh, of course, but I still have to talk them through with the couples afterwards and sort out their albums.'

'Can't you do that while you're down there doing other weddings, and then order them—you surely don't print them, do you?'

She shook her head. 'No. I edit them on my laptop, save them when the couple are happy and get the disk processed by a specialist firm. It's one of the joys of digital photography. And that's another point—we'll need a photographer. I wanted to talk to you about that.'

He lifted a brow. 'That's your department. Got any ideas?'

'Yes—and most of them involve me taking the shots!'

'No,' he said firmly, his eyebrows scrunching down in a frown. 'It's your daughter's wedding. You can't take the photos.'

'No, I know I can't, but I know a man who can,' she said with a slow smile, and Rob smiled back, the frown clearing.

'I was hoping you would. What about Jenni? What will she think of this other person?'

'She's happy. I've asked her. Now I just have

to ask him, see if he's available. He might not be, in which case we'll have to think again, but I'll check with him tomorrow.'

She jotted it on her to-do list, then looked up at Rob. 'Anything else?'

'Not that I can think of. So is that the lot?'

'I believe so, for now.'

'Thank God,' he said, rolling his eyes. 'In which case, as it's a lovely day, why don't we go for a little stroll?'

She studied him warily. She knew him and his little strolls of old. 'Sure. Anywhere in particular?'

He shrugged. 'Wherever you like. I don't mind.'

'There was a glen you took me to, the first time I came up here with you. It was beautiful—so peaceful. I'd love to see it again, maybe take some photos, but I have no idea where it was and I don't suppose you remember.'

'I remember,' he said, his voice suddenly slightly gruff. He cleared his throat and stood up, easing out the kinks in his shoulders with a hearty stretch that made her heart beat just a little faster. 'You'd better change into something warm—jeans and a jumper. I'll see if I can find you some boots. Will Jenni's fit you?'

'Oh—yes. We tend to share them.'

'I might have known you wouldn't have a pair

of your own,' he teased, his voice soft now, and she huffed a little.

'I'll have you know I walk a lot!'

'On pavements. That doesn't count.'

'It most certainly does! I walk miles.'

But he just grinned, and said, 'Tell me that when you're at the top of the ridge,' and opening the door, he ushered her out, that smile still playing around his eyes and making her heart do funny things.

Things it should have got over years ago.

'Ten minutes,' he said. 'I'll meet you in the kitchen.'

And he disappeared off down the back stairs, leaving her to sort herself out.

It really was the most glorious day.

Rob had a small rucksack—'because I know you're going to want to take your fleece off'—and before they left, he smothered her in insect repellent.

She felt like a child, standing with her face upturned while he squirted Deet on his hands and rubbed them together, then wiped them over her cheeks, her brow, her temples, under her chin and down her throat, over the pulse that she knew was hammering under his fingertips.

But he couldn't have noticed, because there wasn't so much as a flicker of reaction, and when he'd done that he gave his hands another squirt and threaded them through her hair, gently massaging the spray into her scalp before stepping back and doing the same to himself before dropping the bottle into the rucksack.

'Right, let's go.'

He turned away, the dogs at his heels, and she followed him, her eyes fixed on his back, trying not to notice the flex of taut muscles as he strode up the steep slope behind the castle, heading for the path that they'd taken before.

She didn't think about his muscles for long, though, because her own took over in protest. After a short while she started breathing harder, then her thighs started to ache, and she concentrated on putting one foot in front of the other until they reached the top of the rise, by which time her thighs were screaming and Jenni's boots were beginning to rub.

She was hot, too, but there was no way she was giving Rob her fleece to carry, so she tied it round her waist and slogged on without a word.

The way levelled out then, to her relief, running along the back of a ridge and heading out into the hills above the village. They were walking in woodland, scrubby trees and rhododendrons mostly, interspersed with conifers and gnarled, twisted birches with nothing but the odd scuttle in the undergrowth to disturb the peace. The path was broader here, and he held back until she fell into step beside him.

'OK?'

'I'm fine,' she lied, wishing she'd put thicker socks on. 'You?'

He eyed her fleece and gave her an enigmatic smile. 'I'm fine,' he echoed. They walked on in silence for a while, but unlike some of the silences they'd shared recently, this one was companionable.

'We used to do this a lot,' she said, after a while. 'Before Jenni.'

He gave a small grunt of acknowledgement, and draped his arm around her shoulders, giving her a brief hug. 'We did. Seems a long time ago. Lot of water under a lot of bridges.'

'Tell me about it,' she muttered, and she was just wondering if it would be a totally stupid idea to slide her arm round his waist when he dropped his and moved away, leaving her feeling ridiculously bereft.

But he was only heading up a narrow path, turning from time to time to help her up a tricky bit, and every time he did that, every time he wrapped his warm, hard hand around hers to steady her, she felt a jolt right down to her toes. Crazy. She had to keep this in perspective, remember that he was only doing this so they could be friends, looking to the future, to the time when they would be grandparents, though how they were meant to be grandparents when they'd hardly even managed to be parents was a mystery to her.

With any luck Jenni and Alec wouldn't be in any hurry to start a family, though, and maybe by the time they did she would have got her feelings for Rob under control.

Huh. Fat chance, she thought, and tripped over a root she'd failed to see. His hand flew out and steadied her, solid and reliable, there for her in the way he should have been all those years ago, and as she trudged after him she tried to work out when it had all gone wrong. Before Jenni, maybe? When he'd gone away to the navy and left her behind?

No. They'd been blissfully happy whenever he'd been at home, which had been quite frequently at first. It was only once he'd gone to sea that the gaps had been longer. Too long.

She gave a little shiver, suddenly oppressed by the trees, but then it opened out, the woodland giving way to glorious open country, glens and mountains stretching away in front of them, gilded by the spring sunshine, and they paused to take in the view while she got her breath back.

And it was spectacular. The colours were amazing in the sun. Greens and golds and purples and a rich, peaty brown—it was beautiful, as lovely as she'd remembered it, and she felt her heart lift. 'It's just stunning,' she said in awe, reaching for her camera, and he smiled.

'It is, isn't it? I never get tired of it.'

'Even in the rain?' she teased, turning to fire off some shots of him, but he just shook his head, his smile wry as she kept on shooting.

'Never. We need the rain. The whole ecosystem of the peat bogs and granite escarpments depends on it.'

'Including the midges,' she said, slapping her neck ruefully, and he pulled the bottle of insect repellent out again and reapplied it, his fingers firm and deft, setting her heart off again and sending shivers of aching need racing all over her body.

'You used to do this before,' she murmured, and his eyes darkened, locking with hers, the expression in them guarded. For what seemed like an age, they stood there, eyes locked, his pupils dark with some nameless emotion that made her want to cry.

'That was a long time ago, Maisie,' he said gruffly, and recapped the bottle as he stepped away from her, giving her room to breathe. He threw the bottle back in the rucksack, turned on his heel and set off again along the ridge, following the path to the head of the glen while she trailed behind him and cursed her stupid overactive hormones.

Except, of course, it was nothing to do with hormones, and everything to do with the fact that she still loved him, and always had.

CHAPTER SIX

HE could hear her breathing hard behind him, but never once did she make a murmur, and after another short climb he stopped and turned towards her.

She couldn't have been looking, her eyes trained on the path, and she cannoned into him, her soft, warm body colliding with his chest with a breathy 'Oomph', and his hands came up to catch her.

She felt so good. Too good, and holding her was making him ache for her all over again. He still hadn't got over holding her that morning, when he'd taken her into his arms and hugged her, and if he didn't let go of her soon, he wasn't going to be able to. He steadied her, then let her go, stepping back and dragging in some of the fresh, moist air before he did something stupid like kiss her.

'Still think you're fit?' he teased to get a rise

out of her and lighten the atmosphere, but she just laughed grimly and tipped back her head and met his eyes in challenge, and heat slammed through him again.

'I'm fine,' she said determinedly, but he knew she wasn't. There'd been a hitch in her stride, just the merest suggestion of a limp, and he thought the boots might be rubbing.

'Good,' he said evenly, and shucking off the rucksack he sat down on a dry rock and pulled it open. 'I thought we could sit here and take in the view for a few minutes before we head back. I can't afford to be out too long, I've got things to do. Guests to see to.'

Guilt brushed her eyes, and he felt an echo of it clutch his gut. He was lying—partly to save her from herself, because he knew she would go on until she was on her knees, and partly because every cell in his body was screamingly aware of their isolation.

They were utterly alone, with only the dogs and the wildlife for company, and it was too tempting. Too—dammit—too dangerous. And he wanted to apologise for lying, but then he'd have to explain why, and he wasn't going there to save his life.

'I'm sorry. I didn't mean to take you away from your work,' she said, but he shook his head, the guilt eating him.

'Forget it. It was my idea to go for a walk. Here—present from Mrs McCrae.'

And he handed her a chunk of gingerbread, then poured two steaming mugs of tea while the dogs lined up and stared hopefully at them both, just in case. Just like him with Maisie.

'Not a chance,' he told them with irony as she reached for the tea, their fingers brushing and sending a current surging through him.

He pulled his hand back, shocked at the strength of his reaction. How could he still want her? After all this time, how could he still need her so badly? Because he did need her, and for two pins he'd have her back.

The realisation held him immobile for a second, but she didn't notice, she was staring out over the glen, her eyes soft-focused.

'It really is so beautiful here,' she said, her voice slightly awestruck, as if she'd only just remembered it. And maybe she had, he thought. Maybe, for the first time since she'd gone away, she was starting to remember the good times. And they had had good times—lots of them. He wondered if she was thinking about them. She wasn't even taking photographs, just soaking it all up, her expression rapt and somehow wistful as she turned to him.

'No wonder you love it so much.'

He nodded. He couldn't speak, because it

wasn't the countryside he was looking at, it was Maisie, and he loved her so much it hurt.

Still, after everything, he loved her.

'We had some good times, didn't we, Rob?' she asked, her voice soft as she echoed his thoughts, and he nodded again.

'Yes, Maisie. We had some good times. Very good times.'

She sighed quietly. 'I loved you, Rob,' she murmured. 'I loved you so much, and I really thought you loved me. What went wrong?'

'I don't know.' It was the honest truth, perhaps the first time he'd faced it. Sitting here with her now, he realised he actually didn't know what had gone wrong. He'd always thought she'd walked away from a good marriage, but now he wasn't so sure. She'd walked away from a situation more intolerable than he'd realised, but there had been more wrong with it than that, and maybe they'd both assumed that love alone would have been enough to make it work.

And of course it wasn't enough. It needed work, effort, application on both sides. And it would have helped a whole lot if they hadn't both been kids.

She turned back, and then her eyes narrowed. 'Is that an eagle?' she asked, her voice soft, and he leant closer and peered along her arm, feeling her thrill as they watched the bird riding the thermals.

'Yes. The male, I believe.'

'Oh, why didn't I bring my long zoom with me?' she wailed under her breath. 'I wish I had some binoculars—'

He was already reaching in the rucksack for them, and he pulled them out with a rueful grin. 'You wanted binoculars?'

She turned to look at him and started to laugh. 'What else have you got in there, Mary Poppins?' she asked him, and he gave a rusty chuckle and passed her the glasses.

'Oh, now, let me see, there's a standard lamp, and—'

'Idiot. Oh, I can't see it any more.'

'No. They're elusive and they blend incredibly well with the landscape. They're nesting over in the next glen, but it's hard to get to—which, of course, makes it a perfect choice as a nesting site, so you were very lucky to spot him, but it tends to frustrate the guests. There are lots of buzzards, though, and that tends to get them pretty excited when they mistake them for the eagles.' He grinned. 'We call them tourist eagles.'

She laughed softly. 'That's mean.'

'No, it's not. We don't lie to them, but if they come back all excited and tell us they've seen eagles and we know they'd be really disappointed if we told them the truth, we let them believe it, even though the buzzards are incredible in their own right. Beautiful birds, but the punters want eagles. It makes them happy, and we like happy customers.'

'Does that include me? Because if it wasn't an eagle, I'd rather you didn't lie to me. I think buzzards are just as lovely. They're one of the things I remember.'

His heart squeezed in his chest, and he managed a smile. 'I'm not lying to you, Maisie,' he assured her softly. 'It was definitely an eagle. I'm just not sure if it was the male or the female. The buzzards have different markings.'

'How can you see from that range?' she asked, and he chuckled quietly.

'One of the advantages of long sight. It makes up for the frustration of holding things at arm's length to read the small print.'

She smiled at that and turned back, scouring the glen for another glimpse of the magnificent bird, but it was gone, so she turned her attention to the gingerbread and he had to drag his eyes off her. Again.

'Jenni tells me you've been renting out the cottages to holidaymakers for a while now,' she said softly after a few minutes. 'How's it going?'

'Very well,' he said, nodding slowly. 'We do low-impact holidays—boat trips, guided walks, a little fishing, some deer stalking, but only with cameras, and the fishing's all catch and release. And to be fair the trout are pretty wily, so they don't get caught often. The visitors come for the walking and the wildlife, mostly, but they keep us out of mischief, and it pays the running costs of the estate. It can get a bit manic, though, in the summer, with them all wanting a piece of you at the same time.'

'How many cottages are there?'

'On the estate? Twelve, but Alec's parents have one, and the ghillie has one, and of course Jenni and Alec will have the gatehouse, so that leaves nine for letting, but two of those only sleep two.'

'And the rest?'

'The biggest takes eight. Our total capacity's forty, so in the summer Saturdays can be a bit crazy, but we have a brilliant team from the village who come and clean and turn them round. And once Jenni's up here she's going to be joining the team full time. We're going to use one of the rooms in the gatehouse as a reception and welcome centre for the guests as they arrive, a first point of contact, and that'll be her focus. She's going to be our front-of-house girl.'

'Yes, she mentioned that. She'll be good at it, I can see her doing that. She's got your easy charm with people, always has had. Maybe it's a shame she didn't study hospitality and tourism. It might have been more relevant than history.'

'No. She's enjoyed history, and it's equally appropriate. She's been working her way through the books in the library here, cataloguing them, and she's found all sorts of interesting old tomes. You ought to get her to show you if you get a moment before the wedding.'

The word seemed to bring her back down to earth with a bump. She chewed her lip, so that he wanted to reach out his thumb and soothe it, then kiss it better.

'This wedding,' she said, her brow puckering in a little frown.

He made himself concentrate. 'What about it?'

'It's a really busy time for you, isn't it?'

'Pretty busy. Still, it won't be a problem. The grounds are always kept tidy for the guests, and the house has been decorated from end to end in the last two years, so there isn't much to do in that way. And trust me, we'll have a fleet of staff to do all the to-ing and fro-ing. It'll be pretty painless, I think.'

Maisie wasn't so sure. She wondered if he'd missed the point, but she'd been to more weddings than he had and she had a better idea of what was in store. Let him think the worst was over for now. There was plenty of time to disillusion him.

'Still, I didn't realise the planning would be such a killer,' he went on, his smile wry.

'I bet you thought it would all be over in a day.'

'That long? Try five minutes.'

Maisie laughed until her sides ached, then sighed softly, wishing they'd had more moments like this, moments of humour. Maybe then they could have made it work, been there for each other when things had gone wrong. 'Well, as I said before, we'll only have to do this once.' She studied him thoughtfully, but his eyes were veiled so she couldn't see their expression. 'Does that worry you? I know what you said this morning, that one is more than enough, but I've often wondered if you mind that your only child is a girl?'

He shook his head slowly. 'No. No, I don't mind. I love her to bits, and I wouldn't change her for anything. And I don't think she's suffered from being an only child. I was an only child, and it has advantages in some ways, but—well, whatever. I would have liked more, but you don't always get what you want and I'm not complaining.'

'You could have married again—had a son to hand the estate on to. I should've thought you'd want that.'

He shot her an enigmatic look. 'No, Maisie. I haven't, I didn't, and I'm not about to now. And I don't need a son. I've got Alec, and I've got a lot of time for him. He's done well for himself, worked hard, and he knows the farm inside out. And he's taken it very seriously—he's got two degrees now, in agricultural science and agro-management, he's very into expanding our potential. He's a real asset. I'm proud of him—and, no, I didn't have a son of my own, but Alec is the next best thing, and I'm more than happy that he's marrying our little girl.'

He eyed her thoughtfully. 'Anyway, you can talk. What about you? I would have thought you'd marry again, have more children. You always said you wanted lots of babies, but maybe having Jenni put you off.'

'No. Not at all,' she said quietly, thinking of the babies they might have had together—the only babies she'd ever wanted. There'd been men she'd met over the years, decent men, men who'd tried to persuade her to have a relationship. Men who might have married her. But they hadn't been Rob, and he was the only man she wanted. The only man she'd ever wanted.

'If I'd wanted more children, I could easily have had more,' she told him matter-of-factly. 'Children are easy to get, Rob. It's bringing them up and dealing with the emotional fallout that's the hard bit. But if you're asking if I regret that our relationship didn't work, that she didn't have two parents in the same place and siblings and a more normal family life, then the answer's yes. But it didn't happen, and no amount of regret's going to change that.'

She turned her head to meet his eyes, and saw a flash of pain in their slate-blue depths.

'No,' he said, his voice quietly sincere, filled with a sorrow she knew was as deep as hers. He reached out and cupped her face in his warm, slightly roughened palm, his thumb stroking lightly over her cheek as he held her eyes.

'I never should have let you go,' he said gruffly. 'I should have followed you, made you talk to me. I should have found a way for us to be together somehow. Why the hell didn't I, Maisie? Why the hell didn't I come after you?'

She swallowed hard, then closed her eyes. 'I don't know, Rob. I have no idea at all.'

She emptied her cup out onto the grass, handed it back to him and stood up, wincing at her aching muscles and wondering how she'd thought she was fit. Wondering about anything except why he hadn't followed her, because that hurt too much to think about.

'Come on, Mackenzie,' she said, turning her back on him and heading down the track towards the castle. 'I thought you had things to do?'

They went to church the next morning, listened to the banns being read from their position in the Laird's loft up above the congregation, and then they were subjected to a hail of congratulations and good wishes from the people of the village. As a consequence it took an age to get away, and by the time they got back to the castle it was time for lunch.

Mercifully, because it meant there was less time to talk, and the less time they had, the better. The tension was simmering between them, and every time she caught Rob's eye, it was as if he was staring right down inside her, looking for an answer.

Well, he wouldn't find it in her, she was sure. She didn't know the answer. She wasn't even sure she knew the question. But despite the tension, they got done everything that could be done over the weekend, and all that remained was a few calls to make the following day. So Rob booked her return sleeper on the Sunday evening, with her standing beside him at his desk in the study overlooking the sea, and she watched the last dying rays of the evening sun stretch across the endless sky, and wondered why she was going back so soon.

It didn't seem so imperative any more, and she found she had a curious reluctance to leave. Not that it was easy, with the tension between them pulling them every which way, and maybe it would be better to be apart just now, let the new, tentative friendship between them settle into their lives without pushing it. Or jeopardising it with some hasty and ill-considered action.

Like resting her hand on his shoulder, stooping down and pressing a kiss to his thick, dark hair with its little threads of silver that somehow made him even more attractive. Like tilting his face back and pressing her lips to his, turning to sit on his lap and sliding her arms around his neck…

'Right, that's that done,' he said, pushing back his chair and turning to look up at her, and she met his eyes and smiled somehow.

'Thank you.'

'You don't have to go,' he said, as if he was reading her mind. 'I can change it to a later date.'

She shook her head before she could let him talk her out of it. 'No, Rob, I need to get back. I've got things to do. We both have.'

By the time she set off the following evening, the rest of the arrangements were falling neatly into place. The hotel was booked for the catering, they were going to the hotel that night for a food tasting, something Maisie was sure they could do without her, and the piper and ceilidh band were booked. And Jeff was free to take the photographs, to her immense relief, because he was the only person she trusted to take the sort of shots she would have taken herself. She had lots of pictures of the castle and grounds, the ruin—and Rob, of course, taken on their walk. She'd put them into a separate file.

He took her to the station, put her on the train

and then hesitated, standing in the tiny little cabin so that she felt all the air had been sucked out of it.

His face was troubled, his eyes guarded, and for a moment they stood there and looked at each other in silence.

Then he reached for her and pulled her gently into his arms, enfolding her against his chest so she could feel the steady, even beating of his heart. 'Thank you for coming,' he murmured. 'And I'm sorry about all the things that have happened. I didn't realise it had been so hard for you here, and I'm really grateful for your help. I'm so glad you came.'

'I had no choice, Rob. I did it for Jenni,' she reminded him gently, and he gave a quiet sigh and let her go, holding her shoulders, staring down into her eyes with an expression she couldn't quite understand.

'Don't leave it too long before you're back,' he said, and ducking his head he brushed his lips lightly over hers, turned on his heel and strode away.

She closed the door and sat down abruptly on the bunk. Her lips tingled, and she lifted her hand and touched her fingertips to the place where his lips had been so fleetingly.

Not fleetingly enough. Her lips were still tingling when the train pulled out of the station over half an hour later, at the start of the long journey away from him.

And not, it seemed, before time.

Life got back to normal, slowly, but somehow it didn't feel quite the same.

There were the flowers, for a start.

They arrived the day she got back, a beautifully presented hand-tied posy of spring flowers, simple and delicate but absolutely perfect. There was a card, written in a woman's hand, of course, not his dark, slashing script that was all but illegible. It said, quite simply, 'Rob. X'

A kiss. Just the one, like the kiss he'd feathered across her lips on the train just last night. She pressed her lips together, sniffed the flowers—they smelled gorgeous, a taste of spring—and she set them in the middle of the dining table that served as her desk, so she could look at them as she worked.

Look at them and think of him.

She had a phone call later in the week, and the first thing she did was thank him for them.

'My pleasure,' he murmured, and she felt the words cruise over her nerve endings like a dancing flame.

'So, how are things?' she asked, picturing him in his study, feet up on the old desk, the sea view stretched out in front of him.

'Fine. Jenni's back at uni, the dress is hanging up in her bedroom here, wrapped in a cloth cover as instructed, we've got the veil and everyone's happy,' Rob reported.

'How was the food tasting?'

'Good. We're still deciding, but the standard is excellent. We were very pleased. And otherwise I think all the arrangements are under way. How about you?'

'Oh, I'm busy. I'm up to my eyes. You were lucky to catch me, I'm just going out to meet a bride to talk wedding photos.'

'Well, I won't hold you up. Take care.'

'You, too.'

She put the phone down, thinking that even a fortnight ago such a phone call would have been unheralded. Brief though it had been, it was another plank on the bridge they were building, and as she raced off for her meeting, his voice was carried with her in her head.

She was ridiculously busy for the next few weeks, both with her photography and with features for the paper. They found out at the office that her daughter was getting married, and immediately sent her to cover a society wedding.

Then there was a spread about the cost of getting married, with budget and lavish options. It was an eye-opener, even for her with all the weddings she'd been involved in.

So was her bank statement. She hadn't looked at the prices when she'd paid for Jenni's dress and her outfit, but she could see the amount on the statement now, and she pulled the receipt out of her handbag and studied it, and winced.

Never mind. Jenni would look stunning in the dress, and she'd been thrilled with her mother's outfit.

Maisie herself still wasn't sure about it. It hung in the wardrobe, waiting for her to find time to accessorise it—or alternatively replace it with something less, well, less likely to 'blow Dad's socks off', as Jenni had so subtly put it.

She didn't want to blow his socks off. Far too dangerous. And after that kiss on the train, however brief and fleeting, she wondered just how easy it might be. She'd felt a simmering energy in him in the last few days of her visit, a raw, untamed side that she'd never seen before, and it thrilled her and terrified her all at once.

But going there would be potentially more foolish now than it had been twenty-one years ago, so she had no intention of poking the sleeping tiger.

Except maybe he wasn't sleeping, just lying with one eye slightly open, waiting for an unwary move. And, meanwhile, the dress hung in her wardrobe, taunting her. So she ignored it, put the wedding out of her mind and concentrated on her work. Until Rob phoned again.

* * *

'Maisie.'

Just the one word, but all her senses were on red alert, her body humming.

'Hi. Problems?'

'No, not exactly. Look, I'm in London, I had one or two things to do, but I'm finished now—can I come and see you? I've got the invitations, and you said you'd write them, so I thought I could drop them off with the guest list—and there are one or two other details. I thought maybe we could discuss them over dinner, if you aren't busy?'

'I thought the details were sorted? Does it really need dinner?' she asked, panicking a little because dinner…well, it sounded a little bit like a date, and she wasn't at all sure she was ready for a date with Robert Mackenzie.

'No, not really, I suppose. I could just drop the invitations off, have a quick run-through of my thoughts and then set off again, but I have to eat at some point, and…' She almost heard the shrug, and then he carried on, 'Anyway, I thought we were supposed to be making friends.'

They were. She thought of their grandchildren, years down the line, and sighed inwardly. She'd just have to keep a lid on her feelings, however hard it was. 'Of course. Sorry. Yes, that sounds OK. I'm not busy tonight.'

'Great. Do you want me to make a reservation somewhere, or will you do it?'

'I'll do it,' she said quickly. She couldn't trust him not to find somewhere—romantic. Intimate. She'd book a table in a noisy, bustling place—she didn't want him getting any wrong ideas, and romantic and intimate were definitely wrong.

'Thanks. That would make sense. And then I can set off tomorrow morning early for the drive home—if you don't mind putting me up, that is.'

He wanted to *stay*? Her heart flipped and started to race, and a million excuses ran through her head, but they were exactly that, excuses, and she had agreed to do the invitations. And dinner. And be friends. But *stay*? After that kiss?

'Of course you can stay,' she said at last. 'You can have Jenni's room. It's your house, after all.'

'Hardly. It's not been my house for the last twenty years.'

'That's a technicality,' she said, and there was a second's silence.

'Maisie, it's your *home*,' he said, sounding stunned.

'Well, whatever,' she said quietly, her emotions tumbling. It was her home—of course it was her home, but at the same time, Rob haunted it, the memory of him soaked into the very fabric, so that she'd never felt she could do certain things in it. Things like take a lover, and bring him back to her bedroom, the room where she'd made love with Rob, so that she could try and erase him from her memory. Not that there had ever been anyone.

'Look, I'm busy, I don't need to get into this now, I'm due out. What time are you coming?'

'I thought I'd leave now. I want to get out of London before the traffic builds up. I should be with you by one at the latest. Is that OK?'

'I should be back. I've got to go and deliver an album to someone. Have you got your key still?'

'Not with me. Don't worry, if you aren't there I can amuse myself. Just call me when you're done. I'll see you later.'

'OK. I'll see you,' she said, wondering how long she'd be.

She looked at her watch. Nine thirty-nine—so nearly ten. She was due with Annette at ten-thirty, but she phoned her to find out if she could come earlier, and was greeted with delight.

'Of course! I'm longing to see the albums, I can't believe you've got them printed so quickly. Do come now. I'll put the kettle on.'

She was there just after ten, and Annette greeted her at the door in a flowing caftan with a bandana round her head.

'Hi, come in, it's lovely to see you,' she said, and kissed Maisie on the cheek. 'Coffee?'

'That would be lovely. How are you?'

'Oh, you know,' she said, wrinkling her nose.

'I'm halfway through my first chemo, and my hair's started to come out in clumps already so I've had it shaved, but I'm too old to look interesting and elegant, so I've wrapped it up and gone ethnic instead! But my scan was clear, no more hot spots, so things are looking good. Fingers crossed. Biscuit?'

'Oh, I shouldn't but I don't care. Yes, please!'

They chuckled as Annette raided a cupboard and produced some utterly wicked chocolate biscuits, poured boiling water into the cafetière and headed through to the sitting room. 'Right, let's see these albums. I can't wait.'

They were in the style of a coffee-table book, with some pages containing just one image, and others containing several scattered casually over the page. And there were some gorgeous ones of Annette with her daughter.

'Oh, Maisie, it's wonderful! Oh, thank you so much,' Annette said, sniffing and mopping her eyes. 'Oh, how silly of me. I'm sorry, I feel really overwhelmed by them, you've really captured the day, they're beautiful, and I just love having them in a real book. Oh, thank you so much. You've been so kind and understanding.'

'Don't be silly. It's been a pleasure working with you all and getting to know you, and I'm thrilled with them. In fact, I've stolen some of the ideas for my daughter Jenni's wedding.'

'She's getting married? Oh, how exciting! When? You haven't mentioned it.'

'June. I found out the day before Lucy's wedding—she just phoned up and announced they were getting married in eleven weeks! So I've been stealing ideas right, left and centre!'

'Of course you have—and it's perfectly possible to do in that time. We did it in less, and I don't think it could have been better for another year of preparation. Oh, I'm so thrilled for you, I do hope you have a fabulous day. So where's the wedding?'

She pulled a face. 'In Scotland—just north-west of Fort William. I'd rather it was here, of course, but that's just unrealistic, and Ardnashiel's a fabulous location.'

Annette's eyes narrowed thoughtfully and she tipped her head on one side. 'Not the castle?'

'Yes—her father owns it,' she admitted.

Her eyes widened, and she smiled delightedly. 'Robert Mackenzie's her father?'

Maisie was startled. 'Yes—do you know him?' she asked, surprised.

'I lectured him years ago. Must be—twenty-something? So did you meet him here?'

Maisie pulled a face. 'Yes. Just after he graduated. I went to look at his house, and we—well, we ended up getting married a little hastily. Jenni was the result. It—er—it didn't work out, though.'

Annette made a soft sound of commiseration and squeezed her hand. 'Oh, I'm sorry. I've been so lucky in that way. Did you marry again?'

'No. No, once was enough.'

'So he was the only one for you?'

Her eyes filled and she looked away quickly. 'Well, you know him. He's that kind of person, really. Hard to follow.'

'Yes, I can imagine. He was a brilliant student—I always wondered what happened to him. So has he inherited the estate now?'

'Yes.'

'Which must make him the Laird, of course.'

Maisie nodded. 'Yes. And, of course, that rather dictates the wedding. It's not very convenient for me, with all the long-distance planning, but it's better for everybody else, and even if we could find a better setting, it wouldn't be right for Jenni to get married in any other place.'

'No—and I imagine it's beautiful. He talked about it once or twice—it sounded as if he really loved it, as if it filled his soul.'

She nodded again, amazed that Annette remembered him so well. 'I think it does, and it is beautiful, especially the countryside around there. I felt that more this time than I have before—I've always found it a bit daunting in the past. It's gorgeous in the summer, but it can be a bit bleak in the winter, and the castle was a bit austere then. He's made lots of changes, though, and it's much more welcoming.'

'There was a dungeon, wasn't there?'

'Oh, yes. I'd forgotten that. It's got a slit in the wall, high up, so the smells from the kitchen could drift down and torment the prisoners. I used to lie awake and wonder how many of the kitchen staff threw food to them, and what it was like down there.'

'Horrible, I expect. The warring Highland clans could be pretty uncompromising. Not that Robert was ever like that.'

'Oh, he can be,' she said softly, wondering if that was why he hadn't followed her. 'Compromise isn't exactly his middle name—but he's learning! The wedding's forcing him to, and he's a good father. He's taking all the wedding stuff very well.'

Annette chuckled. 'It can be a bit full on, can't it?' Her smile faded. 'I'd love to see him again. I was always very fond of him.'

'I'm amazed you remember him.'

'Oh, Robert was unforgettable. As you said yourself.'

So true. Maisie took a slow breath and tried not to dwell on that. 'He's down here at the moment, actually. He had some things to do in London, and he's on the way here now to drop some things off and sort out a few details. Would you like me to ask him to pop in while he's in Cambridge?'

Her eyes lit up, but then she shook her head. 'Oh, he won't remember me.'

'I'm sure he will. I'll ask him—if you like.'

'Would you? I would love to see him, but only if he's got time.'

'I'll ask him.' She could see Annette was flagging, so she gathered her things and stood up. 'I'll leave you in peace now. I ought to be getting back. I'll get him to ring and arrange a time to visit you, if you like?'

'Would you? Thank you so much—and thank you again for the photographs. I know I've said it before, but it was a real pleasure to have you there, and you couldn't possibly have done a better job. We were all thrilled.'

'Oh, Annette, bless you. It was a real privilege to share it with you.' She stooped to kiss her cheek, and then let herself out and drove home.

That word again.

Odd, how it could be home and yet still feel like his house, as if the bricks and mortar held the memory of his presence. No wonder she'd never moved on.

His car was outside when she pulled up, and he was sitting there with the roof down, his head tipped back and his eyes shut, listening to the radio.

'You made good time,' she said, pausing by the car, and he opened one eye and sat up.

'Yeah, the road was good. Am I in your space?'

She laughed. 'There's no such thing as my space. I park wherever I can. Here, take my permit and put it in your windscreen or you'll get a ticket. I'll be back in a minute.'

That was one of the disadvantages of being in a university town as steeped in history as Cambridge was. She was right in the thick of the colleges, close to the river and handy for the town. Any spaces going were either metered or occupied by residents, but her neighbours allowed her to park in their drive, and she turned in there now and headed back to him.

The hood was up now, and he was propped against the car, his long legs crossed at the ankle, a soft leather case at his feet and a heavy-duty carrier bag in his hand.

'Invitations?'

'Amongst other things.' He picked up his case and followed her up the little path to the front door, then into the little terraced house that she didn't feel was hers.

Crazy, he thought. Why hadn't she told him? He'd had no idea that she felt like that—no idea about so many things, he admitted. His mother, for instance, and the way she'd been to Maisie while he'd been at sea.

'Jenni sends her love,' he said as she closed the door behind them.

'How is she? I spoke to her the other day, she sounded a bit hassled.'

'She is. She's been working hard. The dress is lovely, by the way. It looks shockingly expensive.'

She laughed, a little rueful smile playing around her mouth. 'It was,' she admitted. 'But I wanted to do it for her, and it's absolutely gorgeous on.'

'I know. I saw it. I went with them. Mum was very pleased to be included, by the way, and she was delighted with the veil.'

'Which one did she go for?' Maisie asked, unpacking a bag and piling stuff into the fridge.

'Long—very simple. She said she wants some photos up in the ruined tower. She thought the long one, blowing in the wind, could make some spectacular photos.'

'She's right. I'll brief Jeff before the day.'

He laughed and propped himself against the worktop so he could see her face. 'I'm sure you will,' he said drily.

She arched a brow and walked away, putting the kettle on. 'Talking of photos, I've got a message for you from Annette Grainger.'

He did a mild double-take. 'Really? Dr Grainger? How do you know her?' he asked.

'She's the mother of the bride I told you about—the one starting chemo.'

He felt a wave of denial. 'Oh, no. Not her.'

'It's OK, it's not looking too bad. Her scan's come back clear, and she's sounding hopeful. She said she'd love to see you again. I told her I'd get you to ring her.'

'Sure. I'd love to see her. Should I call her now?'

'No, better leave it for a while. She was looking tired—that's where I was just now. She's probably resting. Call her later, before we go out.'

She pulled two mugs out and set them on the worktop. 'I didn't know what you wanted for lunch, so I grabbed a few things—pre-prepared salads, that sort of thing. I thought I'd keep it simple if we're going out tonight.'

He nodded, then shrugged away from the side and rammed his hands in his pockets to keep them out of mischief. He didn't want to think about tonight. 'How do you fancy a picnic?'

'A picnic?'

'Mmm. I thought we could go punting.'

'Punting?' she said, as if he'd suggested eating underwater, and then she smiled slowly, her eyes soft. 'I haven't been punting for years. I went a few years ago, with Jenni and Alec, but I was so busy watching them together and trying to deal with their blindingly obvious devotion to each other that I didn't really take it in. Before then—well, that was really years ago.'

Twenty-something? He didn't want to go there, so he stuck to Jenni and Alec. 'So—how do you feel about them now? Are you more accepting of their relationship?' he asked, and she nodded.

'Oh, yes,' she said calmly. 'I've always been happy about their relationship, it was just getting married so young, but having seen them together in Scotland—well, you're right, they fit together as if they were made for each other. I still think they're very young but, as you say, they know each other inside out, and better this way than the way we did it.'

Her words hung in the air, the tension suddenly ratcheting up a notch, and he let out a short sigh and nodded.

'Yes. I agree. So—picnic on a punt?'

She pulled herself together. 'Yes—sure. Let's see what I've got.'

She hauled everything out of the fridge again, and they made ham salad rolls with a dollop of coleslaw, and packed them up with some cold barbecued chicken legs and juicy cherry tomatoes and a packet of hand-cooked crisps. Then she added a pack of fresh cream chocolate éclairs, and he started to chuckle.

'Well, I suppose the tomatoes are healthy,' he teased, and she blushed and pulled out a bottle of mineral water.

'I wasn't really thinking. I just grabbed stuff quickly. If you're going to complain…'

'I'm not complaining!' he said, throwing his hands up and trying not to laugh. 'Really, I'm not complaining. I'm starving, I missed breakfast because I was working late and overslept. It looks great.'

'Well, we'd better go, then,' she said, zipping up the cool bag, and he took it from her and ushered her out of the door.

They walked the short distance to the river, arriving just as a punt was being returned. 'Two hours?' he asked her, and she nodded.

'One's not enough, not if we're going to take time to enjoy it,' she said, and then wondered if two hours alone on a boat with him would be such a good idea after all.

Exccpt, of course, they were hardly alone. They were surrounded by rank amateurs, and college students taking guided punts to earn a bit of extra money, and on a lovely early May Saturday, the river was heaving.

They set off, him balancing easily on the stern, her sitting in the bows facing him. She had the best view from there. She could watch the river go by, and as an added bonus she could watch Rob, his muscles moving smoothly under the soft jersey shirt he was wearing, his thighs braced as he pushed away from the wall to avoid a group of girls who were wildly out of control.

They looked like girls on a hen weekend, Maisie thought, looking at their silly printed T-shirts and the glasses of champagne, and she wondered what Jenni was doing for hers, if anything.

The punt jolted, and the girls giggled, the girl standing on the back wobbling wildly and letting out a little shriek.

'Steady,' Rob said, grabbing her arm as she flailed, and she straightened up and flashed him a smile that made Maisie want to scratch her eyes out.

'Sorry!' She giggled, and hit the wall again.

He shook his head and smiled at Maisie. 'Kids.'

Kids? There was nothing of the child in that young woman's look, she thought, and wondered if he'd even noticed. Possibly not. She was about Jenni's age, maybe a little older, and it was quite gratifying that he wasn't eyeing her up, because she was very pretty.

'Just because you're so darned good at it,' she said drily, and he grinned and ducked to go under another bridge.

'All that practice. It's great for impressing the girls.'

She knew that. As a girl she'd been very impressed by his skill with the punt. Very impressed with his skill with everything, come to that.

She looked away hastily, studying the backs of the colleges, seeing them as you only did from the river.

'Shall we tie up here?' he suggested when they reached an area of open grass, and they secured the punt to the rings on the side and climbed out, settling down on the grass with the cool bag.

He handed her a roll, and she ate it staring out across the river Cam, studying the glorious architecture of the ancient colleges and wishing things had been different, wishing that they'd settled here, that he'd never joined the navy, that they'd had more children and Ardnashiel had never been part of their lives.

She ripped open the crisps and dropped a handful in her lap, then picked up a chicken leg.

'Penny for them.'

'Not a chance,' she said, and sank her teeth into the chicken.

CHAPTER SEVEN

HE didn't know what to make of her.

No surprises there, he never did know what to make of her. Never had. But today—one minute she was sitting there watching him in the boat and laughing with him at the antics of some of the punters, the next she looked as if her best friend had kicked her puppy.

And she clearly didn't want to talk about it, so he ignored her, lay down on his back on the fresh spring grass and listened to the sound of laughter, the odd shriek or splash, hasty apologies as punts collided with dull thuds. He could hear children playing, people strolling past, a dog barking in the distance. And Maisie rustling in the bag.

'Want an éclair?'

He opened one eye and peered up at her. She was dangling one above his face, just out of reach, and so just for the hell of it he opened his mouth and waited.

And waited.

And then she lowered it, putting the end in his mouth so he could bite it off, the soft, squashy pastry giving way so the cream oozed out and smeared on his lips. He licked them, and her eyes widened slightly. And as he watched her, she took a bite herself, and the sensual imagery slammed through him.

'Hey, that's mine,' he said, sitting up abruptly to take the rest of it from her before she could blow his mind, but she just laughed and took another bite and handed him the box.

'Have your own,' she said through a mouthful of cream, and then licked her fingers.

She was trying to kill him.

He took one and ate it sitting up, one leg drawn up and his arm curled round his knee, avoiding looking at her and eating it systematically and—almost impossibly—without licking his lips. Or his fingers.

He wiped them instead on a tissue, and still didn't look at her. He wasn't playing that game any more. Too dangerous. He'd end up making a fool of himself over her, and he'd done that once before and had never got over it. He wasn't doing it again.

'So, where does Annette live now?' he asked, and the conversation moved to safer topics.

* * *

He went alone to see Annette. He took her flowers—green and white, on Maisie's advice—and rang the bell.

She opened the door almost instantly, as if she'd been waiting for him, and her face lit up.

'Rob! Oh, how lovely to see you. Oh, I would have known you anywhere. You've hardly changed at all—well, except your hair.'

He grinned at her. 'Well, you can talk,' he said gently, touching the colourful fabric wrapped around her head, and she laughed and reached her arms up and hugged him.

'Bad boy. And you've brought me flowers. How lovely, thank you. They're beautiful. Come on in and tell me all about yourself while I put them in water. I gather you and Maisie have a daughter? You are a dark horse. The last thing I heard you were off to the navy.'

'Yes. I did six years in the submarines.'

And in hindsight, although it had been a valuable and humbling experience and had taught him a great deal about himself, it had probably been the most foolish mistake of his life. Hindsight was a wonderful thing.

He talked to Annette about his business in London, still ticking over nicely in the background, about the castle and the estate, about Jenni and the wedding—and then she asked about Maisie.

'What went wrong?' she said.

He nearly didn't answer, nearly told her to mind her own business, but she'd always had time for him, always listened to him, always been there for him.

'I don't know,' he said at last. 'It was after she had Jenni. I was away, I missed the birth, but things were never the same after that. She— I don't know, she didn't seem to want me, although maybe it started earlier than that. Our marriage didn't get the best of starts.'

'No, she implied it was a bit hasty.'

'Yes. We'd found out she was pregnant. Getting married seemed like a good idea at the time, but we didn't know each other nearly well enough then, of course.'

'And later, when you knew each other better?'

He looked away. 'I'm not sure we ever did. I was away a lot, she was unhappy, and she left, came back to Cambridge.'

'And you let her go.'

'I had nothing to offer her that she wanted.'

'Are you sure? Because that's not the impression I got,' Annette suggested softly, but he shook his head.

'She shut me out. She didn't want me.'

'But, like you, she's never married anyone else, never found another man to make her happy. And when I asked her why, she told me you were hard to follow. Doesn't that tell you something?'

He searched her eyes—kind, sage eyes that had seen so much—and he sighed.

'We're different, Annette. We want different things. She hates Ardnashiel.'

'I don't think she hates it, Rob. I think she was unhappy there, but she spoke quite fondly of it today. Said you'd done a lot to it, and it was much less austere.'

'Well, I've done a bit. It'll never be finished, places like that never are, but I love it. It's home, but Maisie never felt like that. It has bad associations for her. I know it was difficult for her being up there with a small baby while I was away, and I've discovered that my parents didn't make it easy for her. I didn't realise that before. But it's too late for us, Annette. She's built a life for herself here now.'

She leant forward and touched his arm, her fingers gentle. 'Maybe you should try again. Maybe she was waiting for you to ask her, and you didn't. Maybe that was what went wrong.'

Could she be right? Had Maisie simply been waiting for him to follow her, to ask her what had gone wrong so they could put it right?

Maybe. He'd begun to wonder—but that had been a long time ago, and now they had the wedding to get through. Not the time to start dragging skeletons out of cupboards.

Nevertheless, the thought played on his mind as he made his farewells and drove back to Maisie's house. He'd lost his parking place, of course, but it was after six and he found a slot around the corner and went back to find her in her dressing gown in the kitchen, making tea.

'I've just had a shower—I thought I'd do that while you were out so the water had time to heat up again for you. Tea?'

He dragged his eyes off the gaping V of her dressing gown. 'Please. Is there a dress code for this place tonight?'

'Not really. Smart casual? What you've got on would do. So, how did you get on with Annette? Did you recognise her?'

He smiled. 'Oh, yes, of course. She's hardly changed. She spoke very highly of you—and she showed me the wedding photos. They were—well, amazing, really. They took me by surprise. I had no idea you were so gifted.'

She gave him a level look. 'Have you ever checked my website? You probably didn't even know I had one.'

He felt a prickle of guilt, 'I did, but I haven't looked at it.' Avoided it, more like, as he avoided anything to do with her on the grounds of damage limitation, but she didn't know that and she took it as disinterest, if the expression on her face was anything to go by.

'Ah, well, there you go. Perhaps you should have done,' she said tartly. 'Here, your tea.'

And plonking it down in front of him, she took hers and disappeared upstairs with it, closing her bedroom door firmly.

He made a mental note to check her website, and retreated to the sitting room—not the room at the front which he had used and which he saw now she was using as a study, but the room at the back, overlooking the pretty little courtyard garden. She'd made it quite lovely, he realised, a lush little oasis. It was filled with pots and tubs, and although it wasn't the sunniest, the late afternoon sun slanted in and filtered through the leaves of the nearby trees, dappling it with a soft, gentle light.

He'd always loved the garden, and they'd intended to put in doors from this room. They'd talked about it years ago, when they'd first met, and he wondered why she'd never done it. Money? Or because she still felt as if it was his house?

He frowned. That was so silly, but also so typical. She'd always been very sensitive to atmosphere. Maybe she'd never really liked the house?

In which case she should have sold it and moved on.

He sighed, took his empty mug through to the kitchen and then went upstairs. Her door was firmly shut, but she was probably getting ready. Good thing. That dressing gown was just a quick tug away from leaving her naked, and even the thought was enough to scramble what was left of his brains.

He went into Jenni's bedroom, opened his case and found his wash things, then went to have a shower.

A cold one.

She had no idea what to wear.

Jeans and a top? A long, casual skirt? A smart little dress? Or the khaki…?

Jeans, she decided. She was pretty sure the restaurant didn't have a dress code. Although if they did…

OK, not jeans. Trousers? Not a pretty little evening dress. Not something that would leave her legs on show.

She opened the wardrobe and there was the wedding outfit, hanging there in its exclusive little garment bag, tormenting her. *It'll blow Dad's socks off!* She grabbed her plain black trousers, shut the door hastily and leant back against it.

Right, so, trousers, and—a jumper? She had a pretty one, but it wasn't really dressy and it might be too warm. A blouse? She had a new one she'd never worn.

She put the trousers back in the wardrobe and pulled out the long linen shift, in a muddy khaki that went with her eyes. It skimmed the tops of her feet, covered the legs that definitely didn't need to be on display—he'd always had a thing about her legs—and she could wear a little cardi over the top. It was her favourite garment at the moment, the thing she fell back on when all else failed. She could dress it up or down, and it was clean. Always an advantage.

She pulled it over her head, zipped it up and dragged a brush through her hair, then looked at herself. A touch of make-up, perhaps—not much, she didn't tend to wear a great deal, but somehow none at all was unlikely and at the very least she always wore tinted moisturiser and mascara.

With a resigned shrug, she put on what she would have worn for a night out with the girls, and stood back, eyeing herself critically. Hmm. She wouldn't want him thinking she'd made too much effort. So just a touch of lipstick. And a spritz of cologne.

Necklace? No. Beads—chunky beads, burnt orange ones to go with that little cardi she'd picked up the other day.

She eyed herself again, then nodded. Job done. She was reaching for the door knob when there was a tap on the door.

'Maisie? I'm ready when you are. Are we going in the car, or is it nearby?'

'It's near,' she said, opening the door. 'We can walk.'

'Good.' He ran his eye over her and smiled. 'You look lovely.'

So did he, but it would have choked her to say so.

'It's just an old dress,' she said dismissively, ridiculously pleased and refusing to show it because she was still mad with him for never having checked out her website, and she wasn't letting him off the hook that easily. Oh, no.

She took a step forward to leave her room and walked into the space he'd occupied a second earlier. A space filled with his fragrance. Oh, he smelt good. Citrus and spice and raw male. Thankfully they were walking and she wasn't going to be trapped inside a car with him!

But as she locked the front door behind them and set off for the restaurant at a brisk pace, he fell into step beside her, and with her first breath her hopes of escaping that subtle, sexy scent were blown instantly out of the water.

'So—the wedding,' Maisie said when their food had arrived and she was picking through the pasta with a fork. 'You wanted to talk to me about it?'

He put his fork down and picked up his wine, swirling it slowly in the glass. 'Yes. Nothing much, just a few details I don't want to trouble

Jenni with. Timings, really, and I thought you've been to lots of weddings, presumably, so you know how they work.'

She nodded. 'OK. I can give you a rough timetable—is this for the caterers?'

'Yes, and the ceilidh band. Oh, and I wanted to talk to you about catering. We had the food tasting.'

'How was it?'

He wrinkled his nose. 'Not sure. Very good food, but I wasn't sure about the balance of the dishes. Jenni and Alec couldn't agree, and they gave me the casting vote, so I thought when you're next up there, perhaps we should go and check it out and you can tell me what you think.'

That sounded to Maisie like another dinner date, but she didn't argue, just nodded agreement and let it go. 'OK.'

'And we were wondering about canapés with the reception drinks. We've got two hours to fill. Do you think we need them?'

'It's up to you. I think they're nice, but they can be expensive.'

He dismissed that with a wave of his hand. 'We aren't talking about a cast of thousands, and in the great scheme of things it's just a drop in the ocean. So I'll email you a list of the options, and could you give me your thoughts?'

'Sure. Is that it?'

'Flowers.'

'Ah. Did Jenni and your mother sort themselves out in the end? She was so set on the monochrome thing, and I don't think she'd even considered having a colour in the flowers. I know she's settled on creams and lilacs now, but was it an amicable compromise in the end?'

He sighed and gave a weary smile. 'I think so. My mother wasn't being awkward, you know, she was genuinely upset.'

'I know that.' Maisie sighed. 'Rob, I don't think your mother's a bad woman. We just didn't hit it off, we both made harsh judgements about each other and it's going to take some time to heal the wounds on both sides.'

'I know. Thank you for trying. I do realise she isn't always easy.'

That surprised her, and maybe it was why she let her guard down, because after that they moved on and Rob asked her about her photography, how she'd got into it, how many weddings a year she did, how many she turned down.

'Lots,' she told him. 'My real job's with the paper, doing my weekly column and features for them. I call it my jobby—sort of a cross between a job and a hobby. I mean, it is a job, and I make sure I treat it as one, being professional and doing things on time and not letting people down, but on the other hand it's my passion, my love, and it really is a hobby. It's had to be, because of Jenni. I would have been a photographer—that was the way I was going at college, with the journalism thing. But life as a female photojournalist is a tough one, and it's not suited to motherhood, and I'm not sure it's really suited to me.'

'So you turned to weddings.'

'Not for years. I did some photography with my newspaper job as part of my features writing, but then someone asked me to do their wedding because they'd lost their photographer, and I stepped in to help them out. And then another friend of theirs saw them and asked me, and it sort of grew from there. It's great fun, and it tops up what I earn from the paper so I can have a few luxuries and do a bit to the house.'

He swirled his glass again, watching the wine intently, then set it down, very slowly and deliberately.

'Talk to me about the house,' he said quietly. 'I can't believe you still think of it as mine. It's yours, and you should be doing things to it—the French doors, for instance. That was why I put it in your name, so you could do what you wanted with it, but you haven't.'

She tried to smile, but it was hard with him being so obviously troubled by her admission. Instead she reached out a hand and laid it over his, the one that wasn't now carefully pushing a few crumbs into a neat, orderly row.

'I haven't been unhappy there, Rob,' she told him softly. 'It's been a great house in many ways—handy for everything, lovely for Jenni growing, a good school—I couldn't have wanted more, so it would have been ludicrous to move. And to be fair, I haven't had the money for wholesale alterations.'

'You wouldn't take it.'

'I didn't need your money, Rob. I was fine. I had the house. That was more than enough.'

His hand turned over, enclosing hers in its warmth. 'But you don't feel as if it's yours.'

No, she wanted to tell him, I feel as if it should be *our* house, as if you have a place there, will always have a place there. But of course she couldn't. 'Ignore me,' she advised. 'I was just being silly.'

'Because you didn't want me to stay.'

It wasn't a question, and she sighed. 'It's—'

She broke off and he put in, 'Difficult?'

She nodded. 'Yes. There just seems to be so much going on under the surface, so much we haven't talked about, so much that we've left undisturbed for so long that we can't even remember it, but it's still there, simmering away under a huge pile of dust. And if we disturb it…'

His thumb stroked idly over the backs of her

fingers, testing the softness of her skin. 'Maybe we need to open the windows and blow the dust away, Maisie,' he said, totally forgetting his earlier decision to leave it alone, at least until after the wedding. 'Get everything out into the open. Talk about the things we haven't talked about.'

'Such as?'

He gave a soft laugh and sat back, releasing her hand before he gave in to the urge to press his lips to that soft, smooth palm. 'Well, if I knew that, I'd be halfway there,' he said, his mouth tilted in a wry half-smile. 'Look, forget it. I don't want to make you uncomfortable. I'll stay at a hotel.'

'Don't be silly. Your things are all there now, it's pointless. Anyway, I can always lock my bedroom door.'

Why, oh, why had she said that? His head came up and he speared her with those extraordinary slate-blue eyes. In the candelight—how had she known the place had had a makeover and gone romantic?—they seemed to glint with fire, and he shook his head slowly.

'You don't need to lock your door. All you need to do—all you've ever needed to do—is say no to me.'

'Well, that's the problem, isn't it?' she said without thinking. 'I don't seem to be able to.'

His eyes became shuttered, and he leant back

a little further. 'You used to manage it. After Jenni was born, the hatches were well and truly battened down.'

She let out a small, shocked breath and looked away. 'That was different. I was—I don't know. Afraid. You'd been away, the birth had traumatised me in all sorts of ways—I wasn't really myself. And you seemed different, too. Indifferent, even.'

'Indifferent? Maisie, I was never indifferent! I was trying to give you space.'

'Really?' She gave a tiny huff of laughter, and rubbed her arms, suddenly cold. 'It didn't feel like it. It felt like you couldn't bear to be in the same room as me.'

'I was afraid to touch you,' he admitted, his voice low as he leant towards her again, his eyes troubled. 'Afraid I might hurt you. Mrs McCrae had taken me on one side and made it clear that you'd had a dreadful time. I had no idea what that might even mean—'

'You never asked.'

'No,' he said, after a long pause. 'No, I didn't. I didn't know how to.'

'You could have just held me. Hugged me. Taken me to bed and held me in your arms all night—except, of course, after I had Jenni, you didn't seem to want to know. And when I was feeding her, you avoided me like the plague.'

'I didn't want to embarrass you.'

She laughed, staring at him in disbelief, and then realised he was serious. 'Rob, you were her *father*,' she said softly. 'You knew my body like your own, and I knew yours. Why would I be embarrassed? I thought *you* were embarrassed.'

He gave a low, tired laugh and looked up, catching the waiter's eye. 'Let's get out of here,' he said. 'I need some air.'

They left the restaurant and walked slowly back along the river, pausing by the spot where they'd picnicked earlier, and he turned to her, taking her hands in his, staring down into her eyes. His were shadowed so she couldn't read them, but his mouth was unsmiling, almost sad.

'Maisie, I'm sorry. If I could turn the clock back, I would, but I can't, and we're stuck with where we are now. And, really, I'm not sure anything's any different, is it? We still don't know each other. We still live at opposite ends of the country. Maybe we should leave the dust alone.'

'Maybe we should,' she agreed, but as she said it, she felt tears well in her eyes. They were laying their love to rest, but it had never died, just starved and withered as surely as if it had been flung into the dungeon at the castle, and just like the smell of food drifting through the slit high in the wall to torment those early prisoners, there had been the bitter-sweet, constant reminders of Rob over the years—phone calls and visits to

Jenni, discussions about matters concerning her, every birthday and Christmas a disappointment for one or other of them. The wedding was just another one, more bitter-sweet than any other, and after the wedding would come grandchildren—christenings, Christmas, more birthdays, more babies. More reminders of all she'd lost.

She freed her hands and turned away, heading blindly back towards the house, and he followed her, a step behind, in silence.

'Coffee?' she asked as they went in, trying to be civilised, but hc shook his head.

'No. I think I'll turn in. I've got a long drive tomorrow.'

'You haven't given me the wedding invitations yet.'

'No. I'll do that now. There's a disk with all the names and addresscs on, so you should be able to print labels from it to save you writing them by hand.'

'There aren't that many, are there? I might do it now, and you can take the Scottish ones with you.'

'There are all the inserts to fold.'

She glanced at her watch. 'Rob, it's only ten. Unless you've changed your habits drastically, you never go to bed before midnight. We could make a start on it together. I can fold, you can write, because your writing's better than mine.'

'It's illegible.'

That was true. It was interesting, individual, but you had to know it to understand it.

'OK, you fold, I'll write,' she said. 'I'll put the kettle on. Or you can go to bed and I'll do it on my own.'

'I thought you wanted me out of your hair?'

'Not so badly that I want to do the invitations on my own.'

He smiled at that, and went to get them while she boiled the kettle.

'Tea or coffee? Or do you want something alcoholic?'

'Coffee,' he said, resigned to a long and sleepless night anyway, and thinking that a clear head might not be a bad idea, to stop him getting up and breaking down her door.

By the time she brought it through to the dining room-cum-study, he'd spread the stationery out in piles on the table, so that she could be writing the names on the envelopes and invitations while he collated and folded the other bits.

'Right, let's see this list,' she said, settling down beside him so that her warm, delicate scent drifted across to him and tunnelled ruthlessly under the hatches of his self-control.

He pulled it up on his little notebook computer, propped it in front of her and turned his attention to folding.

* * *

'Wow. Finally!' she said, handing him the Scottish stack. 'Stamps?'

'Of course.' He pulled a sheet of stamps out, and they stuck them on their separate piles, then he looked up and met her eyes. 'Thanks.'

'No, thank you. I did offer, and you ended up doing it anyway.'

'Consider it penance for all my endless failings.'

'I don't think you had any more failings than me,' she said quietly, picking up the tray and taking it back to the kitchen. He followed her, propping himself up and watching as she put the mugs in the dishwasher and rinsed out the cafetière and turned it upside down. Then she wiped her hands, turned back to him and raised a brow. 'More coffee? Or tea?'

He shook his head. 'No. I really do need to try and get some sleep, I've got six hundred miles to drive in the morning.'

She nodded, rubbing her arms briskly with her hands, making her breasts jiggle slightly. 'Right. I'm going to turn in, too. Do you want to take the bathroom first? I've got one or two things to do down here.'

'Sure. Thanks.'

He washed quickly, trying to get out of her way before she came up, but he was too slow. She was there, sitting on the edge of her bed—his bed, he realised in surprise. He recognised the old black iron frame that he'd brought from home, and it brought memories crashing back over him. Memories of Maisie trailing her hair over his chest, while he lay on his back, teeth clenched, gripping the rails of the headboard while she teased him. Memories of lying with her in the lazy aftermath of their love-making.

Memories of the first time he'd made love to her…

'I'm finished in the bathroom,' he said, and she looked up and smiled.

'Thanks. I'll see you in the morning.'

It was a clear dismissal, but he didn't take it. Instead he stepped into the room, running his hand over one of the big brass knobs on the foot of the bed.

'I didn't realise you'd still got this,' he said, his voice sounding a little taut and uneven to his ears.

'Yes. There didn't seem to be any point in getting rid of it. I changed the mattress a few years ago.'

'Of course.'

Her eyes were wary, huge in her pale face. He ought to leave, to go to his room and lock the door and push the key under it so he couldn't let himself out. Instead he reached out his hand, his fingers cool from the brass, and trailed them over her warm, smooth cheek.

'You're still beautiful, Maisie,' he said softly.

'Rob…'

He dropped his hand and took a step back. 'No. You're right. It would be foolish, wouldn't it?' he murmured. And anyway, he'd promised her, told her that all she'd ever needed to do was say no. Well, she was saying it now, and he had to respect that, had to walk away.

But she stood up, and he just had to taste her, had to kiss her. Nothing more. Just a kiss goodnight.

He bent his head, his lips brushing hers lightly before settling, and with a tiny sigh she lifted her hands to his shoulders and laid them there. To push him away, or draw him closer?

She did neither, just stood there while their mouths clung, the softest, lightest, most chaste kiss imaginable.

And then he eased away. His chest was taut, his heart racing, and he was within a hair of tearing off that wretched dress that hid her from his desperate, hungry eyes.

So he took a step back, and then another, reaching the door and hanging onto it as if it would help to hold him back.

'Goodnight, Maisie,' he said gruffly, and turning on his heel he crossed the little landing in a stride and went into his daughter's room and closed the door.

Firmly.

CHAPTER EIGHT

HE was gone by the time she woke in the morning.

She went down to the kitchen, hearing the sound of the washing machine spinning as she approached, and saw a note propped against the kettle.

'Sheets in washer. Thanks for yesterday, and doing invitations. See you soon, Rob.'

Thanks for yesterday.

Which part of it? The picnic on the river? Putting him in touch with Annette? Dinner?

The kiss?

Her breath hitched in her chest, and she stared down at the blur of sheets in the machine and felt a pang of regret that he'd done that, that he hadn't left the task to her, so she could have stripped them off and carried them downstairs with her nose pressed to the soft cotton, inhaling the scent of him.

She was being *ridiculous*! Thank goodness

he'd done it for her, because her fevered imagination didn't need any more fuel to fan the flames. She'd spent most of last night lying awake thinking of him in the bed next door, just the thickness of a wall away, her body aching for another kiss, another touch.

More than that. Too much more. Dangerously, insanely too much more.

She'd fallen asleep at last, and had missed him leaving. The washing machine must have woken her—it had a tendency to thump when it started spinning. So he'd been gone—what? An hour and a half? So he must have left at five.

She wondered how much sleep he'd had, or if he'd given up and headed off, intending to book into a hotel en route and get a few more hours.

She turned the kettle on and picked up his note. She needed to stop thinking about him sleeping, because sleeping meant bed, and bed meant trouble. Big trouble.

She didn't need any more trouble than she was already in. Dinner last night had been like a drug, sitting with him in a candlelit restaurant, walking by the river—foolish. And he wanted her to go to the hotel in Ardnashiel for a food tasting and go through that all over again?

Including the kiss goodnight?

A shiver of what could have been excitement ran over her skin, and she crushed it ruthlessly. He hadn't meant anything by it. She was reading things where there were none. If he'd wanted to, he could so easily have made love to her last night. She hadn't resisted, but she hadn't allowed herself to beg either, and given free rein, he'd walked away.

He'd probably slept like a log, she told herself in disgust, and making a cup of tea she took it into the study and tackled the accounts that were waiting for her attention.

They were getting busy on the estate, spring giving way to summer and the tourist season getting under way, so there was plenty to keep Rob occupied when he got back.

He was glad of that. Alec was working hard, but it was just as well because it left Jenni free to concentrate on her studies, and in any of his free time he was decorating the gatehouse, ready for them to move in straight after the wedding.

That left Rob, of course, in between a million and one admin jobs at Ardnashiel and juggling his business in London, to sort the rest of the wedding details, and because he didn't want to trouble Jenni, and because he trusted Maisie's judgement more than his mother's on the subject of contemporary weddings, inevitably he'd end up talking more to her.

It would be hard.

Not as hard as lying there all night beside her,

with just the wall between them, so he could reach out and lay his hand on it and feel closer to her. That had been hell, and he'd given up and left when it had became obvious that he was going to get no sleep that night.

He'd pulled over in a service area and reclined his seat so that he could doze for a while, but he'd been glad to get home and go to bed for ten hours of solid, uninterrupted sleep, and when he'd woken up, he'd given himself a serious talking-to and moved on.

No more dreaming about what might have been, no more longing for things he couldn't and was never going to have, no more turning the clock back. He was living in the here and now, and here and now he was rushed off his feet.

But the problems kept coming to find him anyway, starting with the florist.

She had a problem, apparently, so he discovered ten days after he'd got back. Jenni wanted flowers over the arched doorway at the entrance to the church, but the florist didn't know either how to fix them or what, exactly, was required. What about pew ends? Pedestals? And how many tables would there be? And what were the bride's mother and the groom's mother going to require in the way of corsages?

How the hell was he supposed to know? It was a minefield.

He went and studied the church doorway, and discovered that at some point someone had inserted small rings around the top of the arch—for decorating it?

Whatever they'd been for, they were there, so he could tick that box.

As for what Jenni had planned to be fixed there, he was lost—never mind the number of tables and the corsages and all the other stuff.

So he phoned Maisie, and the sound of her slightly distracted voice went straight to his gut and tied it in knots.

'Hi. Florist questions,' he said, getting straight to the point. 'Have you got time to talk?'

'Um—yes, sure. Sorry. I was just editing a feature. Actually, can I call you back? I need to email it now.'

'Sure.'

He hung up, made himself a coffee and paced around his office until the phone rang. Stupidly, it made him jump, and his heart raced.

Unnecessarily. It was the hotel. Had they decided yet on the menu?

'No. I'll call you—we need to have another tasting.'

'Would you like to book it?'

'I can't,' he told her, 'not right now. I might be able to in about half an hour—can I call you?'

'Of course.'

He hung up, and the phone rang again almost immediately. 'Hi.'

'It's the hotel again, Mr Mackenzie. I forgot to say we can't do any tastings on Friday or Saturday nights now, because the hotel's full on those nights for the next several weeks, so it would be best to go for midweek, if you can.'

'Fine.' It meant Jenni couldn't be there, but that was fine. He was happy to go on his own with Maisie. More than happy.

He hung up again, drummed his fingers, made another coffee—and then she rang.

'Rob, hi, I'm sorry it took so long,' she said apologetically, her voice soft and lyrical. Damn. His guts were knotted again.

'That's fine,' he said. 'I've been busy with other calls.'

Well, it wasn't really a lie. 'The florist wants to know what you want over the church door—we've solved the fixing problem, there are rings up there, but she's not sure—she was talking pedestals and garlands and pew thingamies—she just lost me.'

Maisie chuckled. 'It's OK, I know exactly. Give me her email address, I'll send her some photos. What else?'

'Table centres—how many tall, how many low? How many, generally, but we haven't had all the replies yet so I can't tell her. Oh, and what are you and Alec's mother wearing, and what do you want as a corsage?'

'I don't know about Alec's mother, you'll have to ask her. It needs to be something to tone with the other flowers. And does your mother want one? She might well. You'd better ask her, too.'

'OK. And you?'

He could hear her fractional hesitation, sense her reluctance.

'I'm not sure,' she said, surprising him. 'I'm having second thoughts about my outfit.'

'But I thought that was all settled? You bought it when you were with Jenni. She wouldn't tell me anything about it, though, just told me I had to wait and see. She wouldn't even tell me the colour, never mind what it looked like. She just said I'd like it.'

There was a muffled sound at the other end. 'Um—it's cream,' she said after a pause. 'Like really rich clotted cream—and it's lace.'

'Cream? I thought only the bride should wear white or cream?' he queried, struggling with the etiquette.

'It's up to the bride, and anyway, it's a rich cream, almost gold. And Jenni loved it, she told me I had to have it, but…'

'What? You don't sound too sure,' he said, leaning back and propping his feet up on the desk. 'If you're not certain, get something else. I know

Jenni approved it, but you shouldn't let that influence you if you don't feel good in it.'

'Oh, I feel good in it. I love it.'

That confused him completely. 'So what's the problem?' he asked, wondering how something so straightforward could be so hard. 'Doesn't it fit?'

'Yes, but—that's the trouble, really.' He could almost hear her chewing her lip. 'I'm just not sure. It's very…fitted.'

He felt the heat ramp up a few degrees. 'Fitted?' he said, his throat suddenly tight.

'Yes—it's sort of snug, and it tucks in under the bottom and just…well, it fits. It fits beautifully. I'm just not sure it's—I don't know, motherly enough.'

It didn't sound in the least bit motherly. He was going to choke if he couldn't breathe soon, and his entire body was on red alert. 'I'm sure it'll be lovely. Jenni liked it,' he reminded her, desperate now to see this dress that tucked in under her cute, delectable bottom that just fitted so well in his hands.

'Look, it doesn't matter. It's a lovely outfit, and at the end of the day if I go for something that tones with cream it'll go with whatever I end up wearing, if it's not that. I'll talk to the florist. Was there anything else?'

Was there?

'Ah—yes. Food tasting. When can you come up? It's Jenni's twenty-first in a fortnight, and she's coming home for the weekend. She's out with her friends on Friday night, and then coming up on Saturday morning, so you'll probably want to be here, won't you, for that?'

'Oh. Yes, of course. Um…I've made sure I'm free that weekend, and I've got time before and after to allow for travelling.'

'So why not come before? We can't do the food tasting at the weekend, because they're too busy, but they can do midweek. How about coming up overnight on Tuesday, and we'll go on Wednesday evening. Then you can see the florist and sort out any other details and go back the following week.'

There was a small silence, and then a quiet sigh. 'OK. I'll do that.'

'I'll book it,' he said, quickly, before she could change her mind. 'I'll email you the booking reference and the florist's email address so you can send her the pictures and arrange for her to come to the castle and the church and see what we're talking about, and I'll see you next week.'

He hung up before she could argue, dropped his feet to the floor and sucked in a deep breath. All he could see was Maisie's firm, rounded bottom lovingly snuggled in rich, creamy lace, and it was doing his head in.

He booked the sleeper, emailed her all the details he'd promised and went out for a long, hard walk.

With only four weeks to go to the wedding, Maisie went to see Jeff and spoke to him in more detail about the photos.

'I'm going up in a couple of days,' she told him, 'and I'll take some more shots of the church, the castle, the grounds—just so you know what you're dealing with. There's a disk here with lots on already, and I've labelled them so you know what they all are, but you could do with finding your way around beforehand. When will you be able to get there?'

He shrugged, relaxed and certain of himself. 'Maisie, I'll do whatever you tell me to do. When do you want me there?'

'By the Friday morning at the latest? You can see the marquee, work out what shots you want, talk to Jenni and Alec about what they want, then in the morning you can take photos of Jenni getting ready, and walk down with us to the church.'

'What if it rains? Will there be a car?'

'On standby.' She looked him in the eye. 'It won't rain. It's not allowed to rain.' And then she sighed. 'It's Scotland. Of course it'll rain. Oh, damn, Jeff, why is it all so complicated?' she asked him, and he gave a soft chuckle and made her a coffee.

'Chill. It'll be fine. It'll be a lovely, sunny day, and even if it's not, I'll get you some brilliant atmospheric umbrella shots. You'll have a great time.'

He was right, of course. She'd been to lots of wet weddings, and the weather had never put more than a fleeting dampener on the party spirits. She was just used to East Anglia, where the sun shone more often.

'I'll do whatever you want. It's your girl's day, not mine, and you know what you're aiming for. And trust me.'

'I do trust you. I wouldn't ask anyone else. You're a darling,' she told him with a smile, kissed his designer-stubbled cheek and sat back with her coffee and chilled, just like he'd told her to. He was right, she could trust him. He'd do just what she asked, and he'd do it well.

She gave an inward sigh of relief, ticked that box and scanned her mental list.

Accessories. She still hadn't chosen shoes or bag—still hadn't reconciled herself to the outfit, come to that, never mind worked out if she wanted a hat. She finished her coffee, then went home and pulled the outfit out of the wardrobe and put it on.

And swallowed. It really did hug her body lovingly. Very lovingly.

Oh, it was elegant enough, and beautifully, superbly cut. And it definitely suited her.

It'll knock Dad's socks off.

Her heart gave a little lurch, and she pressed her hand to her chest and breathed in. Silly. She put the bolero on, hoping it would make it more demure, but the peep of skin through the lace was somehow more alluring, more sensual.

But she did love it. She turned round, held a mirror up and studied her posterior critically, and then threw the mirror down with a sigh. To hell with Rob. She loved it, she wanted to wear it and he'd probably be too worried about his speech to notice her.

She took it off, put it in a bag and went shopping for accessories.

He wasn't at the station to meet her. Instead of Rob, she found Helen on the platform, looking a little wary.

'Maisie—welcome back,' she said with a tentative smile. 'Did you have a good journey?'

She nodded. 'It was fine. I never sleep very well on the train, but it was fine. I take it Rob's busy?'

'Yes. He's out on the hills with some guests. Alec had to sort something out for the gatehouse, so I offered to come and get you. I hope you don't mind.'

Maisie smiled, reached over and hugged her. 'Of course I don't mind. In fact, if you're not in a hurry, why don't we have coffee at that lovely place on the way?'

'Oh. Well, that would be very nice,' she agreed, returning the smile less tentatively. 'Actually, I could do with your advice,' she admitted. 'I'm not sure about my outfit for the wedding.'

Maisie laughed, picked up her case and followed Helen to the car. 'You as well?' she said, and Helen looked at her in puzzlement. 'I wasn't sure about my dress. Jenni loves it, but…'

'Jenni said you look wonderful in it. She said the colouring was perfect for you, and it was the most beautiful fit.'

'It is. I'm just not sure it's motherly enough,' she said, repeating the words she'd said to Rob earlier, but Helen flapped her hand.

'Do people really worry about that sort of thing these days? I have a philosophy. If it makes you feel good, wear it, if it doesn't, don't, and it doesn't matter what it is. I try not to dress inappropriately, but I do always insist on being me, and it's always stood me in good stead. The thing is, do you feel like you, or like someone else dressed up?'

She thought about that as she loaded her case into the boot and got in the car. 'Me,' she said after a pause. 'I feel like me—but different. Better.'

'Then it's right,' Helen said. 'The trouble with mine is I feel like me, but old and stuffy and tedious rather than better.'

'Is it a new outfit?' Maisie asked, happy to keep the conversation on safe ground, and Helen told her about it, that it was on approval and could be exchanged, that she'd tried several things but not known which to go for.

'I don't suppose you could spare the time while you're up here to help me choose something else, could you?' she asked tentatively, and Maisie was surprised, yet again, at her reticence. She'd remembered her as matriarchal and rather bossy, but this woman was uncertain, almost conciliatory. Had Rob given her a hard time for being mean? Was that it? Was Helen trying to make amends for all the bitterness and unhappiness around the time of Jenni's birth?

'Of course I can spare the time,' she said. 'It'll be a pleasure.'

Helen's face lit up, and she pulled up in the car park of the lochside café a few moments later still smiling, and turned to Maisie. 'Well, here we are. Shall we go in?'

They found a table by the window—the table she'd sat at with Rob when they'd had their revealing and painful conversation—and she vowed that this time she'd guard her tongue and try incredibly hard not to fall out with his mother.

She was being nice today, but Maisie was under no illusions. It was a fragile truce—or so she thought, until they were seated and the waitress had taken their order.

Then her smile faltered briefly, and she met Maisie's eyes, her own clouded. 'Maisie, I—I owe you such an apology. I've treated you badly in the past, and I'm so ashamed of what I did. I didn't know you, I didn't try and get to know you, or give you the benefit of the doubt, and I think I misjudged you terribly. I thought you were using Rob for your own ends, and I had no idea—well, that you'd been so innocent. I really thought you were just after his wealth.'

Maisie gave a soft laugh. 'Helen, I didn't even know he had any when I met him. I knew the house in Cambridge was his to live in, but I thought it was on a lease and he just wanted someone living there for security while he was away. I didn't know anything about housing then, I was still living at home. It didn't occur to me that he owned it. To be honest, it was such a gift I didn't look at it as closely as I should have done,' she admitted with a soft laugh. 'All I could think about was getting away from home, from a father who wouldn't let me wear make-up and a brother who thought I'd been put on earth to take over where my mother left off. Only, of course, once I was pregnant neither of them wanted anything to do with me, my father because I'd brought shame on my mother's name, my brother because the last thing he wanted was a screaming brat in the house.'

Helen clucked softly, and shook her head. 'I had no idea. When Rob moved you up here to have Jenni, so you wouldn't be alone, I had no idea that you would have been quite *so* alone. And—well, we didn't exactly make you welcome, did we?'

Maisie shook her head ruefully. 'Not exactly. But looking at it from your point of view, would I have acted any differently? I don't know that I would.'

Helen gave a strained little smile. 'It's very generous of you to say that, Maisie, but I think you would, you know. You don't have it in you to be harsh or judgemental.'

Maisie laughed at that. 'Oh, Helen, you're so wrong,' she said, her voice filled with regret. 'I thought you were stuck-up and cold-hearted, and I was convinced you hated me and thought I wasn't good enough for your son.'

'I did,' she said honestly. 'But I didn't know you, my dear. And you've done a wonderful job of raising your daughter. It's just such a pity that you and Rob weren't together to do it.'

She sighed. 'Yes. He's missed a lot.'

'He's missed *you*,' Helen said softly, surprising her. Maisie gave a tiny gasp of laughter and shook her head.

'No. No he hasn't. After he came back from the navy, he was different. He wasn't interested in me. Jenni, yes. He adored her. Me? I'm not convinced he thought of me as anything other than the mother of his child.'

'I think you're wrong. I think he really loved you, and I think he still does.'

Her head flew up, her eyes meeting Helen's in disbelief. 'No,' she whispered.

Helen nodded, and Maisie turned her head and stared out over the water. Rob still love her? He could hardly be in the same room with her without them arguing.

But he'd kissed her—so softly, so tenderly.

And then he'd walked away.

Was that the act of a man in love? She didn't think so. A man in love would have stayed, taken what she was so freely, so willingly offering. Or would he? Would he have walked away, and hoped that she'd follow in her own time?

As she had with him?

Suddenly she couldn't wait to see him, didn't want to sit there with Helen talking about him, but wanted to be with him, to talk to him, to see if there might be any truth in his mother's words.

But he was out walking over the hills with some guests, so there was no hurry. She forced herself to drink the coffee their waitress put down in front of her at that moment, and she switched the conversation from Rob to Jenni, to the wedding, to Alec and how the gatehouse was coming on—anything rather than speculate on whether the man she loved still cared about her as anything other than the mother of his daughter…

He couldn't wait to see her.

He would have been there to meet her, but Alec had had a hitch with the kitchen fitters and he'd had to take the guided walk out instead.

He just hoped his mother wasn't causing a riot with Maisie. He didn't think she would, but he couldn't be sure, and he was on tenterhooks for the entire day. They got back at four-thirty, and the guests headed off to their cottage with effusive thanks and he took the dogs in through the kitchen door and found Maisie sitting there with Mrs McCrae, dribbling what looked suspiciously like his best brandy into the bottom of a massive fruit cake.

'Don't tell me—the wedding cake?' he asked, kissing Mrs McCrae on the cheek and earning a swat on the shoulder for his pains, and then he met Maisie's eyes and his heart turned over.

How could the woman grow more lovely every time he saw her? 'Hi, there. Good journey?' he asked, leaning over to brush his lips against her cheek, relishing the softness, breathing in the scent of her and stifling a groan.

'Pretty much as predicted. How was your guided walk?'

'Pretty much as predicted,' he said with a chuckle. 'I'm starving, Mrs M. Any sticky gingerbread left?'

'You know fine well there's not, you finished it yesterday. There's shortbread cooling on the rack, and tea in the pot. And Alec said thanks, and the kitchen's going to be done on time.'

'Really? I wonder what he threatened them with?' he said mildly, breaking off a chunk of shortbread and pouring himself a mug of tea while he munched it.

'I hope you're not going to eat so much you aren't ready for this food tasting?' Maisie said, eyeing the shortbread.

'Not a chance,' he said round a mouthful. 'I'm ravenous. I've probably walked nearly twenty miles today. I'm going to make a few phone calls, and then I'm getting into the bath. I'll see you later, Maisie. Six-thirty OK for you? Our reservation's at seven.'

'Six-thirty's fine,' she said, so with a brisk nod, he grabbed another chunk of shortbread and headed for the stairs, then stuck his head back into the kitchen.

'Don't wear stilts, by the way, we're walking down as it's fine so we can check out all the wines.'

'OK. Dress code?'

'Pretty.'

'That doesn't sound like a dress code,' she pointed out, but then had to watch his mouth twitch into a mischievous grin.

'It's my dress code,' he murmured. 'See you in a couple of hours.'

And with a wicked wink he was gone, leaving her sitting there, her heart drumming, her mouth slightly open.

She shut it, fast, but not so fast that Mrs McCrae didn't notice, and she felt her cheeks burn.

'Shall I wrap the cake again now?' she asked hastily, and without waiting for an answer she closed the greaseproof paper round it and put the lid back on.

The hotel restaurant was busy, even though it was midweek, and Rob was interested to see how many of their own guests were eating there.

No wonder the owner was giving them such a good deal on the wedding breakfast! Clearly their business brought in a lot of trade, but the disadvantage was the lack of privacy. He was recognised, of course, and he didn't want to be. He wanted this to be about them—about the food, too, of course, because of the wedding, but mostly about them, because with every day that passed he grew more uncertain about the reasons for their divorce.

'It's lovely in here,' Maisie said, looking around the restaurant. Modern tables and chairs, slate table mats, and above all the view over the sea from the floor-to-ceiling windows made it a wonderful place to eat, and it didn't hurt that the food was excellent, he thought.

They were shown to a quiet table, tucked out of the way in an alcove but still with a stunning view across the sea to the islands. 'I'll tell the chef you're here,' the waiter said, disappearing, and moments later he arrived, smiling and greeting Maisie enthusiastically.

'So like Jenni. I would have known at once who you were. OK, the menu. You were undecided, Mr Mackenzie?'

He dragged his eyes back off Maisie and looked at the chef. 'Yes. They liked the duck and the chicken. I wondered about that. I thought maybe the lamb would be better, or change the starter to something else—scallops, perhaps.'

'I shall cook you one of everything, and let you share—would that be the best idea? And then you can choose. And wine—I'll bring you a bottle of each, red and white, to get a balance.'

He disappeared, leaving them alone, and

suddenly the small alcove seemed airless to Maisie.

'So, how was the journey really?' Rob asked softly, and she laughed.

'Oh, it was all right. I'm getting used to it, I've done it a few times now, and it's long and tedious, but it's less stressful than flying with all the parking problems and hanging around for check-in. Still, next time I come up will be the last for a while, I expect.'

Something flickered briefly in his eyes and was gonc, and she forced herself to be business-like. 'So—I'm seeing the florist tomorrow?'

'Yes. She's coming at nine. I've cleared my diary. I didn't know if you'd need me, but I'll be about if so.'

Need him? Oh, yes, she needed him, but not in the way he meant.

'Thanks.' She twirled her empty wineglass absently, then set it down. 'So, what else has been going on, wedding-wise?'

'No. I don't want to talk about it. Let's talk about something else.'

She met his eyes and smiled in relief. 'Do you know what? I'd love to talk about something else. Why don't you tell me about your day?'

He shrugged slowly. 'Not much to tell. I walked miles. It was good.'

'See any tourist eagles?'

He gave a soft chuckle, and tore a piece off his roll, shredding it bit by bit. 'No. No eagles of any sort. These rolls are lovely and soft. And warm. Interesting. What flavour's yours?'

'I don't know. It's got seeds in…mmm. Nice. How about yours?'

'Sundried tomato—here, try it,' he said, and held it up to her lips.

She leant back slightly and took it from his hand, but it didn't help because their fingers brushed anyway and it was nearly as potent. She chewed and swallowed. 'Oh, that's lovely.'

'Give me some of yours?'

No way. She pushed the plate towards him. 'Help yourself,' she said, and then to fill the silence she asked, 'How's Alec getting on? I still haven't seen their house.'

'I'll show it to you tomorrow, when the florist's gone. It's coming on well— Ah, here's the food.'

He sounded almost relieved, which was ridiculous as it had been his idea to feed each other. The waiter set down three plates on the table between them.

'Scallops with chorizo, lemon and thyme on wild rocket, pan-fried oriental duck breast on summer leaves, and charred peppers with roasted goats' cheese and chilli oil dressing. Enjoy your meal.'

The sommelier arrived and poured a selection

of wines, then left them to it, and Rob picked up his knife and fork, speared a piece of tender, succulent scallop with a sliver of crisp, spicy sausage and held it to her lips. 'Try this. It gets my vote every time,' he said, his voice soft and yet roughened, somehow, so that it teased at her senses.

She opened her mouth, took the morsel and closed her eyes, because she simply couldn't look at him a second longer. The flavour exploded on her tongue, and after a moment she opened her eyes again and nodded.

'That's lovely.'

'Isn't it? Here, try the duck.'

She stabbed it herself, then moved on to the pepper and goats' cheese. 'Let me try that,' he murmured, and with her heart pumping she put a little on her fork and held it out to him, watching spellbound as his firm, full lips closed around the fork and he drew it off and chewed, slowly and thoughtfully.

'No. OK for the veggies, but the goats' cheese doesn't do it for me. Try the scallop again.'

And once again his fork was at her lips, his eyes locked with hers, and the air between them was brittle with tension.

She didn't know how she got through the meal. He fed her chicken breast stuffed with Brie and wrapped in Parma ham, served on a bed of haggis—haggis, of all things, but as he said, it was a Scottish wedding—and rack of lamb on neeps and tatties—again the Scottish thing—with a redcurrant and rosemary *jus*.

'I like the chicken,' she said, struggling with the whole feeding bit, because he would insist on mixing flavours and offering them to her, a bit from one plate with a bit from another, just to see if the dishes needed adjusting. 'What about the vegetarians?'

'They're having wild mushroom risotto with some pesto something-or-other. I don't know. Jenni liked it. What do you think of the wines?'

'I like the white. I'm not much of a red wine drinker but it's beautifully smooth.'

'I think so. Ready to try the desserts?'

'I think so, but really only a little,' she said. The dessert had been pretty much unanimously agreed, an *assiette* of lemon tart, chocolate mousse and vanilla ice cream in a tiny brandy snap basket. It was beautifully presented, but Rob had asked for just one to share, so this was worse. This was him feeding her tasty chocolate mousse, as light as air and rich as Croesus, on the tip of a spoon—a spoon which had been in his mouth.

'How's the ice cream?' he asked, and opened his mouth, a smile playing round his eyes as he waited for her to return the favour.

Outwardly, they were doing nothing but sharing their desserts. Inwardly—inwardly, he was causing havoc, and when they'd scraped up the last morsel of creamy deliciousness and the waiter suggested coffee, she shook her head.

'No, thank you, I'm fine. I don't need anything more.' Because there would be truffles, and he'd insist on holding one to her lips, or biting one in half and feeding her the rest, and she didn't think she could stand it.

'I agree,' he said, and moments later the chef appeared at their side.

'So, how did you get on?' he asked.

'Excellent,' Rob said warmly. 'A really great meal. And I think we're agreed on the scallops, the chicken and the *assiette*.'

'Excellent choice. Well, we're looking forward to cooking it for you on the wedding day. Fingers crossed for the weather.'

'You do that,' Maisie said with a smile as she got to her feet. Heavens, she felt a tiny bit tipsy. All that wine tasting, she thought, and when the fresh air hit her, she felt suddenly light-headed.

'Are you all right?'

'Yes—a bit tired. I'll be all right after I've had some sleep. I can't sleep properly on the train.'

And the alcohol might have left her system by then. Not that she'd had much, but she didn't drink, as a rule, and any was more than usual.

'It's very dark.'

'It's all right. Here, give me your hand,' he

said, and tucked it into the crook of his arm, his fingers wrapped over hers as they walked slowly back up the hill from the village.

'I can't believe our little girl's going to be married and living there in just four weeks,' she said as they passed the gatehouse and walked down the drive over the stone bridge into the castle forecourt.

'I know. It only seems like yesterday she was a baby. I've been trying to write my speech, and there's so much I want to say, so much to remember. I don't want to leave any of it out.'

'Rather you than me. I'd hate to make a speech.'

He chuckled quietly and led her into the kitchen, then put the kettle on the stove and turned to lean against it, arms folded, his eyes strangely pensive.

'It's so good to have you back here,' he said softly. 'It feels somehow right, as if you're back where you belong.'

She opened her mouth to deny it, but no words came out. It *did* feel right, oddly. Almost as if there was a place for her here now, where there had never been a place for her before.

He shrugged away from the stove and moved slowly towards her, stopping when he was just inches away, lifting his hands and cupping her face tenderly in his palms. One thumb traced the edge of her lips, dragging slightly over the moist skin, bringing a whimper to her throat.

His eyes darkened and he lowered his head, touching his lips to hers, then with a ragged sigh he closed the gap and hauled her up against him, anchoring her head with one splayed hand while the other slid down and cupped her bottom, lifting her hard against him. She gave a little gasp, and he took instant advantage, his mouth plundering hers, the hot, moist sweep of his tongue dragging a ragged little cry from her heart.

It brought an echoing groan from deep inside him, and he lifted his head and stared down at her with wild, tortured eyes.

'Come to bed with me, Maisie,' he said softly, his voice roughened with a need so intense it made her legs buckle.

She closed her eyes, and felt a tear squeeze out from under one lid and slide slowly down her cheek. 'Oh, Rob, I can't. Don't ask that of me, please. It would be so easy, but we can't go there. Not now. I can't let you hurt me again, and you will, I know you will.'

'No! Maisie, no, I don't want to hurt you. I never wanted to hurt you. It was just the wrong time for us.'

'And it's still the wrong time, Robert. It's still the wrong time. We've got a wedding to get through. I can't deal with this complication now.'

'And after the wedding? What then, my love?'

'I don't know,' she said, her voice little more than a whisper. 'Ask me then.'

And without waiting for his reply, she turned and walked out swiftly, running up the stairs to her room and closing the door firmly behind her. Then she turned the key, not to keep him out, because she knew he wouldn't follow her without invitation, but to keep herself in…

CHAPTER NINE

THE meeting with the florist went really well, to Maisie's relief, because by the following morning her nerves were stretched to breaking point and the last thing she needed was trouble with something so fundamental as Jenni's flowers, but the woman was as sensible and willing to listen in the flesh as she had been on the phone and in her emails.

She'd brought along a few ideas for table centres, a pew end, a photograph of a pedestal she'd done before that she thought might suit, and she promised to leave everything for Jenni to see on the weekend when she was coming home for her birthday.

They met up with Rob and Helen for coffee in the Great Hall, and Maisie was glad to have the two women there to act as a buffer between her and Rob.

As it was, when he passed her her coffee cup their fingers brushed and she nearly dropped the cup. 'Steady,' he murmured, his eyes gentle with understanding, as if telling her she had nothing to fear, he wasn't going to make it difficult.

He didn't need to. She was doing that all by herself.

She'd spent half the night glad she'd had the sense to walk away from him in the kitchen, and the other half regretting it. But now she was glad she'd walked away, because it had been the right thing to do, and she gave him a grateful little smile, took the cup and murmured, 'Thank you.'

'You're welcome,' he said, and they both knew they weren't talking about the coffee, but about some new understanding between them that had come out of nowhere, it seemed, an understanding that held her breathless with the promise of resolution of a love so long unfulfilled she'd almost forgotten what it felt like.

Really felt like, deep down inside her where her hopes and dreams had been locked up for so long she was afraid to open it up in case a chink of light would show them to be ashes. But they weren't ashes, they were glowing embers, just waiting for the chance to leap back to life.

She just hoped that in the fire that was sure to follow, she wouldn't get too badly burned…

The week of the wedding came upon them with the speed of light.

Maisie had gone back after the weekend of Jenni's twenty-first birthday, a poignant day for both of them, and Rob had been glad in a way to see her go because the tension between them was palpable.

He missed her, though. Not that he had time to miss her, not really. He was working flat out at the castle, making sure that all the arrangements were in place and nothing had been left to chance, and he knew it would have been harder to concentrate on the detail with her there to distract him.

He remembered, somewhere in the dim and distant optimistic past, thinking that the worst was over once the planning had been done, and he remembered the guarded look in Maisie's eyes. She'd known, he thought with a wry laugh. Known what was to come, and let him keep his illusions a little bit longer.

He was aching to see her again. Two more days, he told himself. Just two more days. Jenni was home, complete with all her baggage from uni piled in heaps in one of the attic rooms, waiting for a calmer time to tackle the unpacking.

The gatehouse was almost ready, Alec having worked himself almost to a standstill to get it finished in time, and when he went over to see how they were getting on, he found them making up the bed with fresh, gleaming white linen.

'Isn't it lovely?' Jenni said, glowing with pride in Alec, and he thought how lucky they were. He swallowed a lump in his throat and nodded, avoiding looking at the bed.

Surely she wasn't old enough, his little girl. Not to feel the wild, tempestuous emotions he and Maisie were going through right now. The need so deep it was flaying him alive. The fear that it would all go wrong and he would lose more than he could ever have imagined.

'You've done a great job, Alec,' he said gruffly, and headed for the stairs, past the little room that might one day house his grandchild.

Grandchild! He wasn't in any way ready to be a grandfather, for heaven's sake! He was only just forty-three, still in his prime—or was he fooling himself?

'What's up, Pops?' Jenni slipped her arm into his and hugged it. 'Are you OK? You look sad.'

'End of an era,' he said quietly, turning her into his arms and hugging her. She tipped back her head and stared up at him.

'You aren't going to cry on Saturday, are you?' she said, and he gave a slightly strangled laugh.

'I don't plan to,' he said, knowing that the tears would be close to the surface for all that. So much emotion. And afterwards…

'I have to get on. I just wanted to see if you were both OK and if you needed anything else.'

'No. A bottle of milk, perhaps, for Sunday morning.'

Ah. Sunday morning, when they didn't realise they wouldn't be here, because he'd arranged a helicopter to whisk them away on their wedding night to a highly exclusive luxury retreat, away from all possible intrusions, to give their love the time and space it deserved to blossom.

'I think we might do better than just a pint of milk,' he said drily.

'Go on, then, push the boat out and buy us some croissants and bacon and eggs. Oh, and decent coffee. And smoked salmon. And champagne, if you're feeling flush!'

'Consider it done,' he teased, the smile easy to find because it was all arranged, and he had no doubt the room service there would provide for their every whim.

Libby and Tricia, her bridesmaids, were in on the secret and had promised to go through her clothes and pack a bag, and Alec's mother was doing the same for him.

All they had to do was get through the next few days…

Maisie didn't sleep on the train.

There were too many emotions, too much to do, too much of all of it, really. Excitement and nervous anticipation and little shivers of dread in case anything went wrong, and under it all, carefully controlled, a little quiver of hope.

He was there on the platform as the train pulled in, and he took her case from her, leaving her with the garment bag containing the dress and the hat box.

'Is that a hat box?' he said, eyeing it suspiciously, and she laughed.

'Don't worry, it's not huge. It's not even a real hat.'

'Not one of those stupid chicken things.'

She laughed again, so happy to see him, and shaking his head in denial, he dumped her case back down on the platform and hugged her.

'Oh, it's so good to see you,' he mumbled into her hair, and she turned her head and kissed his cheek.

'You, too.'

'I've missed you. It's really good to have you back.'

'It's good to be back,' she admitted, and he lifted his head and stared down at her, a quizzical frown on his face.

'Really?' he said softly, and she nodded.

'I never thought I'd say that, but it's true. It feels good to come—' She caught herself just in time, and said, 'Back.' Not home. Don't jump the gun, Maisie, she warned herself.

He picked up the case, slung his other arm

around her shoulders and ushered her through to the car park. He had a Range Rover today, and she raised an eyebrow. 'No sports car? On a lovely day like today?'

He grinned. 'I didn't know how much luggage you'd have,' he said, and slammed the boot shut, then opened the door for her. She climbed in, then turned her head, which was a mistake, because it was level with his and he leant in and touched his lips to hers.

Just that. Nothing else, no words, just a tender, fleeting kiss before he closed the door and went round to get in behind the wheel.

'No time for coffee today,' he told her as they headed out on the road. 'Jenni'll skin me alive if I keep you out too long, and the marquee people are there, so I ought to be at home.'

'I could have got a taxi,' she protested, but he threw her a smile that nearly melted her bones.

'No way. I wanted you to myself for a few minutes,' he told her, and she found her hand wrapped in his, trapped against the hard, solid warmth of his thigh. Just like before.

And just like before, they talked and laughed the whole way back to the castle. He told her about the honeymoon plans he'd made, and she told him about Annette and her progress.

'She's looking pretty tired, but they seem happy with her, and it's looking really positive.'

'Good. I'll have to go and see her again next time I'm down.'

Which implied she would be there, too, instead of here. So had she totally misread his intentions? Had he simply wanted to make love to her, nothing more, nothing less?

But he'd said he didn't want to hurt her, and he knew that would. So was he intending—?

She stopped herself. Now was not the time. She didn't have the emotional energy to concentrate on a love that had waited twenty years. It could wait another three or four days.

'So, tell me what's been going on. What's left to do?'

He laughed a little desperately, and said, 'Ah, yeah. Well—I have no idea. There's an endless list, but at least we're now down to the things that don't matter, rather than the things that do. Mrs McCrae and Alec's mother have polished the church within an inch of its life, the gatehouse is virtually ready, Alec's had his stag do—that was a bit of a laugh. They covered him in soot and treacle and feathers and dragged him through the village, and everyone came out and cheered him on. They all love him, and it was really touching to see it, but we had a bit of a game cleaning him up.'

'Poor Alec,' she murmured, smiling. 'How's his head?'

'Oh, just about recovered, I think. So's mine.

Those boys know how to drink. I have no idea how much of my malt whisky they got through.'

Maisie turned and searched his eyes. 'You love him, don't you?'

'I do. He feels like a son to me, I have to say. It will be no hardship welcoming him to the family.'

'Oh, on which note, how's the speech coming on?'

He groaned, and she laughed and squeezed his hand. 'You'll be great. Don't worry.'

'I'm not worried about the speech. I'm worried I'll make a fool of myself. Jenni asked me if I was going to cry.'

'And will you?'

'I hope not.'

'I will.'

'Don't. You'll set me off.'

They exchanged smiles, and she felt a curious warmth curl around her heart. It was almost as if they were still married, still a couple, still Mum and Dad in the same breath, instead of with a comma and six hundred miles between them.

Except there was still the problem of the six hundred miles, she thought, and then realised, as they turned into the gates and rumbled slowly down the drive, it didn't seem like a problem any more, because suddenly the castle seemed like home. She just hoped the feeling lasted.

* * *

The morning of the wedding, to everyone's relief, was gloriously sunny, not a cloud in the sky, and Maisie sat in the window of her room and watched Rob walk the dogs along the beach and up to the old ruins on the headland. He stood there for a while, motionless, and then, as if he could feel her eyes on him, he turned and stared back at the castle.

She opened the window and waved, and he lifted his hand. It was as if he'd reached out and touched her, and she felt the warmth of his greeting down to her bones.

'Mum? Are you awake?'

She closed the window and turned to hug Jenni, bleary-eyed and sleepy, in so many ways still her little girl. 'How are you, darling? Did you sleep well?'

'Mmm. Still sleeping.'

Maisie laughed and hugged her tighter. 'Silly girl. Excited?'

'Very.' She dropped her arms and took Maisie's hand. 'Come on, I want a cup of tea, and we need to start moving. It's only two hours before the hairdresser comes, and I want to do my nails and make sure I've got everything ready.'

'Are the girls awake?'

'Yes, I called them. They're making tea in the kitchen with Grannie and Jeff, but I wanted you to come. Where's Dad?'

'Walking the dogs.'

He got back while they were all in the kitchen making toast, and joined in, apparently quite at ease with three young women in scanty vest tops and sloppy pyjama trousers. He probably was, to be fair, now that Jenni lived here permanently. And if anyone needed to be self-conscious, she thought, it was her, dressed much the same except that she'd thrown a light robe over the top, and now she was glad she had, because his eyes kept straying to her all the time.

'More toast, anyone?' Helen said, but they all shook their heads.

'No, thank you, Grannie. I need a shower,' Jenni said.

'Mmm, me too,' Maisie agreed, and then caught a flash of heat in Rob's eyes and turned away quickly before he could see the wash of colour across her cheeks.

'I'll go and check everything's under control outside,' he said, and left the room, to Maisie's relief. Mrs McCrae bustled in and hugged Jenni, her eyes filling with tears, and Jenni hugged her back hard, making Maisie's eyes fill as well.

Oh, dear lord, it was going to be one of those days, she realised with a bubble of hysterical laughter in her throat, and almost ran back to her room before it escaped on a wave of tears. She showered and washed her hair, taming it with serum and scrunch-drying it. There was no point asking the hairdresser to deal with it. She'd had almost forty years of learning how to control the wild curls, and she didn't want to look like someone else on such an important day.

She threw on clean clothes and went to see how Jenni was coping, and got swept up in the preparations. The hairdresser arrived, someone opened a bottle of champagne, Mrs McCrae brought up a tray of bagels with cream cheese and smoked salmon, and Jenni's room turned into party central. Jeff was recording it all for posterity, moving unobtrusively around the room as he photographed the dress, the shoes, the girls laughing, the pinning up of Jenni's hair—all the little details that otherwise would be lost.

She wondered what Rob was doing, and then saw him out of the window talking to the florist. She went out to join them, checked that everything was all right, that the table centres were where they should have been, that the pedestals were in the right places, and then she looked at Jenni's bouquet and her eyes filled with tears.

'Oh, it's lovely! Thank you so much!'

It was cream and white, with just a touch of lilac to take the edge off, for Helen's sake, and echo the bridesmaids' posies. So pretty, so perfect for her little girl's special day.

'Hey, come on, you can't start already,' Rob said gruffly, and slung an arm round her shoulders, hugging her to his side. She slid her arm round his waist and hung on.

'She's my baby,' she said, her voice breaking, and he turned her into his arms and held her while she cried the tears that had been threatening for weeks.

When he let her go, she could see his own eyes bright with tears, the lashes clumped, and she gave him another quick hug and went up on tiptoe to kiss his cheek.

'Come on, soldier. We can do this.'

'Yes, we can,' he said, his voice steady and confident, and she had a feeling that he wasn't talking about the wedding at all, and she felt all the stress and worry fade away.

'How are you all doing?'

'OK, Helen. How about you? That looks really lovely,' Maisie said, smiling at her as she did a little twirl in her new outfit that they'd chosen together the last time she'd been here.

'Thank you. I feel so much better in it. Oh, Jenni, you look beautiful. How long? Your father's pacing.'

'We'll be down in five minutes,' Jenni said, as the hairdresser anchored the veil into the back of her hair and stood back.

'Perfect. That's lovely.'

Lovely? Oh, yes, she was lovely, but so much

more. She looked like a woman, serene, confident, sure of her love.

Maisie went out onto the landing, and the girls ushered Jenni out, arranging her dress and veil as they walked down the landing, Jeff firing off endless shots as they moved towards the head of the stairs. As Maisie turned the corner at the top of the stairs, she saw Rob standing there, one foot on the bottom step, his hand resting on the newel post, gazing up at them and looking for all the world like one of the oil paintings around the walls.

His silver-buttoned black jacket and waistcoat were straight out of history, a deep jade ruched tie picking up the colour in the Mackenzie dress kilt and the matching flashes on his black kilt hose, his ghillie brogues gleaming. He looked every inch the Laird, and she felt her heart swell with pride.

'Maisie,' he said, holding out his hand, and she went down to him, her heart in her mouth as his eyes raked over her and darkened. 'You look stunning,' he said under his breath as she reached him, and she lifted a hand and touched his cheek.

'So do you. Who would have known you had such good legs, Mackenzie?' she teased, and then, taking the last step, she turned and watched as Jenni came down the stairs, her eyes filling as she reached her father's side.

'Oh, Jenni,' he said gruffly, cupping her shoulders with gentle hands and kissing her cheek. 'You look…'

He couldn't finish, couldn't say the words. There weren't words for how he felt at that moment, not words he could ever find.

'Don't you start, or you'll set me off,' she warned him, and he laughed softly and took a step back.

'Come and see your flowers. They're beautiful.'

'Oh, they are! Oh, Mum, look!'

'I know, I've seen.'

Seen and cried my eyes out, she thought, and then she noticed Rob wasn't wearing his buttonhole. 'Here, let me pin that on for you,' she said, taking it out of the box and reaching up with trembling fingers to pin it in place.

He returned the favour, his hands steady, his brow creased in a little frown of concentration. 'How's that?' he asked, and she looked down at it and smiled.

'Perfect. Thank you.'

'Right. You and Helen had better go,' he said, and opening the front door he helped them into the first of the three wedding cars waiting on the drive. It was only a short journey to the church; they could have walked, but the weather was never reliable enough for that and, besides, with her stomach in knots and her legs like jelly, she wasn't sure she would have made it.

The church was packed with family and friends, many of them people she'd never met, but Helen greeted them all, introducing her to one or two, and Maisie held her head high and smiled through the speculative glances.

Alec came up to her, his hands shaking as he took hers and kissed her cheek, and she hugged him and told him not to worry.

'How's Jenni?' he asked, and she smiled.

'Beautiful. She can't wait.'

'Nor can I.'

He went back to his place at the front of the church, and she waved to the Coopers, sitting behind their son, Seonaid's hat a delicate confection of lavender, toning with her husband's tartan. She looked nervous, and Maisie winked at her in solidarity, and then turned back to see if her brother had arrived.

And stopped in her tracks, because her father was there too, his face stern. She went over to him, wondering how much more emotion she was going to feel today, and he took her hand in his and gave what passed for a smile. 'I couldn't let my granddaughter get married without seeing her off,' he said.

Why not? He hadn't seen her off, Maisie thought, but she didn't say that, she just thanked him for coming and wondered where they'd seat him. With her brother Peter and his wife, of course, she thought, and greeted them distractedly.

'I'll catch up with you later. The bridesmaids are here, so Jenni won't be far behind. I'd better sit down,' she said, and took her place beside Helen, her heart pounding.

Then the music changed, and with her heart in her mouth she turned to watch as the man who once had waited for her where Alec was standing now walked their daughter down the aisle to the man she loved with all her heart.

Her eyes were shining, her face alight with happiness, and Rob, with his hand over hers in the crook of his arm, walked her slowly down past Maisie and took his place in front of the minister.

When he'd given her hand to Alec, he moved into the pew beside her and she felt his hand brush hers. Their fingers linked and clung, and together they watched as Alec and Jenni made their vows.

The same vows she and Rob had exchanged, the vows that had counted for nothing in the face of all that was to come. But that had been long ago, and really nothing had changed.

She still loved him. There had been no one else for her, and never would be. He was her husband still in everything but law, and if he asked her again, she would marry him once more, would say these vows to him again and mean them, from the bottom of her heart…

The reception seemed to go on forever.

Rob had made his speech, caused a few chuckles and brought tears to the eyes of his daughter and the woman who should still have been his wife. He'd laughed at Alec's speech, laughed even more at the best man's, and best of all he'd got through it all without losing it.

But now the first dance was over, and he could hear the unmistakeable sound of a helicopter in the sky above.

'Whatever's that?' Jenni said, turning to Alec on the dance floor as the music stopped, and Rob and Maisie led them all outside to the lawn and they watched the helicopter land, settling like a feather on the circular lawn up above the castle.

'Dad? What's that?' Jenni asked, and he pulled a face and grinned.

'Your going-away car.'

'But—we're not going away,' Alec said, looking puzzled. 'We haven't packed.'

'Yes, you have,' his mother said, and his father handed the pilot his bag.

'Here,' Tricia said, handing over Jenni's. 'Blame Libby if there's anything missing.'

'But—where are we going?' Jenni asked, so he told them, and their jaws dropped.

'Wow—Dad?'

'Come here,' he said, and she flew into his arms, still his little girl, but not for long. He let her go, handed her over to her husband, slapped Alec on the back and then showered them both with confetti as they ran towards the helicopter. Her veil took off, and Alec grabbed it and bundled it up and helped her into the little aircraft, turning to wave as they took their seats.

And then they were gone, lifting up into the sky, and Rob watched them, Maisie's hand in his, until they were nothing more than a dot on the horizon. Then he turned to her.

'I think we've got a party to host,' he said, and she smiled at him through her tears, swiped them out of the way with an ineffectual hand and turned back to their guests.

CHAPTER TEN

So, it was done.

Her baby was married, whisked away on her honeymoon with tears in her eyes and love in her heart, and now the party was over.

She'd danced for hours, until her feet could hardly hold her, the ceilidh band loud and lively and endless as the caller had kept them all in order and they had laughingly gone wrong anyway. The dashing white sergeant had dashed away, the willow had been stripped within an inch of its life, and they'd finished off with the old Orcadian version of stripping the willow, with two long lines of men and women, crossing and recrossing, whirling each other round until they were giddy and helpless with laughter, and then they'd all joined hands for 'Auld Lang Syne'.

And now the house was quiet, the air still but for a light breeze, and Maisie took herself out to the gun court, rested her hands against the ancient stone wall and stared out over the moonlit sea.

'I thought I might find you here.'

She turned her head, looking at him over her shoulder. 'Have they all gone?'

He nodded. 'I've just seen my mother up to bed. She's exhausted.'

'I'm sure. Do you need to walk the dogs?'

'No. They had a run earlier, one of the ushers took them out. I'll give them a good walk tomorrow, but they're sleeping now.'

He fell silent, the tension between them palpable.

'It was a good day,' she said finally, just to break the silence, and he came and stood beside her, staring out over the sea, his face pale in the moonlight.

'Yes, it was. Better than I thought it would be.'

'They looked thrilled with the helicopter. That was very generous of you.'

He shrugged. 'They aren't having long off, it's a very short break, but I just felt I wanted them to have a little privacy. The gatehouse isn't exactly a honeymoon hideaway and they've waited a long time for this.'

She felt a pang of motherly concern, thinking back to their first night together, and Rob's tenderness and patience. Would Alec be as kind with Jenni?

'He'll take good care of her,' he said gruffly, as if he could read her thoughts. 'He adores her, Maisie. She'll be fine.'

'I know. Your speech was lovely, by the way,' she told him. 'Very touching.'

'I made you cry.'

She laughed, a breathless little sound in the quiet night. 'It wasn't hard.'

'No. It's been a bit of an emotional roller-coaster.' He turned her towards him, staring down at her, his eyes shadowed. 'You looked beautiful today,' he murmured. 'I love that dress.'

'I love it, too. Jenni said—'

She broke off, thinking too late that it might not be wise to tell him what Jenni had said, but he just smiled and tilted his head curiously.

'What?' he prompted.

'She said it would blow your socks off.'

He laughed softly, then gave a quiet sigh. 'How very true.' He turned away again, staring out to sea, his eyes unfocused, remembering Maisie dancing, the sway of her hips, the way she'd doubled up with laughter until she could hardly breathe. It wasn't the dress that had blown his socks off, it was the woman he loved, the woman he should never have allowed to slip through his fingers. Did he dare to try to win her love once more?

'Maisie, I don't know if I can do this again,' he confessed softly, finally voicing the thoughts he'd had all day. 'I've held on all these years, never married again, never even got close, but now you're back here and it feels as right as it could, but even so, I'm afraid to let myself trust it.'

He breathed in deeply, then let his breath out on a harsh, ragged sigh. 'What if I'm wrong, Maisie? What if you come back here and find you still hate it after all? What if I let you back into my heart, and you leave me all over again?'

'I don't hate it,' she said quietly. 'I don't think I ever really did hate it. I hated being lonely, I hated being without you, and I had no friends, but I was never unhappy with you, Rob. I was only unhappy without you, or when you held yourself back from me. And when I left because I couldn't stand it any more, you didn't come after me. I thought you would, thought you'd come to Cambridge on leave, so we could have a chance to work on our marriage, but you didn't. Only to visit Jenni, and then not for six months.'

'I couldn't,' he told her. 'I was so confused, so hurt, so angry. My parents gave me your letter when I got back, told me you'd left me. I was devastated. I thought it was better to leave it for a while, to let things settle, then maybe we'd be able to talk. I think I was waiting for you to realise you'd made a mistake and come back to me, but you didn't, and why should you? And I'm not going to blame my parents. They didn't help, but

I should have talked to you, should have realised something was wrong. I should have come after you.'

'I wrote to you again, weeks later when I knew you were home, but you didn't answer my letter. You didn't even acknowledge it.'

'I never got a letter,' he said, and he shook his head slowly, his expression resigned. 'My father.'

'Not necessarily. Things get lost.'

His smile was wry. 'No, Maisie. They don't.' He sighed softly, his expression bleak now. 'I know I've let you down, but I still love you, Maisie, more now, maybe, than I did then, because I know now what I've lost.'

She closed her eyes, breathing slowly, steadying her heart. He still loved her. Nothing else mattered—only that. She reached up and cradled his face, turning it gently towards her. 'Rob, after the food tasting, when you kissed me and I stopped you, you said you'd never wanted to hurt me, it was just the wrong time for us. But it's the right time now. I don't want to hurt you, either. I love you, too, Rob. I've never stopped loving you. I just couldn't live here without you, and I was faced with another five years of that. I never left you. When you asked for a divorce, I was devastated.'

He stared at her. 'I thought that was what you wanted?'

'No. I wanted you, Rob. I've only ever wanted

you, but I was too young to know how to tell you that, too young and inexperienced and proud to fight for you. But it's different now. We're different now—older. Wiser.'

She took a deep breath for courage and held his eyes.

'Ask me again, Rob. Ask me now.'

He looked around, looked at the lights still on in some of the guest rooms, and shook his head. 'Not here. Not like this. Meet me here in five minutes—and you might want to change your shoes.'

The ruin. He was taking her to the ruin, the place where they'd always gone to be alone. The place where Alec had asked Jenni to marry him only ten weeks ago.

She went inside and slipped off her shoes, then ran up to her bedroom. How quickly could she shower?

Very, was the answer. She pulled on clean underwear, and then because he loved the dress, because he'd suggested she change her shoes, and only shoes, she put it back on again, zipped it up and put on her little flat gold pumps, the ones she wore with her jeans.

Then she ran back down to the gun court and found him waiting, still in his kilt, but he'd lost the jacket and waistcoat and tie, the shirt was undone at the neck and he had a wicker hamper in one hand and a blanket over his shoulder.

'Ready?' he asked, and she nodded, slipped her hand into his and squeezed it tight, then they went down the worn stone steps to the beach, along the shore with the suck of the sea in the shingle for company, picking their way carefully but hurrying nonetheless because after all this time the suspense was killing them both.

The moon was bright, lighting their way along the familiar path, but Rob led her, turning every now and then to make sure she was all right, helping her up steps, over rocks, round the rough patches.

And when they reached the ruins of the old castle, he led her gently by the hand to their crumbled tower in the corner overlooking the sea, and he spread out the blanket on the ground, knelt down on it and held out his hand to her, drawing her down to him.

She knelt in front of him, just inches away from him, and he took her hand in his, his eyes steady on hers even though she could see a pulse hammering in his neck.

'I love you, Maisie,' he began. 'I've loved you since the first moment I saw you, and I wish with all my heart that I'd been able to make things right for you, that I'd had the courage to come and find you, the humility to ask you to have me back, instead of hiding away up here and throwing away so much that was good and precious in our lives. But I didn't, and I lost you, but I've never forgotten you, not for a moment.'

She felt a tear slide down her cheek, and brushed it away, and he lifted his hand and smoothed the last trace from her skin with a hand that wasn't quite steady.

'There have been other women,' he went on softly. 'Redheads at first, but they weren't you, so I switched to blondes and brunettes, and then I realised I was cheating all of us, I was sick of pretending, sick of shutting my eyes so I could convince myself it was you, ashamed that I was using women, nice, ordinary, decent women, to forget you. And it didn't work anyway, so I stopped. It was easier that way, less painful, and it meant I could look at myself in the mirror in the morning when I shaved. But I hated it, because I'd vowed to be faithful to you for the rest of our lives, and we'd thrown it all away.

'But I want it back, my love. I want you back, and if it means I have to fly down every weekend and divide my time between here and Cambridge to do it, then so be it, because when you went away this time, the life went out of the Highlands for me. I got through it, but all I could think about was when you'd be coming back and how long it would be until I could see you again. The castle's nothing without you, just a pile of rock on the edge of the sea somewhere just shy of the Arctic Circle.'

She smiled at that, but it was a poor effort, a wobbly smile that turned somehow into a tiny sob, and he squeezed her hand and pressed it to his lips. 'I understood then what you meant about living here without me; I was just getting through the days till you returned, my life suspended. It was like being in a coma, going through the motions, but nothing seemed real—even the wedding preparations hardly scratched the surface. And I began to realise what it must have been like for a young woman, alone, friendless, with a small, demanding baby and no one to turn to, no one to hold you or tell you it would get better. No one to love you.'

'I thought you loved me,' she said sadly, confused. 'But when you came back, you were so different. All I wanted was a hug, but you didn't come near me.'

'I was afraid to hurt you, afraid of my emotions. I wanted you so much—I'd been shut up under the sea in a metal tube for months, and the thought of holding you, making love to you again, was all that got me through. And I didn't trust myself.'

'You should have said—'

'We both should have said. It wasn't just that. Maybe that was just a good excuse. I was really unhappy in the navy, but when I came home and needed you to hold me and tell me I'd get through it, you were so wrapped up in Jenni and so obviously unhappy I just had to bury my own problems and concentrate on yours. But I couldn't. I wasn't mature enough to do it, and so I lost you.'

Tears were coursing down her cheeks now, but she just blinked them away. 'I'm so sorry. I didn't realise what you were going through. That must have been so awful.'

'Well, you know the saying, "What doesn't kill you makes you stronger". I survived it, and it made me a better man, in the end, but the cost, to both of us, to Jenni, just doesn't bear thinking about. The children we might have had. The time together, for the last twenty years—so much, just gone. And I don't want to waste any more of our lives, Maisie. I need you. I love you. Come back to me, my love. Marry me again—and this time, let's do it right.'

'Oh, Rob…' She sucked in a shaky breath, and fell into his arms, the tears falling like sweet summer rain, washing away the hurt.

His lips touched her cheeks, kissing away the salty trails, his thumb smoothing them out while he fought to hold back tears of his own. 'Yes or no, Maisie. Tell me now, for pity's sake.'

'Yes. Oh, yes, my love,' she said, lifting her face

to his so he could see the love there for him, shining silver in the moonlight. 'Of course I'll marry you again, and I don't care where we live. I love it here, so long as you're here with me. I can still do my photography, and I can write features and send them to magazines and newspapers, if I want, or I could just help you here, help you to build up the business, work alongside you, if you want me.'

'Want you?' He laughed a touch crazily. 'Oh, my dearest, darling Maisie, of course I want you. I can think of nothing more wonderful than having you by my side every day of my life.'

'My family are down there. My father came, even after all the things that have been said, even though he's old and ill, he still cared enough to come to Jenni's wedding. I'll need to spend some time down there. And I've got other friends. Good friends who've stood by me. I can't forget them.'

'I wouldn't want you to. And, anyway, I've got the business in London and I go down from time to time, as you know, so we can keep the house in Cambridge as a base and go down together, and you can catch up with your friends and family while I keep my firm on the straight and narrow. And now we can leave this place with Jenni and Alec, it's not such a problem to get away. It's going to be theirs, after all. And my mother might like to spend some time in Cambridge, and Jenni and Alec. It won't go to waste. Talking of which...'

He drew her gently into his arms, kissed her tenderly, then shifted so he was sitting down, one leg bent at the knee. He patted the rug beside him and she settled there, watching as he opened the hamper and pulled out a bottle and two glasses, a little basket of canapés left over from the wedding and a big chunk of Mrs McCrae's fruit cake.

'What are you doing?'

'Feeding you. I don't know about you, but I hardly ate anything, I was too wound up, and I'm starving. Champagne?'

She started to laugh, and he gave a chuckle, then put the bottle down and lay back, laughing till the tears ran down his cheeks, Maisie cradled against his chest.

She lifted herself up on one elbow when she could breathe again, and stared down at his beloved face. 'Make love to me, Mackenzie,' she said softly. 'I've waited such a long, long time.'

'And you're going to have to wait a little longer,' he told her, kissing the tip of her nose before sitting up and reaching for the champagne. 'I'm taking a leaf out of our daughter's book, and doing it properly this time round. Only I'm not waiting two and a half months. We're getting married in two and a half weeks, my darling, so pull up a glass, get stuck into the food and start planning.'

She wore the dress again, with the fascinator she'd worn for Jenni's wedding as a veil, the net over her face hiding her eyes from him as she walked down the aisle on Alec's arm.

Jenni was behind her, waiting to take the simple posy she had made of flowers from the castle garden, and Helen and the Coopers and Mrs McCrae made up the party.

Or that was the idea, but word had got out that the Laird was marrying his lady again, and the church was packed to the rafters, all the estate workers up in the Laird's loft above them, anyone who could get inside crowded in around the back of the nave, and the rest were outside, cheering and waving as she walked in to marry the man of her dreams.

As she reached his side, he held out his hand to her, his eyes glowing with love, and she went to him with a smile that came from the heart. Their vows were the same they'd made all those years ago, but this time they said them with new conviction, a deep-seated sincerity that left the other in no doubt that this time their love was unshakeable.

He slipped the ring on her finger, the same ring he'd put on nearly twenty-two years ago, and then she gave him his, a new one because he'd thrown his own into the sea in a rage of despair when their divorce had come through.

And then he kissed her, his eyes warm with the promise of what was to come, and after they'd signed the register, witnessed by Jenni and Alec, they turned and walked back down the aisle and out of the church together, arm in arm, in a hail of confetti and good wishes. He kissed her again, just to give the crowd something to make them happy, and then with a smile and a wave he led her away, down to the hotel where they were having a lunch party.

She could hardly eat anything. Her nerves were strung tight, her heart was racing, and every time he caught her eye, she knew he felt the same.

As if he'd read her mind, he passed on coffee and got to his feet, holding out his hand to her. 'Sorry to bail out on you, guys, but we're off now.'

'Off?' Alec said, his face a picture, but Rob just laughed.

'You'll cope. We'll be back the day after tomorrow. We've been waiting twenty years for this day, and I think you'll agree we've earned it.'

'Oh, Mum…'

Jenni got to her feet and hugged her, Alec too, and then they left the table, with Mrs McCrae dabbing her eyes and Helen trying to look disapproving and failing dismally, and he ushered her out to the car, which was waiting in the car park.

'So where *are* we going?' she asked, taking off the fascinator and dropping it down behind her seat as he put down the roof.

'The place we sent Jenni and Alec. We've got a lodge in the grounds, with a hot tub and room service.'

Her heart rate hitched up a gear, and she rested her head back as he drove swiftly through the glorious scenery, pulling up after a couple of hours outside a beautiful old country house hotel on the shores of a loch. They checked in, and the receptionist asked if they wanted to book dinner.

'No,' he said firmly. 'We'll get room service.'

And the moment the door was closed behind them, he drew her gently into his arms and stared down into her eyes. Then he lifted his hand and cradled her face.

'I love you, Mrs Mackenzie,' he said gruffly, and, lowering his head, he touched his lips to hers in a kiss of promise.

He lifted his head, and she reached up and laid her hand against his cheek, relishing the feel of stubble against her palm, the contrast between them, yin and yang. 'I love you, too,' she said, her heart slowing now because there was no hurry. They had all the time in the world, and from the look of him, Rob intended to take it.

He crossed to the window and tilted the blinds, and the ring she'd put on his finger in their simple ceremony caught his eye. It felt strange after all these years, but he'd get used to it. And for now it was a constant reminder of what he'd so nearly lost. He'd thrown the other ring away, but this one he knew he would never take off, because it was engraved inside, with one simple word.

Forever…

* * * * *

0610/02

Coming next month

AUSTRALIA'S MOST ELIGIBLE BACHELOR

by Margaret Way

Corin Rylance is super-handsome, super-rich, and way out of farm girl Miranda Thornton's league. Until Corin's sister takes Miranda under her wing and puts her within touching distance of Corin...

THE BRIDESMAID'S SECRET

by Fiona Harper

When glam editor Jackie arrives back in Italy for a big **Bella Rosa** wedding and sees her old boyfriend Romano, her groomed façade disappears. She has a long-kept secret to tell him...

CINDERELLA: HIRED BY THE PRINCE

by Marion Lennox

Struggling cook Jenny gets hot under the collar when she accepts a job on gorgeous stranger Ramón's luxury yacht, and discovers Ramón's not a humble yachtsman – he's a secret prince!

THE SHEIKH'S DESTINY

by Melissa James

Without a kingdom to rule over and a public to serve, Sheikh Alim El-Kanar believes he has no future. Can nurse Hana give him a glimmer of hope?

On sale 2nd July 2010

Available at WHSmith, Tesco, ASDA, Eason and all good bookshops.
For full Mills & Boon range including eBooks visit
www.millsandboon.co.uk